REFINER'S FIRE

A NOVEL BY

SYLVIA BAMBOLA

MULTNOMAH
BOOKS

REFINER'S FIRE
published by Multnomah Books

© 2000 by Sylvia Bambola
International Standard Book Number: 978-1-59052-852-5

Cover image by Peter Samuels/Tony Stone Images
Background cover image by Jay Simon/Tony Stone Images
Design by Kirk DouPonce/David Uttley Design

Published in the United States by WaterBrook Multnomah, an imprint of the Crown Publishing Group, a division of Random House Inc., New York.

MULTNOMAH and its mountain colophon are registered trademarks of Random House Inc.

For information:
MULTNOMAH BOOKS
12265 ORACLE BOULEVARD, SUITE 200
COLORADO SPRINGS, CO 80921

Library of Congress Cataloging–in–Publication Data
Bambola, Sylvia.
Refiner's fire / by Sylvia Bambola   p.cm.   ISBN 1-57673-694-6
1. Ambassadors–United States–Fiction. 2. Ambassadors–Romania–Fiction. 3. Christians–Romania–Fiction. 4. Brothers–Romania–Fiction. 5. Romania–Fiction. I. Title.
PS3552.A47326 R44 2000 813'.6–dc21   00-008204

146651086

Dedicated to all the Christians of the Underground church who suffered and died for their faith during Nicolae Ceausescu's regime in Romania (1965–1989).

And dedicated to all persecuted Christians worldwide. At this printing, seventy-seven nations continue to actively persecute their Christians. It is believed that more Christians have lost their lives in this century than in all previous centuries combined.

In this you greatly rejoice,
though now for a little while
you may have had to suffer grief in all kinds of trials.
These have come so that your faith—of greater worth than gold,
which perishes even though refined by fire—
may be proved genuine
and may result in praise, glory and honor
when Jesus Christ is revealed.

1 PETER 1:6–7

The story and characters in this novel are fictitious. Any resemblance to actual persons or events is strictly coincidental. The two exceptions are as follows: First, some historical facts regarding Nicolae Ceausescu's regime are mentioned; second, various incidents described in this book are factual while the characters themselves are not. These events represent a composite of true happenings, collectively or individually, experienced by members of the Romanian Underground church.

In addition, I have employed poetic license in some descriptions of places and settings where deemed necessary for the flow of the story. One example is the creation of the entirely fictitious Diplomat's Club.

ACKNOWLEDGMENTS

Special thanks to the Romanian Missionary Society and the Slavic Gospel Association for their monthly newsletters which faithfully tracked the plight of Christians behind the Iron Curtain during those many years of Communist rule.

Richard Wurmbrand, in his book, *Tortured for Christ,* profoundly affected my understanding of the Romanian Underground church. As a Romanian pastor who was imprisoned many years himself, Wurmbrand relates firsthand the suffering, beauty, and power that characterized the Underground church during those harsh years under Nicolae Ceausescu. His story provides much of the factual information associated with the persecuted Christians depicted in *Refiner's Fire.*

1

MAGDA SAT STOOPED ON THE OVERTURNED CRATE, combing the dirt with her bony fingers. It was dry and sandy, not like the soil back home. She rubbed it between her palms, then brought it to her nose. No, it was nothing like home.

"Mama, are you going to give me away?"

Magda let the dirt in her hands fall to the ground. She looked at the small, thin blond squatting in the dust next to her. Brown powder caked his face like a mask.

"You did not wash today, Alexander."

"Aunt Sonia said you were going to give me away."

Magda bit her lip and turned aside. "Aunt Sonia likes to hear herself talk."

"See, Alexander, I told you so," Yuri said. "Aunt Sonia was only teasing. Just like when she says she's going to put us in the garbage for the garbage truck to take if we're bad."

Magda's mouth formed a hard line. "I don't want to hear any more talk like that."

"People shouldn't tease, right, Mama?" Alexander shaped a mound of sand between his legs and poked holes in it with his finger.

"No, people shouldn't tease."

"Somebody said there's a great big God that lives up in the sky. Is that a tease, Mama?" Yuri asked, pushing dirt onto Alexander's pile to form a larger mound.

Magda glanced at her small, dark-haired son. "Who has been talking about God?"

"One of my friends."

"What did this friend say?"

"He's not his friend!" Alexander said. "Yuri hardly knows him."

"Well, he's nice to me, not like some of those other boys who are so mean and always want to beat you up if they think you hide your bread. Some even beat you for no reason and—"

"And once one of them—he was a giant, Mama, honest— he tried to steal my shoes, but Yuri and I—"

"What did your friend say about God, Yuri?"

"He said that God made us, that He made everything. Did God make us, Mama?"

"I have heard it said that God made man out of dirt, but I don't know about such things."

Yuri smiled. "God must've used dirt just like this."

"Well, I've seen your grandfather grow cabbage on rocks," Magda said.

"Rocks?"

"Not rocks exactly, but a rocky patch of ground where no one could ever grow anything. If Grandfather could do that, then why couldn't God make man out of dirt? That is, if there is a God."

"Tell us again about Grandfather's farm," Alexander said.

"Yes, tell us, Mama."

Magda began combing the dirt again, digging her fingers deeper. "I am tired. Enough talk."

"Please, Mama," Alexander said. "Just tell us a little."

"It's useless talking about things that are lost. It's only pain and sorrow to hold on to the past." Magda tightened her fist around the dirt in her hand and felt a sharp prick. She opened her fingers and saw a piece of glass the size of a raisin and watched as blood and dirt mixed.

She had seen this before, but that was years ago. Why couldn't she forget?

"Now see what you made her do, Alexander!"

"I'm sorry I asked, Mama. I didn't—"

"Hush, it's all right," Magda said.

"Doesn't it hurt?" Yuri asked when his mother didn't utter a sound.

"Silence is its own language, little one. Complaining is useless." She pressed the wound firmly, trying to stop the bleeding. The glass had cut deep. "You'll learn soon enough that no one is interested in sharing your pain."

"Can I see it, Mama?" Alexander asked. "Can I see the glass?"

Magda cleaned the glass on her tattered skirt then held it out for her twins to see. It was blue-gray, the color of the sky before it rains, and sharp on one side.

"I wonder what it's from?" Alexander said.

"It's like a seed," Yuri said. "It looks just like a big seed."

"No, it doesn't. Seeds don't look anything like that."

"Once a farmer in the barrack showed off his seeds. Some of them looked like that."

"How come he didn't show them to me, Yuri? How come only you got to see them?"

"Because you weren't there."

"Mama, tell Yuri that's not a seed."

11

Magda sighed. "He knows it's not a seed. He said it was *like* a seed."

Alexander watched his mother intently as she jiggled the glass in her hand. "What'll you do with it, Mama? If you're not going to use it, do you think I could—"

"It will be useful for cutting thread when I sew. I'll keep it." Magda slipped the glass into her pocket.

"How did it get here, Mama?" Yuri asked.

"Maybe if God made everything from the ground, then the ground is where everything must return."

"But he only made people from the ground."

"Then, Yuri, there is no answer. Then this little glass was here for no reason." Magda closed her eyes. Just like they were all here for no reason. She visualized the blood and dirt. If only all pain could be removed as easily as this bit of glass. With her uninjured hand, she again began combing the ground. "There is no reason," she repeated.

"Let's dig for our own glass," Yuri said.

Alexander's eyes grew wide. "Maybe we can find other things too. I bet we can find lots of other things. Right, Mama?"

Magda opened her eyes and looked past the twins. "You boys wear me out. Go talk to Aunt Sonia. She's full of answers."

"No, Mama, we want to stay with you," both boys said.

"Then stay quiet and let me rest."

The boys watched silently as their mother continued combing dirt. Soon the young fingers also began sifting the soil. Her movements became theirs, as if imitation could gain them entrance into her world.

Finally, Yuri turned to his brother. "I think I know why that glass was here."

"No, you don't. You always try to act so smart."

"Well, I am older."

"No, you're not."

"By five minutes."

"That doesn't count."

"I'm older, and Aunt Sonia said because I'm older I should look after you."

"Well, I don't have to do what you say."

"Yes, Aunt Sonia said so, and she's smart. She used to live in a city."

"Mama, did Aunt Sonia really come from a city?" Alexander asked.

Yuri jabbed his brother in the arm. "Shush. Mama doesn't want to talk."

"Aunt Sonia said people that come from the city are smarter than people from a farm. Is that true, Mama?" Alexander said.

Magda sighed. "Yes, Aunt Sonia came from Cluj, a beautiful city in Transylvania. And I don't know if city people are smarter than farm people, or if they just think they are."

"Did you ever see Cluj, Mama?" Yuri asked.

Magda cradled her head in her hands. "No."

"How come?"

"I just didn't."

"Why didn't Grandfather ever take you?"

"He promised I'd go for…for my eighteenth birthday. He wanted me to see the monuments and restaurants, the pastry shops."

"Pastry shops! I wish I could go to a pastry shop," Alexander said.

Yuri leaned closer to his mother. "Why didn't you go? If Grandfather *promised?*"

Magda's hands squeezed her head. How could a five-year-old

understand that was a thousand years ago when promises meant something.

"I did pass by once, just once." Magda pictured the dusty back roads clogged with sweaty, tired people fleeing for their lives. "So, perhaps…perhaps in a way, you could say I saw part of Cluj."

"Will you take me to Cluj someday, Mama?" Alexander asked.

"Well, I…who can know what the future holds?" Magda looked away, not wanting her sons to see the tears that had suddenly filled her eyes.

"I wish we could go there now," Yuri said. "Right now, and leave this place and never come back. Alexander and I, we hate it here, don't we, Alex?"

The thin blond nodded.

"Yuri, you must never call your brother Alex but only Alexander. It is a noble name, a name he must grow into. And someday…someday he'll live up to his great name."

Magda had turned her full attention to Alexander. She looked into the large, frightened eyes that became even more alarmed by this sudden scrutiny. He seemed so small, so help-less. What was she going to do? Where was this God when she needed Him? She turned away when she felt the tears again.

"Well, it'd be nice if we could all go to Cluj right now," Yuri said. "All of us, you and me and Alexander and Aunt Sonia."

Alexander nodded. "Aunt Sonia says——"

"Aunt Sonia, Aunt Sonia. I am sick of hearing about what Aunt Sonia says. Go find her, both of you, and leave me in peace. Just leave me in peace."

"Mama, I don't want to find Aunt Sonia," Alexander said.

"Quiet! Not another word!"

14

Alexander's eyes began to fill. When Yuri saw his brother wipe his tears, he leaned over and kissed him.

"Stop kissing me. I'm not a sissy."

"You look sad, little brother."

"Stop calling me little brother!"

Magda glanced sideways. "I didn't mean to be harsh. I'm not angry with either of you. I'm just...I'm just..." Magda sighed and shook her head. "Go get your mess kits."

The line in the mess hall inched forward, and Alexander pressed his mess kit against his protruding ribs and allowed the crowd to push him along. His brother stood to one side, holding back a little, fighting the surge of the crowd as though wanting to control his own steps.

"I still have my bread from yesterday," Yuri whispered.

"I can never save mine. I'm too hungry. How do you do it?"

"I like saving it for you."

"You think I'm a sissy, just because I can't help eating all my food."

"No, Alexander. Honest! I'm more of a sissy than you are. I cry more."

"I had a cut once, as big as the one Mama got today, and I didn't cry, remember?"

"Yes, you were very brave." Yuri leaned closer to his brother and whispered, "The bread is in my pocket. I'll share with you."

Alexander wiped his runny nose on his sleeve. "Okay, but I'm so hungry I could eat *him*." He nodded toward a burly man, several feet away, ladling food.

Yuri giggled as he looked at the large-bellied cook with

hairy arms. "He doesn't look like he would taste very good."

"No, he's so shaggy, and he…he's scary."

"It must be nice to be a cook. Then you can eat all day long and never go hungry."

The cook's stomach protruded beneath the white apron and at times seemed to get in the way of his duty.

"I know why he's so fat," Alexander said.

"Why?"

"Because he eats bad boys."

"He does not."

"He does so!"

"Who said?"

"Aunt Sonia."

Yuri shuddered. "Stay near me and don't say anything to him, not one word."

"I will, but I'm not a sissy, Yuri. I'm only doing it because you asked me."

Magda walked behind them, hunched over, trying to make herself smaller. It would be easy to hide in this crowd. Her fingers tapped nervously against one thigh, then began roaming the frayed edges of her blouse.

She had to avoid Sonia. She couldn't endure her badgering today, her smug self-assured ways. Not today. Didn't Sonia ever tire of dishing out advice like this fat cook with his ladle? As if Sonia knew everything. As if Sonia understood. How could a woman who had no children possibly understand?

Her fingers crawled over the blouse fabric, searching, probing, as if looking for a place of refuge. Her rough thumbnail snagged a thread.

Did people from Cluj think they were the only ones with feelings? She must avoid Sonia. *Hide, hide,* her mind whispered as her thumb twirled around and around in the thread.

Magda realized suddenly how long the thread was, and she secured it carefully before pressing her thumb against the edge of the cloth. With a quick twist of the wrist she snapped the thread free. Perhaps she would mend the new tear in her skirt with the needle she had carefully hidden in the seam of her mattress. Here, there were always greedy eyes in search of opportunity.

When she slid the thread into her pocket, her hand brushed against the glass that had cut her palm. She had forgotten it was there. Now she had three treasures to safeguard: the glass, the thread, and her most prized treasure, the photo hidden inside her blouse. She hunched even lower. If Sonia had her way, she would take everything from her.

The line slithered forward. A man with bulging eyes argued with the cook, then tried to grab the ladle. The cook lunged for the man's throat and barely missed getting stabbed by his fork.

"*Mergeti!*" Magda growled at him. "Go!"

Alexander dropped his mess kit at the sound of his mother's harsh voice. As he bent to pick it up, the man with the bulging eyes stepped backward and accidentally kicked it a few yards away. Alexander fell to the ground, large tears running down his cheeks, and groped the floor in panic. He could hear the grumbling of the people in line. He was on all fours now, crawling blindly, unable to see through his tears. Suddenly his brother was next to him.

"Take mine," Yuri said, shoving his mess kit into Alexander's hand. "Hurry! Mama is holding our place. I'll find yours."

People had started to push against Magda, but she held her place until her sons returned. She looked down at them and smiled sadly. Her little men in boys' bodies. Childhood stolen.

What would their futures be? How deep would fate's razor cut into them? She couldn't think about it. She didn't want to think.

"Let's eat something," she said, gently nudging the boys forward.

A large, hairy hand scooped a ladle full of stew onto each of the boys' plates, then onto Magda's. She watched the last drop of gravy trickle onto her mess kit. The brown watery liquid ran to the bottom, leaving naked blisterlike particles. Magda knew the meat was mostly gristle, but she didn't care.

"Magda! Magda, over here."

Magda looked around. It was difficult to discern the direction of the voice through the loud, strange talk, the noise of a thousand scraping forks, the maze of bodies.

"Magda!" An arm waved and pointed to a table. "Come! Come!"

Magda groaned when she recognized Sonia, but she and her sons made their way through the crowd to the table where Sonia was.

Sonia gestured for Magda and the boys to sit, then buried her face in her plate. An assortment of women and children were clustered around the table but not one of them looked up. They were too busy sloshing food into their mouths. Brown liquid ran down chins, large and small, then swift fingers wiped it into eager, hungry mouths.

Magda looked at her own plate. With her fork she began pushing similar items together: potatoes on one side, peas on the other, the meat in the middle. She would eat the peas first. There were eight of them. Carefully, like a jeweler mounting a pearl in its setting, she placed one pea on her tongue and let it melt before swallowing. One by one the peas disappeared.

But as Magda saw Sonia licking the last drops of gravy from

her plate, her fork moved faster. Here, there were no second helpings. Quickly the three potato cubes disappeared, quicker still, the two pieces of gristly meat. Food in the belly could not be taken away.

Sonia leaned across her empty plate. "Well, Magda, what're you going to do?"

Magda wiped her mouth with the back of her hand and made no reply.

Sonia pounded the table. "Magda!"

Magda shrugged. "I don't know." She looked at her boys. Her hand went out to touch them, but recoiled midway, like a timid sparrow, and returned to its nest on her lap. "I don't know."

"Well, you better decide quickly. There are other sons, and mothers not so inclined to foolishness."

"Foolishness? My heart is breaking and you call it foolishness? Do you think it's easy giving one of my boys away? I must think of him."

"Exactly. And that's why you must give Alexander to the American. He'll provide a good home."

Magda eyed her fair-skinned Alexander, his soft, blond curls lying matted over his head.

Alexander's frightened eyes met hers. "Mama, are you giving me away?"

"Hush, child, this is grown-up talk."

"But Mama—"

"I said hush!"

Yuri squirmed beside his brother. He had no way of knowing how such things as the color of one's hair or eyes had the power to alter one's life. Without saying anything, he put his arms around Alexander.

"Think of your son, Magda, and what's best for him. Think

with your head, not your heart. What can you give Alexander? You're a woman alone, a foreigner among foreigners. You have no prospects of a job or marriage. No man wants a woman with two sons. It'll be easier to get a husband if you have only one extra mouth to feed."

Magda's eyes hardened. "Men. Is that all you think of? Did you ever hear me say I wanted a husband? No! Once I get back on my feet, I'll take care of myself and the boys."

"And just how do you expect to do that?"

"You know the Agency has promised us a new home. They'll relocate us."

Sonia laughed. "It takes time. They say there are still a million of us scattered in camps throughout Europe, all in need of a place to live. It takes time. How much time do you have?" Sonia put out her two hands, palm side up. "In one hand you have a promise that someday the Agency will help you begin a new life, and in the other hand you have the means to rebuild your life *now.*"

"Sometimes I wish I had never met you."

"Ha! Who would've helped you when the Nazis came pouring into our country like sludge from a cesspool?" Sonia spat on the floor. "The murdering, raping pigs! Well? Where would you be?"

Magda gnawed her finger. "I...don't know."

"Who would've helped you deliver your twins? Did you see anyone stop on the side of the road when you were screaming with pain? No. What was one more woman delivering her babies to the dirty, frightened rabble that passed us? Only I stopped. Remember that. Only I stopped. I could've left you there. You were nothing to me, a stranger. But I stopped. I *stopped.*"

"Sonia, *please.*"

"Please what? Please talk some sense into you?"

"Please don't ask me to do this. You of all people, you who have known my babies as long as I have."

"Yes, your sons call me 'aunt' for a reason. I've taken care of them and you. Aside from you, I'm the closest thing to family they have."

"Then for pity's sake, let's find another way."

"There is no other way."

"There has to be!"

"There is no other way."

"Why do you keep insisting on this?"

"Because you mustn't let this opportunity pass."

Magda bit into her lip. "I would've died; my sons would've died without you. I know this. You've been good to me, to us. But that doesn't change the fact that you are what you are."

"Just what does that mean?"

"I know what a cheat and a liar you can be."

"What are you suggesting?"

"How much are you being paid?"

Sonia reddened, then smiled slyly. "Yes, you do know me well."

"How much?"

"Enough," she finally said. "But that isn't the only reason I speak. You may not believe this, but I think of you and of Alexander. This is your best hope. Don't ruin it. This chance won't come again."

"I need more time."

"Soon. It must be soon. The American grows impatient."

The camp, like a giant kettle, simmered beneath the noon sun and filled the air with the odor of urine and unwashed bodies.

Magda moved snail-like along the fence, with the boys trailing behind. She couldn't get Sonia's words out of her mind. She pleaded with her brain to stop thinking, but it didn't work. She closed her eyes. Words. Words. So many words, like the steady drip of a faucet. She squeezed her eyelids trying to stop the drip. Too late. It was seeping through her eyes now, large shimmering drops of water, tears, useless tears that could change nothing. Still they poured from her.

Suddenly, she was back in Romania, a daughter of the Carpathian foothills. She saw the farmhouse, a silhouette against the glowing sunrise, and lush green vineyards that formed graceful arbors. In front, she saw herself sprouting like a young walnut tree. Then they came, goose-stepping, grinding the sprout beneath their black boots, leaving the seed of hatred implanted within the torn, crushed limbs. Both land and girl raped. The withered ruins outlined by a dying sunset.

Magda tore at her eyes. *Stop! Stop!* But the picture only loomed larger until her senses were filled with it. The father unarmed, fighting off many soldiers, the crack of rifle fire, the burnt smell of gunpowder, the red, red blood; the screams of anguish, the mother running, the crack of rifle fire, the burnt smell of gunpowder, the red, red...

Magda moaned, but still it came. The memory. Before her lay the bodies of her mother and father, so near each other, their blood puddled around them. It was this vision that made everything that followed worse, made surviving seem wrong somehow. It even came between her and the boys. Sometimes it made loving them hard.

Magda clung to the wire fence. She tried to get her bearings. For a moment nothing was familiar. Where was she? She looked for blood on the ground. There wasn't any. She looked for sprawled bodies. She saw only a sentry box in front of her. She listened for rifle fire but heard a creaking noise overhead instead. She looked up. There, swinging to and fro on rusty hinges, hung a sign with large foreign lettering, REFUGEE CAMP 10. Although she could not read it, she knew what it said. It said she had no home, no country. She was a person without rights, dependent upon the charity of foreigners.

Magda walked back toward the barracks, and her boys followed. *No more thoughts. Please, God, if there is a God, no more thoughts.* Still they came. What was she going to do? What would become of her? What would become of her sons?

Angry voices distracted her when she entered the barrack. One man, holding a small, bony girl by the pigtails, shouted and gestured with his fist. Another man stomped his feet while his jaws opened and closed like a fanning bellow. Because their language was foreign, she could not tell why they fought. Perhaps the child was found stealing. It was a familiar scene: accusations, counter-accusations, endless bickering. There was never any peace.

Magda hurried into her cubicle, but the angry voices followed her. She covered her ears with her hands. She wanted to run, somewhere, anywhere. If it wasn't for the exploding pain in her head she might have done so. The long hot walk, her stirred emotions, her near empty stomach, all helped produce a headache so severe that the slightest flutter of the eyelids intensified the pain. It was this pain that brought her to the cot.

She didn't know how much longer she could go on like this. Life was too hard. She was growing weary of it. Sonia was right. She had no future. Could life be over for her? She was only twenty-two.

The boys climbed up beside her. She hardly noticed them, but they watched her intently.

"What's wrong with Mama?" Alexander whispered.

"I don't know," Yuri mouthed. "But be quiet!"

Alexander leaned closer to his brother. "Is Mama going to give me away?"

"Shush. Can't you see Mama's not feeling well?"

"But Yuri—"

"No. Mama would *never* give you away."

Magda stretched out and put an arm over her forehead to block the glare from the overhead light that burned day and night. With her free hand she pulled her treasured photo from its hiding place in her blouse.

"Look, Yuri, it's our picture," Alexander said.

"Hush!"

"I love that picture."

Magda held the picture up slightly so the boys could see it better. "I love this picture, too," she said softly. "We're so safe in it, so safe. Nothing can reach inside where we are here and touch us. Nothing can hurt us." Magda brought the photo closer to her face as though she were going to kiss it. "I tried. I tried so hard. I'm sorry I couldn't do better."

"Mama, don't cry," Yuri said. "Please don't cry."

"Magda?"

Magda turned to see Sonia's head peeping over the tattered blanket that divided their cubicles.

"We must talk."

Magda shook her head. "Not now. Go away. I'm not well."

"I promised the American you'd make up your mind this afternoon. He wants to see the boy again, and you must decide. It's either yes or no."

"I need more time."

"Time has run out. He's leaving Germany."

"Stop pressuring me! I can't think when you pressure me. And I need to think this out."

"Think, think, think. That's all you say you want to do, but I don't believe you've done much of it. All you do is put off making your decision. But the time for putting off is over. You must decide."

Magda pressed the photo to her chest. "What can I do? What should I do?"

A sound like steam from an iron escaped Sonia's lips. "How many more times must we go through this? I've told you how much the American wants Alexander, that he's promised to provide a good home. And his wife has finally consented to adoption."

"Then let her find another mother's son."

"I've already told you how much Alexander looks like this American woman. No, it's either Alexander or no one."

"If she cannot bear her own sons, then let her go childless."

Sonia shook her head. "The American has been stationed in Germany since the Allied occupation. His tour is up. He must return to America. You cannot delay any longer!"

With a trembling hand, Magda slid the photo into her blouse. "You don't understand what it's like. You have no children. You can't imagine…you can't. Why are you so cruel? Where is your pity?"

"You can cry and scream, you can say anything you want, but I will not leave here without an answer."

Magda looked imploringly at her inquisitor. "I don't know what I want to do."

"Want? What does it matter what you want? It's the only way to get money; to buy a chance to live like a human being again, free from this place."

"Money, money, money! That's all you think of. And now you want me to give up my child for money. Why should I be surprised? A woman who sells herself is capable of selling anything."

"It was all right when I sold myself to keep *you* alive. You didn't speak so disapprovingly of me then. Who got you food when you were as weak as a lamb, and who got milk for your babies when yours dried up?"

Tears shimmered on Magda's cheeks. She quickly brushed them off. "It's true. I owe you much. And what I said was mean, hateful…I'm sorry. But this is different." Magda compressed her lips defiantly. She knew she was drowning. She could feel herself slipping away. "You don't understand."

"I understand. I understand that you have a fool's pride," Sonia answered, moving closer to the woman on the cot. "You think you have a choice, but you don't. You have no education, no skills. There are so few jobs. If you're lucky, you can get employment now and then, where, for a couple of pennies, you do the work of a man."

Magda was sitting up now. She rubbed her hands together, trying to hide her calluses, but said nothing. The boys cowered behind her.

"What's happening, Mama? Why are you and Aunt Sonia fighting? What's wrong?" Yuri said.

Alexander began to cry.

"Hush, children, Aunt Sonia is about to leave." Magda narrowed her eyes at her tormentor. "Go away; you're frightening my sons."

Sonia folded her arms across her chest. "I won't go until you tell me what you plan to do when winter comes. You have holes in your shoes and no warm wrap. How do you expect to survive the first snow?"

26

"The Agency will give us shoes and blankets."

"Are you sure?"

"They promised."

"But are you so sure?"

"Yes…certainly shoes. Maybe blankets."

"What if there aren't enough to go around? Are you willing to take that chance? And your boys, will they survive another winter in this place? Will your pennies be able to provide for them?"

"I don't know."

"Well, I know. I've seen it and so have you. This is what will happen. To make up the lack, your sons will begin to steal. They're still young, so at first they will steal only little things, but as they grow so will their stealing. And one day they'll get caught and someone will hurt them badly or send them to jail. And you, you'll see this coming and think, 'I must do something,' so you'll follow my trade. Oh, yes, Magda, you'll end up working on your back like the rest of us. And one day, when you bring a customer to the miserable little room the Agency will get for you, that customer will see Alexander or Yuri and decide he'd like one of them instead. This is your future because the only thing you know is farming and the only language you know is your own, and only Romanians speak Romanian."

Magda padded across the dirt yard. Her temples throbbed. All afternoon she had skirmished with Sonia. Finally, the confession came. The American was getting nervous and had promised Sonia a bonus for each of them if he could have Alexander today. He wanted the boy desperately and was willing to double the original price. Sonia had been relentless. Tears and curses had not stopped her. And in the end, Magda came to the bottom of herself.

Because the officer was leaving, things had to be rushed along. The American had powerful friends. The necessary papers were already prepared. The long, tedious legal process had somehow been bypassed. All that remained was for Magda to agree and sign a paper or two.

Magda had cursed Sonia loudly, then she threw herself on the cot and wept. Her eyes were dry now, but her head still throbbed. She walked slowly, her left hand holding Alexander's, her right holding Yuri's. Next to Yuri walked Sonia. All of Magda's muscles ached with tension. No one spoke.

Now she could see him leaning against the gate, under the large, white sign that swung to and fro with an irritating metallic sound. Her heart pounded as she wondered how they would manage. She did not speak his language. It would be awkward. She fought back tears and the urge to turn and run. This was not real. This was not happening. A mother did not give away her child just like that. Yet Magda knew it happened all too frequently, and many were not as fortunate as Alexander. They were given to the prostitution rings. At least her son would have a normal life. She had to believe he would have a normal life. Once she had heard someone say, "War was hell." It was a half-truth. The full reality was war was hell, and life *after* war was hell.

Sonia greeted the American in English. "Hello, Colonel Wainwright."

Next to him was a man Sonia had never seen before; he held a clipboard with long pages attached. Sonia gave him a polite nod, then focused on the colonel. The tall, lean

American smiled weakly as he looked around the camp.

"The boy is yours. The mother has consented," Sonia said.

The colonel's smile deepened, and he looked at the shy, blond boy. "Tell her she won't be sorry," he said without glancing at Magda. "Tell her the boy will have a good home in America."

Sonia translated for Magda who stared boldly at the stranger, studying every detail of his face, as if by studying his outer features she could determine his inner ones as well.

"And the money? Where's the money?" Magda snapped, digging the knife deeper into her own heart, slashing at her guilt and her longing for a normal life. "If I'm to sell my child, then I must see the money first."

After Sonia translated, the American looked at Magda for the first time. He made no effort to conceal his disgust as he pulled two envelopes from his pocket. One he gave to Sonia. The other, larger envelope, he handed to Magda.

Both women counted their money. It was all there, just as promised. With the money, Magda could begin a new life. *A new life.* It had cost her only one son. How she loathed herself. She looked again at the American colonel and accepted his disgust as penance. What did he know about hunger or cold or depravity, a man so clean and crisp in his uniform of power? See how far off he stands, not wanting to get her dirt on him. But her dirt would get on him because it was on Alexander. Did this colonel think he could transplant a seed without getting dirty? Didn't he know they were all dirty? Cradle and grave, that's what the earth was. She wished she believed in God, then she would have someone she could entrust Alexander's safety to, then she would have someone to blame. She had not asked for sons. Sons broke mothers' hearts.

Magda watched as Sonia stuffed her money back into the envelope. Her friend was well satisfied. It was more money than Sonia could earn in a year, even as a prostitute. When the envelope was safely tucked inside Sonia's pocket, Magda gave her a sign to proceed. This business had to be done quickly or she wouldn't be able to go through with it. *Hurry! Hurry!*

On cue, the man with no name shoved papers in front of Magda. She signed the designated areas. Then he nodded to the colonel that all was in order.

Quickly, Magda pulled out the treasured photo from its hiding place in her blouse and transferred it to Alexander's pocket. He was Alexander Wainwright now. That knowledge terrified her.

"Never forget!" she said in Romanian, then she thrust Alexander's small hand into the American's.

"No, Mama!" Alexander shrieked, trying to get away from the American's tight grip. "Don't leave me!"

Magda backed away, gasping for air, suffocating on her pain. She tried to pull Yuri with her, but he yanked his hand from hers and threw his arms around Alexander and kissed him. Large tears streamed from the dark, almond eyes.

"Don't worry, little brother," he whispered. "Someday we'll see each other again."

Then Magda took Yuri by the hand and led him away.

It would be okay. She would make it okay. She would survive this, *even this,* she told herself, as she walked briskly across the dusty ground. She walked faster and faster, almost running, almost carrying Yuri, trying to flee from the woeful cries of the little son she would never see again, a little son carried away by an American, carried away forever. Yes, life after war was hell.

2

ALEXANDER WAINWRIGHT REMOVED HIS PULLOVERS from the suitcase and began placing them in the middle dresser drawer, first the red, then the hunter green, and finally the white on top. Then he began filling the top drawer with his underwear to the left, undershirts in the middle. The socks went to the right, also separated into colors. For as long as he could remember he had kept his drawers in this manner; his "system" he called it. He could put his hand in any given drawer, and without looking, pull out the desired garment.

Once, feeling very smug, Alexander told his wife, "Life should be like a chest of drawers. What you put in, you get out." She had smiled in that peculiar way she had when she wanted to be irritating and answered, "Bravo, darling, but are we talking about your drawers or mine?" She had no system and had difficulty finding anything. He laughed as he thought of it. Loretta had a way of keeping him humble.

Alexander had finished his closet earlier. There, his shirts, arranged from lighter to darker, hung from the pole like a rainbow. His shoes were also sorted by color in two khaki shoe organizers fastened to the back of the closet door.

He zipped up the last of the suitcases and tucked it under

the bed. Unpacking was a pleasant chore. It afforded one both the opportunity to reorganize and cull. An orderly, uncluttered existence was a great prize. Why didn't Loretta understand this? She never complained when they moved, but it would take her months to unpack, and she never did so with order in mind.

Loretta also hated throwing out. Everything had meaning and recalled a special person, place, time, or event. The problem wasn't so much that she kept everything, but that she wasn't organized enough to find it later. That's why he never entrusted her with his treasured folder of travel brochures. He thought of her and smiled as he placed them in his nightstand drawer. He collected travel brochures like some people collected stamps, and they were always of places he had never been but hoped to go.

Loretta teased him, calling it his rootless side in search of itself, the orphan looking for his home. This irritated Alexander. She was always trying to scratch and scrape down to the bare wood, and for someone who was sensitive about most things, she seemed rather insensitive about this.

But he liked being Alexander Wainwright. He saw no point in trying to remember who he had been. He hated her murky insinuation that he should bring his past into the light, that he needed to come to terms with it. Well, he had come to terms with it. Once upon a time a baby named Alexander was born and when he grew up he became an American ambassador. *Ambassador* wasn't too shabby. He had a promising future. Everyone in the corps said so. What else did he need to know? He couldn't help it if that wasn't good enough for Loretta. She just couldn't leave anything alone. Alexander glanced down at his travel folder, then closed the drawer. Maybe that was one of the reasons he was so crazy about her.

With his unpacking finished, he had only one thing left to do. It was the thing he always saved for last. He retrieved Loretta's picture from the spot on the bed where he had carefully placed it, and carried it, ceremonial-like, to his nightstand. He moved it three times before he was satisfied, then took a deep breath. New beginnings. He loved them.

He glanced at the phone next to Loretta's picture. He had placed an overseas call two hours ago and still no return call. Where was she? He had told her he would phone.

Alexander loped down the massive oak staircase and into the dining room. The first thing he noticed was the crystal chandelier that sprouted from the center of the ceiling like a giant mushroom. He watched as it sparkled and shimmered, first like a thousand frozen tears, then like a thousand frozen droplets of blood, all suspended in air. He wondered at this as he walked in a circle beneath the fixture, then realized why the color changed. At certain angles, the crystals captured the mauve tone of the ceiling. He had never seen a chandelier as large or so unusual.

Alexander walked the length of the room. It was fifty feet long, with a fireplace at one end and a multicolored tapestry on the wall of the other end. He nodded his approval. An adequate reception hall needed to be large enough to hold over a hundred people. This room could easily hold that many. Loretta would like it.

Next he went into the kitchen. It was also large, with white European cabinets and ample white countertops. He checked to see that all the necessary appliances were in place. They were. Then he spotted a hearth in the corner. He put his fingers in the opening and felt the warm ashes that were pushed to one side; on the other was a dusting of corn flour. He laughed to himself. Loretta would never have time to use it for baking bread.

He walked out the back door without finishing the rest of the house. He had already seen the rooms deemed most important by Loretta and was sure she'd approve.

The grounds were bricked on three sides and iron fenced on the fourth. Silver-coned floodlights dotted the perimeter like owls searching for prey. The gardens themselves were disappointing. Weeds overran flower beds. Colonies of crabgrass choked large sections of the lawn. Fruit trees were in need of pruning, and many of the shrubs were brown or discolored.

He had not expected to find the cloistered garden of Villa Taverna, but he had expected a *garden,* not a tangle of unrecognizable vegetation. Life wasn't going to be easy here. He'd need the serenity of a beautiful garden at day's end. He would insist that his staff rectify this immediately. Then he laughed. This was Romania, remember? His servants didn't work for him, they worked for the secret police. Still, he could try. Tomorrow he would see about it.

Alexander returned to the house and continued his assessment. In addition to the dining room and kitchen, there were several living rooms, ten bedrooms, five bathrooms, and a study. One thing was certain. Ambassadors lived well, even in Romania.

He repeated his reconnaissance once more, this time with an imaginary Loretta. He tried to guess what her favorite chair would be in each of the living rooms, her favorite bath. He studied the wallpaper and tried to guess which she would leave and which she would replace. He smiled when he saw the bird and butterfly paper in one of the bathrooms. He made a mental note to tell her about that.

On his third trek through the house, Alexander began looking for bugs. He didn't need to—tomorrow the professionals
from the embassy would come over and do it right—but he
was playing a game, just to see how many he could find. That
and to pass the time.

Alexander probed walls, lampshades, and tables. He found
two bugs along one wall and another in a curtain fold. He went
from room to room, picking off miniature microphones, here
and there, like so many grapes off a vine. By the time his sweep
was complete, he had fifteen. He flushed them down the toilet.

Alexander had not seen any of the servants, though he had
heard soft chatter waft through the halls during each of his
three rounds. Upon his arrival at the residency, no one had
greeted him, no one had tended to his luggage, and no one had
offered him coffee.

Again he heard soft chatter coming from one of the rooms.

"Hello! Anyone here?" he shouted into the hall.

No answer.

He waited quietly for the chatter to resume. When it did, he
followed it on tiptoes, and found himself standing in front of
one of the ten bedrooms. The door was ajar and Alexander
Wainwright pushed against it.

"Hello," he said again, feeling embarrassed about acting like
a prowler in his own house.

Two women, in slow, mechanical movements, were putting
fresh sheets on a bed. Neither answered nor acknowledged his
presence.

"I'm Ambassador Wainwright."

The women stopped their labor and stared at the American.

"Do you speak English?"

A large, stocky woman with a gray and yellow headscarf

nodded. She looked like a drill sergeant.

"I'm a day early. I know you didn't expect me until tomorrow."

Alexander smiled at the drill sergeant, then at her timid companion. Neither uttered a syllable. He cleared his throat; he shifted his weight from his right to his left leg; he leaned against the door frame, then straightened again, feeling foolish as he waited for one word in response. There wasn't any.

"Well," he finally said, backing out the door. "I just wanted you to know I was here."

It wasn't until he reached the end of the hall that the soft chatter resumed. He entered the master bedroom, closed the door, and walked over to the nightstand. He picked up the five-by-eight color photograph of his wife. An attractive woman with short, honey blond hair and a bright, toothy smile stared at him. A hint of freckles dotted the bridge of her nose. The picture had been taken three winters ago, shortly after they had arrived at their last post. Her hair was longer now and she had more freckles. Loretta's freckles always sprouted in summer, like unwanted weeds, across both cheeks.

He had an irresistible urge to kiss the photo, but just then the phone rang.

"Hello, Ambassador Wainwright speaking."

"Darling! It's soooo wonderful to hear your voice."

"Hi, Loretta. I've been waiting for your call."

"I know, I got your message. You sounded like a lost puppy."

"I miss you. You can't believe how much I miss you. I hate this being alone, being apart. How long before you come?"

"Soon. I've been running my legs into stumps, trying to finish up here. But yesterday I found Lucy."

"The cook?"

"Oh, Alex, she's perfect. Has a notebook full of recommendations. They say she makes a Gruyère soufflé that you have to anchor to the counter or it'll float away. And then there's her personality…well, the whole package is wonderful. She's a gem, Alex, a pure gem. The problem is, gems cost money."

"How much?"

"Well, darling, there's a vast difference between a cubic zirconia and a diamond."

"How much, Loretta?"

"Let's just say you're not going to make your representation allowance this year either."

Alexander groaned. "You know how much I wanted to meet budget."

"I know, and I would take it up with the home office if I were you. After all, if they continue to insist upon all this compulsory entertainment, then they should make certain your allowance can cover it."

"Loretta, you're missing the point."

"And quite frankly, darling, as long as you and other diplomats continue to tap into your own resources to make ends meet, well, I hardly think there'll be much incentive for the higher-ups to come across with a raise. Of course, my solution is far easier—we could just drastically curtail this nonsensical dining around."

"You're beating an old drum, Loretta."

"Yes, and one of my favorites. So…what do you say? Does Lucy make us Gruyère soufflés?"

"I don't know, Loretta."

"Come, come, darling. No guts, no glory. If you're bound and determined to climb the ladder up to Bonn or Paris, you'll need long arms to keep reaching into your pockets. The other day someone told me it cost the British more to run their embassies in those cities than it did Buckingham Palace!"

"I know…I know. But maybe you could go with a zirconia. Do we really need soufflés that float?"

"McAllen told you how it would be over there. You remember his story about that Chinese translator who was reassigned to Mongolia because he shared two meals with a foreign diplomat? Now, how can I run a household under those conditions? I need at least one servant who'll want to serve, and I'll need someone friendly around the house to talk to and not disappear after I do."

"Well—"

"And what about the tension factor? You know how edgy things can get when there's servant problems. And none of the servants, Alex, none of them will be ours. You know they'll all be Securitate."

"Okay, Loretta, get the diamond."

His wife made kissing sounds into the phone. "Did I ever tell you I love you madly?"

Alexander laughed. "Only when you want something."

"I only want you, darling; you know that. And speaking of you, tell me everything."

"Obviously, I got here safely. Exhausting trip, but uneventful. Only two servants here, and they're avoiding me like the plague. And the garden, you won't believe it, Loretta, it's a jungle. I was almost attacked by the aralia."

"I'm sorry to hear that. I know how much your gardens mean to you. But this isn't Rome, darling; you can't expect the Taverna. Certainly you can make the garden bow to your wishes. I've seen you do it before."

"Yes, but not in a country like this. I mean, who was it that told us about the U.S. ambassador to Moscow whose garden went unattended for weeks because his gardeners 'couldn't find the tools'? These Communist countries are tough."

"Yes, that's why you're there. Tough countries need tough men."

"Yeah, that's true, Loretta. Even McAllen, and you know what a son of a gun he is, even he admitted that I was going places."

"Talking about going places, how about taking me through the rest of the house?"

"Beautiful. The house is beautiful and large, very large."

"Not on the scale of the American residence in Buenos Aires, I hope?"

"No, thank God. Can't even imagine what that monstrosity would cost to run."

"So our little 'golden ghetto' is still golden even in Romania?"

"Loretta, one thing I've learned—American ambassadors live well no matter where the country."

"More the pity."

"Don't start."

"Maybe if American ambassadors lived more like the natives lived, they'd be closer to the reality of what's going on in that country."

"Loretta, most ambassadors don't want to live like everybody else."

"I'm just thinking of the isolation, especially now that we're behind the Iron—"

"Say, remember the story about the ambassador who had bird and butterfly wallpaper stripped from an old house in Dublin, dry-cleaned in Manhattan, repaired in Hong Kong, then glued on canvas for use in the garden room of his residence in London?"

"Yes?"

"Well, I think that same ambassador must've lived here."

"You're kidding?"

"The same wallpaper's in one of the guest bathrooms."

Loretta laughed.

"Seriously, thank you for being so frugal. I know I give you a hard time sometimes, like with the new cook, but thank you."

"What brought that on?"

"The wallpaper. I know you'd never do something like that. You always amaze me with just how beautiful you make things without going to extremes. I just wanted to say thanks."

"Well, darling, behind every good man is a good woman. You know that." There was laughter in Loretta's voice.

Alexander held the phone closer to his mouth, almost caressing it. "I'm just trying to tell you that I couldn't imagine life without you."

"I love you too, darling, and can't wait to see you."

"Me too." The ambassador's eyes misted. "You want to hear about the dining room now?"

"Oh, of course! It's the most important room in the house."

"Well, I wouldn't say that. I can think of a room I like better."

"Yes, darling, so can I, and I wish I were in it right now. But I don't think Lord Palmer would agree."

"Oh? How's that?"

"You know—that wonderful quote of his: 'Dining is the soul of diplomacy.' Anyway, did you ever stop to calculate it? I mean, a major capital can contain a hundred and twenty missions, and if each just had two functions per year, that'd make two hundred and forty parties! I'm exhausted just thinking about it."

Alexander chuckled. His wife always made him laugh. "So, do you want to hear about your new dining room?"

"Yes, every detail."

Alexander described the room to his wife, then said, "Want to hear what I did for fun today?"

"Love to."

"I debugged the house."

"No kidding?"

"Yep, found fifteen of them."

"Did you kill them?"

"Kill them?"

"You know, squish them, stop them from crawling around."

"Loretta, you're being silly."

"I feel like being silly. I haven't seen you in days, and I'm having silly-withdrawal. Everyone in D.C. takes themselves soooo seriously."

"Like me?"

"Well, yes, but at least you let me be me."

"So come home."

"I will…soon." Loretta paused. "Alex, do you think the phone is tapped? I mean, do you think anyone is listening to us now?"

Alexander thought a moment. "Remember me telling you about that wooden eagle Moscow gave back in the midforties to the U.S. ambassador 'in appreciation of American assistance' during World War II? And seven years later, someone discovered it was hollow and bugged?"

"Yes."

"Well, where do you think it hung for seven years before the bug was discovered?"

"I don't know."

"In the office of the State Department's deputy assistant secretary for security. The assistant secretary for *security*, Loretta. So what do you think?"

"I think this tour is going to be murder on 'pillow talk.'"

Alexander sighed. "You do know the former ambassadress had a nervous breakdown?"

"Yes, darling, you've told me three times. Stop worrying about me. I know things will take getting used to. It's not going to be easy, but you've always said I was tough. And what of...what of you? How are you doing with it? How's the 'Ambassador Extraordinary and Plenipotentiary' doing on his first day in Bucharest?"

Alexander looked at the photo on his nightstand. He reached out a hand and ran his fingers gently down the picture of his wife's face. "I know sometimes you laugh to yourself when you hear me addressed that way."

"No, I don't...well...maybe just a little."

"That's okay. I guess it's because you know how much I love it. You hate me taking myself too seriously. But today, Loretta...today you wouldn't have laughed."

Colonel Yuri Deyneko silently prayed as he sat in front of the desk of Valentine Tulasi, number two man in the Securitate and a cousin, once removed, of Elena Ceausescu. He watched the short, beefy Tulasi press his belly against the edge of the desk. A belly of this proportion was not produced by rationed food or sustained by food coupons. He watched Tulasi remove his glasses, wipe them carefully, point them as though they were a loaded gun, then return them to his face.

"Yuri, I do not understand your stubbornness. You're a patriot. You know your duty."

"I have served my country for twenty years. My record speaks for itself. I will not defend it."

"Yuri, Yuri. It needs no defense. You're a loyal, outstanding officer. You have an impressive record, and you're highly respected by both your superiors and those who serve under you. And...and you've come up through the ranks without making enemies. I must say this is an astonishment, a true astonishment. You know in our arena enemies multiply like fruit flies."

Colonel Deyneko continued to sit quietly.

"Yes, you're an oddity. You are to be both admired and feared."

"Feared, sir?"

"You carry influence, Yuri, the power to sway men. We want someone like you to be on our side."

"But I am already a loyal officer."

"Yes, that too, that too. And it is precisely because you are so loyal that I am puzzled. Why will you not seize this opportunity to bring honor to yourself and your president? Few are offered such a high post in the Securitate." Tulasi rose from the desk, walked to where Yuri sat, and stood draped behind his chair.

Colonel Deyneko could feel Tulasi's hot breath on his neck, but remained frozen, not moving a muscle, resisting the temptation to turn around. "I am content as an officer in the regular army," he answered into the air.

"Perhaps, perhaps. But contentment is not everything. Have

you considered that your status would be heightened greatly in the Securitate? We are not children here, Yuri. We are men of understanding, you and I. So why must you make me spell it out? You know that the Securitate is always looking for friends who will be our eyes and ears."

Colonel Deyneko's mouth formed a thin smile. "Your Securitate hardly needs more friends. It is already over seventy-five thousand strong."

"Yes, seventy-five thousand handpicked men. The elite, Yuri, only the elite."

"Handpicked from orphanages?"

"Young saplings are easier to bend."

"Surely the Communist Party's Central Committee is not in need of more Praetorian Guards?"

"Is that what the regular army calls us, Praetorian Guards?"

Yuri nodded.

"And what else?"

"I'd rather not say."

Tulasi's pudgy face wrinkled into a smile. "This is an informal discussion. You're free to express yourself here. I insist you answer."

"Fanatics—they call you fanatics."

The smile slid off Tulasi's face. "Fanatics? Now you see why we are always looking for more friends! With the regular army outnumbering us two and a half to one, we need all the friends we can get. These attitudes of the army are less than satisfactory; in fact, they are downright distressing. You can see why it breeds insecurity among the Securitate."

Yuri continued his silent prayers.

"Of course, I do not count you as one of our enemies. You are a fair-minded man, and a man of honor. The Securitate can use

44

someone of your caliber. It would be shortsighted not to consider the advantages. It is not wise to take such an offer lightly."

"I prefer to remain as I am."

"I'll be candid, Yuri. It's no secret that officers of the Securitate regard regular army officers as inferiors. You must realize what a high honor we are offering you."

"I prefer to remain as I am, sir."

A hissing noise escaped from Tulasi's lips. "Do you love your country, Yuri?"

"Yes."

"And President Ceausescu. Do you love him as well?"

Yuri remained silent.

"Yuri, I am asking you if you love your president."

"It is not necessary for the fulfilling of one's duty."

"Don't be evasive."

"I have taken an officer's oath to defend this nation should that become necessary. I am prepared to die in fulfillment of that oath. That should be sufficient."

"But you do not *love* your president."

Yuri knew of a man who languished in the bowels of Tirgu-Ocna prison for the sole crime of criticizing one of Ceausescu's long-winded speeches. He took a deep breath. "No," he said.

Coarse laughter sprayed Yuri's neck, then Tulasi returned to his desk. "Colonel Deyneko, you are a brave and honest man. It is precisely because of these qualities that I trust you and wish for you to join us." Tulasi appeared disappointed by the lack of interest on Yuri's face. "Confusion, confusion. The world is full of confusion, Yuri. And you have just added to mine."

"In what way, sir?"

"Your career was built, first doing, then overseeing manual labor, such as bridge construction?"

"Yes, sir."

"That is menial labor."

"Yes, sir."

"Menial and inferior."

"Menial and honest."

"Perhaps, perhaps. But I believe we can agree on this one fact, that it is *hard* work."

"Yes, sir."

"Well then, why continue this hard labor when there is an easier way out? Forgive me, Yuri, but there is something unreasonable about a man who doesn't want to connect himself properly. After all, doing favors for the right people can accomplish more in a few months than a lifetime of hard work."

"I do not mind hard work."

"I see. Then there is nothing I can say to entice you?"

"No, nothing."

"Is that your final word?"

"Yes, sir."

Tulasi sighed. "So be it. But your refusal causes you to fall into disfavor. I am at a loss. I do not know what to do with you. Perhaps a special assignment will give you time to think things over."

"I am under the jurisdiction of General Lentine."

"You are under *my* jurisdiction," Tulasi snapped, and for several seconds he squinted angrily at Yuri. "Yes, you are under my jurisdiction. Temporarily, at least."

"Am I being relieved of command?"

"Not exactly. Transferred for special assignment. You will report to me until further notice."

Yuri smiled. "A great honor."

Tulasi looked annoyed. "Your assignment, Colonel," he said,

throwing a folder across the desk.

Yuri picked it up and noticed the bent and frayed edges. He placed the folder, unopened, in front of him.

Tulasi removed his glasses and wiped them again. "We expect your full cooperation, as well as detailed weekly reports."

Yuri nodded and said, "Yes, sir." God would have to help him through this.

"Good. This is more like it, Yuri. Now, let's begin." Tulasi leaned across his desk and waved his glasses impatiently in the air. "It would be easier to follow my briefing if you *opened* your folder."

Yuri complied, but instead of looking at the contents he watched Tulasi settle contentedly in his chair.

"The new American ambassador was scheduled to arrive tomorrow, but our sources tell us he came today. Americans, so impetuous and always in a hurry!" Tulasi paused and replaced his glasses. "You will act as his chauffeur. I assure you, Yuri, your position is of paramount importance. Study this man. Find his weaknesses so that we can turn them into our strengths. He is a peacock, and it should not be difficult. But he is also a military man, like yourself."

"West Point?"

"Yes, his father also. But the son is not the father. He served only his mandatory five years. This man is ambitious. Ambition, Yuri, can be a powerful asset or a powerful liability. Let us see how we can mold it to our purposes."

"Is he a political appointee?"

"No, a career diplomat with a good record. But he likes to play it safe, no black spots on the slate. This is also good. Ambition will make him go to great lengths to keep the slate clean. Can you now see how it works, Yuri? Are you beginning to grasp what we are looking for?"

"Yes, I see," Yuri said without enthusiasm.

Tulasi removed his glasses, then wiped them before inspecting them in the light. "It is difficult to see through dirty lenses. But things become very clear, Yuri, if you understand that man's character is like a chunk of Swiss cheese, full of holes. Our job is to find those holes. The only problem is that we must find them in the dark. We must probe and search and listen until we know where those holes are." He frowned when he saw the puzzled look on Yuri's face. "My simile does not please you?"

Yuri shook his head. "I am a simple man. To me, cheese is for eating."

"But that is exactly right! Cheese and men, both are for eating. So, let us see how we can devour this Ambassador Wainwright."

Wainwright! The name exploded in Yuri's head. He had heard that name spoken a thousand times. His hand trembled slightly as he picked up a large black-and-white photograph from the folder on his lap. An unfamiliar face filled the page. No, it was nothing. Just a coincidence, that's all.

Yuri brought his hand to his mouth and made a coughing noise. Calm, must stay calm. He closed the folder. "I will study this file thoroughly. If our Swiss cheese has holes, I will find them."

"Good, good. Now you're getting into the spirit of things. I'm glad we had this little talk. It has been beneficial. We both see more clearly now. I believe you have come to recognize that we are different sides of the same patriotic coin. While I have come to see that you are not the simple man you make yourself out to be, Yuri Deyneko."

Yuri sat at his small kitchen table looking at the portfolio in front of him. With his finger he traced the name on the edge of the eight-by-ten glossy: *Alexander Wainwright.* A lump formed in his throat. He rose to his feet and began pacing from one end of the apartment to the other.

He was a tall man able to cross the one-room, fourteen-by-fourteen-foot apartment in six strides. With each stride, his mind shouted, *Alexander.* For years, Aunt Sonia had talked about the American Colonel Wainwright who had given them the money to rebuild his grandfather's farm. Sonia had called him "benefactor," "guardian angel," "the hand of Providence," but she had never called him "thief." She never mentioned that it was Colonel Wainwright who stole Alexander from him.

What did Aunt Sonia know about brothers who were so close they could read each other's thoughts?

He closed his eyes to dike the tears as he recalled the desolation he felt after losing his brother. How could one so small endure such a great loss? Only his mother understood. She would look harshly at Sonia when she spoke about Colonel Wainwright in her son's presence. After years of putting up with her prattle, his mother had finally forbidden Sonia to mention that name again.

Yuri walked the length of the apartment several dozen times. Back and forth, back and forth. "Oh, great and merciful God," he finally whispered, "I do not know how to pray about this. I both want this man to be my Alexander, and hope it is not so."

He returned to the table and stared down at the pleasant face. He strained to see in it a five-year-old boy, but could not.

He fumbled through the papers, scanning them quickly as he went. No, it was not there, the place of birth. An oversight by the Securitate. No doubt they considered it an unimportant detail.

"Oh, Alexander! Alexander!" Yuri cried as he dropped onto the metal kitchen chair. Not a day went by when Yuri did not think about his brother; when he did not try to imagine what he was doing or what kind of man he had become. Not a day went by when he did not pray for him.

With shaking hands he covered his face. He had seen nothing in the photo that reminded him of that emaciated five-year-old. Time had a way of wrapping memories with burlap, leaving only minuscule portals of recall through which the shapes of history were often bent and twisted into altogether different patterns. It was foolish to think he could bridge forty years with a single photograph. Yet how unthinkable that this American ambassador could be his brother.

But if he was? What then?

The head held so straight and ridged in Tulasi's office now bowed freely in utter submission. "Lord, You who know all things, You who know the beginning from the end, have pity on me. Remove the scales from my eyes that I might see and know if this man is my Alexander."

3

A LEGION OF PHONE CALLS TRAMPLED the morning as embarrassed undersecretaries and junior diplomats called the residence to make their apologies for having missed the arrival of the ambassador. The first secretary had not met him at the airport. The official limousine had not transported him to his residence. There had been no dinner prepared or appropriate reservations made.

"We hope this gross omission, Mr. Ambassador, has not caused you any inconvenience," the first secretary said. He tactfully avoided mentioning that the ambassador had failed to notify his staff of the change in plans.

By noon things had settled down, and Alexander Wainwright was determined to address the matter of the garden. He had heard various sounds all morning: footsteps on the bare wood floors, whispers floating along hallways, pots clanking in the kitchen, and whistling outside a window. Once he actually saw a figure out of the corner of his eye, but when he turned, it was gone. He decided he would have to take the offensive and began following the sounds. He found the drill sergeant and her companion in the same bedroom. The bed was made, and the women were idly looking out the window and talking.

Alexander stuck his head in the doorway. "If you will follow me now, please."

Next he ducked into one of the hall bathrooms. There, on a little footstool, stood a woman with a feather duster in one hand. Her other hand groped the top of the mirror frame.

"Come with me," Alexander ordered, without introducing himself.

She gave him a startled look, then quickly climbed down and fell in behind the others. He marched down the oak staircase with the women bobbing behind him like a passel of quail. Onward they tramped to the kitchen. A man and woman were removing pots and pans from a cabinet.

"Follow me," he said.

The staff trailed him out a side door and into the arbor section of the garden. Through the vine-covered latticework, around the weed-infested flower beds, and into the fruit tree area, Alexander Wainwright led his silent band. He stopped when he spotted three men clustered around a plum tree. One of the men whistled as he kicked the dirt, then said something in a low voice to the others.

The ambassador and his bevy of five had been so quiet that the three men were taken by surprise. Alexander cleared his throat, then gestured impatiently with his hand for the men to join him.

"I am Ambassador Wainwright. I've heard most of you, seen some of you, and only spoken to one of you, and I wanted to formally introduce myself." He looked from one face to another. Blank stares cloaked every countenance except for the whistler's, the man with the dirty digging shoe. His face was open, expectant.

"My wife will be joining me next week," Alexander said.

"When she arrives, she'll supervise the running of the house, and you'll take all household problems to her. Until that time, my only requirement will be breakfast. I'll eat the other meals out. In addition, I'd like the names of those staff members who will be sleeping at the residence. I don't want to hear you in the middle of the night and mistake you for a prowler. My only other concern is this garden."

Alexander paused to allow the staff time to survey the pitiful condition of the grounds, but no head turned except the whistler's. This man looked around with a frown, then said something into the ear of the man next to him.

"What was that?" Alexander said, leaning forward. "I can't hear you."

The whistler's mouth curled upward, but his eyes did not smile. Instead, they focused intently on Alexander's face.

Alexander felt uneasy, then chided himself for being intimidated by this bumpkin of a man. He had locked horns with his share of powerful people. Why should this whistler make him uncomfortable?

"What was that you were saying?" Alexander said.

"Pardon me, Mr. Ambassador, but I was telling Miki that the soil around the fruit trees is too heavy and needs compost for better drainage."

"Are you the gardener?" Alexander straightened his frame to its full height, then noticed with disappointment that the whistler was still a few inches taller. "Well, are you?"

"No, Mr. Ambassador."

"Then who are you?"

"I am your driver."

"Then is Miki the gardener?"

The man nodded.

"And the other man?"

"The assistant gardener."

"But you are my chauffeur?"

"I am."

"A chauffeur who tells the gardener his trade?"

The man laughed. "I have spent many years on a farm. Just before you came to greet us, Miki asked my opinion of the soil. If the soil is not right, the trees will be more susceptible to the curculio beetle and he was wondering if—"

"And what is *your* opinion?" Alexander looked at the head gardener.

The head gardener said nothing.

"I imagine since you're a gardener you know how to handle this curculio beetle without having to consult a chauffeur?"

Still, the gardener said nothing.

"I'm also assuming you'll be able to turn these grounds around."

More silence.

"I've never seen such neglect. I take pride in my gardens, and I must insist that they be kept up."

Miki stood like a plaster statue, eyes riveted on a spot near his feet.

"I'm also assuming there are no lack of tools here!" Alexander's voice went up an octave. He took a step toward the gardener. "I fully expect you to restore these gardens. They were beautiful once and I see no reason why they can't be so again." He took another step. "You must understand that these grounds are unacceptable. I am extremely fussy about my garden!"

Miki broke eye contact with the ground and gave the chauffeur a desperate look. No one said anything for a long time.

Finally, in exasperation, Alexander also turned to the driver.

"Doesn't he understand English?"

"Your entire staff understands and speaks English, Mr. Ambassador."

"Then why won't he answer?"

The driver's eyes narrowed. "This is Romania, Mr. Ambassador."

"I'm aware of that!"

"Then you should have done your homework, sir. If you had, you would know that he is afraid."

Alexander stepped backward as though he had been struck. "Just what is he afraid of?"

"Of appearing too friendly to an American. It is a serious offense."

Alexander's face reddened. "I see. And what is your name?"

"Yuri Deyneko."

"Well, Yuri, how is it that you're so brave?"

The driver shook his head. "And another thing, Mr. Ambassador, you need not worry about hearing the servants at night. No one dares sleep at the residency."

Alexander took several small backward steps. Then he spun around and turned his back on the band of silent mutineers. The heat of his foolishness streaked his face in red blotches. He would fire the lot of them, starting with the chauffeur. He would not spend another day, no not another minute, with that man. But would he be able to get replacements? And wouldn't those replacements only be more secret police or their stooges? Maybe he'd just fire the chauffeur, make an example of him, the arrogant yokel. Still, the driver was the only one who talked to him. That alone might make him worth keeping. He'd have to think this through.

By the time Alexander got to the vine-covered lattice, he felt more in control. He *had* done his homework. He knew that in Communist countries servants reported even on each other and that any friendly actions toward an American today could be in a report to the Securitate tomorrow. Why had he not applied this understanding to the gardener? He had acted like a novice instead of the veteran he was. He had made himself look foolish. He could not let that happen again. He lifted his head and walked more erectly.

"Driver," he said, as he continued walking straight ahead and without looking back, "I need the car."

The black limousine crept through the streets of Bucharest heading for Str. Dionisie Lupu 9. On the front of the car fluttered two miniature flags: an American flag and a special ambassadorial flag showing thirteen stars on a solid blue background.

Inside sat Alexander Wainwright feeling rather glum. His first trip to the U.S. embassy should be more joyful. He always loved riding in the official limo with the flags waving. Often cars would move aside and make way for him. In a few days he'd be presenting his letter of credence to the chief of state, President Nicolae Ceausescu. It would be his first official act here in Bucharest, and much pomp and ceremony usually surrounded such an occasion. If this were Paris or London, a horse-drawn coach and footmen would pick him up on the day of presentation. Judging by events so far, Alexander didn't think he'd see much ceremony on this tour.

"Vanity, vanity, all is vanity," he whispered.

He was glad Loretta had not been here to see his poor

behavior. When his ego made him foolish, he never saw his foolishness reflected in her eyes. She would just look at him in that special way of hers, a mix between sympathy and love. He adored her for that. He knew how much she disliked when he took himself too seriously, but she was always kind about it. Still, he was glad she had been spared that little scene in the garden.

He watched silently as Bucharest passed before him. One dirty, gray building after another gaped like a huge sad face and was virtually indistinguishable from its neighbor. Sandwiched between were the infamous state housing apartments, gray, eight- to ten-story flat-roofed buildings. They were the most depressing with their dark, blank windows and mold and rain stains running down like tears on their faces.

Alexander watched the people move along the sidewalks. He began to notice how gray the people were; how sad their faces, how their bodies, one so like the other in dress and demeanor, produced a clonelike repetition. Never had he seen a more unattractive country or populace.

He reminded himself that Iron Curtain assignments were generally given to the promising few. Such a post was the mark of a "coming man." His performance here would determine his next post. He had his eye on one of the plums: Paris, London, Moscow. Any of them would do. His ultimate goal, however, was the UN. But the future American ambassador to the United Nations could not afford many mistakes.

Caution was one word his superior, Rod McAllen, had whispered into his ear before parting; that and the all too familiar, "Don't rock the boat." Every career man received these worn, trite instructions. Well, he had no intentions of rocking anything. Two years, that was the usual tour in a hostile mission.

Two years in this unfriendly, God-forsaken country. He would put in his two years, pay his dues as it were, and then get out. In the scheme of things, what were two years anyway? A mere inhale and exhale of the cosmos. They would pass quickly. The trick, as Rod McAllen so cleverly put it, was to "keep your nose clean."

Alexander sighed and closed his eyes. Right now he wouldn't mind having Rod for company, then laughed at the absurdity of it. He couldn't be that homesick.

From time to time, Yuri Deyneko glanced in his rearview mirror at his passenger. He felt a heaviness of heart as he watched the man in the back. What did you expect? he chided himself. Did you think it would be easy? No, he had not expected it to be easy. But he had not expected this profound disappointment either. It was clear the American did not want to be here. Tulasi had called Alexander Wainwright ambitious. Yes, ambition brought him here and ambition will carry him away. For this American, Romania was only a springboard to better things.

But it had all been there in the file for Yuri to see: the privilege, the vanity, the ambition. So why was he disappointed? Because a long time ago, before Yuri met Jesus, the "lover of his soul," he too had been acquainted with arrogance, with this cousin to ambition. So what right did he have to despise another for it? *Let him who is without sin cast the first stone.* But God forgive him, Yuri did despise this American for disappointing him, for not being larger than life. How could such a great country like America produce such a small man?

Yuri had come this morning with enormous expectations. He had carried with him a desire to like this man, but he could not. He had hoped for a sign, an instant feeling of kinship or recognition, to see perhaps that little brother's face in a grown man. There had been nothing. No physical clues, no chemical reaction had told Yuri they belonged. Now, that feeling of hope, of expectancy, was replaced by another. Yuri didn't want Alexander Wainwright to be his brother.

The limousine turned down Str. Dionisie Lupu and stopped in front of number 9, a cold, austere building surrounded by high wrought-iron fencing. The sidewalk in front of the building was deserted, although several people walked on the opposite side of the street. Alexander Wainwright noticed two men in rumpled suits standing at one end of the compound and another two, clonelike, standing at the other end, directing people away from the front of the embassy. Alexander surmised that they were secret police.

A large side gate opened for the limo, and Yuri pulled in. There was another smaller gate in front for pedestrians—visitors or Americans in need of assistance—but it was seldom used. The driver stopped at the private back entrance, and Alexander stepped out before Yuri could open the door.

"I'll see myself in," he said. He bustled through the door and stopped at the receptionist's desk long enough to introduce himself and ask directions. At last he stood at the entrance of his new office. It had a warm feel, full of the familiar: the tilt-back leather executive's chair and large mahogany desk, the matching leather couch, the wall of bookshelves, the large painting of George Washington, and the twelve-by-twelve color photo of the thirty-fifth president of the United States. Obviously the former ambassador was a Kennedy fan. Well, he would leave it. He would leave everything just as it was. He liked it and felt at home. But then, he was home.

Before Alexander could even try out the desk, two men came bounding into the office. The first and second secretary introduced themselves, and there were handshakes all around and some good-natured laughter over the ambassador's "secret" entrance into Bucharest. The first secretary, Donald Walters, appeared overly enthusiastic, and Alexander wondered if it was Walters's attempt to cloak the feeling that already he had gotten off on the wrong foot.

More polite conversation followed. The ambassador's first impression of Bucharest was sought. His night's sleep was inquired about. His plans for lunch were made. At last, Alexander Wainwright sat behind the desk.

Alexander was a man of discipline and routine. He knew it would take several days for everything to settle down. Then he could slip into his familiar pattern of work at nine, an hour for browsing through newspapers and overnight cables waiting on his desk, meeting at ten with the section heads where they shared information and discussed what needed to be done. There was usually a visitor, perhaps a businessman or journalist, in the morning, and another in the afternoon. Diplomatic dining around occupied the evenings, which consisted of two or more dinners and cocktail parties per night. Crammed in between would be the courtesy calls on other embassies, and of course, those endless reports to the home office. Such was the life of an ambassador and Alexander Wainwright was anxious to get started.

"Okay," he finally said, cutting off the small talk. "I'd like to meet the troops."

Donald Walters smiled. He was one of those bright no-

nonsense whiz kids, and had acted as the deputy chief of mission in Alexander's absence. "Your staff is awaiting you, sir."

Alexander followed Walters into the conference room. It was large, furnished in Early American, and covered with pictures on loan to the State Department by various American art galleries.

"Gentlemen," Alexander said to the seven men who rose to their feet as he walked in.

Each in turn introduced himself. The political counselor, the economic counselor, the administrative officer, the public affairs officer, the information and cultural officer, the defense attaché, and the CIA deputy station chief all shook the new ambassador's hand.

"Be seated, please," Alexander said after all the pleasantries were over. "Let's just get right down to business. It'll take me a few days to get my feet wet and I'm counting on you all to see me through. I think you'll find me easy to get along with provided you understand my pet peeves. I don't like hedging nor do I appreciate inaccurate data. Save the diplomatic snow job for the outside. In here, I expect honest communication. If someone messes up, forget the face-saving exercises. Just come to me, give me the facts, and we'll take it from there. These things can usually be worked out. In return, I'll play it straight with you and protect you when necessary. But if you snow me and cause this agency embarrassment because of it, you'll find me a most unpleasant individual and you'll find yourself transferred. I always give my people this speech the first day. I find it can save misunderstandings later. Okay, now that that's over, I'd like to hear what you've got to say." At that, Alexander took his seat.

There was a flutter of paper as the group picked through

their files. Donald Walters sat beside Alexander and began the discussion.

"As you know, Mr. Ambassador, the tension has been steadily building between the U.S. and Romania over the past couple of years because of Romania's continuous human rights violations. And you know, better than anyone here, the nature of the current political climate back home. The pressure by Christians and others, especially over the Volkovoy case, has been relentless. Of course, this being an election year, both Republicans and Democrats want to be perceived as defenders of human rights and have jumped on the bandwagon. Today we received word from the State Department that our embassy is to lodge an official protest with the Romanian government."

"What reaction can we expect from President Ceausescu?" Alexander asked, looking directly at the CIA deputy station chief.

"Open hostility," Arnold Houser replied. "And if you push him too hard, he's liable to close down shop. He's a mean hombre, and he's not about to pussyfoot with us. With his favored nation status gone and with pressure on U.S. banks to stop their rolling over of his country's current loans, and certainly no new loans, he's a man with nothing to lose. He hates his own people. He wants to modernize Romania and doesn't care how many bodies he's got to bury to do it. In my opinion, Mr. Ambassador, you'll be speaking into a deaf ear."

The others nodded their agreement.

"I don't see how things could get much worse," added the economic counselor. "The nation is on monthly ration cards. Each person can purchase only four pounds of meat, four eggs, butter, and flour each month. In the past, rural families could supplement their food by growing produce. It's not so easy now. Ceausescu's boys have bulldozed hundreds of villages and have targeted an additional seven thousand. Once a village is destroyed, the people are forced to move into unheated, poorly erected apartments. Then they're obliged to pay rents they can't afford. The economy's on the verge of collapse. Even in the face of all this, Ceausescu doesn't want western handouts. It's the proverbial dog biting the hand that feeds it. I know it sounds crazy, but it's almost as though the Romanian government wants to destroy its own people. Glasnost has improved human rights in every Communist country except Romania. Ceausescu continues to drive his country in the exact opposite direction."

Alexander pictured the gray, colorless government housing he had passed, and the gray, colorless citizens. Romania's future appeared equally gray. But what could he do? He was only one man with his first allegiance to his government and post. *Caution. Caution.* The word blinked like a neon light in his mind. Sometimes it was best not to think of these things. He would have to stay detached, keep a cool head. Besides, maybe things weren't as bad as the reports indicated.

"Okay, we have our orders, gentlemen," he finally said, "and Ceausescu be hanged."

"That's not a bad idea, sir," Arni Houser said. When he saw the look on some of the faces he quickly threw up his hands. "Just kidding. Just kidding. There is one thing, sir. Ceausescu will retaliate."

"In what way?"

"He'll increase surveillance, stage anti-American demonstrations, certainly hype up anti-American propaganda, try to embarrass the U.S. in some way, and he may even blow up an embassy car or two."

"Any real danger?"

"I doubt it. The cars will be empty. It'll just be for show, for intimidation."

"All right, but let's brace ourselves for the worst. We don't want to be caught with our pants down."

"Will do, sir."

"And Arni…"

"Yes, sir?"

"Do a background check on my driver; a thorough check."

"Any particular reason?"

"Let's just say my gut tells me we need to spotlight this one."

Arni nodded, then Alexander turned toward the first secretary. "I'd like to see that communiqué from State."

Donald Walters pulled a telegram from his manila folder and handed it to Alexander, who scanned it quickly. It was short, ordering him to immediately lodge an official complaint over human rights violations. It was signed by the secretary of state. Beyond that, it did not contain a suggested course of action nor a clear policy to follow. He doubted if there was one. That would have to be determined later. But whatever it was, he would be required to court and maintain a relationship, however meager, with Ceausescu. It was just the thing a diplomat dreaded. Alexander knew of foreign service officers who faced crisis situations in their host countries without ever getting any direction from the home office. Whoever said, "Never let the left hand know what the right hand is doing," had to have been a diplomat.

Alexander forced a smile. "Let's get something out to Ceausescu right away, requesting an appointment with him after I present credentials. Stress that it's a matter of grave importance. Dispense with the flowery greetings and warm felicitations. And for heaven's sake, don't spoil it by filling it with nonsense. Don't say how grateful and honored I am to be here. I want it clean and crisp. Ceausescu must know right off that I mean business."

Yuri Deyneko took a leisurely stroll around the spacious, shrubbed grounds of the American embassy. It was a place he never expected to visit. Now he worked here. Already it was proving an unpleasant assignment. He had relived the agony of losing a brother. He had felt the intoxication of hope, and finally the bitterness of disappointment after meeting Ambassador Wainwright. He had prayed for guidance and received none.

He smiled to himself as he headed back to the limo. He was used to the workings of God. The Master's plans always included a larger purpose, and He rarely made things simple. *"Suffering produces perseverance."* Yuri tried to shake the feeling that he was in for a major renovation. Well, so be it. He reached the car and leaned against the hood. During the past difficult years, he had come to know one tenable truth: No matter what, God could be trusted.

What would Tulasi think about all this? Yuri smiled as he visualized the round face and glasses. Clarity was not won by a simple act of wiping one's spectacles. It was won by pain; *"suffering produces perseverance; perseverance, character."* Yuri opened the car door. What did the full-bellied Tulasi know of these? Tulasi despised men of character. He threw them in prisons. He tortured and killed them. *"Suffering produces perseverance; perseverance, character; and character, hope."*

Hope, that's what Yuri lived on, and sometimes that was all he had to keep him going. God would see him through this just like He had everything else. Yuri slid behind the wheel of the car. Yes, God would see him through.

He noticed a crumpled piece of paper on the seat. It hadn't been there before his walk. He unfolded the paper, and a crude but familiar drawing of a fish stared back. A message was waiting for him at the secret place. But to go now, while on duty, was madness. Still, someone had taken a great risk to get him this drawing. The message had to be important.

Yuri got out of the car and wandered through the large side gate. He passed the four Securitate guards in front and nodded politely. The guards returned the nod when they recognized him. He walked down the street some distance before removing his chauffeur's cap, which he stuffed into his pocket.

At a newsstand, he purchased a copy of *Scintela,* one of two papers published by the Romanian Communist Party, folded it and tucked it under his arm. From there he hopped a bus that took him to Str. Bursei 4 and the Central State Library, where he got off.

Within minutes, he was standing in the designated section. His eyes raced over the bound books until finally he came to Ion Budai-Deleanu's *Gypsy Epic,* an eighteenth-century satirical picture of Romania's feudal order. It was hardly a sought-after book. Yuri pulled out the volume, positioned his newspaper to obscure the book from another's view, then leafed through the pages. A small white paper separated pages forty-five and forty-six. Yuri took the note, closed the book, and returned it to the shelf.

He did not read it until he was once again safely inside the limo. His heart leaped as he recognized the familiar neat handwriting. Normally the identity of the sender was unknown. Even the person who dropped the fish drawing into the limo did not know the location of the secret place or the contents of the message or the dispatcher. It was as if everyone had a little piece of the puzzle, but no one had the complete picture. If a person were caught and tortured, there wasn't much he could give away. Because even if one didn't want to talk, even if he was willing to go to his death, there were drugs that could loosen the tongue, that could make the mind and will bend in spite of themselves. There were things done in secret, in dark, deep rooms, that were horrible beyond understanding or imagination. Yuri had seen them, and he had seen what was left of those who had been there. No, this was better. The less one knew, the less he could betray.

But Yuri knew who wrote this note. "Beloved," he said softly to the paper and caressed it almost as though he were caressing her. His empty arms ached. It had been so long since he had been with her, since he had touched her, had looked into her face, had seen her smile. He could almost feel her silky dark hair between his fingers, smell the freshness of her clothes as if they were washed with the Carpathian winds. She never wore perfume. She could not afford such luxuries or its dangers. Scents could be traced.

"Anna," he whispered. The sound of her name made him so lonely he wanted to weep. Inside that great heart of his—an ox heart his fellow soldiers had called it, because Yuri never seemed to be hurt by anything—he did weep.

He forced himself to focus on the words. "Gustov ill. Penicillin needed." There was no signature, just a drawing of a fish with the letter *A* inside the fish body.

Because of all the publicity about him in the West, Gustov

Volkovoy had recently been transferred from prison as a diagnosed mental patient. He was declared "unbalanced" and "dangerous to the state." But those who understood such things knew it was because no amount of torture had been able to break Gustov or make him renounce his faith. With pressure building from the West, it seemed more beneficial to the country's image to incarcerate a dangerous mental patient rather than make him a martyr of the faith.

Yet in many ways Gustov's fate was more precarious now than when he was imprisoned. In the psychiatric hospital, drugs as well as torture were used. Yuri knew of many Christians who had gone there. Some were never seen or heard of again. Others were released, after years of confinement, unrecognizable. Yuri knew of a Christian driven mad after starving rats were forced day and night into his cell. Day and night this Christian had to defend himself. He couldn't sleep. Finally he broke. Another Christian was made to take so many hallucinogenic drugs that his mind snapped. Now this once bright, vibrant man mumbled incoherently and ate his own excrement. And there were others, hospitals and prisons full of them. Yes, Yuri knew what Gustov was up against. A stay in the State Mental Hospital meant that everything possible would be done to drive him mad. No wonder he was ill.

There was another side. Gustov had been in and out of one prison after another and always God had provided a guardian angel. Yuri certainly believed this was true in the spirit realm, but for Gustov it was also true in the physical. There had always been someone who had helped the pastor through his ordeal. In his last prison it had been a guard who would slip him extra food. Now in the mental institution, it was a Christian orderly who had been sending secret messages to

Anna keeping her informed of her brother's condition. It was the merciful hand of God, visible over and over again.

Yuri held the note over the ashtray and lit it. The paper burned quickly. He closed his eyes and prayed for God's grace and peace to come over Anna and Gustov.

"So here you are! I was looking for you. You left without a word to anyone."

Yuri opened his eyes. Through the partially opened window he could see the angry face of the new American ambassador. Yuri smiled and shrugged as he picked up the newspaper. "I went for the *Scintela*," he said, trying to sound sheepish, like a naughty boy who had been caught in some mischief.

"In the future, kindly remain at your post until relieved. And if you do need to go somewhere, get permission first."

"I apologize, your excellency."

"Just take me to the Diplomat's Club," Alexander said, opening his own door.

Yuri watched him through the rearview mirror and felt a sudden twinge of compassion. The possibility of the American being his brother still plagued him. He could not trust his feelings. Emotions alone would not tell him. But even if the incredible were true, even if they were related by blood, could they ever be true comrades, one in spirit? That notion seemed impossible.

Whoever this man is, Lord, please guide him. Give him strength and wisdom. Then, as Yuri started the car and pulled away, he felt an unexpected stirring in his heart. It was the same stirring he always felt when he knew God was speaking to him. And in an instant, as surely as he knew his own name, Yuri Deyneko knew that God was going to use this American and that somehow their paths, their very destinies, were entwined.

"That restaurant, sir, the Diplomat's Club, it is very inferior," Yuri said. "We have better eateries. I would suggest—"

"What's your name again?" Alexander asked.

"Yuri, Yuri Deyneko, your excellency."

"Well, Yuri, perhaps I can use your suggestions some other time. Today my plans are already set."

"I have heard that the *fripura de vaca,* the roast beef, is always overcooked. Also avoid the grilled sausage or *militei.* It is much too fatty. Now our plum brandy, our *tuica* or *slivovitza* as we natives call it, is excellent, but I am afraid that at the Diplomat's Club they try to improve it by adding water."

Yuri had been watching the ambassador in the mirror, hoping to provoke a smile, however small. But the ambassador's face was expressionless. And instead of saying anything, he leaned over and closed the window that separated them.

Alexander Wainwright pushed away his plate of dried roast beef, then disdainfully swirled his watery slivovitza in the glass. He had lied to his friend across from him—no, it was not the food; the food was delicious; he was just too full to finish. He would learn later everyone pretended that the food was good here, to justify coming back again. Mostly, the clientele were all diplomats.

"Now see here, Ali," said the friendly voice of Charles Riley, a middle-aged American newspaper correspondent and long-time friend, "don't let this human rights business get you down. It's not something you need to worry about. I mean, why get overly concerned about something you have absolutely no control over?"

"Ever the crustacean."

"What?"

"Always minimizing. Always wanting to be perceived as hard-boiled. But I know what's happening here bothers you too."

"You'd be surprised."

"No, I wouldn't. I've known you too long."

Riley sighed. "We do go back, old boy. I suppose you can't room with a person for two years without getting to know him pretty well. Ah, the good old days. How I try to forget them! But it's hard to forget West Point. I'm afraid I'm scarred forever."

"It wasn't so bad."

"For you maybe, not for me. It was hell. Pure hell. They all hated me, you know."

"That's because you didn't work at it, Charles. You were too lazy, socially and academically."

"A little harsh, but considering the source...I mean they didn't call you Mr. Neurotic for nothing."

"I like to be prepared, that's all, which brings me back to—"

"You saved my hide enough times. That's for sure. Those serious military types would've used me as the butt of their jokes if it weren't for you."

"They loved me, what can I say?"

"Of course you were never as arrogant as I was...am. But I can't help it that I'm a genius. Notice how the gifted are always hated?"

"Charles, about—"

"Know what I disliked most about the Point? All that marching around in a circle. Seemed rather silly, don't you think? And all those 'yes, sirs' and 'no, sirs.' No room for individuality. They wanted to make clones of us, dear boy. Little gray clones. Now you take journalism. What an arena! Especially the international scene. You know a person can

71

really blossom there. I mean, think of it, I can travel, be on the first line of the opening paragraph of history, report it, along with my own slant, of course, and actually get paid. Now, Ali, that's what I call a career!"

"You know you're the only person I've ever allowed to call me Ali?"

"That's because you're one of the few people who appreciate true genius. When I talk, you listen. That's to your credit, dear boy, to your credit. Just like your last assignment when I warned you about the military takeover. You listened. Turned a potential disaster into a political victory. Earned you plenty of brownie points too. Got you here, didn't it? That's what I mean. I'm a bloomin' genius."

Alexander took a sip of his brandy. "Yeah, it got me here. Now all I have to do is manage to stay here in one piece."

Charles Riley reached across the table and patted his friend's arm. "Don't worry about this human rights thing, Ali."

"Easy for you to say. But I'm the one in the tar pit. And if I'm not careful, I could end up like Brer Rabbit."

"Nonsense. All you have to do is follow orders, like always, and you'll come out all right. But as far as changing anything, just forget it, dear boy, forget it. I tell you, Ali, this government is bent on genocide. They'll not be satisfied until they've killed off their entire race. But you're in for hard times, make no mistake about that. This Christian, Gustov Volkovoy, has captured the fancies of the West."

"Thanks to your series of articles."

"What's more, he's become a symbol of religious persecution around the world. Even non-Christians have joined the protest. So, Ali, you must be careful, very careful indeed. There's nothing that stirs the emotions like religion."

"Romania's human rights violations aren't just aimed at the religious. Political dissenters don't fair well either."

"That's true, but Christians are still the scapegoat of choice. They're really having a rough time of it. Rumor has it there's a very active underground church here. Just don't get drawn in. Public opinion is strong now. Many eyes will be on you, watching to see what'll happen here."

"I know."

"Even the politicians have gotten on this bandwagon, although most of them don't give a hoot about these poor wretches. But they'll be watching just the same, and they can be dangerous too. If you slip up, they'll crucify you just for the publicity. In the meantime, the Romanian government seems to be getting crankier by the day. Listen to this article in yesterday's *Informatia Bucurestiului*." Riley unfolded the paper that lay on the table between them and began to read, translating the Romanian into English.

"'The disturbing rise in youth experimentation with religion continues to astonish the State. This, despite the law which forbids anyone under eighteen years of age to participate in church services and the fact that our youth are taught in school the danger of such unhygienic practices as Communion or baptism. It is therefore strongly suspected that outside forces are at work in an attempt to subvert our country's philosophy of separation of church and state and to bring discord among our populace and their government. Stronger measures, therefore, will be taken against all hooligan activities such as illegal prayer meetings and formation of underground churches. In addition, severe penalties will be meted out to those found guilty of proselytizing,' etcetera, etcetera." Riley's voice trailed off as he searched his friend's face.

"Another crackdown. Looks like we can expect things to get worse."

"Almost a certainty."

"It's hard to understand."

"What is?" Riley asked.

"How they take it. Why...why they take it."

"What can you expect from peasants. Sheep, the entire lot."

"A little pompous and cruel, Charles."

"Well, how do you explain it then?"

"I don't know. It's tough to say. Conditioning, maybe. All I know is that these people are afraid. I had a gardener this morning afraid to talk to me about my garden. Afraid to answer my questions about the plum trees, for heaven's sake! If he can't talk to me about trees, how can he talk to his government about his rights? And how do you deal with that?"

"Well, not here, that's for sure," Riley said in a hushed tone as he leaned over the table. "If we're going to get into anything of real significance, you have to understand that our table is probably bugged."

Alexander Wainwright picked up his fork and began stabbing the dried roast beef. "How many ration cards do you think it'd take to put this much meat on my gardener's table?"

"Get a grip, old boy. You've seen starving people before, and you've seen despots before. And what's more, you'll see them again. That's the way of it, Ali. Besides, Loretta's the bleeding heart, not you. Your policy has always been to avoid getting involved with the natives. It's a good policy. Stick to it."

"Yeah. 'See no evil, hear no evil, speak no evil.'"

"That's right. Just keep thinking New York City and the United Nations."

"Am I that superficial?"

"Yes and no." Riley laughed, but when he saw the look on his friend's face he added, "What do you want, Ali? After almost twenty years in this business you know the ropes. Stop acting like a novice. You've heard that quote by Sir Henry Wotton, 'An ambassador is an honest man sent abroad to lie for his country.' That's what it's all about, dear boy. A game. Just a game. But it has rules, and if you want to win, you can't break them. And your number one rule is 'Don't rock the boat.' So if you're smart, just keep your eyes closed for the next two years."

"You haven't kept your eyes closed. I've read your articles on Volkovoy. They don't sound very objective to me. Makes you want to blow up every prison in this place."

"Different racket, dear boy. Journalism and diplomacy are miles apart. My job is to uncover. Yours is to cover up and make nice."

"Right now, I think I'd rather blow up prisons."

Charles Riley cursed softly under his breath. "This is for posterity, remember? Seditious overtones, they're going to sound just jolly on the instant replay!"

Alexander Wainwright rode silently in the back of the limo, thinking about Charles Riley's words. This new crackdown by the state would mean more human rights violations. He wondered just how far the home office wanted him to go. How tough could he be and to what effect? Life here was going to be a balancing act, he could see that. Politics as usual was out. He would have to hunt and peck his way through this assignment like a blind pigeon waiting for his morsels from the State Department. Sometimes those boys couldn't get their act together and by the time they came up with a definitive policy on something, the crisis was over. What he needed was a clearer picture of what he was up against.

He studied the dark-haired driver. What would he say, this chauffeur, this member of the secret police, this outspoken and irritating man? Would he be as willing to educate him on things like human rights and persecuted Christians as he was on gardeners and dried roast beef? Alexander opened the glass partition between them.

"Tell me, driver, what do you know about the so-called underground Christians?"

"Underground Christians?"

"Yes, the Underground church. Certainly you've heard of it, given your passion for newspapers? There was even an article in yesterday's *Informatia Bucurestiului*. Surely you know something?"

Yuri Deyneko watched the ambassador through the rearview mirror. "Your excellency, Romania is a very religious country. Our constitution guarantees all of its citizens 'freedom of conscience.' There are millions of Christians here, thousands of churches. Why would any of them want to go underground?"

"I don't know. You tell me."

"Your excellency, forgive me, but you will come to understand that our police, our government is never happy unless there is a mystery to solve. Perhaps there are a few malcontents, yes. And in order to find and flush them out, the police will shake every bush, every leaf of every tree. It is their job, and they love their work. Perhaps zeal on their part tends to bring out exaggeration."

"Then there is no Underground church?"

"Well, there must be. Our newspapers have said it is so."

Alexander eyed his driver. Who was he? There was a quietness and confidence about this man that irritated him. Alexander settled back into his seat and closed his eyes. Arni Houser would come up with proper identification rather quickly. Then he would know who he was dealing with.

"Is it…is it your wish, Mr. Ambassador, that I try to find out about this Underground church for you? That is, if it were possible to do such a thing?"

"Mrs. Wainwright will be here in a few weeks," Alexander said with eyes still closed. "After she settles in, I'd like you to spend a little time showing her some of the sights."

"And the Underground church, what of—?"

"She's rather inquisitive…adventurous. She'll want to visit just about everything. I'd like you to see to it. It's important that she's happy here."

"And the Underground church?"

"She'll probably run you ragged. She has inexhaustible energy. Start with the important sights."

"Important sights?"

"You know, the Palace Square, Congress Hall, the points of interest."

"To a native, all of Bucharest is important, your honor."

Alexander opened his eyes. "The important sights I would like my wife to see are your standard tourist attractions. I'm sure even you natives will concede that there are some sights more excellent than others."

"Of course. There are many such attractions: The Faculty of Medicine, the Palace of Justice, The Athenaeum, the Palace of the Grand National Assembly, the Ministry of Agriculture, the General Post Office, the Central Army Club. What is your pleasure?"

Alexander yawned. "I'm sure my wife will want to see everything. Work it out with her."

"But you are not interested, your excellency?"

"I'm interested only in seeing that my wife is happy."

"I understand, sir. A man needs the aid of his wife."

"Are you married?"

"I am not as fortunate as you to have a wife by my side."

Alexander detected sadness in his chauffeur's voice. "How is it that you never married?"

"In Romania, sometimes it is best that a man stand alone."

Alexander closed his eyes again and rested his head against the seat. Let all these gray, gaping-faced people deal with their own misery. He was only here for two years. It would go fast. He had to keep his sights on his goal. London, Paris, the UN. This was just a jump-off point. Two years, that's all he had to do, two years. Two years in which his mandate was not to change things but to make as few waves as possible.

4

LORETTA WAINWRIGHT LEANED, EXHAUSTED, against the exit of the Village Museum. Next to her stood the imposing Yuri Deyneko. She had spent the past seven hours seeing two hundred and twenty bona fide village houses that contained over seventeen thousand exhibits, all illustrating the ethnographic differences of five Romanian provinces: Transylvania, Oltenia, Wallachia, Moldavia, and Dobrogea. She had seen carpets, wood carvings, costumes, ceramics, woven fabrics, household utensils—all homemade. She saw windmills, watermills, farm equipment. In short, she had seen an entire nation of over ninety-one thousand square miles compressed into twenty-seven acres of exhibition.

"It was wonderful!" she said.

The dark chauffeur smiled. "There are only thirty-seven more museums in Bucharest to see, plus twenty-four theaters and sixty-three institutes for scientific research. After that we can begin with the government buildings."

"No," she said, gazing out at Herastrau Park. "I think I could spend the next two years just seeing this."

The twenty-seven acre Village Museum, nestled in the southwest section of the park, comprised but a small portion of the park proper. There were endless flower beds, libraries, an open-air theater, an amusement park, a huge playground, and a spectacular view of Herastrau Lake.

"It's magnificent," she repeated in a hushed tone, as though viewing a Rembrandt or Michelangelo. "I never—"

"Never expected to see anything so lovely in this country?"

Loretta smiled. "No, in Bucharest. Bucharest is so…so *gray.*"

Yuri eyed her casually. She had been in Romania for only two weeks and this was the second time he had taken the ambassadress to see his city. The first time they went to the domed Palace Hall in the center of People's Republic Square, still called Palace Square by everyone except the most ardent Communists. He had spent three hours with her then, another seven today. He had come to think that Ambassador Wainwright was a fortunate man.

"Yuri, what a rich heritage you have," Loretta said, still leaning against the carved wood doorway. "Descendants of the Dacians, Romans, Slavs."

"You did your homework."

"I like to learn about the places we're stationed."

"And you find us interesting?"

"Very. You must be proud of your history."

"Histories, like the people who make them, are imperfect, madam."

Loretta Wainwright laughed heartily. "But of course they are."

"And that amuses you?"

"I'm always amused when the obvious is stated. But I apologize for laughing. I didn't mean to be rude. It's just that you sounded a bit like my husband, and it struck me as funny."

"In what way?"

"I think you take yourself a little too seriously."

It was Yuri's turn to laugh, and it felt good. He had not laughed in a long time. "Perhaps we are alike, your husband and I."

"They say that opposites attract. Does that mean that similarities repel?" Loretta glanced at her companion.

"You are a very wise woman, Madam Ambassadress." He was surprised when he saw a pink rash creep up Loretta's face. "I have embarrassed you?"

"Not really. I just hadn't expected to receive a compliment from the secret police."

"Your candor is wonderful. So refreshing and charming."

"You only think so because you're not used to American women."

"Then, you are a typical American woman?"

"Actually, I'm just a simple Midwesterner."

"Like I am just a simple driver?"

"Well, perhaps we are also complex."

"Yes, simple and complex at the same time. Interesting. But you, madam, enjoy people."

"Yes, very much. Don't you?"

"Perhaps Americans are easier to like."

"What an odd thing to say."

"By the time you are ready to leave Bucharest, you will not think it is so odd."

Loretta noticed a hardness wash over her driver's face. His lips formed a thin, dark line, and he looked so unlike the smiling man of a moment ago.

"It looks like I have much to learn," she said. "I guess that course in August is a good place to start."

"From the University of Bucharest?"

Loretta nodded. "I've seen it advertised everywhere."

"Yes, there is much publicity."

"You know about the course?"

"Naturally. The university makes much of it. And it is advertised everywhere, as you have said."

"I understand people from over twenty-six countries attended last year."

"Yes, probably twenty-six people in all. Such advertising is meant to make a good impression, not necessarily to be accurate. I see that it has succeeded on you."

Loretta smiled. "I guess I'm an easy sell."

"That is not to say you will be disappointed. It is a good course and covers Romanian language, culture, and literature."

"You attended?"

"No, someone I know did—well, never did, but wanted to. The university has been giving this course for years." Yuri could still see Anna's excited face the day she registered. But he didn't want to remember what came next. That summer, the government ordered a sweeping, bloody crackdown on all Christians. Gustov was arrested for the first time and Anna went underground. "The application deadline is quite soon— June 15. It is the same every year."

"June 15? I...I still have time," Loretta said, but there was a strain in her voice and the smile faded from her face.

"Do not look so worried, madam. My friend waited until the last day to file her registration."

"I'm not worried."

"Well, there is something else on June 15."

"What's that?" Loretta forced a smile.

"An outdoor concert here at Herastrau Park. If you wish, I will take you."

"It sounds delightful."

"Then you will go?"

"I'm wise, remember?"

Ambassador Wainwright stood in front of the mirror holding his white starched shirt on one hand and a fizzing glass of Alka-Seltzer in the other. He studied the deep circles under his eyes. Was he ever going to get another good night's sleep? He had one cocktail party and one dinner party to attend this evening, and he still hadn't gotten over lunch.

His wife walked in from the adjoining bath, her terry cloth robe slightly open. Smiling sweetly, she removed both the glass and shirt from his hands and put them on the dresser, then snuggled against him.

"My shirt's going to wrinkle," he said.

"Stomachache bad?"

Alexander nodded as he ran his hands up and down the length of her spine. "I'm going to look a mess," he said, eyeing the crumpled shirt on the dresser.

"It's that awful food at the Diplomat's Club. This is your third Alka-Seltzer this week."

"I know. I feel miserable."

Loretta stood on her toes to kiss his forehead. "Poor baby."

"I'll be all right as soon as the Alka-Seltzer kicks in."

"The poor baby needs a treatment." Loretta's lips trailed kisses from his forehead to the middle of his chest.

"I'm useless tonight, no point in even trying."

"Silly boy, is that all you think about?" Loretta laughed, then pulled him toward the bed and pushed him down. "I had another treatment in mind. Turn over."

"We don't have time for this. We're going to be late."

"They'll never notice." Loretta knelt beside him on the bed. Her hands began kneading the back of his neck and shoulders.

"Ooooh, that feels good."

"You're one big knot, darling."

"Yeah, you feel how tight I am?"

Loretta massaged his muscles, working the neck, then the shoulders, the arms, and finally the back.

"I wish you could've seen that wonderful museum."

Alexander lay sprawled, facedown, his body relaxing into the mattress, forgetting the half-finished Alka-Seltzer and the starched white shirt.

"Oh, I know you usually hate those replicated chunks of plebeian history, but I think you would've enjoyed this."

"At least you had fun," he said with a yawn. "Was it hard being with our sour 'friend' for seven hours?"

"I like him, Alex. He reminds me a little of you."

"I think I'm insulted."

"Wouldn't it be wonderful if we could stay home tonight?"

"Impossible."

"Nothing is impossible, darling."

"This is. You know how strained things are. I'm going to need all the friends I can make."

"Who'll be there?"

"The Andorran and Spanish ambassadors."

"You've already powwowed with the Andorran chap."

"Hardly scratched the surface. Besides, it'll be useful seeing both ambassadors together. They have seniority in this town and know all the ins and outs."

"Is the Andorran dean of doyen?"

"No, the Spanish ambassador is. Beat out the Andorran by a year."

"Well, he'll be the next doyen. Andorra won't let him come home until he makes it. It always amuses me how these small nations keep their ambassadors in a host country for years and years just so they can achieve seniority."

"I don't know why you find that amusing. Dean of doyen is a position of high status. As the spokesman for the diplomatic community he carries a lot of weight. You can't blame these little countries for wanting their moment in the sun."

"First off, darling, the doyen is only the spokesman for the diplomatic community in collective matters. And that's hardly the gargantuan weight you make it out to be. And I don't blame them for wanting it. I just find it amusing, that's all. To me it's testosterone on a national level. Males strutting their stuff."

"After all these years, you just don't get it, Loretta. Power makes the world go round, and everyone wants a piece of it."

"Does he ride a stallion?"

"Who?"

"The *powerful* Spanish ambassador. You know, like the Spanish ambassador to London who rode his white Arabian in Richmond Park every morning."

"No, but I hear he's just as colorful."

"Well, I'm certainly glad he's not as white as you are."

"What?"

"Your face, darling. You don't look well. You're drained and need rest."

"No, Loretta. Just get off that track right now. Tonight's important."

"Pooh! That's what you say about every cocktail party and dinner. And they usually end up a big nothing."

85

"Are you trying to tell me I'm obsolete?"

"No, darling. Just this nonsensical running around every night."

"Impossible, Loretta. Just forget it, we're going. But maybe we don't need to leave just yet." He locked one arm around her waist and pulled her next to him.

Loretta Wainwright walked toward the parked black limousine. "Thank you for taking me to the concert," she said to the man walking next to her.

"You did not seem to enjoy it. Perhaps the next concert will be more to your liking. By then, you will better understand our language and the songs will be easier to follow." Then leaning closer, Yuri added, "To tell you the truth, I never liked Dumitrescu's oratorio either."

Loretta nodded absently, her thoughts galloping ahead far from the park and the concert. She tried to rein them in, but they were like a wild stallion and would not be curbed.

"You are not happy, madam," Yuri said.

"I'm giving a dinner party tonight. Perhaps it was imprudent of me to go this morning. I've left too much undone."

"But that is not all."

"No…you're right. June 15 is a hard day for me. It brings back memories."

Yuri nodded sympathetically as he opened the car door for her.

"Thank you for a wonderful morning." Loretta tried to sound cheerful as she stuffed her painful memories back into the envelope of her mind. "By the way, I've submitted my application. Come August, I'll be a student again."

"Congratulations, madam."

◦◦◦

Anna Rosu cradled Ion's head in her lap. Blood streamed down his face and created a macabre abstract on his right cheek. She moved quickly, first mopping up blood then pressing the wound tightly.

"Hold his hands," she instructed, when she saw the bleeding lessen.

An elderly man stooped over the reclining body and gently picked up the injured man's hands. Though he looked frail and old, his trade as shoemaker kept his hands and arms strong. He could still make younger men wince in arm wrestling.

"Will this hurt?" Ion said through clenched teeth.

"Close your eyes," Anna said.

"Will that make it hurt less?"

"No, but it will help if you don't watch." Anna sprayed the right side of his face with Novocain. When she was finished, she shook the canister; it was almost empty. Not so long ago a canister like this would last two or three months. This was only a week old. Yuri would have to send more, if he could. It wasn't always easy to get, even for Yuri who could get most things. He was always getting her things. She wondered how often he risked his life, then realized she didn't want to know. She pushed Yuri from her mind. Not now. She could not think of her dear Yuri now.

The old shoemaker's grip tightened around Ion's wrists when he saw Anna thread her needle. "Be brave," he whispered. "Ask the Lord for strength."

"Can you feel this?" Anna asked, poking his right cheek with her finger.

The young man nodded.

"I'm sorry, but I cannot spare more Novocain. I must stitch it as is."

Ion's lips moved rapidly in silent prayer.

Anna held Ion in a headlock, then with her free hand pierced his cheek with the needle and began stitching the two-inch long gash. She worked quickly, ignoring Ion's moans and pleas for her to stop.

From time to time she would glance at Teofil Bucur to make certain he was still in control. His long bony fingers remained like iron cuffs around the younger man's wrists, and he had pinned Ion's arms along each side of Ion's body. The old man was practically sitting on top of Ion now, trying to prevent him from impeding Anna's work.

"She's doing a fine job," Teofil said. "You're fortunate that Anna is such a good seamstress. I believe the scar will be thin."

Anna continued stitching small Xs neatly down Ion's cheek. "When I became a seamstress, I never expected to be called upon to sew men."

"There's no one else who could do it as well," Teofil said.

Anna's eyes misted. "But so many, Teofil? When will it all end? And now, more and more I am forced to stitch what I know my needle and thread cannot mend."

Teofil relaxed his iron grip when he saw the seamstress make her last stitch. "You're a soldier in God's army and we're at war. In war there are wounded and there are…there are casualties."

Anna swabbed the right side of Ion's face with iodine.

"Owww, that hurts more than the needle," Ion said, still prone on Anna's lap.

"You don't want that pretty face of yours getting an infection now, do you?" The iodine had discolored his skin and made the wound look even worse. She bent over and gave Ion a careful kiss on the forehead.

"Tell us about the others," she said to Ion, but her eyes were watching Teofil.

"Dead, all dead," Ion said, rising from her lap.

Anna walked over to the little sink in the corner and washed the blood from her hands. Then she went by the window where Teofil now stood. She put her arms around him. When he turned to her, she could see pain etched into his eyes. She had seen that pain before, when Teofil had lost his wife, then again when he lost his only son, and now, losing his best friend.

"Did they suffer?" Teofil asked.

Ion sighed. "The flesh is weak. It feels pain, even when the spirit is willing."

"And Pastor Tson? What…did…how did Anatol die?"

Anna hugged the old man closer and shook her head. "Teofil, you don't need to know this. Ion, don't tell. You only need to know that Anatol Tson was a wonderful pastor, a loved pastor, and now he's with his Lord. And Teofil, you will see him again. You will see them all again."

The old man sank against the seamstress. His bony shoulders heaved as loud sobs came pouring out.

Ion walked toward the old man as though he were going to hug him, then stopped and began tearing at his hair. "I hate them! I hate them all! Butchers, the lot of them. And we're like lambs. Must we all be slaughtered?"

Teofil separated himself from Anna, then wiped his eyes. "Ion, you are a young…a newborn Christian. But even so, you must not say such things. I know you've seen much, have lost much, still—"

"Lost much? My family…my family was everything!"

"So was mine, Ion."

The tall, young man swayed back and forth like a bruised reed. "I'm not you, Teofil. I wish I were. I wish I could be more like you. But I can't forgive. I can't forget. I have prayed and prayed and prayed but still the hatred, the bitterness burns me like acid. It churns and bubbles in my stomach until I'm sick with it."

Teofil put his arm around the young man's shoulders, then pulled a clean handkerchief from his pocket and handed it to him.

Ion just stared at it, then a cold, hard sound came from deep within his throat as he tried to laugh. "Who should I cry for, Teofil? Myself? You? My parents? My sister? Who?"

Teofil gently put the cloth to the young man's eyes. "Cry for us all and be cleansed. Let the tears wash the acid away. Let the Lord's peace come to you and fill you."

The young man pushed the shoemaker's hand away. "Do you want to know something?" His voice was a near whisper. "Do you want to know why the police let me go?"

Teofil led Ion to the couch and made him sit down. "Because God has further need of you."

"No!"

The shoemaker nodded his head. "Yes, God has further need of you and has spared your life."

A single tear ran down Ion's face. "Oh, Teofil! How is it that you are so loving, so trusting? How is it you always see the good, even when evil sits before you?"

"You are distraught."

"No, Teofil, I won't let you do it, not this time. I won't let you try to make something good out of this. It wasn't God who spared my life. It was my own hate."

"You're talking nonsense."

Ion again tore at his hair. "No. No, you don't know what happened. But if you knew…if you knew…I'm so ashamed. Oh, Teofil, I'm so ashamed!"

The strong, bony hands now tenderly stroked the young man's shoulders. "Tell us what happened."

Ion rocked back and forth, then turned away. "I don't want to. I cannot."

"Bring it to the open, Ion. Don't let it fester in the dark. It's not good to let a thing fester."

"I let my Jesus down," Ion said slowly, pronouncing each word as though it were a sentence. "I know how bitterly the apostle Peter must've wept. I have cried those same tears today. But I tell you this, I would rather die than to humiliate my Lord again. I'd rather die!"

"Tell us what happened."

Ion sighed. "When the police questioned me, when they examined me, they believed me when I said I wasn't part of the secret prayer meeting, that I was just passing…that I…they believed and let me go. They were unable to see Jesus in me, Teofil. They only saw the hate. They only saw the hate and let me go. They believed me." The young man began to sob.

Teofil continued stroking Ion's back. "Don't feel shame for surviving."

Ion buried his face in his hands. "Their clubs were flying everywhere…and there was blood…so much blood…and screams. Everyone was screaming and trying to run away. But they rounded us up like cattle and herded us into a corner. Then they separated Anatol and the other church elders, put them against the wall. They knew just who they were, Teofil. They knew just who the leaders were, knew every one of them and separated them. Did you know that death has a smell? It does. I could smell it. Everyone could. I could see by their faces that they could. We all knew our pastor and our elders wouldn't be going home today. The police questioned the rest of us and let most of us go. But they didn't even ask Anatol and the others anything…they didn't ask…they just started beating them with their clubs, over and over again. They didn't even give them a chance to say a word. And I didn't do anything. I didn't even try to help. I just stood there. I just…stood there."

Teofil stroked the young man's hair. "Tomorrow they will say there was a riot, that a mob killed Anatol and the others. This is what you will read, Ion. Lies…lies. But you know the truth, and you will tell the others at the next meeting. You will tell everyone how bravely Anatol and the elders died."

"How can I, when I was such a coward? How can my lips speak the names of these brave men?"

The old man sighed. "Don't you know we are all cowards? This is not a life you can live alone. Only God's Spirit can equip us for such an undertaking."

"Then why has He not equipped me?"

"He will, Ion, if you're willing to let go of the hate."

Ion finally used the handkerchief in his hand to wipe his tears. "But it's so strong, so strong, Teofil! I don't know if I can."

The shoemaker smiled. "You can. God will help you with this too. Trust Him, Ion. Let Him touch your heart with His love. Let Him pluck that stony heart from you and replace it with His tender heart of mercy. Ask Him to give you a love for the Securitate."

"Impossible. I could never, never love the Securitate."

"With God, nothing is impossible. Do you believe that, Ion?"

Ion shook his head. "If God can do this thing…if He can

change my heart…then I am willing for Him to do so."

Teofil nodded and waved for Anna to join them. "Good, good. We will pray now and you will see what a mighty God you serve."

Anna came and knelt beside the two men and they all prayed together. They prayed for Ion, they prayed for the families of the dead men, they prayed for their church, and then they prayed for the police who had mistreated and killed their dear friends.

Loretta Wainwright bustled about the kitchen. Why in the world had she gone and wasted the morning at a concert with Yuri? But she knew why. Every June 15 she overbooked her day, trying to busy herself to the point of forgetfulness. She quickly poured a salmon mousse into a fish-shaped mold and watched as some of it dribbled down the outside of the pan.

"Haste makes waste," the cook said with a slight brogue, as she watched out of the corner of her eye.

Loretta wiped the spill, then covered the mold with plastic wrap and put it in the refrigerator. "Lucy, make sure you don't put anything on top of this."

"Missis, I've been in this business longer than you have." The cook smiled sweetly as she wrapped the filet mignon with bacon.

"That's why you're here, Lucy. Now, if only you'd read *Diplomatic Ceremonial and Protocol* you could take over my job completely."

"What kind of book is that, missis?"

"A big, thick, boring book. Three hundred and fifty pages to be exact. Three hundred and fifty pages of rules and regulations."

"You mean like manners?"

"Yes, I guess it's like manners, at least what's considered proper procedure and behavior in diplomatic circles. Did you know there's an absolutely right and wrong way to raise and lower a flag, to mourn, to seat people at the dinner table? And of course there's an appropriate time to wear white gloves, an appropriate time to write in pencil or pen. The book covers everything. Everything."

"Seems like an awful lot of fuss to me."

"You don't know the half of it. Take a significant dinner party—that's what we're having tonight. According to our hefty protocol book, a significant dinner party usually consists of twenty-two to thirty-two people—"

"You said set the table for twenty-four."

"—and is a black-tie, seated affair. It's held after seven, and the men, if they're properly attired, will wear a white waistcoat, starched wing-tipped straight-collared white shirt, white chamois gloves, black patent leather shoes, a top hat, and black cape."

"Phhh. Utter silliness."

"Oh, it's worse than silly, Lucy, it's a royal pain. First you have to line up the important guests: one or two ambassadors from other countries, their wives, several visiting dignitaries and influential businessmen, a visiting senator, congressman, or White House staff member, and of course, various members of the embassy staff. And you have to be very careful that all these people are compatible. Suppose Senator X is not speaking to Ambassador Y. Well, it simply wouldn't do to have them sitting elbow to elbow, now would it?"

Lucy shook her head slowly as she absently patted the filet mignon.

"Even the staff selection's a nightmare. You have to make sure you rotate invitations. It's bad form to single out any one member either by underinviting or overinviting. Then the seating…forget the seating, Lucy. I'd rather get a root canal than figure out the seating."

"You would? I hate the dentist too, missis. Got a thing about drills. Gives me the willies."

"You want willies, try seating diplomats. Rank has to be safeguarded. The senior ranking guest and spouse must be seated by the host and hostess, then the next ranking official, and so on."

"Sounds like a big to-do about nothing. Has anything significant ever come out of one of these hooplas?"

"Once, Lucy, just once did I ever hear of that happening."

"Was it one of yours, missis?"

"No, it was before my time. In 1941, actually. A drunk Japanese naval officer told a Peruvian military attaché that if war broke out between Japan and the U.S., Japan's first move would be to bomb Pearl Harbor." Loretta absently wiped her hands on a dish towel. "When I was younger, I really thought something historic always happened at these parties. Talk about naive." She pushed the hair off her face and began wiping up the counter. "I should never have gone out this morning."

Lucy shook her head. "I'd athought the same thing, missis. It's not that you're naive, it's just that you're the type that wants to give it all. Give your best. There're them that care and them that don't. You're a carer. And don't worry, missis, everything'll be ready in time. Just tell me this…do I set the table for twenty-four or thirty-two?"

Loretta smiled and squeezed her cook's arm. "Twenty-four, Lucy, just twenty-four."

"By the way, I had a run-in with the drill sergeant while you were out. She's a cagey one, that one."

"You weren't too hard on her, were you? You know perfectly well that she's afraid of you. Personally, I think it's that red hair of yours."

"Now, missis, how you love to tease." Lucy washed her hands at the sink then began washing the asparagus.

"What happened?"

"Well, after I finished the soup and put it in the refrigerator to chill, I made myself a cup of tea and was just fixing to settle down in one of the living room chairs and have myself a little rest, when I saw her in the study. Her back was to me, so she didn't know I was watching. But I saw her, clear as crystal, going through all the papers on the mister's desk. She was *snooping* again!"

"And what did you do, Lucy?" Loretta asked in a near whisper, pretending to be shocked by her story.

"Why, I told her to scat and that she should be ashamed of herself, prying where she had no right."

"And did she?"

"Oh, yes, and ever so fast, too. But not before I gave her one of my fiercest looks, the one I used to use on my brothers when they were misbehaving, and I'm telling you, missis, I thought she would faint dead away, right then and there."

"Well, I'm sure she didn't see much. The ambassador never keeps anything of importance in that desk."

"I'm powerfully glad for that. Still, it's the principle of the thing. Such bad manners! I bet she never read that protocol book of yours."

"Certainly not," Loretta said with laughter in her voice.

"You know, my brothers never developed genteel ways, no

matter how hard my mother and I tried to instill them. But I tell you, not even those scrappers would do such a thing."

"Did the sergeant say anything to you?"

"No. She never does. It's the third time this week I've surprised her and she never says a word, only looks a little terrified and leaves. I'll never get used to these snoopers over here. When they're not going through things, they're listening or watching. I tell you, missis, it's not good for the nerves, not good at all."

Loretta gave her cook a little hug. "Come now, Lucy. You survived Boston and three scrappy Irishmen."

"Yes, but with them you knew what you were up against. My brothers weren't sneaky, and my neighborhood, it was just plain bad. Everyone knew it; it was all around you, out in the open. Here it's…well, it's sneaky, that's all."

"I guess you're right, Lucy." Loretta stood by the counter deveining shrimp and piling them up until they looked like a miniature Tower of Pisa.

"Missis, no sense in you fluttering around my kitchen any longer. I can finish up the shrimp coquille. You might as well go upstairs and rest before dinner."

"Well…I could use the time to do my nails and give myself a facial. You sure you can handle things?"

"As sure as I know the sergeant will be snooping again tomorrow."

"Thanks, Lucy. You're terrific."

"I have to be. I'm out for your job."

Loretta laughed. "Don't try too hard. You won't like it."

Anna sliced two loaves of black bread and put them in a paper bag. Each loaf yielded ten generous pieces. She would have time to go to only one area tonight, and she knew her bread was ample for the group there.

"Don't you think you should stay home?" she asked the tall, thin man in front of her.

"No, I want to come. I must come."

"You look like a balloon, Ion, with your swollen face. Besides, you could pop one of your stitches. You don't want to make me stitch you all over again, do you?"

"Anna, I'll be careful. I won't talk much. I'll just stand quietly in the shadows. You must let me come."

Anna put her hands on her hips, hoping to appear stern. "If you go out tonight and pop a stitch, I warn you I won't use Novocain this time. I have precious little as it is and none for patching foolish young men who don't take proper care of themselves."

"Anna, please."

She turned her attention to the paper bag and began folding it carefully.

Ion paced back and forth in the small kitchen. "I've never missed a night, not one. I don't want to miss tonight."

"Ion, she has been gone three years. It's a long time. It's doubtful she'll come back this way."

"Maybe not, but I can't stop hoping. I'll never stop hoping...and praying. They say there's a new one, a new girl that's been showing up. Maybe...maybe—"

"Not tonight. You cannot go tonight. If there is a new girl, I promise I'll speak to her. I promise I'll find out everything I can."

Ion stopped pacing and sat down in one of the metal kitchen chairs. "All right. All right, I'll stay. But you've seen Dora's picture. You know what she looks like. If it is Dora, promise me…promise me you'll come back and get me."

"Ion, new girls come and go all the time. Don't get your hopes up."

"Promise me!"

"Yes, if it looks like your sister, I will come for you," she said with a sigh, but she meant it.

Ion smiled, then winced and touched his face. "It hurts."

"I only stitched you a few hours ago. Flesh doesn't heal that fast."

"Maybe we could pray for a miracle."

"You've had two miracles today; don't be greedy."

"Two?"

"Yes, God spared your life and He has begun to mend your heart."

Loretta took small sips of her vichyssoise as she listened politely to the gray-haired wife of a U.S. senator. The senator had come over on a fact-finding mission regarding Romanian human rights violations in response to mounting public pressure. He had been here a week and this was his last night in Romania. He was a well-meaning and sincere man who had hoped to take some concrete evidence back to the Internal Security Subcommittee of the United States Senate. Instead, he saw what Ceausescu allowed him to see: model prisons, workhouses, and detention centers.

He had been sullen during cocktails and now sat morosely stirring his soup. He had yet to put one spoonful of it to his mouth. His wife sat chirping gaily, having talked nonstop since being seated.

"Madam Ambassadress, your gown is simply stunning! I

can't keep my eyes off it. A Lacroix?"

Loretta fingered the olive green bodice of her taffeta gown and smiled. "No. I'm afraid Lacroix is too mini for me."

"Well, whatever it is, it's very attractive, and certainly suits you."

"Thank you. I've also been admiring your dress."

The aging guest patted her front. "It suits me too, don't you think?"

Loretta blinked back her surprise at this boldness. The dress, a sleeveless pink crepe with gold braiding, was sacklike and made the woman look like a stuffed sausage. "Yes, it's very suitable," she managed to say.

"It took me ever so long to find it. I shopped for days. But it's so gratifying when you find just the right thing, don't you agree?"

"Yes, it's always worth the extra effort."

"Men generally don't understand this. My husband says I spend entirely too much time shopping. But shopping is hard work. Not at all the relaxing pastime some husbands think." The gray-haired woman giggled nervously then took a small sip of her soup.

"I think all husbands should spend some time at Macy's during their one-day sales," Loretta said. "It would give them a better understanding of the word *aggression.*"

"Yes, I think so too, and maybe they'd appreciate the effort that goes into a bargain." The senator's wife plunged her spoon back into her soup, then looked worriedly at her husband. "Bucharest is very lovely. Well, actually I was able to see only a small portion of it, but what I saw was lovely."

"Yes, very lovely."

"The weather seems ideal this time of year, too. The last

time the senator and I traveled, it rained and rained. It puts such a damper on a trip, rain I mean. Don't you agree?"

"Yes, weather can certainly spoil a vacation." Loretta turned to the French ambassador at her left. "How do you find the weather here, your excellency?"

The swarthy, middle-aged diplomat smiled graciously. "Charming, just charming. Actually, this is one of my favorite seasons here in Bucharest."

"Really?" the senator's wife said. "And are there any other seasons you favor?"

"Why, the remaining three, of course," the French ambassador responded with a straight face. He glanced at the Romanian deputy to the Grand National Assembly who sat at Loretta's right.

The Romanian official beamed and began describing the delights he had discovered while visiting France.

Loretta leaned into her chair, content. The conversation, previously bottled up in the pink sack dress, now flowed freely around her. She glanced down the length of the table where her husband sat. Wives of the ranking diplomats flanked him, and Loretta wondered if her husband's conversation was more profitable to the national interest. She strained to hear the dialogue but could only glean bits and pieces.

"I've been admiring your dress, Madam Ambassadress," Alexander Wainwright said. "A St. Laurent?"

The French woman nodded and smiled, and said something about rain. Loretta couldn't hear what it was because the woman spoke in a low, soft voice.

"No, we haven't gotten much rain here in Bucharest…yes, I know that June's part of their rainy season…yes, it's one of my favorite seasons too," Alexander said.

Loretta stopped trying to listen. She nodded politely at the people around her as though acknowledging something they had just said. She sighed and took a few more sips of the vichyssoise, then began wondering what Yuri Deyneko's friends were talking about.

Anna Rosu pulled Teofil's old Dacia into the darkened alley and silently blessed the shoemaker for his generosity. Teofil was one of the few people Anna knew who could afford a car, and that car was unselfishly shared with whomever needed it. The Dacia had seen many years on the road, most of them making secret trips on behalf of the Underground church: trips to deliver supplies to needy Christian families, trips to clandestine faraway meetings, trips to haul and disperse illegal Bibles and Christian literature.

Whenever a Christian needed the car, Teofil never refused, never asked questions, never expected anything in return. But tonight, after Anna had discouraged Ion from coming with her, she could see that Teofil wanted to question her. She saw it in his eyes when he stepped from the shadow of the doorway into the kitchen. But he didn't say a word. He only looked at her in a queer sort of way. What must he think? Dear Teofil. How she hated to deceive him. How she hated to deceive all the wonderful Ploiesti Christians who had given her their love and trust. But she had to. The danger was too great.

She sat in the car a moment and prayed for God's strength. Then she picked up the bag of black bread from the seat, got out, patted her pocket to make sure the bundle of tracts was there, then locked the car.

Light from the corner street lamp probed the opening of the

alley like timid fingers afraid to venture too deep. Anna saw a group of colorfully dressed girls huddled together laughing over…what? A joke? Her heart ached when she saw them, so young, some with flowers in their hair, as though trying to create an allusion of freshness to belie their own wilted, plucked lives. Her heart overflowed with love. She could not explain this love or how God had managed to place it inside her, but it was there. It made her want to wash their feet, to tend their wounds, to shake them to their senses, to kiss them like a mother, to tell them how much her Jesus loved them, and then to gather them to Him.

But she knew it would have to be done gradually, slowly, one piece of bread at a time, one tract at a time, one kind word at a time. There were no quick remedies in this alley of sin and sorrow.

"Anna! Look, everyone, it's Anna!" a bony girl with wispy brown hair shouted.

Anna smiled as she walked up to the group. "How are you, Mirela?" She hugged the girl and could feel her protruding ribs. "Are you well?" Anna asked with a frown.

"Very."

Anna had a special fondness for this thin, sweet girl. She suspected it was because Mirela was only thirteen, young enough to be her daughter. Her parents had abandoned her when their village was bulldozed under Ceausescu's orders. Alone and half starved, Mirela had found her way to Ploiesti and into these back alleys.

"Floare, Elisabeta, Simona, Felicia, how good to see you all," Anna said, hugging each one in turn. But one arm never let go of Mirela.

"It's good to see you too, Anna, but I hope you don't intend to stay too long," Simona, a tall, zaftig woman, said. "It's bad for business, and business hasn't been all that good lately as it is. Too much competition these days."

"You don't look like you've been going hungry," Felicia said, nudging Simona with her elbow. "So I see no reason to rush our guest."

"What's in the bag?" Mirela asked, looking at Anna with large, doe eyes. "Did you bring us bread again?"

"Yes, bread for both the soul and the body."

"Oh, here she goes!" Simona snorted. "Not here two minutes and already she seeks to indoctrinate us."

"Hush!" Felicia said. "Anna doesn't want to indoctrinate us, do you, Anna?"

"The truth sets you free. It doesn't enslave or brainwash. Don't you want to be free?"

"Anna, be careful," Floare said. "It's not wise to speak about freedom. That kind of talk is dangerous. You never know who will hear. Tell us your story, like always, but carefully."

"Yes, Anna, be careful," Mirela said, huddling closer. "You're getting too bold. We heard what happened today, to the other...to the others. We heard what happened to Anatol Tson."

"Be quiet, Mirela!" Floare said. "What do we have to do with what happened today? Those people—those Christians—they're not our concern."

"But Anna is a Chris—"

"Quiet!" Floare shook Mirela's shoulder. "Anna comes to give us bread and tell us stories. That's all. That's all! Do you understand?"

"Ladies, please sample some of my freshly baked bread. I think it's extra good today, though I know I don't sound very modest." Anna pushed the first piece into Mirela's hand, along with a Scripture tract, then kissed her on the forehead. "And while you eat, I'll tell you a story about a very rich man and his unhappy son."

Mirela's eyes brightened. "You've never told us this one." She crammed the bread into her mouth and ate half of her slice before Anna had finished passing out the bread and tracts to the others.

While the women ate, Anna told them the story of the prodigal son. Most of the women had eaten three slices of bread each before Anna finished her story.

"I don't understand how a father could take back such an ungrateful child," Mirela said. "This father was a very kind man. How could the son leave him and then squander his life and fortune?"

"If I'd done that, my father would've beaten me, then thrown me into the streets where I belonged," Floare said.

"Yes, no parent would put up with such disrespect," Elisabeta said.

"Some parents don't deserve respect," Simona said. "My father's a drunk. And he's a pig of a man. He's lucky I didn't slit his throat. I would've, too, if I'd stayed."

"This story of Anna's cannot be true," Felicia said.

"Yes, it can!" Mirela said. She looked imploringly at Anna. "It is true, isn't it, Anna?"

Anna began passing out the remaining bread. "Take this home, ladies, for later."

"It is true, yes?" Mirela said.

Anna squeezed Mirela's hand. "Yes, it is true. Such a father exists. It's our heavenly Father. And we, all of us, Mirela, are like that ungrateful son who left home and squandered ourselves."

"You ladies having a picnic?" asked a large, staggering man with whiskey breath.

At once the women separated.

"No, we were playing a game to see who could make up the best story," Simona said, shoving her black bread into a skirt pocket.

"Can I play too?" The man's belly hung over his belt like a sack, and he began rubbing it as though it hurt.

"Maybe. But it'll cost."

The drunk put his hand into his shirt pocket and pulled out a roll of bills and threw some at Simona's feet. "That enough?"

"For who?" Simona asked.

"For all of you," the man said, laughing coarsely.

Simona folded her arms across her broad chest. "One. It's good for one."

He shrugged, then moved closer to the women and began looking them over one by one. He stopped at Mirela. "You. I'll take you," he said swaying back and forth and making a loud belch.

Mirela looked as if she were going to cry.

"You don't have to go," Anna said. "I'll help you find work. You could try—"

"There's nothing else." Simona stooped down and picked up the fallen bills and handed them to Mirela. "There's nothing else."

Mirela gave Anna one last look, then took the money from Simona.

"There's a Father who loves you," Anna said softly. "Remember that, Mirela. There's a Father who loves you."

"Maybe," Mirela answered slowly. "And maybe not."

Suddenly, Anna heard a coughing sound from deep within the alley. She strained to see what made the noise, but saw nothing. When the coughing persisted, Anna decided to investigate.

"Don't go down there," Simona said, catching her arm.

"Why?"

"Because *she's* there."

"Who?"

"No one you want to know. Not if you want to stay healthy."

"TB," two of the girls said in unison.

"We think it's TB," Simona said.

"TB? How do you know?" Anna asked.

"I've seen it, that's how. I've watched others die with it. They all looked and sounded like her. She's begun to spit blood. She tried to hide it, but I saw her yesterday. I can tell you one thing, she won't come near me. I showed her my knife and told her I'd help her bleed faster if she ever tried."

"But if she's sick, she needs our help," Anna said.

"*Our* help? Don't speak for us," Simona said. "You've no right."

"Surely you won't leave her to die in the alley? Where's your pity?"

"She's a stranger. She's nothing to us," Felicia said. "Why should we care where she dies? We cannot afford to be kind. Who'll support us if we get sick? Who'll care for us? We've all let her know she's not welcome. We keep chasing her away, but always she comes back."

"She lives here now," Elisabeta said, "in the back of the alley, under an old crate. The other day we saw she wasn't there and we wanted to destroy it, but no one had the courage to touch anything."

"They say you can get it just by touching someone who has it," Felicia said. "Or just touching their things."

"I still don't believe that," Elisabeta said.

"No? Then why didn't you touch anything?" Simona said. "I admit it. I wouldn't touch anything of hers, except with my knife if she comes too close. I wanted to burn it, though, that crate and those rags of hers. It'd be safe enough, I think, but the others wouldn't let me."

"You'd bring the police down on our heads," Felicia said. "What would you have said when they saw all that smoke and came to question us?"

Simona let go of Anna and crossed her arms over her chest. "The police don't frighten me. They're among my best customers."

Everyone laughed, except Anna.

"Maybe I'll still burn her out," Simona continued, after the laughter subsided. "She doesn't have the looks to attract her own customers, and when she starts that awful coughing, she scares ours away."

"I think she must still get a few," Felicia said, "because sometimes I see her with a man. And sometimes I see her carrying bread and cheese back to her crate, so she must be making some money."

"Her name isn't Dora, is it?" Anna asked.

"We've never asked her her name!" Simona said. "We don't need to know. She won't be here long, we'll see to that. We cannot have a sick, ugly woman scaring away our customers."

Anna left the group and began walking toward the coughing sound.

"Don't meddle in this!" Simona shouted. "We don't want you to start bringing her your black bread and stories. You won't be welcome here anymore if you do!"

Anna stopped and looked at the buxom woman. "What if that were you, Simona? Tell me, what would you have me do?"

"Well, I...I suppose you'll do what you want, so go. Go! I won't stop you."

"Thank you, Simona," Anna said softly, then turned and walked into the blackened alley.

She had not walked more than twenty feet when her eyes adjusted to the dark and she could see someone standing and leaning against the side of the building. Covered in tattered, dark rags the figure looked like a cloud of soot that had drifted out of someone's chimney and settled against the alley wall. Directly behind the dark figure, Anna could see an old crate turned on its side and more rags that served as a bed. The woman's eyes were closed.

Anna came as near as she dared.

"What do you want?" said a rough voice, suddenly.

"I...I wanted to see if there was anything I could do."

"Why?" the woman asked, not bothering to open her eyes.

"Because—"

"Because you want to make yourself feel good? Because you want to tell your friends tomorrow how you helped a poor, sick prostitute?" The woman finally opened her eyes. "Well, little do-gooder, what do you want to say?" The woman brought a handkerchief to her mouth and began hacking into it.

Anna hesitated, then reached out and began to gently rub the stranger's back. "Would you like to sit down?"

The woman laughed, then hacked again and shook her head. "Do you see any chairs?"

Anna gently led the woman toward the crate. "Perhaps if you just rested a—"

"I was listening to your story about that father and his son. I've never heard such foolishness!"

Anna helped the woman to the ground, to where the rags were placed like bedding, then she squatted next to her. "I wish I'd known you were here. I would've saved you some bread."

The woman squinted and looked hard at Anna. "What is this game you play with your bread and stories?"

"Bread and stories both are food, and I have more than enough to share with those who are hungry."

Suddenly, Anna felt a cold, clawlike hand on her face. "You're familiar to me. Your voice, your face…"

"I travel down many alleys, perhaps you've seen me in one of them."

"No…no, I think not," the stranger said, still holding Anna's face.

Anna removed the woman's hand. It was weak and thin, like dried parchment, and offered no resistance.

At once the stranger began hacking into her handkerchief. The rags that covered her seemed to heave and twist with each cough.

"Who are you?" the woman asked when the coughing finally stopped. "You're so familiar, but I cannot place you, I cannot think. Sometimes it's difficult for me to think. But I must, I must think. What? Did you know that when you cough you cannot breathe? Think. I must think. Yes, I know you. But where? What was I saying? Oh, yes, yes, I know you. Who are you?"

"I am Anna Rosu."

"Anna Rosu, Anna Rosu. No, I don't know Anna Rosu. I know other Annas but no Anna Rosu."

"You're tired and sick. Tomorrow, first thing, I'll bring you food. I'll come back with black bread and a proper blanket. And then we can talk."

"Anna Rosu, Anna Rosu. Anna, Anna, Anna." Suddenly the woman began to laugh. She laughed and laughed until a wave of convulsive coughing stopped her.

"I haven't lost my mind yet. No, not yet. I do know you! I told you I knew you. You're Anna Volkovoy. Anna Volkovoy!"

"You're mistaken. The name is Rosu."

"Don't play with me, Anna. We grew up together. I come from your village. I am Eva, Eva Stanciu. Surely you remember me? Eva Stanciu. I was Eva Stanciu. Was. Was. No, I still am Eva Stanciu. And you are Anna Volkovoy. What a world, what a wonderful world we live in!" she said, laughing and coughing at the same time. "Just when I saw no hope, just when I was about to give up, you, Anna Volkovoy, my treasure, my deliverance, you suddenly appear! It's too funny. Too, too funny and wonderful. Is it not wonderful, Anna? Is it not wonderful that you have suddenly appeared? Don't you see the humor of it?"

"It's cold tonight, colder than usual. I wish I had a sweater to leave you," Anna said, draping some of the rags around Eva's shoulders.

"Soon I'll have sweaters enough. Yes, sweaters enough even for the cows at the end of the alley. But I won't give them any. Why should I? They'd burn me out. Yes, I heard! Burn me out! No, let the cows freeze. But I'll have sweaters and blankets and food—yes, lots of food. When the Securitate hears, I'll have food enough, I think. Thank you, my little pot of gold, for coming. Thank you."

Anna's eyes grew wide. "The Securitate? I don't understand."

"But you're Anna Volkovoy. Surely you know how valuable you are to the Securitate? Oh, how long they've searched for you! I've known many in the Securitate. Many. They are relentless. They never, never stop. They'll do anything to get what they want. Will even pay money. I've known many. Yes, many. But not now. I must think. Think. What was I saying? Many. No. Think. Oh yes, you Anna, you are worth a fortune. You're my pot of gold."

"I...I don't understand."

"Of course you do. A pot of gold, a pot of gold, Anna Volkovoy is a pot of gold! And it will be gold enough to keep me in a warm bed, keep me under a dry roof, and keep my belly from shriveling. The Securitate will pay me handsomely for what I know."

"Why would you do such a thing? What have I ever done to you?"

"You heard the other women, what they said! They keep trying to run me off. Now that fat cow wants to burn me out! Can you believe that? She'll do it too. They'll all do something...something bad to me...I don't know. What then? What will happen to me? Where will I go? It's the same in every alley. They chase me away. Always they chase me away. But no one ever tried to burn me out before. Only that fat cow! What am I going to do? What can I do? As soon as they hear my cough, they try to chase me away. And...and they see I'm not so young and know I'll not be able to draw men for them. I was beautiful once. Did you know that? Now you see what I'm up against? If I cannot stay here, where will I go? How will I survive? It's becoming harder and harder to get men to look my way. I was beautiful. Once. Did you know that? I told you. But you knew that. You knew me when I was beautiful. But they're gone now…my looks. What'll happen to me when I can no longer earn money? How will I live? Am I a dog to be chased from alley to alley? Is there nothing left for me but to lie in my own vomit and die in the streets? But no, Anna Volkovoy, now I have found you. I know people who would pay much for this information. It will be my way out."

"That isn't the way. Let me help you. I have friends who'll take you in, will give you—"

"Lies! I won't listen to your lies! Promises. Everyone promises something when they want from you. Promises are lies, just lies. No, I won't listen. Once the favor is given, only the lie remains. I won't give you a chance to have your friends take care of me. I know how that works. You think I'm ignorant? I know the Securitate. I've known many. Many. You think I don't know how easy it would be for your friends to make me disappear…forever?"

"You don't understand. My friends would never—"

"No, Anna Volkovoy, I will not listen. You are a gift, a golden gift, yes, a golden coin that's been given to me, and soon, very soon, to be spent."

Yuri Deyneko pulled a lightweight brown sweater over his head (Bucharest in June could be chilly) and combed his hair in front of a cloudy eight-by-ten mirror that hung over the small kitchen sink. When he finished, he placed the comb next to his toothbrush and shaving equipment. There was no bathroom in the apartment, only a communal one down the hall. The apartment consisted of a small kitchenette and a main room that served as dining room, living room, and bedroom. It was sparsely furnished but clean, with freshly painted walls.

He looked again into the cloudy mirror. He wished he had time to get a haircut, but Anna would not notice. She never did. She always thought he looked handsome. Love *was* blind. His hands shook slightly as he smoothed the hair over his right ear. Already the anticipation was building. He could barely wait to see her.

He opened the refrigerator and carefully withdrew four eggs and a five-pound sack of flour. He placed the eggs in a small paper bag, grabbed the car keys, and carefully balanced eggs, flour, and keys in one hand. He opened his apartment door with the other. A few yards down the hall he stopped and knocked gently on the door of apartment forty-one.

It took a while, but finally a young woman answered the door. Two small children were wrapped shyly around her legs and a third cried in the background. Her apartment mirrored Yuri's in size and layout, except that five people occupied this flat. The husband worked double shifts at a large ball bearing factory in the city and was rarely home.

"Nadia, please do me the service of accepting these eggs and flour. I eat out so much, you see, that I'm afraid they'll spoil."

"Yuri! How fine to see you." The woman brushed the stray hair from her face and smiled. There was a tooth missing on the bottom. She was only in her twenties but looked almost forty. "I don't know what to say. This is such a gift! You shouldn't do this. Last month it was two pounds of meat and the month before—"

"A man alone doesn't eat much. You will do me this service, please," he said, holding the food closer to her.

"I bless you," she said, taking the packages from him. There were tears in her eyes. "Can I offer you hospitality?"

Yuri shook his head. "Give your husband my greetings."

Nadia hugged the eggs and flour to her chest. "I will—and thank you. Thank you."

Yuri smiled as he walked briskly down the hall, but the smile faded when he saw a man enter the building.

"How goes it, Yuri?"

"Well. It goes well."

"You don't wear your uniform?"

"Even the army must rest," Yuri said.

"Then you look for pleasure tonight. A sweetheart?"

Yuri shook his head. "I go for a ride, for tranquillity. I go to enjoy this cool, crisp evening."

The man frowned as he unlocked his door. "No, getting a sweetheart is what you should be about. The years are passing. What do you wait for?"

Yuri laughed. "I look for tranquillity. Going for a drive is a simpler thing than going for a sweetheart, and more restful."

"You'll never find a wife that way, Yuri Deyneko," he said and entered his apartment.

Outside, Yuri carefully studied the street before climbing into his exhausted '72 Yugo. A black Dacia, parked twenty yards away, caught his eye.

Yuri wanted to floor the pedal, to fly over the pavement, to close the miles that separated him from Anna. With great discipline, he pulled away slowly and proceeded down the highway as though he were a man with no place to go. He watched in the rearview mirror as the black car also pulled away.

He was desperate to see Anna, but he was also apprehensive. He had been contacted again. The familiar fish drawing had been waiting for him in the car, and when he went to the secret place, he found another note, written by the same dear hand. He was to meet Anna in the familiar place, and his heart raced with the prospect. He had not heard from her since that business with the penicillin. Yuri's sources told him the penicillin had saved Gustov's life. So what could be important enough to risk such a meeting? Anna's note had simply said, "Must see you."

Yuri maneuvered down the side streets of Bucharest, winding and turning sharply here and there until finally he lost his tail. He had been followed all week, not by the secret police, but by the CIA. Valentine Tulasi had sent word to Yuri, warning him of this new development, which was working to his advantage. It kept Tulasi off his back and somehow promoted a new worth in Tulasi's eyes. Someone distrusted by the CIA was worth trusting by the Securitate. Yuri smiled at the foolishness of the secret police. He had seen God use even more foolish means to protect his people.

Yes, his Jesus had made things easier tonight, Yuri thought as he came upon the lights of Ploiesti, a large, sprawling, ugly town just forty miles from the capital in the heart of the oil producing region. During World War II, German troops gathered at Ploiesti to secure its oil supply. In the sixties its large, modern refineries were held up by the government as examples of advanced technology. The oil was not so plentiful now. And Ploiesti was worn and outdated, a reflection of Romania's change in status from oil exporter to heavy oil importer.

Yuri accelerated in order to pass through quickly. This was a dangerous place, filled with tough oil workers who liked to drink. It was also filled with the unemployed. As more and more villages were demolished, sons left their fathers in hopes of making enough money to support themselves and send back what they could. Fights were common as oil workers retaliated against peasants competing for their jobs. Daughters left their mothers to work in the ever-swelling Ploiesti bars as table maids, and often ended up in the Ploiesti streets instead. There was no lack of prostitutes in the dying oil town and it was said that at night on the blackened side streets, women lined up like dresses on a rack waiting to be tried. He wished Anna had not settled there. But she insisted that was exactly where God had directed her to go. How could he fight both God and his wife?

Once out of Ploiesti, he headed north. His destination was ten miles farther, to a wooded area where a small orchard farm lay nestled at the base of the Carpathian Mountains. The smell of pine floated through the open window. Yuri loved the quiet countryside. It reminded him of a simpler time, when days were happy and carefree. Or was it only because they had been viewed through a child's eyes? His longing to be out of the congested capital was growing with each passing season. He was weary of his dual life, of the secrecy and deception. If only he could resign from the army and live peacefully with Anna in the Carpathians. *How foolish a man's dreams can be.*

He slowed the car around a sharp curve, then turned onto a wide dirt road and followed it to the end. There in a clearing stood a modest thatched-roofed house and barn. The house was made of whitewashed rough-hewn planks and was surrounded on three sides by a narrow wildflower garden. It could have been a Monet painting.

At the back of the house was another dirt road that led to the orchards. This area of the sub-Carpathian hills was renowned for its excellent vineyards whereas orchards flourished more in the Oltenia and Wallachia area. But the same family had owned this orchard for ten generations and for ten generations it had thrived. Yuri teased his friend every harvest, asking him how many trees had he prayed over that year? Prayer had always come out of this farm. Around the perimeter lay a thick unclaimed forest that had cloaked many Christians during prayer services and meetings throughout the years.

Yuri noticed a fir tree with part of its trunk peeled next to the driveway, and it reminded him of the peeled fir tree where Anna had hung her cross and wreath years ago. It was customary in some regions for a marriageable girl to hang a cross and wreath of dried flowers on a fir tree to announce her availability. Yuri remembered his rage when he saw it, and his disappointment that Anna did not understand that *he* was to be her husband.

Yuri parked the car. A man cautiously opened the front door of the farmhouse and peered through the small opening. When he recognized Yuri, he ran out to meet him. They embraced, then walked toward the house. Yuri noticed the parked car on the side and glanced at his friend.

"Yes," said the man, "that is her car. She's waiting inside."

Yuri bounded up the two steps leading to the front door and entered. Hungrily, his eyes scanned the simple abode; the large common room where the family ate their meals at an oilcloth-covered rectangular table and sat after dark in the stuffed sofa and chair along the far wall. To the side was the kitchen with an open hearth where the woman of the house still did some cooking even though she had a wood-burning stove. Along one wall, tied bundles of herbs hung on pegs to dry. In a corner stood several partially filled barrels of flour, barley, and oats. The aroma of the evening's meal still lingered in the room along with the clean smell of soap. The wide plank wood floor was swept; the kitchen counters scrubbed and tidy.

Yuri saw only an elderly woman standing by the stove. He concealed his disappointment at not seeing Anna and warmly embraced the mistress of the house.

"She's inside." The woman pointed to a closed wooden door at the end of the kitchen. "It is yours for the night. My husband and I will take turns watching the window. We'll warn you if strangers come."

"God bless you," Yuri said as he disappeared into the bedroom.

Inside, sitting on the bed, was the most beautiful woman Yuri had ever known. Curly chestnut hair framed a glowing, but very average looking face. It wasn't her physical assets that made Anna so beautiful to Yuri, it was the warmth and love that flowed from her like a bubbling spring. Her large, brown eyes sent a thousand kisses to him as he stood by the door.

"Anna," Yuri whispered softly, her name sounding like a prayer.

Anna rose quickly and pressed tightly against her husband as they embraced.

"Darling Yuri," she said, kissing him hard on the mouth.

"The room is ours for the night if you can stay," he finally said.

"I can stay."

"You'll be in no danger?"

Anna shook her head.

"For sure?"

"There's no danger," she said, holding him tightly, refusing to think about Eva Stanciu. She would not share this news with Yuri. It would be too difficult for him not to ask her to change identity. But if she did, if she changed her name, obtained forged papers, and relocated, the Securitate would go

after Teofil and Ion and all the other dear Christians who had
befriended her. And only the severest torture would convince
the Securitate that these friends were not party to her deception. No, she would not tell her husband about Eva Stanciu or
any of the other events of the day. It was enough that her God
knew about them. Her fate, Yuri's fate, the fate of all her
friends, as always, rested in His hands.

"While I was waiting for you, I realized today is June 15,"
she said softly, nuzzling his hair, clinging to him, wondering if
this would be their last night together. She prayed that God
would give her strength for whatever lay ahead.

"Yes, the day after June 14."

"You don't fool me," Anna said, putting her head on his
chest. "You know perfectly well what day this is, and I won't let
you go until you confess."

"Then I shall never confess."

Anna lifted her head and again kissed Yuri on the lips.
"You're impossible, but I love you."

"Those were the very words you used when I proposed."

"Yes, I believe they were."

"Did you mean them?"

"Every word! What kind of a man takes an eligible girl's
wreath from the tree and then doesn't propose for almost five
months! I never thought you'd get around to it, Yuri Deyneko!"

"You were afraid of ending up an old maid."

"No, I was afraid of ending up without you."

Yuri kissed his wife tenderly. "Thank you for that," he said,
then separated himself. "So, what is so urgent?"

Anna's eyes filled. "It's Gustov. He's in a bad way. They torture and drug him day and night. Our contact doesn't think he
can stand much more. He doesn't think Gustov will last six

months." Anna began to sob. "I'm sorry. I promised myself I wouldn't cry like such a baby."

Yuri embraced his wife. Her sobs came harder now, and they tore at Yuri's heart.

"We have chosen this way of life," Yuri said as he sat down with his wife on the bed. "We know and accept our fate. We must also accept it for the people we love."

"I know." Anna wiped her eyes with a handkerchief. "But sometimes it's more than I can bear. Sometimes I wish they'd just catch me and shoot me. At least it would be over."

Yuri cradled her in his arms. "And then you'd leave me broken-hearted."

Anna let her head drop against Yuri's chest. "All this hiding and looking over my shoulder. Not even able to see you for months at a time. I grow weary, Yuri. So weary."

"I know, my love. I know."

"I've accepted God's will for Gustov, but I can't shake the feeling that I mustn't give up so easily. It's so strong! Perhaps God will make a way of escape for my brother. Perhaps He doesn't want him to die in a psychiatric hospital."

"Perhaps." Yuri gently caressed her hair, her face, her arms. He was storing these moments, hoarding them like food that he would feed on until he saw her again. "Still, you must consider the possibility that God's will for Gustov is martyrdom."

Anna shuddered, and Yuri began to work his hands across her neck, then down her back. He could feel her tension begin to melt away. "Let it go, Anna."

"I can't."

"Are you God? Do you know His purposes? Can you say, 'Thy will be done,' when it's the blood of others, but not your own? Already God has used Gustov mightily. His plight is known in America and they are demonstrating against Ceausescu's regime and the treatment of Christians here. Maybe God will use world opinion to break the back of this evil."

"But it's so strong, Yuri, this feeling."

"Anna, you cannot fight God. Gustov is not yours. He will live or die, as God sees fit. Nothing else can be said."

"Yes, that's true, but I believe God wants to save Gustov. I believe He wants us to do something, but I don't know what."

Yuri became very still. His hands and breathing stopped simultaneously, as though something powerful were happening inside him. "Perhaps it's to me that God is directing this feeling. Perhaps He wants me to do something."

"But what, Yuri, what?"

"I don't know. We must pray on this."

Alexander Wainwright sat propped in bed reading a Zane Grey novel. The empty foam-lined glass on the nightstand contained the residue of his Alka-Seltzer cocktail. The "significant" dinner party had left him with a giant headache and heartburn so fierce a fire extinguisher couldn't put it out.

"Coming to bed, Loretta?" he shouted, placing his book, text-side down, on his chest.

Loretta finished applying night cream to her face, then turned off the bathroom light. "It wasn't a very productive party on my end. How about you? Any profit to the national interest?"

"Nope."

Loretta walked to her dresser, which was cluttered with makeup, jewelry, some unopened mail, grocery bills, and a black clutch bag. Slowly, she began moving the items from one side of the dresser to the other. "You know what day this is?" she asked absently.

"Saturday." Alexander picked up his book and pretended to read.

"It's June 15."

"Loretta, don't."

"You didn't remember, did you?"

Alexander closed his book and placed it on the nightstand. All evening he had watched her like an overprotective nanny.

"Of course I remembered," he finally said.

"He would've been eighteen today."

Alexander patted the spot next to him in bed. "Come over here."

Loretta obeyed and slipped between the sheets. "I'm sorry. I do this every year. I try not to, but it just comes out."

Alexander hugged his wife. "It's okay."

Loretta rested her head against his shoulder. "Do you think there really is a God?"

"I think so, but I'm not sure."

"I want to believe, but it's hard. I keep thinking if there is, why would He want to take our only son from us?"

Alexander remained silent. With his free hand he began massaging his pounding temples.

"And why couldn't we ever have any more children? Are we being punished for something? What have we done wrong, Alex?"

"The answer's beyond us, Loretta. It's no use asking these questions. Forget about it."

"I wish I could. I wish I were more like you. You've been able to put this behind you. I don't know how, but you have. I just wish I could."

"Someday you will."

"I just have to, Alex. I can't go on hurting forever. I can't go on like this forever."

"You're one of the toughest women I know. You'll get through this."

"How did you?"

"What?"

"How did you?"

"I…I don't know. I just don't think about it. I'm a 'level one,' remember? That's what you tell me, anyway. Nothing gets past that first layer of skin."

"That's only when you're with other people. You're certainly not like that with me, and you weren't like that with your son."

Alexander sighed. "I don't know what to say to you, Loretta. If I knew, so help me, I'd say it. You ask impossible questions."

"Did I ask them last year?"

"Yup."

"And the year before?"

"Yes, and the year before that. You ask every year."

"I forget. I block it out and then I forget. I promise I won't ask you next year."

"You promised that last year."

"I did?"

"Yes, and I'm going to tell you now what I told you then. We have a good life; let's try to concentrate on that."

He felt the familiar stab in his heart. Loretta's discontentment and restlessness played itself out, wherever the post, in her becoming overly involved with the natives and their politics. It was harmless enough, but deep down lurked the knowledge that *he* wasn't enough for her. A friend once told him that Loretta needed to "get some religion." His friend was being sarcastic, but after thirteen years of seeing his wife's broken heart resurface every June 15 and then bury itself in everything from politics to strays, he wondered if that wasn't such a bad idea.

"Maybe it's time you found out if there's a God," he said, gently stroking her blond curls.

Loretta lifted her head slightly to look at him. "What do you mean?"

"I don't know. Take a course or something."

Loretta laughed. "You simpleton."

"What'd I say?"

"Nothing, that's just the point."

"Well, I made you laugh, didn't I?"

"Uh-huh."

"Feeling better?"

His wife shook her head. "It's there; it's always there. It's no one's fault. I just don't know what to do about it."

"Take some Alka-Seltzer."

Loretta laughed again and snuggled closer to her husband. "You always come up with the best ideas."

They lay quietly together for some time, she with her head on his chest, he with his arms around her, the tensions of the day beginning to melt from them.

"Loretta, did you go out with Yuri this morning?"

"Uh-huh."

"Where?"

Loretta propped herself on her elbow. "Well, he took me to a morning concert at Herastrau Park. A small orchestra was performing Gheorghe Dumitrescu's *Tudor Vladimirescu,* free. When Yuri explained to me that it was an oratorio about Romania's struggle for social and national liberation, I understood why it was free." She laughed softly. "Three hardy souls did all the arias and recitatives. You would've cried from bore-dom."

"Did you enjoy it?"

Loretta replaced her head on his chest. "Way over my head."

"And the driver?"

"He has a name."

Alexander grunted. "And Yuri?"

"I think as bored as you would've been."

"Why do you think he took you?"

"Because he promised. Last time we were at Herastrau he told me about the concert and asked me if I wanted to go."

"Hmm."

Loretta propped herself up on her elbow again, "What is it, darling, why do you ask?"

Alexander pointed to his ear to remind her that the room was probably wired. Loretta nodded and pulled a pad and pen from her nightstand drawer.

She scribbled on the pad *What's wrong?* then handed it to her husband.

CIA says he's a colonel in the regular army, Alex wrote back.

Loretta whistled the tune to *Dragnet. Not secret police?*

"Don't know. Maybe. But they don't think so."

Loretta wrote furiously, *Why send a colonel to do a subordinate's job?*

"Don't know," Alex said as he took the pad from his wife. *Limit your time with him. He may be dangerous.*

Loretta nodded and began tearing up the scribbled sheet of paper. She got out of bed, went to the bathroom, and flushed the pieces down the toilet. "Pillow talk isn't what it used to be," she shouted from the bathroom. "Thanks, comrades."

When she returned to the bedroom, she found Alex opening up another foiled pouch of Alka-Seltzer. She slipped under the covers. "Make one for me," she said.

5

ALEXANDER WAINWRIGHT SAT GLUMLY STABBING the militel with his fork. It was fatty as usual, and he wondered at his foolishness for having ordered it again and for continuing to come to the Diplomat's Club. He ate lunch here at least once or twice a week, along with most of the other high-ranking diplomats in Bucharest. He glanced over at his friend, Charles Riley. The reporter was enjoying big sips of his slivovitza, which did not seem so watered down today.

"I understand Ceausescu has imposed a travel restriction," Riley said between sips.

"Yes, now we need special permission if we want to go beyond a fifty-mile radius."

"Did Washington retaliate?"

"Slapped the Romanian ambassador to D.C. with their own travel restriction."

"Certainly cranks up the tension."

"We're really isolated now, Charles. We can't go anywhere and people can't come to us. Ceausescu's doubled the police outside the embassy."

"He's trying to intimidate you."

"For crying out loud, Charles, three Romanian citizens were

arrested last week, practically in front of my window. What's Ceausescu thinking?"

"I told you, intimidation. He and his clan are masters. They want to keep you, as well as their own people, on edge."

"Ceausescu won't see me. Did I tell you that?"

Riley shook his head.

"All our phone calls and correspondence to his office are being handled by a flunky." Alexander tried another bite of the fatty sausage, then pushed it away. "Let's go for a walk."

The black limo stopped in front of Palace Square and discharged its two passengers. The pair walked quietly along the footpath. Finally the ambassador broke the silence.

"Things don't look good, Charles. This dirty sock of a country could unravel in front of us."

"You may be right, Ali. The climate becomes more unhealthy all the time. You can actually *feel* the tension."

"My staff is certainly feeling it. CIA has doubled my guard."

Riley turned to look behind Alexander. "Yes, so has Securitate," he said, as he saw four men in black suits following the four CIA bodyguards. The three-tiered entourage looked like an official procession.

"It's like living in a fishbowl," Alexander said. "Loretta's been great about it, but I find it unnerving."

"I always said Loretta was one in a million."

"One in ten million."

Riley chuckled. "Okay, let's call her Saint Loretta since you've already canonized her."

"Remember how she stayed at the clinic for two days during

the worst of that cholera epidemic? How she cared for all those kids? None of the other diplomat wives stayed. Only Loretta."

"You're not telling me anything new. I wrote a whole story on it. What's the point, dear boy?"

"You don't know what it's like having to be 'on' all the time. Always wearing a smile, being a gracious guest or host night after night, having no privacy in your own house, trying to forget that everything you say, and I mean *everything,* is being recorded. But not forgetting completely because you don't want to slip and give away some sensitive information. I mean, it wears on you. For heaven's sake, we can't even make love without thinking someone's listening, someone's hearing this. But Loretta takes it all in stride. She's really terrific."

"Yes, dear Saint Loretta."

"Give it a rest, Charles. I'm just trying to say I couldn't last at this post without her."

"I know, dear boy. All kidding aside, I like her too, but you found her first. Maybe if I had stayed at the Point and finished. There really is something about a man in uniform that gets the girl every time."

"Thanks, Charles, for trying, but I don't want to feel better. I want to go on feeling miserable for a little while longer. Do you mind?"

Riley laughed. "Not at all. Indulge yourself."

"The point is, Loretta's done a lot to help me in my career, and frankly, I'd hate to let her down."

"What are you talking about?"

"Unraveling, that's what's happening here. And I just hope my career doesn't unravel with it."

"Oh, you are low today. Just tell me, is this on the record or off?"

Alexander gave Riley a dirty look. "Off."

"Well, since you put it that way, I offer my condolences. When's the funeral?"

"The Christian Coalition's pushing hard for the cutback of all aid to Communist countries. It looks like the senate will go for it."

"There's still a strong conservative element there."

"The House also seems to be buckling. The Coalition has mounted a tremendous grassroots offensive, and letters by the hundreds of thousands are urging a cut in aid to our UN 'enemies.' The budget deficit's unnerving everyone. People are starting to panic that their taxes will go up. And the Coalition's begun to pressure major banks to halt all lending to Communist nations."

"And Romania is first on their list?"

"Bingo. Now Romania has already given up most favored nation status, but if they're refused any more loans, you know what'll happen?"

"A funeral. Death of a nation. And I say, let it die. It's rotten, Ali. It's a rotten, stinking corpse already, only it doesn't know it."

"But *I* don't want to die with it."

"Don't be melodramatic. Your career, dear boy, will survive. Just keep your head. That's all. Keep your head."

Alexander smiled wistfully. "The Seventh Floor is paved with heads. You know State. They give as little guidance as possible, so if things get fouled up, the field office takes the hit. One wrong turn on this and I could be back in the bush country with my mosquito nets."

"Not the end of the world."

"That depends on which side of the net you're standing."

"So, what do you want from me?"

"You know how isolated we are at the embassy. No one talks to us except the other embassies, and they're just as isolated. You're the only foreigner I know who has his finger on the pulse of this country."

For the first time, Riley laughed. The only pulse he had his finger on was that of his Romanian girlfriend, and he was quite certain she was secret police. "I'm afraid you've overestimated my position here. Ever since I did those Volkovoy articles, I've been restricted in where I'm allowed to go and what I can see. They're squeezing hard, trying to dry up my contacts. People are frightened to be seen with me. Now I get most of my information hanging around sleazy holes-in-the-wall, buying lots of slivovitza for anyone who'll let me, hoping that someone will slip and say something. But honestly, dear boy, I think most of the time I'm just buying drinks for the secret police. I think they must have a jolly laugh over it every night when they go home."

"But you still overhear things, and you're able to get impressions that are denied us."

"I suppose."

"I want to know what I can expect, what my people can expect."

"I'm not going to tell you anything your CIA boys haven't already told you. But for starters, Ceausescu won't stand idly by while his country goes under. He'll want a scapegoat. At the very least, expect an increase in anti-American propaganda. Maybe some 'spontaneous' demonstrations. And of course, he might try to discredit or embarrass you."

"And the worst?"

"He'll close down shop, expel you."

"And the Romanian people. What of them?"

"They're tired, Ali, and hungry. Many of them don't have jobs, a roof over their heads, or heat in the winter. You won't hear them cry if Romania falls, as long as Ceausescu falls with it."

"That's all you've got?"

"That's it. Told you I wouldn't have anything new."

"All right. Thanks. But keep your ears open and tell me if you hear anything."

"Of course, dear boy. Does that mean I can charge my bar tab to the embassy?"

Alexander laughed. "At least you've made me feel better, you and your jokes."

"Who's joking?"

Alexander walked toward the waiting limo. "Can I drop you somewhere?"

"No thanks. It's a nice day for a stroll." Riley stopped on the sidewalk. "You still didn't tell me if I have to pay for the slivovitza?"

"I've seen the size of your bar tabs," Alexander said, not even bothering to look back at his friend. "Forget it."

"In that case, I'd better look for some fringe benefits elsewhere," Riley said, sticking his right index finger in the air. "I think I'll go take someone's pulse."

Yuri Deyneko sat behind the wheel watching the ambassador and reporter in the distance. What was he going to do? He prayed a while then closed his eyes and pictured his wife. The first thing he saw was her tears, and he tried to block it out. Their evening together had been bittersweet. They had spent the night talking and making love. They had also spent much

time in prayer, most of it for Gustov. It was during those times
that something began to stir in Yuri's heart. If the West had
made Gustov their symbol for human rights, perhaps they
would be willing to rescue that symbol. The thought, like an
embryo, began to form and take shape in Yuri's mind. Maybe
the U.S. Ambassador would help. It had seemed a ludicrous
assumption at first, but gradually, it appeared less foolish. What
if this was God's answer for Gustov? What if this was God's way
of escape? But if Yuri was wrong—if he approached the
American, revealed who he was and what he wanted, what
then? He envisioned disaster. They had continued to pray. Still,
the nagging feeling had not lifted. Finally, his lips gave birth to
his thoughts, and Yuri had said the unthinkable. "I will speak
to Ambassador Wainwright."

Now, as he sat watching the two Americans, his faith, so
strong the night before, began to give way. He had promised
Anna he would follow the leading of the Lord. But what if he
had misunderstood God's direction? So many lives hung on his
slender thread of decision. He had to be sure.

He thought of the protests going on in America. At least
someone on the outside knew what was happening here. Do
not forget us, American church! he cried silently. Pray for us,
weep for us, carry protest signs for us. *But do not forget us!*

Maybe this was the sole reason for Gustov's suffering, Yuri
thought, closing his eyes again. Perhaps gaining U.S. attention
was enough. Perhaps it was not necessary to go further.
Perhaps he had missed God after all. He had been so sure last
night. Oh, where was his faith now?

As Yuri rested his head against the seat, a vision began to
form behind his closed eyes. At first it appeared as a micro-
scopic seed. How insidiously it had taken root in his heart!

How quickly it grew into this sizable obstacle! It was hideous and full of torment, and after several moments of studying it, Yuri was finally able to call it by name. Fear. Fear was the real issue here. Last night he had accused Anna of not trusting God with Gustov's life. Today, he was afraid to trust God with hers. What if something happened and Anna was discovered, arrested, imprisoned…killed? This was the obstacle that held him from his sure course. He felt ashamed. *Oh, you of little faith!* Who was he to question his Lord? His instructions were clear and he would follow them.

"To the compound," Ambassador Wainwright said, sliding into the backseat.

Yuri opened his eyes and looked into his rearview mirror at the tall, stately man. The question of whether this was his brother had faded more and more into the background of Yuri's mind. Gustov's problem was all-consuming now, that and the problems facing his country. Yuri wished he could pour his heart out to this American, to tell him of his suffering land, to tell him of his wondrous God, and in that telling, light a spark in him. He watched the American in the mirror. *American ambassador, how I wish you could be that agent of healing,* his heart cried, but with his lips he said, "And how was your lunch, sir?"

"Fine, just fine."

"Mr. Riley looks well. Did he also enjoy his lunch?"

"You know Riley?"

"I've never had the pleasure, sir. But I have read his work. His writings on Gustov Volkovoy were inspired."

"How is it that a chauffeur reads American newspapers?"

"Colonels need to keep informed."

"Colonel Deyneko, I assume?"

"You show no surprise."

"No."

"Is your CIA's dossier on me very large?"

"Moderate."

"It is as expected."

"Is it?"

"Your CIA is usually thorough. But you are wondering why I speak now."

"Something like that."

Yuri was still parked by the curb and turned to face the ambassador. The partition between them was open. "Because I find I need to trust you."

"Are we on tape?"

Yuri laughed. "The secret police have no need to bug your car. They have put me here."

"What about your friends back there? Do they have some gismo pointed at us, picking up every word we say?"

"I have told you no extraordinary means of surveillance are being used."

Alexander crossed and uncrossed his legs, trying to decide whether he should continue this conversation or end it now. "What did you want to talk about?" he finally said.

"Gustov Volkovoy."

"What about him."

"He is dying. He has no more than six months to live."

"Why are you telling me this?"

"America needs to know what is happening here. It needs to know that this country is a butcher shop that bleeds its people."

"Is this an official complaint?"

"No."

"Are you defecting?"

"No."

"What then?"

"I am asking you to get Gustov out of the country."

"You're asking the impossible."

"The CIA could do it. And I would see to it that they had inside help."

"It's *impossible!*"

"You do not trust me. You are saying in your mind, 'This is a trap.'"

"It has all the earmarks."

"I beg you, Mr. Ambassador. Gustov's life depends on it."

"Why should you care about this Volkovoy? Who is he to you?"

Yuri sat silently for a moment, then leaned so far over the backseat that Alexander could see the flecks of black embedded in his brown pupils. "What I tell you now could cost my life. He is…he is my brother-in-law."

Alexander turned his face away and sank into the leather seat. "I don't believe you," he finally said.

"Then let me convince you."

"No, I will not pursue this. You may have a legitimate grievance against your country, but I can't help you with that. Unless this is a defection, I—"

"I will not defect, Mr. Ambassador."

"Then there's nothing I can do."

"Because you are afraid."

"Because I am an official of the United States government with no jurisdiction here, and because my first responsibility is to my staff at the embassy and to my country. I do not have the luxury of crossing that invisible boundary between what I must do and what I would like to do."

"Because you are afraid."

"This issue is dead." Alexander began to close the glass partition between them.

"And so is Gustov Volkovoy," Yuri said just as the glass slid shut. He took one last look in the rearview mirror. No, it was impossible. This man could never, never be his brother.

The little brass bell over the entrance jingled when a woman in rags opened the door and stepped into Teofil Bucur's Leather Shop. For a moment she seemed confused, as though she had made a mistake and might leave, but finally she settled in an uncomfortable looking stance and just stared wide-eyed. The shop was only one room but was divided into two distinct industries. To the right was the leather shop with its heavy-duty sewing machine and large drill-like punch. Hides of various species and sizes hung on hooks along the wall. On the floor, leather scraps formed miniature mountains and the bitter smell of tannic acid floated over the mounds like vapor from a volcano. Against the far wall and almost in the corner, a thin, old man sat hunched over a table. He did not look up.

The rag woman shuffled to the left side of the room. Here a smaller, daintier sewing machine hummed as Anna Rosu sat busily stitching the cuff of a flannel shirt. Against the back wall was a neat array of colorful fabrics, ribbons, buttons, zippers, and spools and spools of cotton thread lined up in rows by color.

Although Teofil Bucur owned the shop, had owned it for forty years, he had begun renting out half of his space to Anna almost three years ago. And although the store now served a dual purpose, the name Leather Shop remained and had come, by word of mouth, to mean in most Ploiesti minds both a place where one could get a shirt as well as a pair of shoes, either new or repaired.

The rag woman leaned against the counter and coughed into her handkerchief. Without looking up, Anna Rosu continued to join the interfacing ends with a lapped seam. She had been up all night with Yuri and was tired and unable to command her fingers to work the heavy, durable flannel.

"I'll be with you shortly," she said.

The stranger coughed again into her handkerchief, then said, "I couldn't do it. I tried, but I couldn't do it."

Anna finally looked up. Her face went white when she saw Eva Stanciu. Her eyes darted past the bundle of rags in search of the Securitate.

"I couldn't do it," Eva repeated.

Anna's heart pounded. *To live is Christ, to die is gain.* She only hoped her weak flesh would not disgrace her beautiful Jesus, and prayed for courage.

"I tried, but I couldn't…I couldn't do it."

Anna looked carefully at the worn, sick woman with her caked makeup and lined dirty neck, her sunken cheeks and dark empty eyes, and only then realized Eva was alone.

"Come sit," Anna said, when Eva staggered and looked as if she were about to topple.

Eva allowed the seamstress to direct her, without protest, to a cushioned armchair in the corner.

"I walked back and forth, back and forth, but I could not go in."

"What are you talking about?"

"All morning I walked in front of police headquarters. Back and forth, back and forth. I'm so tired. Yes, this chair is good.

It's been so long since I've sat in one. I'm so tired. So tired."

"What about police headquarters?" Anna pressed.

"You know all about that, Anna Volkovoy!"

Anna shot a quick look over to Teofil who was punching holes into a new leather belt. His eyes grew large as they met hers. Without saying a word, he went to the front door, locked it, then hung a CLOSED sign.

Eva tried to rise from her chair when she saw Teofil pull the shades, but she was too weak and fell backward.

"You plan to kill me, yes, I see. You'll kill me and dispose of me like a bundle of garbage. Like a bundle of—" The woman began to cough, and her thin shoulders shook up and down.

Anna picked up a clean piece of cloth and began dabbing the perspiration that dotted Eva's face. Then she gently rubbed her back. "No one is going to hurt you. You're safe here."

The coughing stopped and the frail body sank deeper into the chair. Eva's thin clawlike hand took the cloth from Anna and blotted her mouth. Blood streaked the fabric.

"Can you tell me about this morning? Are you strong enough to talk?"

"You won't get away with this. I know people in high positions. I have known many. Many. They kill people too. They'll find out. If you do anything to me, they'll find out. They find out everything. In the end, they find out everything."

"Eva, think. I need to know about this morning."

"Yes, think, think. I haven't lost my mind yet. Not yet. I still have that. Think. Only do not hurt me, Anna Volkovoy!"

"You must stop using that name. *Please,* Eva, you must stop."

The frail woman nodded, then let her head slump to her chest. "I am tired. So tired."

"You went to police headquarters this morning, then what?"

Eva's head remained slumped, and she closed her eyes. "Nothing. Then nothing."

"You didn't go in? You didn't tell them about me?"

Eva shook her head.

"Why?"

"Every time I tried, I couldn't. I couldn't. It was as though something held me back. Once I thought I felt a hand, but no, it was nothing…maybe, maybe it was nothing. I couldn't go. I couldn't do it. I tried, but I couldn't do it."

Anna turned to Teofil, who now stood behind her. He embraced her, and she could hear him whisper, "Praise God!"

She too praised her God. Her heart swelled with love for Him. And gratitude. Oh, how generous He was! How kind! There was no doubt in her mind that it was He who had stayed Eva this morning.

"It's a pleasure to make your acquaintance, Anna Volkovoy," Teofil whispered.

Anna returned his embrace. "Forgive me for my deception, and forgive me for having now involved you in this."

"It is God who orchestrates our lives, Anna, not us. We come and go as the Master bids. Don't concern yourself. You've done nothing wrong."

Suddenly, they heard loud coughing and turned to see the cloth Eva pressed against her mouth soaked with bright red blood.

"Teofil, get the doctor!"

"He won't come. He never comes…here."

"Then go to the hospital and ask them what to do. And get some medicine."

"For a woman who's bleeding?"

"For a woman who has TB."

"TB?" Teofil said softly, then took a deep breath. "But of course, Anna, I'll go, and you must try to get this sick woman upstairs where we can take care of her."

Anna's eyes misted. "Teofil, I don't care for myself, but if you take her in and she should talk, she'll bring you trouble. They'll think that you knew about me all along. It will go badly for you."

"Go upstairs with her, Anna. God has sent her here and I won't be the one to turn her away."

Loretta Wainwright watched Yuri Deyneko through her bedroom window as he buffed the sleek, black limousine. She had seen him do this before, only this time he was not whistling any of those merry little tunes. Her husband didn't want the colonel hanging around the embassy and had ordered the car kept at the residency.

She knew all about their explosive encounter. Alexander had written down every detail for Loretta to read. He had also cautioned her to avoid all contact and to curtail all outings. In her husband's opinion, Yuri Deyneko was capable of anything.

Who was this man who gave her husband nightmares? she wondered as she stared through the window. Since Alexander's conversation with Yuri, he had been agitated and out of sorts. For the past three days and nights, he had eaten and slept little.

The Romanian colonel was burdened too. She could see it in his slow gait, in his brooding face, in the way he buffed the car as if the rag were a fifty-pound weight. It was impossible for her to believe Yuri capable of fabricating such a gross lie. But how could Gustov Volkovoy be his brother-in-law? Would

Yuri have attained his rank in the Romanian army if he were related to such a hated national figure? And what was a colonel doing as a chauffeur? No matter how she added it, it always tallied trouble.

Loretta watched Yuri buff the left fender. He went over the same spot time and again, like a man whose mind was far from his work. Was it on Gustov Volkovoy? She had read all of Charles Riley's articles. They had kept her up nights. They had made her walk the floor of her fifty-foot-long dining room for more hours than she cared to count. She shuddered to think that while she gazed out this very window, thousands of Christians, like Gustov Volkovoy, were in prisons all over Romania, being tortured and starved. She watched Yuri drag a heavy hand over the car and visualized another hand with a whip being drawn across a bare back. As he raised a hand to wipe the sweat off his forehead, she pictured another fist crashing against a cheek. As he picked up a water bottle and drank, she pictured the cracked and bleeding lips that were denied water. Was this the reason for his great burden? Was Yuri picturing these things too?

In all her years of marriage, Loretta Wainwright never once deliberately went against her husband's wishes. But before she could stop herself, she opened the window and shouted, "Yuri, I'll be needing the car."

Throughout the ride to Herastrau Park, Loretta sat quietly in the back. Her mind rebuked her over and over again. *What are you doing, Loretta? This is madness!* When the car finally stopped in the parking lot, she allowed Yuri to open the door for her.

"Let's go over there," she said, pointing to the playground.

The grounds were deserted except for a woman and young boy of about five. As the woman pushed him on a swing, she kept looking up at the clouds that swirled dark and menacing overhead. She said something to him, and he began to cry. She tried to bring the swing to a stop, but the young boy continued to pump his legs and almost slipped off. The mother said something Loretta did not understand, but she recognized that universal language of a mother scolding her child not so much because he had been naughty but because he had frightened her. When the boy began to cry again, the woman picked him up, kissed him on the cheek, and started to carry him off. Take away the outer layers of language, dress, and customs, and we are not so different, Loretta thought.

"Buna dimineata," Loretta said to the woman.

The woman slowed her pace as she approached the American, smiled shyly, but neither answered or stopped.

"Esti grabit Vrem sa placam, ca e semana ploaie?" Loretta continued, speaking louder than normal so the harmless nature of the conversation could be overheard and not compromise the stranger.

The woman looked confused, smiled politely, nodded after a moment's reflection, then resumed her journey carrying her child.

"What did you say to her?" Yuri asked with a smile.

"You're in a hurry to leave before it rains?"

He chuckled and shook his head.

"Okay, what *did* I say?"

"You are in a hurry, we want to leave because it looks like rain."

Loretta laughed. "I have been studying this language of yours, but I still can't speak it."

"But you try, that is the main thing."

"I guess." Loretta sat on the swing and held it steady by digging her heels into the ground.

"Why are we here, Madam Ambassadress?"

"You're a blunt man, Colonel Deyneko."

"It is out of respect."

"I know." Then looking anxiously around she said, "Is it safe?"

"Safer than most."

"Out of respect, I'll be blunt as well. I want to hear about Gustov Volkovoy."

"Why?"

"Because I want to help."

"Your husband does not share your feelings."

"Don't judge him too harshly. He's a good man. But he can't risk the U.S. position here."

"He does not believe me. He does not believe that Gustov and I are relatives."

"No."

"But you do?"

"Yes."

"Why?"

"Because I just do."

Yuri smiled. "Yes, I suppose it is for the same reason I trust you. But what of your husband? Does he know you are speaking with me?"

"No. I'll tell him when I think it best. I love my husband, and I won't do anything to betray or embarrass him or the United States."

"I understand, but what can you do?"

"We have a friend, a reporter, Charles Riley."

"I know of him."

"If I bring him information, he'll publish it."

"He has already written about Gustov."

"Yes, and with marvelous results. If I can give him new material, well, it'll keep the pressure on."

"On who, madam?"

Loretta was quiet, then finally she shrugged. "Public opinion can change things, Colonel Deyneko."

"If you please, between us I wish you to call me Yuri."

"You could tell me exactly what to say to Charles, so no one is compromised or put in danger."

Yuri paced in front of her for a few minutes without speaking. "I will pray on it," he finally said.

Loretta rose from the swing. "Yuri, are you...are you a Christian?"

Yuri nodded.

"You're with the Underground?"

Again he nodded.

Loretta let out a deep sigh. "I hadn't expected that, or maybe I did. I don't know."

"You are distressed?"

"This complicates things. This is more dangerous than I had counted on. It seems now that your life is also on the line."

"Why?"

"Because until I can convince my husband that you're telling the truth about Gustov, I can't tell him about you and the Underground. With the house bugged, well, he could betray you without meaning to, just with a misspoken word."

"He could do that now, with what I have told him about Gustov."

"No. He never mentions that name, ever, just in case you

are telling the truth. But it's for Gustov's sake, not yours."

"And Charles Riley? He is your husband's friend. Will he help you without the ambassador's knowledge?"

"Charles knows the position my husband's in. He'll protect Alexander by not involving him. And as for me, a reporter will never betray his source. We can trust Charles."

Yuri nodded thoughtfully, then glanced up at the dark clouds. "I will let you know. Is that all?"

"What's the Underground church like?" Loretta asked, looking into his kind eyes. She did not see a Romanian colonel before her now. She saw a quiet, humble man, a man of great courage.

"How does one describe a thing so beautiful or a love so great? The Underground church is a church purified by fire and blood."

"I can't believe that you, an army colonel working for the secret police, could be part of that. It's incredible."

"You would be surprised just how many of us there are in positions of authority. But I was not always with the Underground. I was already a grown man before I even realized it existed."

"How is that? I mean, how did you discover it?"

Yuri looked again at the clouds that were growing increasingly dark. "It will rain soon."

"You don't want to talk about it?"

Yuri shrugged. "These memories are painful. It is difficult to think or speak of them."

"I'm sorry. I didn't mean to pry."

"No, it is good for you to know. Remember outside the Village Museum you said that I must be proud of my heritage and history?"

"Yes. Your answer reminded me of something Alexander would say."

"I answered in that way because I have witnessed my country's history during its hour of shame. We are still living in that hour."

"The human rights violations?"

Yuri nodded. "I did not always see this shame. There was a time when I saw it as a season of glory. We were going to forge a new, modern nation. How ambitious I was! Such a vain, young soldier in search of fame."

"It's hard to picture you that way."

"Why? It is the photograph of every man with an unregenerated soul. An empty soul must fill itself. And what poor filler we choose. Power, wealth, pleasure. And still they do not satisfy. This was the state of my soul before I was assigned to guard duty at Tirgu-Ocna prison."

"That must've been a very long time ago."

"Not so long. Only eighteen years."

"That's where you became a Christian?"

"No, that was where I first became mindful of them. I had heard rumors of what went on in these places, the torture and the horrible savagery. But it did not prepare me for what I saw. I learned quickly that there were two types of guards. The first did their duty without trying to become animals, the second *were* animals. In this second group were inquisitors who extracted confessions through torture, and instructors who taught by punishment. These men loved their work."

"How long were you there?"

"Two years. For two long years I lived in the belly of a beast. For two long years I watched starving men fight over potato peelings, saw all manner of perversion, saw men's bodies and minds destroyed. Day after day, the filth of what I witnessed piled higher and higher; first the brutish acts of the torturers against the prisoners and then the acts of prisoners against each other."

"But I thought they were Christians?"

"Tirgu-Ocna is host to all manner of prisoners, from petty thieves to murderers, as well as political and religious prisoners."

"But where do the religious prisoners come from? I've seen your churches in Bucharest and the people going in and out of them. Do the police just pick them at random? Do they raid an entire church? I don't understand."

"Most of the pastors and priests in the State-affiliated churches are appointed by the State and act as stooges. They report on their own congregations. Some participate in both the seen and Underground church and are true believers, but their road is very difficult. If they do not inform on their people, the State will remove them and put others in their place who will. So they tell only enough to keep the secret police happy while trying to protect the people, but it is a difficult balancing act. The Christians in prison are usually the ones who have participated in illegal prayer meetings, those not authorized by the State. The illegal prayer meetings have no stooges. And without stooges, the government cannot control. They are very afraid of this, losing control. Some of the other imprisoned Christians have passed out literature or taught their children about God."

"It's illegal for a Christian to tell his children about Jesus?"

"Yes, unless those children are eighteen or older."

"That's hard to believe. And they're imprisoned for that?"

"Yes, for that. And the religious prisoners are the ones most mistreated. They are the ones the guards love to work on. They are the ones dragged in over and over again. And after enduring the torture and savage beatings of their captors, they endure taunts and mistreatment by other prisoners. They are picked on, pushed around, stolen from. At that time I had no understanding and did not know how they could endure such treatment. My mother was not a believer, and I never went to church. Her life had been difficult. She had to earn everything by hard labor. 'Let God take care of others,' she would say. 'I will take care of myself.'

"But I would listen to the Christians talk among themselves and hear them speak about their God. I would laugh when they spoke about the Spirit of God. What was that? A wind blowing through the trees? A tongue of fire? Who could say exactly? And that was just the point. There was no one who could say, *exactly*. I would laugh when they spoke of God the Father and His love. I had not known the love of an earthly father. If earth could not provide a father to care for one small son, how could heaven provide one who cared for millions? I laughed when I heard them talk about Jesus, about loving their enemies. This Jesus was not a very intelligent fellow, I told myself, otherwise He would have understood that if you loved your enemies, the next thing you knew they would be at your door with a rifle. Power and strength, these were the keys. They are what make people sit up and take notice. I did not realize, then, just how much power and strength Christians had."

Loretta was standing now, almost leaning toward Yuri, not wanting to miss a word. "What happened to change your mind?"

Yuri stared past her as though he were inside Tirgu-Ocna,

walking past those cells. "Too many things to speak about. But it was a gradual revelation, something that happened day by day as I watched the Christians, saw how they loved each other, saw how they loved the other prisoners who abused them and even how they loved their tormentors. It was an astonishment. But my heart was still very hard towards them, because I believed they were such foolish people."

"But you changed."

"Yes."

"What happened?"

"God broke my hardened heart," Yuri said, his eyes filling with tears.

Loretta hesitated, then cleared her throat, embarrassed by her own boldness, but needing desperately to understand. "Please tell me what happened."

"It was long ago. A single incident."

"But a single incident that broke your heart?"

"Yes."

"I'd like to hear about it."

"I do not know if you can understand by just the retelling. You had to have been there. You needed to see it."

"*Please,* Yuri."

Yuri looked at her for so long that Loretta blushed. Finally, he nodded as though he had seen her emptiness and felt pity for her.

"One day a theft occurred. Five loaves of bread were taken from the kitchen. The guards stole food all the time and would take it home or sell it to some of the prisoners, but on this day, the prison commandant heard about it and was outraged. The prison was searched from top to bottom. Each prisoner was inspected. The commandant was determined to punish some-

one and threatened to systematically torture every single prisoner in Tirgu-Ocna. He arbitrarily selected ten men and
ordered they be whipped with chains in full view of everyone.
They would be beaten until they either confessed or died. If
they died and did not confess, then the commandant assured
everyone he would choose ten more. He was prepared to beat
the entire population of the prison to death in order to get his
confession. But before the first ten received a single stroke of
the chain, a voice cried out, 'Wait.'

"The voice belonged to a tall man with graying temples. He
was haggard, with cheeks that looked like empty pockets on
his face. He looked like a man of fifty, though he was only
thirty-two. His crime was pastoring an Underground church,
and despite the harsh treatment he received, he continued
preaching to whoever would listen. I saw him, almost daily,
being dragged back to his cell after the guards worked him
over. He would be bruised and bloody, but always, *always* he
would tell them, 'Jesus still loves you and so do I.'

"Now this hungry, broken man stood tall and bold in the
courtyard, telling his jailers to wait. He had not been one of the
ten chosen to face the chains, so his plea came as a surprise. All
eyes were on him.

"'I will take responsibility for the theft,' he said. There was
not one person in the camp who believed he was guilty. I was
astonished. Why would this man say such a thing? He knew
the commandant would kill him. Within seconds the ten grateful prisoners were removed from the wall, and before the entire
camp, the pastor was strapped to a post. He was positioned so
that everyone could see his face. His final words rang out as the
commandant gave the order. 'Jesus loves you and so do I.'"

Tears welled up in Yuri's eyes as he remembered that pastor's face. "This man died in front of us. The commandant made a grave error in allowing us to see that dying face as it looked out on the very inmates who had treated him with such contempt, had stolen his food, had beaten him unconscious so they could destroy the treasured Scriptures he had scribbled on little papers. These inmates had spit on him, had laughed at him whenever he tried to speak of his Jesus. And yet he died for them, because he *loved them*. What kind of love was this? This impossible love? What kind of people were these Christians? No human being could endure what they had to endure and still be so full of kindness, generosity, and love. Who were these lovers of the unlovely who looked into empty men's souls and did not turn away in disgust, who could pass through the fires of hell itself and still come out saying to their tormentors, 'Yes, I love even you.' And how could such a love be ignored?"

Tears brimmed over onto Yuri's cheeks, and he wiped them with the back of his hand. "*How foolish!* I thought. It made me angry. It frightened and confused me. It made me weep for the sheer greatness of it. The pastor's love had been like a sweet flower blooming in this prison wasteland of hate. And even after it had been plucked, the fragrance of that love haunted me. Why? How could anyone love so? In this land where men were only apes posing as men, love did not exist. Eight months at Tirgu-Ocna had taught me that. But now, this crushed flower poured out its sweet fragrance and cried not, 'Love me for I am beautiful,' but said to the dust and waste, 'I love you!' What manner of man was this? I asked. And who is this Jesus?"

Loretta's eyes had also filled. "They beat him to death?"

Yuri nodded.

"Didn't anyone have pity on him?"

"Just as I saw God in the faces of these Christians, I saw Satan in the faces of the torturers. No, they did not pity. They loved their work. Sometimes their eyes would glow with joy as they beat and broke men. Once I heard one of them say, 'I am Satan.'"

"Surely you don't believe in the devil?"

"Madam, Romania is a country where evil lurks in caves by night and hides behind men by day. It is the home of Dracula. Do you know what people call President Ceausescu?"

Loretta shook her head.

"Draculescu."

Loretta was suddenly cold; she folded her arms across her chest and shivered.

"Yes, Satan is real and I have seen him in the dungeons of Tirgu-Ocna."

Loretta stood in a corner of the foyer looking at Yuri, who had followed her into the house to see if anyone from the embassy had called for the car. He had seen the sadness in Loretta's eyes, and he pulled her gently to the side.

"I failed to tell you of my gratitude for your kind offer," he said in a hushed voice. "I know the difficult position you are in."

"Then will you let me help? Will you let me take some information—"

Yuri put his finger to his lips. Loretta nodded in understanding.

"I will think on it and advise you tonight," Yuri said.

Loretta nodded, and there were tears in her eyes. "Yuri, thank you for telling me about…thank you."

Yuri smiled, picked up Loretta's hand, and brought it to his lips. "Bless you, madam," he said, then walked out the door.

❧

"Let me drive you home, Mr. Ambassador," first secretary Donald Walters said as he watched Alexander Wainwright cradle his head in his hands.

"It's a beaut, Don." Alexander rubbed his temples.

"Brain implosion?" Walters said with a smile, then thought better of it and tried to look glum.

"I think it finishes me for the day."

"Then please, sir, let me take you home."

Alexander pushed a few papers neatly into a pile, put his pen in the top drawer, and pulled the burn bag from under his desk and handed it to Walters. "Okay, Don, but take care of this when you get back."

Walters nodded and tucked the bag under his arm.

"I was going to send something to State today, but maybe tomorrow we—"

"I'll bring the recorder. You can dictate, Mr. Ambassador, and I'll see that it's sent."

"Fine." Alexander rose from the chair and began walking out of his office.

"Looks like rain, sir," Walters said, grabbing the black umbrella that hung from the coat rack. "Better take this."

Alexander took the umbrella and walked down the hall and out the back with the first secretary. He slipped into the front seat of Walters's car.

"Perhaps you should close your window, Mr. Ambassador. It may pour any minute," Walters said as he passed through the embassy gate.

Before Alexander could react, a fist flew through the window and grazed his right temple. A mob had suddenly appeared from nowhere and surrounded the car. Wild, angry men began pounding on the car windows and shouting, "American dogs! Down with the American capitalist dogs!"

Alexander used his umbrella to beat back arms and fists, and inch by inch, he managed to close his window. The attackers began to push and heave on the sides of the car, rocking it back and forth. At one point Alexander thought the car was going to go over on its side, but Walters put it in reverse and floored it, then slammed on the brakes and spun it around in the opposite direction. The mob ran after the car, but scattered when four Marine guards descended on the street with rifles firing into the air. The streets suddenly became deserted and quiet. The only people visible were the ever present secret police in front of the embassy and the Marine guards holding their silent, smoking rifles.

"Our first anti-American demonstration, Mr. Ambassador," Walters said as he punched some numbers on a pad and picked up the car phone. "Arni, where the devil were your boys? No…I didn't see it coming…yes, the ambassador's fine…yes, I'll tell him." Walters looked over at Alexander. "You *are* fine, aren't you, sir?"

"Yes, I think so."

"Well, Arni sends his regrets. Said he'll have more Marines guarding the perimeter by this time tomorrow. A small unit has already been ordered over and is on its way."

Alexander looked back at the empty road. "That was good driving, Don. You kept a cool head."

"Thank you, sir, but I don't think they were planning on doing too much damage. Just wanted to rough us up a bit."

"Secret police?"

"Definitely. Staging one of their spontaneous protests. It'll be in the newspapers tomorrow. Probably had a few boys with cameras here. Don't be surprised if you see your picture on the front page."

Alexander picked up the umbrella that had fallen by his feet. "Well, this certainly came in handy. Maybe we should start carrying one around as standard combat gear."

"You did get the worst of it, sir, with that open window and all. I'm sorry about that."

"Actually, I think it cured my headache," Alexander said, and the two men laughed.

"Loretta!" Alexander Wainwright shouted as he ran through the foyer and out to the kitchen. "Loretta!"

"The missis went out," Lucy said.

"Out where?"

"Don't know, sir. She never said. I just saw her get into that big black limousine and drive off."

"When was that?"

"A few hours ago."

"Are you sure?"

"I saw what I saw, mister."

"Did she say when she'd be back?"

"She wasn't in a very talkative mood this morning. A little sour—no, not sour, more like sullen. You know, withdrawn and sad like. Kinda sickly, too. Maybe she wasn't feeling well."

"I think she's okay, Lucy."

"I don't think she's well at all."

"Lucy, I think I'd know if my wife was sick. And right now I'm more concerned about her safety. You won't believe what hap—"

158

"Well, I'd look into your wife's health, if I were you. There's a problem brewing, if you ask me."

"For heaven's sake, Lucy, Loretta's as healthy as a horse."

"Really? Would a healthy woman pace half the night? I couldn't tell you how many times she walked the length of the dining room and back, but it won't surprise me none if I were to find a groove in the floor."

"You heard her?"

"Didn't you?"

"Yes…she's…I think she's having trouble sleeping."

"Would you cry over a thing like that?"

"What?"

"I heard her crying."

"Crying?"

"Like a baby. And the night before it was the same."

"I…didn't know."

"I'm worried about her. She should be seeing a doctor. I don't think she's feeling well. Small wonder, with what's going on around here. They're everywhere, mister, *snooping*. It's enough to drive you into an ailment even if you were healthy as a horse. It's a good thing you have me here, I can tell you that. They'd probably poison the food if they had a chance. But you're not to worry because no one comes into my kitchen."

"I'm not worried about food right now, Lucy."

Alexander walked out of the kitchen and saw Loretta standing in the foyer with Yuri Deyneko. He watched as Yuri and Loretta huddled together, as they spoke in low, betrayal-like tones. And then Yuri, as calmly as you please, picked up Loretta's hand and pressed it to his lips. As calmly as you please and as if that hand belonged to him, as if he had a right to it, as if his lips had a right to it. Then, instead of Loretta becoming indignant, instead of Loretta slapping that arrogant face or those lips that trespassed so easily, she smiled. She *smiled!*

Alexander wanted to plant his fist squarely into the smug face of Yuri Deyneko, to pummel it until those lips could never kiss another thing, ever. And then he wanted to cry.

He waited behind the partition, like a thief in his own house. When he heard the door close and saw Loretta by herself, he pushed himself off the wall and pretended that he had just come from the kitchen.

"Loretta! There you are. I was just in the kitchen looking for you."

His wife smiled and came over to him. "Oh, I was in the garden, darling. And you can't imagine how bad it still looks."

Alexander's heart began to pound wildly.

Loretta threw her arms around him and gave him a big hug. "You've been so busy you've hardly had time to putter in the dirt. I'm afraid the servants have taken advantage of your inattention. The grounds are rather pitiful."

"Well, let's go out there now," he said with a tremor in his voice.

"But it's going to rain. It's going to come down in buckets any minute."

"I need to talk to you," Alexander said, guiding her toward the back entrance to the garden. "I want to tell you what happened on the way here."

Loretta looked at her husband's white face. "What is it? What happened, darling?"

Alexander bit back the tears. "Nothing, I hope."

"What?"

He looked away as he led his wife through the arbored side of the garden. "It wasn't all that bad." He cleared his throat, trying to regain control. "A little mishap at the embassy."

Loretta walked to the bench next to the plum trees and made her husband sit down. She placed one hand over his. "Now, tell me all about it."

Alexander looked down and saw it was the same hand Yuri Deyneko had kissed just moments before. His chest began to pound again. Never once, *never once* had he had an affair. There was a time in Zaire when he toyed with the idea. He had even kissed the woman's hand like Yuri had kissed Loretta's. But it just hadn't been worth it. He pulled his hand from Loretta's. He closed his eyes and let his head drop forward, but he didn't say a word.

Loretta rose from the bench and went behind her husband and began to massage his temples. "Go on, darling, tell me what happened."

Alex took a deep breath and opened his eyes. "Well, Don Walters and I…"

A few hours later, Alexander Wainwright watched his wife from the bedroom window. He watched as she huddled close to Yuri Deyneko, too close, and then he watched the chauffeur give her a note. Moments later, he watched through a crack in the partially closed bathroom door as his wife read the note, then tore it up and flushed it down the toilet.

"I sent Yuri home," she shouted from the bathroom. Loretta had been most insistent that they cancel all their evening plans and spend time at home so Alexander could rest. She was distressed over the assault on Don Walters's car. Under different circumstances, Alexander never would have agreed, but he was too distraught about his wife and Yuri to argue. Now he wished he had. At least in a crowded party he wouldn't be alone with his thoughts. *Stop thinking about Loretta and Yuri,* he commanded his mind as he climbed into bed.

"You look awful, darling," Loretta said, emerging from the bathroom. "I'm so glad we're staying home. I'll have Lucy send up dinner."

Alexander watched as his wife moved gracefully across the room, as she smiled sweetly before leaving. His headache was back. Too much thinking. He tried to fight back the dark thoughts beginning to bubble up like crude oil. Not until that afternoon had *adultery* ever entered his mind in connection with his wife. The concept was too alien, too absurd. But now his mind's eye watched again as his wife and Yuri moved close together, as Yuri's lips pressed against her fingers, as she stood by the limo and Yuri handed her the note, as she read it in the bathroom and flushed it down the toilet. He tried to keep the sludge from taking over, from contaminating his reason, but his thoughts spewed out like an uncapped well.

My wife is having an affair! She's having an affair!

6

THE BRASS BELL RANG AND IN STEPPED A MAN neither Teofil
Bucur nor the seamstress who shared his shop had ever seen.

"Good morning!" the stranger said, moving toward Anna
Rosu's side of the room. His angular face was a crinkle of smiles
and amiability.

Anna rose from her seat behind the sewing machine and
walked to the tiny counter. "Good morning," she said.

The man was clean shaven, his hair misshapen, as if a relative rather than a barber had cut it. His black suit was well
worn and ill fitting, his white shirt frayed around the collar;
one of the top buttons was chipped. But his shoes were new
and expensive. The shoes startled her. That and his eyes. In
spite of the tiny smile lines around them, his eyes were hard as
marbles.

"Good morning," Teofil said, not rising from his chair
where he was busily resoling a large work boot.

The man nodded in Teofil's direction but did not leave his
post by the seamstress.

"Anna Rosu?"

"Yes."

"I'm Pastor Vladimescu. Gheorghe Vladimescu. I'm replacing

163

Pastor Tson. Unfortunate situation. Very unfortunate. He was a good man. He'll be missed. I never had the honor of meeting him, but he'll be missed I know." Vladimescu coughed nervously, then leaned over the counter until his face was only a few inches from Anna's. "I'll take over where he left off. Everything will be as before. Nothing will change. Nothing. I've been visiting the members of my church, introducing myself and giving my assurances. I understand you're an especially devoted member."

Anna reached out, took the pastor's hand in hers, and began shaking it. "It's a great pleasure," she said, smiling warmly. "Teofil, come over and meet our new pastor."

The old shoemaker rose and stepped gingerly over the piles of leather scraps on the floor. "An honor, an honor," Teofil said, vigorously pumping the stranger's hand up and down.

"Yes, well, the honor is mine," Vladimescu said. "I was just telling Miss Rosu how I plan to continue the work of Anatol Tson…with all of your help, of course."

"Of course," both Anna and Teofil said in unison.

"Yes. I wanted to begin by offering to help care for that poor soul who's taken shelter in your home—Eva Stanciu. Some of the other church members have told me what you're doing for this unfortunate creature. It's commendable, most commendable."

Anna smiled sweetly. "Thank you, but we're managing. It wouldn't be right to burden you—you're so new to us and need to get used to things. But I thank you, Pastor."

"Yes, well, if you should need me, of course I'll be instantly available."

"Thank you. That is comforting."

"Yes…well. Strange that I have no record of Eva Stanciu

164

being a member of the church. Was she not one of Pastor Tson's flock?"

Anna shook her head.

"Strange then that she picked this place for refuge and convalescing."

"Nothing strange about it. She came into the shop one day, collapsed in the chair, and has been here ever since."

"She came into the shop? Then she knows you?"

"This is a place of business, Pastor. People come here to make purchases or solicit repairs." Anna moved around the counter so she could stand next to the new pastor.

Vladimescu took a few steps backward. "Then you didn't know her?"

"I certainly don't know everyone who comes into this shop for service."

"And why did she come, again? Or did you already tell me that?"

"There's nothing to tell. She collapsed before she had a chance to make her intentions known. Perhaps she wanted me to make her a blouse or skirt. She was poorly dressed."

"Could she afford such extravagance? I understood that she was a street dweller, without a home."

"She's a prostitute, and prostitutes generally have money enough," Teofil said.

"Yes, well...tell me, have you won this poor creature to the Lord yet?"

Both Teofil and Anna shook their heads.

"Perhaps I can try. Would you let me see her? Speak to her?"

"Now here's a brave fellow, Anna," Teofil said.

"Brave?" Vladimescu said.

"Already willing to lay his life down for the sheep, and Eva

Stanciu not even a sheep of our Lord's flock yet."

"Lay my life down? Certainly I'm most willing to give up my life for the cause of Christ. But how…that is, I mean to say, what is wrong?"

"Personally, I believe the danger is greatly exaggerated, don't you, Anna?" Teofil asked.

Anna nodded and smiled at Vladimescu.

"But I have seen Eva *spray* the room when she coughs," the shoemaker said, patting the stranger's shoulder. "A bit nasty. The spray goes everywhere, you know. I try to avoid going in when I hear her hacking. It's only a small room and you can imagine, everything must be contaminated by now. But I haven't heard her coughing too much today, have you, Anna?

Anna shook her head.

"They say it's in the sputum," Teofil said.

"What's in the sputum?"

"The germs, the *tuberculosis* germs," Anna said. Both she and Teofil began leading Vladimescu toward the stairs that led to the second floor apartments.

The pastor stopped short. "Yes…well…no one told me about that. I mean…that is to say…if Eva Stanciu is so ill, she may not be receptive to the gospel message right now. Let her rest. When she's better, I'll come. Just let me know and I'll come at once." He began to back away. "I'll eagerly await news of when I can return."

The little brass bell jingled and Vladimescu disappeared just as suddenly as he had come.

Teofil smiled at Anna. "It seems the Securitate has sent a jellyfish to do its work."

"Don't be deceived, my friend. Jellyfish may have no backbone, but they have a painful sting all the same."

Teofil went back to his table and picked up the boot he had been resoling. "Yes, jellyfish may have a sting, but they're at the mercy of the currents."

Anna walked over to him and gave him a kiss on the forehead. "And what do currents have to do with anything?"

Teofil's eyes twinkled. "Currents are at the mercy of our God."

Anna tiptoed into her bedroom and found Ion sitting on her small cot, spoon-feeding vegetable soup into Eva Stanciu. She was happy to see that Eva was finally awake. She walked the few paces to the cot and tousled Ion's hair. He had been sitting with Eva for hours, waiting for her to wake up, putting cool compresses on her head, and praying for her recovery. They had all taken their turn at this. Their patient had been drifting between various stages of consciousness for three days.

"How is she?" Anna said softly.

"A little confused, but hungry."

Anna smiled down at Eva. "It's good to see you awake."

Eva Stanciu pushed the soup away. "Where am I?"

"You're safe. But you must eat something to get your strength back," Anna said.

Eva began to paw at the covers, trying to get out of bed. With one hand Ion pushed her back onto the pillow. He rose and took the bowl of soup with him.

"It'll be useless now. You must calm her, then I'll try again." He crossed the room and left.

Anna closed the door behind him, then went to the cot and sat down. She began tying a bow with the lace ribbon that edged the neck of Eva's nightgown. It was Anna's, the only good one she owned.

"There," Anna said after she finished the bow, "you look lovely."

For a moment Eva just stared at Anna. With her clean, scrubbed face Eva looked vulnerable, almost innocent.

"Where am I?"

"You're in my room."

"*Your* room?" She looked around the small space furnished with only a cot, a faded stuffed armchair, and an old three-drawer dresser. In the corner was a bedroll Anna had been using. When it was unfolded, there wasn't any room to walk.

"How…how long? How long have I—"

"Three days. You've been unconscious for three days."

"How did I get here?"

Anna smiled. "I believe God has sent you to us."

"God? What has God to do with this? How did I get here? Think. I must think. The Securitate. Yes. It was because of the Securitate. Think. Think. Yes, I remember. I remember! The Securitate. I was on my way to the Securitate." Eva looked up in horror. "I must get out of here!" She tried to rise, then fell backward against the pillow. "What have you done to me? Why can I not move?" She attempted to scream, but nothing came out except a flat gravely sound.

"Don't upset yourself. You're sick and weak." Anna gently took Eva's hand in hers.

"I know what you're up to, Anna Volkovoy! You would…you would try to silence me! You would try to *kill* me! But I've told you, I couldn't do it. I couldn't tell them about you. So you see, it's not necessary. Not necessary at all. I won't tell anyone. Let me go. Please, don't hurt me," Eva said, pulling her hands from Anna's.

"No one is going to hurt you. You're safe here. It's best you stay until you're better."

Eva lunged for Anna's throat, then collapsed against the pillow and began to cry.

Anna watched her for a moment, then sighed. "If you really want to leave so badly, I won't stop you." She went to the closet and took out a white off-the-shoulder blouse like Simona had worn, and a skirt with matching jacket. She draped the clothes over the armchair. "Here, I made these for you. I used your old clothes for size, but without measuring you—well, I hope they fit."

Eva stared at the beautiful blouse and long floral skirt. Large tears began to stream down her drawn cheeks. "These are mine? These are for me?"

Anna nodded, then quietly took a brush from the dresser and began brushing Eva's matted hair. "You have pretty hair. When we were both young in the village, I always admired it. I confess I was a little jealous."

Eva wiped her tears on the back of her hand, but her eyes never left the clothes on the chair. "Jealous?"

"Yes, the color was—*is* still so beautiful. I always wished mine had some gold in it."

Eva finally tore her eyes from her new clothes, and for the first time she smiled. "I too was jealous."

"Now what could the village beauty be jealous of?"

"Of you and Yuri. Of the way Yuri loved you. I always thought the two of you would marry. The whole village thought so. But things change, don't they, Anna? Why do things have to change? Of course, when your brother got into trouble and well…well, naturally Yuri had his career in the army. Why is my mind so clear when I think of those days? I wish things didn't have to change. Why do they have to, Anna?"

"Because they just do." Anna rose and went to her dresser, pulled a green satin ribbon from the top drawer, and returned to the bedside. She began tying back Eva's hair with it. Her fingers worked quickly, skillfully. When she finished, she was pleasantly surprised. The ribbon and freshly combed hair had softened Eva's haggard face.

"You're beautiful!" Anna said, stepping away from the bed as though viewing a newly created masterpiece.

A blush colored Eva's cheeks. "You mock me."

"Oh, no." Anna rushed to the dresser and picked up a small hand mirror. "See for yourself."

Eva held the mirror in front of her. For a long time she did not say a word. Then suddenly she threw the mirror on the bed and began to sob.

"You shouldn't have done this," she said between sobs. "I wanted to betray you, to turn you over to those…those animals. You don't know what they're like, but I do. I do. I've known many. Many. They would've hurt you, they would've shown you no mercy. I've seen what they do. I have seen."

Anna sat on the bed and cradled the sobbing woman in her arms.

Eva tried to push her away, but she was too weak. "You don't know about me. If you knew, you would never have done these things."

"I do know."

Eva shook her head violently. "No! No, you cannot know. You cannot possibly know what I've done. I've helped them, Anna. I've denounced many people, many people like you. Christians. Yes, many. And they've died. They're dead. I know the Securitate. They're ruthless, Anna, ruthless. Once they have their hooks in you, they never let go."

Anna continued to hold the sobbing woman. "It's all right."

"No, it's not all right. It can never be all right."

Anna hugged her tighter. "Yes. Truly it's all right."

"Stop. Please stop. I can't take your kindness. It's unbearable."

Anna began to rock Eva like a baby. "Hush, you're safe. We'll take care of you. You will stay with us."

The sobs began to subside and for a long while Eva clung to Anna as though afraid to let go.

"Why, Anna? The clothes…the ribbon…this bed. Why are you so kind to me?"

"Oh, Eva," Anna said in a merry, lyrical voice, "because Jesus loves you and so do I."

Valentine Tulasi carefully wiped his glasses, then returned them to their perch on his nose. "Your efforts have been very disappointing, Yuri. Very disappointing."

Yuri Deyneko sat tall in his chair, his face frozen in a mask. It had taken years of practice to perfect this emotionless visor. Not even Tulasi, with all his skill, could read it.

"I am an impatient man," Tulasi continued. "You have failed to grasp the true nature of your assignment. I tire of your lackluster performance. Your reports are rote, with no insight. And where is the documentation on conversations, overheard or engaged? Since my order to step things up, it seems you have deliberately dragged your feet. I'm appalled, to say the least. Do not think my commands can be ignored without penalty."

Yuri followed Tulasi's every move as he huffed and puffed around the office. He had been anticipating this interview for some time, and he knew he would need his wits. He prayed silently.

"Come, come, Colonel Deyneko. What have you to say?"

"I'm working on it, sir."

"Yes, Yuri, you're working on something, but *what?* I have seen only three messages from you in the past few months and they say nothing. Nothing!"

Tulasi's glasses were off again, and he stood near Yuri, waving them in the air. "I will not have this. I will not have this inefficiency from you!"

Yuri watched Tulasi's round face in silence.

"You have nothing to say?" Tulasi said, sitting down behind the desk.

"I'm at a loss. I don't understand your concern."

"Don't play the fool with me, Yuri Deyneko. You are in full understanding of my meaning."

"No, sir, I am not. I am doing my duty. If my efforts do not please you, perhaps you should replace me."

"You're tough, Yuri; I'll give you that. But I'm tougher. No. There will be no replacement. You will continue surveillance and continue your reports."

"As you wish."

Tulasi replaced his glasses. Beads of perspiration had broken out on his forehead, and he patted his face with a handkerchief, then pointed to a wooden plaque on the wall. "President Ceausescu himself gave me that award. Do you know what it's for?"

"No, sir."

"For outstanding achievement in maintaining security during a crisis. *Security.* That is what I do best. Nothing escapes me. Not the smallest detail. You sit before me like a man in full control. At least that's what you wish me to believe. I have studied you closely, Yuri. I have read your entire dossier. I

172

know your strengths: the quiet way you go about moving mountains; how you command men; how they obey you; how they even *admire* you. I know about every post you have served. I know how you, as a young guard at Tirgu-Ocna, were transferred to the Iron Gates. Difficult times, those early years of construction. There were those who believed the power plant would never be built. And when other men were being stripped of their rank, you were making a name for yourself there. It was you who rallied the men to work harder; to work with a spirit of excellence. Yes, I know about all your achievements. I know that later, when you got promoted, it was always your construction crews that outworked and outbuilt all the rest. The engineers quarreled over who would get you because your jobs had the least flaws; your crews were always the best. Your record is impressive. Promotion came to you, even though you never sought it. You're an interesting man, Yuri, and in some ways an intimidating man. But you do not intimidate me. Do you know why?"

Yuri looked straight ahead.

"Because *I* am in control here. We are carpenters, you and I. You're a builder of roads and bridges, while I'm a builder of men. Do not think for one minute that your past record will stop me from dismantling you. If I choose, I can break you."

Yuri watched as perspiration ran down Tulasi's forehead. He watched as Tulasi dabbed, rested, dabbed. Tulasi's face reddened when he realized he was being scrutinized.

"You think I'm afraid of you, don't you, Yuri Deyneko?"

Yuri shook his head. "I had no such thought."

"It's true; I do sense your strength and power. And I admire you for it. But it will not help you if you come between me and what I want."

173

Tulasi rose from his chair and began to walk around the room again, encircling the desk and the seated colonel. He made three circles then stopped next to Yuri. "Before you go, kindly explain to me the meaning of the reports I've been getting on you from our agents at the U.S. residence. The reports concern you and Ambassadress Wainwright. It seems you have been observed in intimate discussions, passing notes, and once you were actually seen kissing her." Tulasi's fingers rested menacingly on Yuri's shoulders.

"Her hand, sir. I kissed only her hand."

The fingers on Yuri's shoulders tightened, and he smiled. How puny was this man's power that he needed to demonstrate it with his hands.

"You are amused?"

Yuri continued to look straight ahead. "Amused? No, sir."

"Would you care to explain your actions."

"I was following my instructions."

"Instructions? Did anyone instruct you to dally with the ambassador's wife? I didn't know you were a womanizer, Yuri."

"My instructions, sir, were to discredit the American ambassador or find information we could use to do so."

"Well?"

"The ambassador is very fond of his wife."

Tulasi's eyes narrowed. "What does that have to do....oh, yes...I see...brilliant. Brilliant! Yuri, you do amaze me." Tulasi's sausage fingers relaxed their grip. "The ultimate humiliation. You are planning to seduce the wife. Yes...good, good. Perhaps some compromising photographs on the front page of our newspapers. Yes, I like it."

Tulasi returned to his desk. He sat for a while, enraptured, cleaning his glasses, his lips curved upward in a smile. His smile was menacing and sharp like a sickle, and suited this man who cut and harvested men's souls.

Yuri remained silent, nauseated by what he had just done. When one played in dirt, one got dirty. His words had soiled both him and Loretta. He sent up prayers of contrition, then prayers chastising God for not showing him a better way, then prayers of contrition again.

"You're a handsome man, Yuri." Tulasi's face beamed with joy. "But even for a handsome man, the seduction of an ambassadress is a difficult task. How, then, are you winning her affections?"

"Americans are softhearted."

"Yes, they are foolish and gullible."

"I have found something that pulls on the heartstrings of this woman."

Tulasi leaned as far over the desk as his huge belly allowed. "And what is that?"

"Gustov Volkovoy."

Tulasi snapped backward in his chair and the color drained from his face. "I...I do not understand."

"She's concerned about the criminal, Gustov Volkovoy. It seems there is much attention being given him in the United States."

"Yes, I know. But how does this tie in with you?"

"She asked me about him. And about the Christians in the Underground church."

"She asked you? But why? Why would she do that?"

"Because I told her *I* was a Christian."

Deep throaty laughter filled the room. "Brilliant! Brilliant!" Tulasi said, then laughed some more. "I cannot remember when I've enjoyed myself more. You're a genius. I could use twenty more like you. I see now why you have such an excellent record. You're a very resourceful man." He rose, walked over to where Yuri sat, and began pumping his hand up and down. "My compliments, Colonel Deyneko. My compliments."

Alexander Wainwright sat on the bench beneath the plum trees. He watched as several birds pecked for grubs among the crabgrass. The gardeners were nowhere in sight. Since his initial conference with the house staff, Alexander had seen the gardeners only a handful of times. One flower bed in the corner had been weeded, but the remaining were still overrun. Only a small section of the fruit trees had been composted. The lawn was in need of cutting, and the unruly shrubs continued to snag hair and clothing.

He had never had a garden so poorly tended, and it occurred to him that the country and these grounds were similar. In both, grubs and weeds were master; one visible, one invisible. One spread over the surface, like Communism, and one worked underground, like the Securitate. But the results were the same. In time, everything was destroyed. He hoped he wouldn't be here to see it. Demolition and cleanup were hard work.

Loretta was right; he was a level one. He never let people get too close. Getting close to a person meant getting close to his problems. Heartache by association. He had enough heartache, he thought, as he pictured Loretta. What grub had come into their garden? What was eating away, unseen, at their marriage?

On two other occasions, he had seen Loretta take a note from Yuri. That made three notes in all that he had seen. Who knew the number of those he had not? He chided himself for thinking such evil about his wife, but just when he would begin to believe nothing was happening, Loretta would do something else to plunge him back down into that pit he couldn't seem to climb out of. She would get another note from Yuri, or sneak out of the house and not tell him where she was going. She had become withdrawn, secretive, and sometimes he would awake in the middle of the night and hear her crying in the bathroom. A guilty conscience trying to cleanse itself? He remembered Lucy telling him of the nights she had heard Loretta cry. Just how long had this been going on? And how much longer could he take it?

He found it more and more difficult to concentrate at the office, and at a time when he needed all his wits. The political situation was as strained as it could be. Donald Walters had been picking up the slack admirably, but how long could he be expected to do that? Alexander knew people were talking. He would see heads together, whispering, then they would separate when he was sighted. This was the second time this week he had left the office early. And this was the second time this week Loretta had not been home when he arrived. How much of his marriage had the grubs eaten?

Alexander had already decided that no matter what, he would not divorce his wife. No matter what Loretta had done, it could not be as terrible as life without her. Forgiveness and reconciliation would be slow, but he was prepared to duke it out. But first he had to break this hold Yuri had on her. He had to get her back, though he didn't know how. His career no longer seemed so important. London, Paris, they would be lonely and dull without Loretta.

He put his throbbing head between his hands. *Loretta, what have you done?*

❦

Loretta stood near the water's edge and looked out over Lake Herastrau. The water, a crystalline blue, shimmered in the sun. She watched as light pirouetted from point to point, like a lithe ballerina. There were no concerts at Herastrau Park today except for the concert made by children's voices as they romped in the distant playground.

"I have given Charles Riley your last note."

The man beside her nodded. There was a new sadness in his eyes Loretta had not noticed before.

"I read it of course. You said Gustov is on his death bed."

Yuri Deyneko took a deep breath. "Yes, that is what I said."

"I'm sorry," Loretta said in a near whisper. "There's nothing more I can do. Charles will do his best with the story. But it…it won't be enough, will it?"

Yuri shook his head.

Loretta began to cry. "Something's happening to me. I can't explain it, but it's as though my heart is breaking. I can't get all those stories about the Underground Christians out of my mind. Sometimes at night I wake up sobbing. Poor Alex. He doesn't know what to make of me anymore. I can see it on his face. *I* don't know what to make of me anymore."

Yuri gently took Loretta's arm and turned her toward him. His kind eyes stared into hers. "It is conviction. You have fallen under the power of God, and He is convicting you."

Loretta's eyes brimmed. "I don't know what it is, but yes, I believe it's God doing something. For as long as I can remember, I've had this emptiness inside. Nothing has been able to fill it. No matter what I've tried. Does that sound crazy?"

Yuri released her arm and stared past her.

"No. No, I know it doesn't sound crazy to you. You've talked about your own emptiness. Alex, he doesn't seem to have any needs. He seems content. He loves his job. It's just that he worries so much. But I've always been looking for something. And after my son died of meningitis, well, things got worse. Only, for the first time, I think I'm going to *die* if I don't fill the emptiness."

"Look to God for the answer. I cannot help you," Yuri said.

"But you can. You *must!*"

"What is it you want, madam?"

"I want to go to an Underground prayer meeting."

"What you ask is impossible. It is too dangerous."

"Please. *Please,* I must go."

"Why?"

"I want to see these Christians. I want to pray with them. I want to meet their…I want to meet their Jesus." Her voice quivered with desperation.

"You do not need to go to a prayer meeting to meet Jesus."

"Maybe not, but ever since you told me about the Underground church, I've had such a hunger to see it, to experience it. It's like something has been drawing me, pulling me. It's a force so strong that if I don't go, I don't know how I can go on with anything. A person needs a reason to go on living. *I* need a reason. To say that it's a matter of life or death sounds too crazy, I know. But I have to go. I just have to!"

Yuri was silent for a long time. "I understand," he finally said.

"Then you'll take me?"

"It will not be easy, but yes, I will take you. However, there is something you must do for me."

"What?"

"On the day we go, you must come to my apartment. You will need to stay for only about an hour."

"Why?"

Yuri shuffled uncomfortably, then turned away. "For safety reasons."

"I...don't understand."

"My assignment from the secret police was to find information that would embarrass the ambassador. There are those in the Securitate who believe we are...that we are having an affair."

"What?"

"Forgive me, but you must understand that in my country, deception rules. Our government deceives us, and we deceive our government. That is how we survive."

Loretta began to walk away, trying to put distance between her and Yuri.

"Madam, wait! You do not understand," Yuri shouted, trying to catch up to her.

"No, I don't. I don't understand any of it. And what's more, I don't want to." She was walking as fast as she could. "Just take me home."

"You do not believe what I am saying. You tell yourself this is a snare. This man is fooling me and wants to hurt my husband."

"I told you—I told you right from the start—that I wouldn't do anything to embarrass my husband."

Yuri's large hand clamped onto Loretta's arm pulling her to a stop. "I am married also, and I love my wife as much as you love the ambassador." His voice was low, his eyes blazing. Then he let go of her arm.

Loretta stared at him, balancing his words, balancing everything she knew about him, balancing the cautions of her husband, balancing the tenuous position the Americans held here, balancing her future, balancing the void that filled her.

"Your wife is with the Underground?" Loretta finally asked.

Yuri nodded. "You will meet her when you go."

"And the other matter. Why is that necessary?"

"To avoid suspicion. I must show the Securitate proof of what I have led them to believe. My life rests on this. Someone in the secret police will see us go to my apartment. That will be enough to satisfy them for some time."

"But they'll want more. They'll want to discredit my husband with it."

"The Securitate wants a compromising photo of us. That will never happen, so they will have no photographs they can use against him. I can talk my way out of the rest."

"I don't know…it's so chancy. What if something happens?"

Now it was Yuri who began to walk away. "You want me to risk my life and the lives of my wife and friends in the Underground, but you are not willing to risk anything."

Loretta followed him. "How soon can we go?"

"A few days perhaps. I will let you know."

Loretta wished she had never agreed to come. She felt like vomiting all over the hall of the gray apartment building. She wore a smart, cream-colored suit, and half clutched, half wrapped the jacket around her. Beside her walked Yuri Deyneko.

When he stopped, she stopped and stood watching him insert a key into the lock and open the door. Suddenly a man stepped into the hall from his apartment several feet away.

"Good morning, Yuri."

"Good morning."

The man walked toward the couple. There was a smile on his face. "I see you're not looking for tranquillity today," he said in Romanian. "It is overdue that you bring your sweetheart for a visit. Overdue."

Loretta blushed under his gaze and moved closer to Yuri hoping his bulk would hide her.

"She's a friend," Yuri said.

The man continued to eye her approvingly. "Well, that at least, Yuri Deyneko, is a beginning."

Yuri pushed Loretta through the door. "Since my companion does not speak Romanian, you'll understand that I consider it rude to converse with you any longer. I must say good day."

The man laughed and slapped Yuri on the back. "No, you're not looking for tranquillity today, nor do I think you'll be getting much rest either, my friend."

Yuri closed the door, happy that Loretta's knowledge of Romanian was still elementary.

"What did he say?" Loretta asked as she walked into the middle of the apartment.

"It is of no importance. Please seat yourself." Yuri gestured to one of the kitchen chairs.

Loretta placed her purse on the oilcloth-covered table and sat down. She absently drummed her fingers on the table and surveyed the small apartment. A brown stuffed chair and lamp occupied the far wall to the left, and a single metal bed, like the kind one saw in a dormitory, occupied the wall to the right. There was a small round table next to the bed. How like this man the apartment was: simple, functional, straightforward. Loretta had never seen such sparse living quarters. The only decoration was the silver-framed photo on Yuri's bed table. At first she thought it might be a picture of his wife, but even from a distance she could tell it was a group shot.

"Can I offer you tea?" Yuri asked. "It is good Russian tea, but I have no lemon." He had already filled the kettle with water and put it on the stove.

"No, thank you."

"I am sorry, but I am out of coffee."

"I don't like Romanian coffee. Too thick and sweet."

"Yes, like Turkish coffee."

"My husband says a spoon will stand straight up in it, but he loves to exaggerate." She cleared her throat.

"I know. This is awkward for me, too. But time will pass quickly. Try to relax."

Loretta took a deep breath. "Yes, I'm beginning to. Now that we're inside, it's a bit easier."

Yuri walked to the cupboard and removed a mug. "Are you certain you will not join me for some refreshment?"

Loretta shook her head. "You live modestly for an officer of your rank. I doubt you'd find an American colonel willing to live this simply."

"Few Romanian colonels either." Yuri placed the mug on the counter. It was chipped and the decal across the center was faded and unreadable. Loretta could see only one more mug in the cupboard and it looked worse.

"What do your fellow officers say about you living so simply?"

"They criticize. They don't understand why I do not live in a manor befitting my position."

"And why don't you?"

Yuri laughed. "I find better uses for my money."

"You give your money away, don't you? To the church, to other Christians?"

Yuri shrugged. "Many Christian families are destitute."

"It seems most Romanians are destitute."

"Yes, but a man can lose his job or be given an inferior-paying one if it is discovered he is a believer. And if a man is arrested for practicing the faith, the State will take everything from him, leaving his wife and children in poverty. Many times both a husband and wife are arrested, then the children must care for themselves. Sometimes...sometimes young Christian girls will even go into prostitution to help support the family. And often, after a few years, they will leave the faith because this life embitters them and steals their soul."

"I had no idea. Why don't people help them? Surely, if everyone pitched in—"

"It is a great crime to help the family of a Christian in prison. It carries harsh penalties. I have known many who have paid dearly for doing so."

"What kind of penalties—what happens?"

Yuri checked the kettle on the stove and saw it was about to boil. "Imprisonment, for some. Beatings for others. Once, a friend of mine helped a little girl who lived on the streets. When this girl was only five, the secret police broke into her home and forced her to watch while they kicked the abdomen of her pregnant mother until she died, all the while they screamed, 'We don't want any more of your kind giving birth!' Then they dragged her father away. When the Securitate found out what my friend was doing, they beat her severely. She is paralyzed now and sits in a wheelchair all day."

"I'm sorry, Yuri," Loretta said softly and looked away.

"You will see her today, this little girl, and when you hear her pray, you will know what a victory God has won in her life."

"I can't tell you how much I'm looking forward to the prayer meeting. I've been anticipating it for days. I'm even missing my first day of class, but I don't care. The summer course seems rather unimportant in lieu of everything else that's been happening."

"Anna never made any of her courses either." Yuri said. "It suddenly became unimportant to her as well."

"So, that's the 'someone' you were talking about who wanted to go but never did?"

"Yes."

"I just know I'm going to like her."

"It is difficult not to."

"You must miss her very much."

"Yes," Yuri said, then blushed. "It has been too long since I have seen her. It is hard to be apart."

"She must be very special."

Yuri retrieved a small tin of loose tea from the counter and placed it next to his cup. "For me, no other woman exists. Perhaps it sounds foolish coming from a military man. Soldiers are considered great womanizers. At least I have been told this." He laughed at the description. He was usually clumsy and shy around women.

"Do you have a picture of her?"

"No, it is too dangerous." Yuri put a spoonful of sugar into his cup and tapped the spoon against the rim. "Actually, I do have one picture. I will show you."

He walked over to the night table and removed the five-by-eight photograph. Aunt Sonia's Communist friend had taken the picture and purchased the silver frame as a gift. Before Yuri went into the army, Aunt Sonia had given it to him, "to remember us by," she had said. Now he handed it to Loretta, carefully, as though it were a large jewel. With his finger he pointed to one of the figures.

"There, that one is Anna."

"But she's only a child!"

"Yes, she is quite young here, which tells you that I have known her a very long time. We grew up together."

"She looks so happy," Loretta said, studying the photograph of a dark, curly headed girl. She was barefoot and wore a shapeless dress.

Yuri nodded and went to the stove to remove the boiling kettle. "We were all happy then," he said, pouring hot water into his cup. "Life was hard for us, but we were very happy together."

"Who are these other people?"

Yuri brought the cup to the table and bent over Loretta. "This is me next to Anna, and behind Anna is her mother, my Aunt Sonia, and—"

"Where is Gustov?"

"Oh, he was not born yet. My Aunt Sonia is pregnant there, but I do not think you can tell in the picture."

"So Anna is quite a bit older."

"Yes, Aunt Sonia became pregnant with her just prior to leaving the refugee camp. It ended her days of prostitution forever."

Loretta looked startled. "She was a prostitute?"

Yuri smiled. "Does it shock you that Anna and Gustov could have a prostitute for a mother?"

"No…yes…well, they're both so devout. I only thought that…well, I assumed their parents were deeply religious."

Yuri laughed good-naturedly. "'God delights in using the foolish things of this world to confound the wise.'"

"I didn't mean to sound pompous," Loretta said, her face burning.

"Do not be embarrassed."

"I'd like to know more about Anna and Gustov, more about all the people of the Underground church. Will you...will you tell me?"

"There is not much to tell. After the refugee camp, my mother, Aunt Sonia, and I went back to my grandfather's farm. That's where Anna was born. Four years later Gustov followed."

"Then Anna and Gustov are half-sister and brother?"

Yuri nodded. "Every town has a Communist official in charge of controlling cults or religious activities. In reality he is a member of the secret police. Gustov is the son of such a man."

"And where is Gustov's father now?"

"Oh, who can say? This official won Aunt Sonia's affections by showing up at the farm with provisions and gifts. Their courtship lasted until Sonia became pregnant, and then he began bringing his gifts to another farm further down the road."

"So he left? Just like that?"

"Yes, just like that. Aunt Sonia said it did not matter, but she never had any more interest in men after that. But we had Gustov, and he was more than compensation."

"You love him very much."

"Like a brother. He and Anna are all I have left."

"Your mother and Sonia are dead?"

Yuri nodded.

Loretta studied the picture once more. "Then this woman next to Aunt Sonia must be your mother?"

"Yes, that is my mother."

"I know that face. I've seen it before. But that's impossible, isn't it?"

"My mother was ordinary looking. With a babushka, she looked like a thousand other peasant women. You have probably seen a similar face in one of your *National Geographics*."

"No…no, I tell you I've seen this woman before. Wait. I think it—" Loretta dropped the picture, splintering the glass. Her hands began to shake.

"Are you all right?"

"I'm so sorry. Your picture…I've broken your picture."

"It is fine, only the glass is damaged. But you are not cut?"

Loretta shook her head and began clutching the jacket around her. She was very pale. "Yuri, I *have* seen this woman before. Alex has a picture of her!"

Yuri slowly lowered himself into his chair. There was a strange look on his face, but he said nothing.

"It's a picture his mother gave him before he was adopted. And Yuri, you were in that picture too. I wouldn't have known you the way you are today, but this picture of you here is not so very different from the one Alex has."

Yuri continued to sit very still, saying nothing. Loretta watched him as his eyes clouded over and stared past her.

"How long have you known that Alex was your brother?"

"I have suspected it from the beginning. But I did not know for sure until this moment."

"You never said anything. You never even hinted."

"What could I say?"

"I don't know. Something. I don't know. It's all rather…

rather incredible." A distressed look pinched Yuri's face. "It's been hard, hasn't it? Not knowing for sure. Pulled between your duty and then thinking, perhaps…and Alex, behaving so badly."

"No harder than it will be on your husband."

"Oh, how am I ever going to tell him?" Loretta said softly. "How can I even explain being here? How is he going to deal with all this?"

"He will probably dislike the idea as much as I do."

Loretta put her shaking hand over Yuri's. "I know this is difficult, but also, certainly, it must be…it must be joyous, too? After all these years, to find your brother. That has to mean something."

"It means danger and complication." Yuri pictured the fat face of Tulasi and the mischief he could work. "Your husband—Alexander—will not be happy. This will not be good news. It will make his job here more difficult, if not impossible. And what of his career? He is a man of great ambition. Certainly you can see how this information could destroy his future. For all these reasons, I think it best you say nothing."

Loretta rose from the chair and began pacing. "Do you think that's fair? Making the decision for him? Alex has a right to know."

"You will not be doing him a good turn, Madam Ambassadress."

Loretta laughed. "Yuri, for heaven's sake, stop calling me that. Please, call me by my first name. After all, we're relatives."

"Yes, God has had His little joke," Yuri said with a sad smile. "But I do not believe Alexander will think it is very funny."

Alexander Wainwright paced back and forth in his bedroom.
In one hand he held a note from Loretta, in the other a quart
bottle of Johnnie Walker Red Label. He had come straight
home after lunch and found Loretta's note explaining that several weeks ago she had asked Yuri to take her to see some of
the countryside. Since she wanted to travel more than fifty
miles, special travel passes were required and Yuri had only
now obtained them. She promised to be back in time for the
French ambassador's dinner party. Loretta had not said one
word to him about it this morning.

Alexander flung the note to the floor and stomped it several
times with his foot.

"A note, Loretta! You couldn't even tell me face to face!" He
took a big swig from the bottle. He was going to get good and
drunk. That's how Loretta would find him when she got home,
plastered. Maybe plastered enough where he wouldn't be so
concerned about hurting her feelings, plastered enough to
curse and yell, plastered enough to get some straight answers
and put an end to it.

He pictured Loretta and Yuri together in the car, driving to
who knows where. Maybe a picnic lunch? Loretta liked pic-
nics. The simple things, those are what Loretta enjoyed. It was
funny how complex people always seemed to like the simple
things.

He took two more gulps of the Johnnie Walker and continued to pace. "What else are you doing, Loretta?" He saw her on
a blanket with Yuri; they were kissing. He took another swig
and cursed under his breath. "I'll kill him."

He heard the sound of a car and ran to the window, but it

was only a car passing near the residence. Tears began to stream down his face as he listened to the sound fade away. He pressed a wet cheek against the glass and just stood there looking out, hoping that any minute a car would pull up and he would see his wife step out; that any moment someone would tell him it had all been a mistake; that nothing was as it seemed. After a while he left the window and began pacing around the room. No, no one was going to tell him that. Reality could not be changed into fantasy. He gulped from the bottle. There was no such thing as Santa Claus or the Tooth Fairy…or Snow White.

Seventy miles south of Bucharest a dark gray Yugo sped toward a campground in Tulolt. Loretta sat in the front seat quietly gazing out the window. The further from Bucharest they traveled, the fewer cars and the more oxcarts she saw. Also the further away from Bucharest, the less gray and modern everything became. Instead of the monotonous high-rise apartments, whitewashed wooden houses clustered together to form small inviting villages. Farmers tilled their fields with horse-drawn plows. Women, wearing babushkas, carried bundles of sticks and twigs for the cooking fires. Children tended small grazing herds of sheep. Loretta suddenly felt as though she had stepped back in time.

She tried to concentrate on the tranquil scenery in hopes of quieting her nerves. Between the revelation that Yuri was her brother-in-law and the anticipation of actually meeting members of the Underground church, she was in a state of great anxiety. She was also frightened. How could life ever be the same for her? And what about Alex? What was all this going to do to him? She didn't agree with Yuri. There was no way she could keep this information to herself.

"Vorotna Monastery," Yuri said pointing to a large stone compound with five spires. Fir trees, so large and full that they touched, formed a solid green semicircle on one side. Green sloping mountains framed the other.

"It was built by Stephen the Great in 1488 to celebrate one of his victories against the Turks."

"It's lovely," Loretta said, straining to see as much as possible in the few seconds allowed. "1488. America wasn't even discovered yet. Sometimes I forget how old Europe really is."

Yuri slowed the car. "If you look carefully, you will see the painted frescoes on the outside walls. Inside there are beautiful friezes of the church calendar. We have several other Moldavian churches like this, with magnificent exterior murals. The one at Moldovita illustrates the siege of Constantinople; the one at Sucevita 'The Ladder of Virtues'; at Humor it is the 'Hymn to the Virgin'; and at Arbore, the lives of the saints. Romanians have always been a religious people."

Loretta looked backwards trying to take it all in. When the monastery was finally out of view, she turned around. "How did this happen, Yuri?"

"What?"

"I see churches and monasteries wherever I go. How could such a religious country be reduced to a place where its citizens must meet in secret to pray?"

"It is a difficult question, and I do not know the answer. I only know that after the war, my country, like most of Europe, was devastated. We were a backward nation before the war began, but conditions were made very severe by the Nazi looting and destruction. When people are in want, it is easy for unscrupulous men to gain power. We did not make it difficult for the Communists to take control."

"But after they got into power and you knew what they were really like, why didn't you stop them?"

"There is a saying here, 'The best way to cook a frog is to put it into a pot of cold water and slowly turn up the heat.' The Communists know this too. Little by little, they turned up the heat until they killed the soul of our nation."

"Can't anything be done?"

"Only God can do anything now. But God is more than up to it. Even now, He is stirring hearts and minds. I do not think it will be much longer before you see something happening in this country."

"Like what?"

"I do not know," Yuri said, as he came upon the entrance of the campground. Just beyond the gate, the one road forked into five, like spreading fingers of a hand. He took the extreme left. "I do not know what will happen. Only God knows. But someday, things will be different."

Loretta sat quietly as the car traveled a mile more into the forest. When the road ended, Yuri parked the car and they continued on foot for another quarter of a mile. On either side, dense forest and vegetation gave Loretta the feeling she was in a tunnel. Then suddenly, between the tangle of vines and shrubs, soft-lobed gentian formed mats of brilliant blue. As if not to be outdone, clusters of foxglove spiked like miniature steeples ringing their bell-like flowers of pink and white. It all looked so wild and beautiful. Loretta stopped. She was filled with delight as if she had just discovered the Garden of Eden, abandoned and overgrown, but still virginal and magnificent. She half expected to see an angel with a flaming sword step in front of them to bar the way.

"I've never seen anything like this," she said.

"Yes, it is very special."

They continued on the path, hushed and reverent, as though they were walking down the aisle of a cathedral. At last they found themselves in a small clearing with grass up to their knees. Again Loretta stopped in delight. In front of her the grass gradually gave way to a large patch of sunflowers; most of them were waist high, but some came up to her shoulders. It looked like a field of fire. Perhaps it was this fire that guarded the entrance to her Eden. Hesitantly, as though fearful of getting burned, she put out her hand and touched a petal. It was soft and moist.

"I've never seen such beautiful sunflowers," she said.

"They are all over the Soviet Union. They are grown to make sunflower oil cakes and used to feed livestock."

"But how did they get here, in the middle of nowhere?"

Yuri smiled. "Anna and I planted them—well, not planted exactly. Fifteen years ago we got married right here in this field. We had little money. There was no bridal bouquet. Anna carried only one sunflower. After the wedding we broke the disk and scattered the seeds. This is all from that one flower. Every year the flowers come up and new seeds fall to the ground. It was not just for us that we planted them. It was a memorial to God. Anna and I prayed that God's seeds would be planted here as well, and they have. For years, Christians have used this spot for their secret prayer meetings. Just as the sunflower seeds have changed a landscape, so the seeds of prayer have changed lives. Many people have been touched by God here."

They came out the other side of the flower patch, and Loretta saw a sizable group huddled together in the clearing. She heard a sweet melodious sound as they began to sing.

A woman with long curly brown hair noticed the pair and left the group. At first she walked slowly, then, as though she could no longer contain herself, she began to run. Her hair blew behind her and seemed to lift her, like wings.

"Anna!" Yuri cried as they met in the middle of the clearing. For a while Yuri and Anna seemed a tangle of brown, as arms and lips connected and hair swirled like a cloud over both of them. After some moments, they walked arm and arm toward Loretta.

"This is Anna, my wife," Yuri said, his eyes beaming with love and pride. "Anna, this is Loretta Wainwright."

The slim dark woman smiled and shook Loretta's hand. Then, as though it was the most natural thing in the world, Anna linked arms with her husband and the American, and the three began walking toward the assembly. Anna said something to Yuri in Romanian, then looked shyly at Loretta.

"Pardon. I speak poor English. You will excuse if I talk with Yuri in our own tongue?"

"Of course. But Yuri, you must go with your wife," Loretta said, disengaging herself. "I'll be all right. I'll just stand over here and listen for a while."

"You do not mind, then?" Yuri asked, squeezing Loretta's hand gratefully.

"How could I?"

Loretta watched as Yuri brought Anna to a spot just a few yards behind the rest of the group. The couple sat on the grass. Loretta inched closer to the main body that seemed to form a spiraling circle. She stood next to an attractive woman wearing a pretty white blouse and long floral skirt. She watched the wind playfully toss about the green ribbon that tied back the woman's hair. This woman seemed better dressed than the others and Loretta wondered who she was.

As everyone sang, Loretta looked from face to face, wishing she understood the language. Men, women, and even the few children that were present all had their eyes closed, their faces tilted upward in adoration of their God. Loretta could see their poverty in their tattered and mismatched clothing, yet she had never seen such happy faces. At that moment, nothing else existed for them. Loretta looked around, half expecting to see light shining down from heaven and onto these devoted heads. She looked away as though her defiled eyes were not worthy to gaze on such a sight, and she began to weep. Despite all their poverty and lack, she had never seen people so *full*.

Suddenly the singing stopped. Then one by one, as though moving around the circle, they began to pray. Some prayers were long and others only a few words.

Finally a young girl prayed, and Loretta stood frozen as the words were spoken. She did not understand one of them, but she could feel their power. Love poured from the child's lips, petitions and yearnings of the soul. Loretta could sense that these words were soaring into the very throne room of God.

How long the child's voice rang out toward heaven, Loretta did not know. All she knew was that when it was over, she found herself on her knees. Then suddenly a group of believers surrounded the woman next to her. This woman, with her pretty floral skirt, had also fallen to the ground. Loretta watched as they placed their hands on the woman's head, as they prayed prayers she did not understand, as they sang strange songs, as they hugged and kissed her. She watched the woman first writhe as though in pain, then sob deep sobs as this pain ebbed and flowed from her. She watched the woman's face change in front of her, transformed into joy itself. Then the little group of believers raised their arms and voices into the air, and Loretta had never heard such adoration, such love. For the first time in her life, she knew she had come face to face with the living God.

Loretta Wainwright stood by the car saying her good-byes. Her heart was still full from the meeting in the clearing though she was not able to come to terms with what had happened there. All the way home she had been a mix of euphoria and sadness. She had touched the hem of the garment of utter peace and contentment, yet she knew what upheaval awaited her. How was she going to tell Alex all that happened today? How was she going to tell him about these beautiful people? And how was she going to tell him that Yuri Deyneko was his brother?

Loretta threw her arms around Yuri. "Thank you. Thank you so much for today. I don't know what to do with it all yet, but…thank you."

Yuri smiled, his eyes brimming with kindness and understanding. "And the other matter? What will you do with that?"

"I don't know. Maybe I'll do what you always do. Pray on it."

"Then you are on the right track," Yuri said as he slipped into the front seat of the car. "It is always the best place to start."

Upstairs, Alexander Wainwright had half walked, half dragged himself to the window when he heard the car pull up. He watched through bloodshot eyes as his wife embraced the driver. For a moment he thought he was going to throw up on the windowpane. His head was spinning, and he watched as two Lorettas walked toward the house.

He stumbled around looking for the Alka-Seltzer, and when he found it, he ripped the foil pack so hard that the wafers broke into several powdery pieces and fell to the floor. He opened another and managed to get them out whole and into a glass. He staggered to the bathroom and filled his glass with water. Then without waiting for the wafers to properly dissolve, he began pouring the contents of the glass down his throat.

When Loretta opened the bedroom door, the first thing she saw was her husband, foam mustache over his lip, holding a partially filled glass.

"Oh darling, you have one of your stomachaches again," Loretta said, coming to his side. She threw her purse on the bed then gave him a hug. "I've never seen you look this bad. Is that why you came home early?"

Alexander crinkled his forehead and nodded, looking like a little boy in need of sympathy.

"Why don't you go to bed for a while, take a little nap? You'll feel better when you wake up." She took the glass from his hand and gently led him across the room. "Lie down and I'll put on some soothing music. It'll help you relax and go to sleep."

Alexander lowered himself to the mattress. Maybe everything was all right. Maybe nothing was as it seemed. Maybe... he opened his eyes and saw a large grass stain over the hem of his wife's skirt. He felt the rage bubble up again and he pushed her away.

"You were out with Yuri again!"

"Yes, I wrote you a note," Loretta said, reaching over to stroke his head.

Alexander knocked her hand away and tried to sit up, but

he fell backward onto his pillow. His bloodshot eyes grew large, fierce. "Is that how you relieve *his* stress!"

"What? What are you talking about?"

"Yuri. I bet he likes it when you rub his forehead."

"Alex, what's wrong with you? Why are you talking like this?"

"What else do you do for him?"

"Have you gone crazy?" she said, backing away from him. The heel of her shoe hit something, and she turned and found an empty Johnnie Walker bottle on the floor. "For heaven's sake, Alex, you're drunk."

"Not drunk enough, Loretta. Not nearly drunk enough."

"Alex, let me get you some coffee."

"No! You stay right here. Don't go anywhere. We're going to have this out, here and now."

"Have what out? What are you talking about?"

"You know very well what I'm talking about!"

"I don't have a clue. Honestly, Alex, look at you. I'll get you some coffee, and when you're sober, we can talk about anything you like."

"I don't want to be sober. When I'm sober it hurts too much." Tears were beginning to well up in his eyes.

Loretta walked back to the bed. "What it is, darling? What's wrong?"

"You, Loretta, you're what's wrong. You've broken my heart. You've broken my—" Alexander picked up his half-finished Alka-Seltzer cocktail and threw it against the wall, shattering the glass. Then he fell backward onto the bed.

Loretta bent over him and began to gently stroke his head. "It's all right. Rest now. Everything's going to be fine."

7

ALEXANDER WAINWRIGHT TIPTOED OVER TO THE BED, each step an agony, and looked down at his sleeping wife. The clock on the nightstand said five past seven. He had been up for hours, quietly nursing his behemoth hangover. He had never felt sicker. Finally, around six, he could stand erect without feeling as if he were going to puke, and he had called Don Walters. "Be here in an hour," he had told him. "Pressing business." The truth was that Alexander did not want to be around when his wife awoke. He vaguely remembered the scene with Loretta the night before. Well, he sure handled things. He sure straightened everything out.

He watched his wife curl around her pillow. She looked so innocent and sweet; it was hard to believe her capable of the slightest treachery. His hand reached to brush the blond curls off her forehead, then recoiled.

"Next time, Loretta, you won't get off so easily," he whispered.

His wife stretched and rolled over. "Ummm, Alex? Is that you?" she said sleepily.

Alexander quickly picked up his briefcase and fled, silently closing the bedroom door behind him.

∞◦∞

"Good morning, Mr. Ambassador," Donald Walters said, opening the car door for Alexander Wainwright.

Alexander grunted, trying hard not to move his head as he settled in the car. He wondered if anyone had ever died from a hangover. Only once before had he come close to feeling this bad. He was ten and had smoked an entire pack of Marlboros with his friend. Alexander thought he was going to die then too. He remembered pleading with God for his life and sprinkling his supplication with repeated promises to "be good."

As the car pulled out and jerked his head backward, Alexander prayed that same prayer.

"What was that, sir?"

Alexander put his fingers to his temple. "You don't need to shout, Don; I'm right here."

Walters glanced anxiously at his passenger. "The ambassadress called me last night and requested that I fill in for you at the French ambassador's dinner. She said you were ill."

Alexander continued to hold his head with his fingers so it wouldn't bob.

"If I may say, sir, you don't look well at all. Are you certain you want to go to the embassy?"

"Yes." The word sounded like a hiss.

"Then allow me to assist you in this pressing business you spoke about on the phone."

"No need."

Walters eyed him. "As you wish, sir."

Ambassador Wainwright watched the red second hand of his Bulova jerk around the clock face. Twenty after nine. He felt as though he had put in a full day already instead of just two hours. He tilted slowly back in his chair and closed his eyes. Was it his imagination, or did he feel slightly better? Perhaps he was just a few hours away from feeling human. That's what kept him going. The belief that eventually he would feel normal again.

He wondered if he should take an Alka-Seltzer, but the thought of all that white fizz made him feel sicker. Besides, he needed to stop taking so many. He pictured it eating the lining of his stomach as his stenographer had warned. It had become a standing joke around the office that when State sent the pouch of mail to the embassy, it always included a new box of Alka-Seltzer.

Maybe work would help. He pulled himself closer to his desk. Work had always been like a tonic to him, a snake oil that cured everything. He began thumbing through the latest telegrams when suddenly he heard the screeching of tires, men shouting, then the crashing of metal and gunfire.

Alexander flew out of his chair and in a minute was in the hall heading toward the front of the building. All the other offices had emptied, and people swarmed toward the noise.

"What happened?" Alexander asked when he saw Donald Walters.

"I don't know, sir, but please stay back. I heard rifle fire." Walters stepped in front of Alexander and barred him from moving closer to the entrance.

The next instant the front door flew open and a stout, elderly man, half dragging, half carrying a woman, stumbled in. He had a small, soft briefcase handcuffed to his wrist.

Alexander moved forward.

"Mr. Ambassador, please!" Walters said.

"It's okay, Don. Where's Arni?"

"Here, sir."

"Let's find out what this is all about."

Donald Walters had already reached the couple and was trying to find a chair for the woman, who appeared unconscious. An undersecretary wheeled an armchair from one of the offices and Walters placed the woman in it. There was blood on her blouse, and Walters saw a bullet hole near her right shoulder.

"She's been shot!"

"Call an ambulance!" someone shouted.

The elderly man with the chained briefcase became hysterical. "No! No! Sanctuary! Sanctuary!"

Three people surrounded the man, but aside from "Sanctuary!" they could get nothing more from him.

The entry door remained wide open and from where Alexander Wainwright and Arni Houser stood, they could see the scene outside. A car had crashed into the small iron gate in front of the embassy and remained with part of the gate on its hood. Both front doors of the car were wide open, and the motor was still running. Outside the fence, but near the car, stood four men with guns drawn.

Houser stepped in front of Alexander. "Let me, sir," he said. It wasn't until he was standing outside on the first step that he realized the secret police were pointing their guns at a small unit of Marine guards positioned around the embassy perimeter. Every Marine had his rifle drawn.

"A Mexican standoff," Houser said as Alexander stepped next to him. "Maybe I should go break this up."

"Careful."

"Mr. Ambassador, I'm not paid to be careful."

Houser took several steps forward, and ten Marines, in unison, slapped their rifle butts against their shoulders. The four secret police were now in the sites of ten rifles.

"This is the property of the United States government," Houser shouted. "You will not come any closer."

One of the secret police took a small step forward. "We have no wish to trespass. We only want the two criminals."

"What criminals?"

"The two Romanian citizens who have entered your embassy illegally."

"What have they done?"

"That is not your concern. Surrender them so they can face Romanian justice."

"I repeat, what have they done?"

The spokesman turned to the other three and began speaking rapidly in Romanian. Finally he turned once again toward Arni Houser. "Will you surrender the felons?"

"Not until you tell me their crime."

More silence. The Marines remained frozen in position, each with his finger on the trigger of his rifle. The four secret police looked at the Marines, then at Arni Houser, and then back at the Marines. Finally, the speaker holstered his gun, and the other three followed suit.

"At ease," Houser ordered. Immediately, the rifles dropped from the shoulders.

"Get someone to clean up this mess," Ambassador Wainwright said looking at the mangled gate and car. "And let's double the watch."

Within minutes the secret police were all back at their posts at each side of the embassy, but one of them spoke rapidly into a walkie-talkie.

Inside the embassy, the unconscious woman had been wheeled into one of the offices. Someone had found a first-aid kit and it lay open on the desk. Alexander entered the office and watched as the elderly man dressed the woman's wound. The briefcase still dangled from his wrist.

"Has anyone had time to question them?" Alexander said to the three secretaries gathered in the room.

"Not yet, sir," Donald Walters said. "We were worried about the woman. I think she'll be all right. At least her bleeding has stopped."

Alexander looked directly at the intruder. "Do you speak English?"

The man nodded but continued to work with the bandage. Finally, after the gauze was properly secured and he said a few words in Romanian to the woman, who was coming around, he turned to the ambassador.

"I am Dr. Josef Tulasi, and this is my wife, Marian," he said with a heavy accent.

Alexander looked at the woman slumped in the chair. Her eyes were open and she was moaning softly. "How is she?"

"A bullet wound through the flesh of the shoulder, but not the bone. She is shaken and in discomfort, but not seriously hurt."

"Dr. Tulasi, what's this all about?"

The short, stocky man found a chair and wearily sat down. He removed a monogrammed handkerchief from his suit pocket and dabbed his perspiring forehead. One hand hung limp over the side of the chair, weighed down by the briefcase.

"Sanctuary. My wife and I request sanctuary."

"Why?"

"Conscience, sir. It is a matter of conscience."

"Please explain."

"I have worked for the Securitate as prison physician for years. The position gave me stature and favors I otherwise would not have had. But it also gave me...nightmares. I have seen things. I have seen things no man should see."

"I can't give you absolution, if that's what you're looking for."

"No, no. If there is a God, only He can forgive. I cannot. No, it is too terrible. You cannot imagine what men are capable of. You do not want to imagine such things."

"Dr. Tulasi, I must establish if this is a political defection."

"Political? I do not know...I am not a politician, I am a doctor."

"I understand that, but I need a clearer picture of why you're defecting."

"I have told you why. Because of what I have seen. A man's eyes can witness only so much suffering. I cannot look on it anymore. No, not anymore!"

Alexander threw up his hands in frustration. A wave of nausea swept over him and forced him into a nearby chair. He slid down in the chair and tilted his head slightly backward.

Donald Walters walked over to the Romanian. "What's in the briefcase, Dr. Tulasi?"

The doctor picked up the case and hugged it to his chest. "Papers, files, proof of what goes on in those prisons."

"May we see them?"

Tulasi hugged the case tighter. "No one will see these until I receive a promise of sanctuary."

"It's your call, sir," Walters said, eyeing Alexander and noticing that he had turned a pale shade of lime.

Alexander looked at Arni Houser.

"You're the boss," Houser said.

Alexander sighed. "'The buck stops here.'" No one responded. He thought for a moment, but it was hard with his head pounding like a jackhammer. "All right," he said, picturing the sour face of McAllen and dreading the telephone call to State.

"I have your word?" the doctor asked, still hugging the case.

"You have my word."

The doctor nodded and flipped the case flat on his lap. With the unshackled hand, he reached into his shirt pocket and pulled out a key. Within minutes the case and its contents covered the office desk.

"Here are names of prisons and prisoners, dates they were jailed, cause of death. I also have papers showing how the names of some prisoners were changed to conceal their whereabouts so family and friends could not find them, and would think them dead. And here are details and descriptions of the methods used to extract confessions and inflict punishment." The doctor pushed himself away from the desk. "You look at them; I cannot." He rose and went over to his wife. "Do you have pain pills? My wife is in great discomfort."

Alexander did not look up from the desk but continued shuffling through the papers. "This is unbelievable."

"Sir, my wife!"

"Don, in my top drawer is a bottle of aspirin."

"Yes, sir."

"And bring some for me."

Loretta Wainwright was bitterly disappointed when she awoke and found her husband gone. She had hoped they could spend the day together and go somewhere to talk. They *needed* to talk. Things had gotten terribly out of hand. She could only imagine what Alexander thought. Poor Alex. How many hours had he and Johnnie Walker spent working up a case against her? How miserable he must have felt. Where had his thoughts taken him? She knew her husband's propensity for worst-case scenarios. She almost cried as she pictured his anguish. She just had to talk to him, to rid him of his foolish notions.

She walked to his side of the bed and picked up her picture. She unfastened the back, then carefully separated the picture from the cardboard. There, wedged between the two, was an old black-and-white photo of a woman and two small boys. She stared at it for several minutes. There was no doubt. This was the same woman in Yuri's picture. And one of the little boys was Yuri, the other her husband.

The first time she had seen it was after their honeymoon. They were busy in the discovery of each other and wanted no secrets. Alex had told her all about it, the little he could remember, anyway: his mother and brother, the refugee camp, and the adoption. Then he told her he never wanted to discuss it again, and he never had.

Only those few times when Loretta replaced her old portrait with a new one did she ever look at this tattered snapshot. She kept it wedged between her photo and the cardboard like a hidden treasure although she didn't know why exactly. She only knew the picture evoked a tenderness in her own heart and stirred deep feelings of loss. Both she and this woman had lost a son. And Alex? He too had lost so much: a family, a childhood, a sense of security, an identity. How do you measure these? And how were they ever to be regained? Certainly not by climbing the ladder to the UN. No matter how important Alexander became, he'd always feel like a throwaway child. Would he ever be able to prove to himself he was worth keeping?

Loretta put the frame back together and returned her picture to the nightstand. She put the photo of Alexander's family on her dresser. She looked wistfully at the telephone but knew there was no use in calling him. The lines were tapped. Well, she'd just wait. Sooner or later he'd have to come home.

Alexander Wainwright, Donald Walters, and Arni Houser sat huddled around the desk. Someone had brought coffee in for the doctor and his wife and someone else found half a box of two-day-old pastries. Aside from that, little attention had been paid to the couple.

"This is unbelievable," Alexander said over and over again as he read accounts of torture and brutality; of Christians put in deep, dark cells under assumed names and their families told they had died; of priests and pastors put in "refrigerator cells" while the prison doctor watched as they were nearly frozen then thawed, frozen then thawed, over and over like packaged meat; of families who sent life-saving medicines that were withheld by the guards because the prisoners would not recant their faith.

"What kind of people do these things?" Walters said, pushing the papers away in disgust.

"Animals," Alexander said. "And Arni, make sure your people know the type of scum we're dealing with."

"He's not here, sir," Walters said.

From time to time, Arni Houser would quietly leave the group and go into the front corner office. There he would peer out the window and get a visual update of the situation. The wrecked car had been removed by the secret police and parked several yards down the street. Seven Marines patrolled the front perimeter, another four were on the roof, and still more were posted on the sides and back of the complex. A makeshift repair was performed on the gate and though somewhat twisted, it was back on its hinges.

This time when Houser checked, something new had been added. Forty secret police in special uniforms stood along the street, twenty on each side. They were spaced about five feet apart and each one carried a Soviet-made AK-47 automatic assault rifle. On both ends of the street, armed guards were rerouting traffic.

"You need to see this, sir," Houser said when he returned.

Alexander left the papers and followed the station chief. He let out a whistle when he looked through the corner office window. "Looks like they're not going to let the birds out of the cage."

"No, sir. Not alive, anyway."

"We'll have to break out the mattresses. This could take a while."

"Looks that way."

"Set the doctor and his wife up in one of the back offices."

"Good choice, sir. It'll make them easier to guard."

"Posting a guard, is that necessary?"

"Yes, sir, it is. We have a lot of auxiliary personnel here, file clerks and whatnot, who are *locals.*"

Alexander nodded. "You're right. Do it. Then I want you and Don in my office. I'm calling State."

Alexander Wainwright picked up the phone and dialed the direct line to Rodger McAllen, bureau director for Eastern

Europe and the USSR, at the State Department. Alexander spent a few moments scribbling something on paper, then he put his hand around his throat and winked at Don Walters and Arni Houser.

"Let's try to keep our heads, gentlemen," he said, then in the next breath, "Hello, Rodger! Alexander Wainwright...I'm fine, thank you. And you?... Glad to hear it. I wanted to call you with an update. Tuesday, I will be going to the Japanese embassy to make an official call and present my card. Because a situation regarding their fishing violations off our Pacific Coast has recently occurred, I thought a visit was timely. Don is here and concurs. It's of grave importance that I show our friendship and desire to establish excellent communications here in Bucharest. I'll send details of the outcome. I wanted to tell you first. I will follow through with your suggestions on this. I hope by week's end to have some news. Look for courier correspondence on this. That's it."

Rodger's raspy voice came over the phone. "Hold it a minute, Alex. Someone's at the door."

Alexander held the receiver loosely to his ear, waiting for Rodger to play back his tape and decipher the message. The word *update* told Rodger to look for a coded message. *Tuesday,* the third day in the week, indicated that the third word in every sentence was the key, not counting the first sentence. The message Alexander had given McAllen was, "Situation here grave. Details to follow by courier."

"Okay, Alex, I got rid of 'em. Some secretary selling Girl Scout cookies. Now regarding your situation, the only suggestion I have right now is don't foul it up. I'll be in touch."

Alexander heard a click on the other end of the phone, and after pressing the receiver button, he began dialing again.

"Don, start the paperwork on a glass room. We're going to need it."

"Right, sir."

"Just one second, gentlemen." Alexander pressed the receiver to his ear and wondered why all this had to happen on the day he had the worst hangover of his life. "This won't take long…Loretta? Alex. Cancel all plans this evening. I won't be home. We have a situation here." Then without giving his wife a chance to say anything, he hung up.

Yuri Deyneko sat tall in his chair, watching the nervous man in front of him pat his perspiring forehead with a handkerchief.

"My agents have told me of your great progress with Ambassadress Wainwright. Outstanding job, Yuri, outstanding!" Valentine Tulasi lifted his glasses to wipe the bridge of his nose. "I fear that my agents are a far more satisfying source of information than you are. But no matter, no matter. Let's forget that for now. It's sufficient to say that we're pleased with you, very pleased. The ambassador is quite beside himself. This will be a bigger coup than I had hoped. You'll have some photographs for us soon?"

"It is hard to say."

"Well, no matter, no matter. I'll leave those details to you."

"Thank you, sir."

Tulasi brought the handkerchief to his mouth and coughed into it. "Yes, Yuri, we are very pleased. So pleased, in fact, that I have another assignment I'll entrust to you."

"I am honored."

Tulasi coughed again. "Yes, well, this is a very delicate matter, and of extreme importance. It is a matter of national security.

And…and very delicate." Tulasi studied the emotionless face of the man in front of him and sighed deeply. "What I am trying to say is that a very delicate…very embarrassing situation has occurred. It has come to my notice that Dr. Tulasi and his wife have defected to the Americans."

Yuri's eyes grew large with disbelief.

"The traitors managed to get into the U.S. Embassy despite the presence of our secret police. But we have the situation well in hand. They will never get out of the embassy alive." Tulasi rose from his chair, walked a few paces, then sat back down, pulled himself close to the desk, then pushed himself away again. "That is why I've asked you to come. You will expedite matters."

"What is it you wish me to do?"

"You will assassinate them both."

"Sir? Surely you don't mean it. They are, after all, your… parents."

"They are traitors! Traitors! Traitors! Traitors!" Tulasi banged his fist on the desk. "They have disgraced their homeland. They have disgraced *me*."

Yuri shook his head. "I am a soldier. I cannot do it. I do not kill civilians in cold blood. I am not a butcher."

"You are under my command and you will do as I say!"

"I respectfully decline this mission."

"You dare refuse!"

"Yes."

Tulasi's face was aflame. "Don't press me, Yuri Deyneko! I am a man to be *feared*. It is precisely because you are a soldier that you will follow orders or be shot!"

Yuri stared straight ahead. His mind formed prayers of the most urgent kind.

"Did you hear what I said?" Tulasi's face was purple with rage. "You will follow your orders or be shot! Well? I am waiting for your response. For an indication that you understand my order. Do I have it?"

"Yes, sir."

With a trembling hand Tulasi wiped his forehead again. "Someday you will push me too far. Then I will shoot you myself!"

"I do not remember ever meeting a Dora," Eva said, in response to Ion's relentless questioning. She sipped her tea as she tried to rack her brain. She wore no makeup and still looked radiant. It was hard to believe this was the same woman who was so near death only a few weeks earlier. "God is in the healing business and He is in the process of healing me," Eva would say to whoever would listen. And while her cough was not completely gone, it was considerably diminished, and there was no longer any blood in her sputum. Every day she grew stronger. Even her mind had improved and no longer wandered. Anna was certain it was because the Master had lifted Eva's burden of sin from her, and with it, a tormenting guilt.

"Sometimes when we were very little, she'd call herself Dor. Does that sound familiar?" Ion said.

Eva shook her head. "I have come across many women in my travels. Oftentimes we used different names, sometimes we didn't give any name at all. So you see, I may have met your Dora without knowing it. If only you had a picture, then I'd know for sure."

"But I do have a picture!" Ion jumped from his chair and disappeared.

215

Anna shook her head as she cut a large piece of bread, then a smaller piece of cheese and handed them to Teofil. "Eva, you must make certain of your facts. He's very tender and easily stirred when it comes to his sister."

"I can see that. Dora is all he talks about—when he's not talking about the Lord, that is. I only hope I can offer him good news, assuming I have any news at all." Her eyes misted as she looked first at Anna, then at Teofil. "Not everyone has been as fortunate as I have. God has been very, very good to me. I cannot praise Him enough."

Anna poured herself a cup of tea. "Ion constantly prays for his sister. Perhaps God's mercy has caught up with her as well."

"It is God's fondest wish to pour out His mercies upon us all," Teofil said. "But sometimes we run too fast."

"What do you mean?" Eva asked.

"It's possible that sometimes we don't want God's mercy to overtake us, and God never violates our free will. He won't force us to accept His love or His blessings."

"It must be God's love and blessing that has brought Eva to us," Ion said, entering the room with his sister's picture. "Perhaps it will be Eva who'll unite me with Dora once again."

"You don't know how it is with us...with us prostitutes," Eva said. "We don't *want* to be reunited with family. We can never go back. Never. It's too painful. Our lives are too painful. There is no going back, ever."

Anna reached across the table and took Eva's hand in her own. "Ever? Can you really say that, Eva? You who have experienced our beautiful Jesus? You who have seen that there is no depth from which His loving arm cannot reach and retrieve?"

"Yes, that's true, but for those who don't know about such things, there's no going back. And there are many...many who do not know. And, Anna, I will tell them. I'll tell all those who will listen, and for as long as I can, about our dear Savior. I'll walk the streets as you did, to give them bread and to give them love."

Ion pushed his sister's picture across the table toward Eva. "What Christ has done for you, I pray He will do for my Dora."

Eva picked up the worn photograph and stared at it for a long time.

"Well, do you know her?" Ion finally blurted.

Eva nodded; her face had gone ashen. "I've seen her, yes."

"What is it?" Ion said. "What have you to tell us?"

Eva looked sympathetically at the young man. "She's dead, Ion. I'm sorry."

"Dead? But…how can you be sure? Did you see her die?"

Eva sighed. "It was in Buzau. I saw her in one of the alleys."

"Then she was alive? Did she say anything? Did she speak of me?" Ion was standing now, pacing the small kitchen floor and pulling at his hair.

"No, no, she was already dead. She was found that way. They were taking away her body. But I looked at her face. I got a good look at her face. And I remember…I remember thinking how young she was. Too young to die, I thought."

Ion stared wide-eyed into the air. "This can't be. Dora cannot be dead."

"Ion, I saw her."

"But how? How can one so young exist one day and be gone the next?"

"She had a hard life. A life on the streets takes its toll."

Ion looked pale and ready to cry. Both Anna and Teofil went to his side and directed him back to his chair.

"Sit down," Anna said. "I will get you tea."

Ion hunched low in his chair. "How did she die?" he asked softly.

Eva opened her mouth to speak, then looked at Anna and was silent. Anna bent over Ion and hugged him. "Are you certain you want to hear this? It cannot be good, Ion, and bad news always brings pain."

"I need to know. Eva must tell me."

"I do not know, not for sure, anyway. I only know what I heard," Eva said.

Ion hunched lower as Anna placed a steaming cup of tea in front of him. "Then tell me what you heard."

"They said it was pneumonia."

"Pneumonia? But if she was sick, why wasn't she in a hospital?"

"She didn't want to go, Ion. She wouldn't go."

Ion stared down into his tea as though looking for an answer. "I don't understand," he finally said.

"They said Dora would pass out night after night in the alley, with no covering, no shelter. That's how she got pneumonia."

"What does this 'pass out' mean? Why was she passing out? I don't understand any of this."

Anna stood bent behind the young man's chair, hugging him. "Ion, why do you do this? Why do you torture yourself?"

"Let Eva continue!" Ion said, with a severity that surprised everyone. "I must hear all of it."

"All right, Ion. I'll tell it. They say she wanted to die, that she was trying to drink herself to death."

"Dora never drank."

"Maybe not when you saw her last, but yes, among the other ladies, she was known as 'the drunk.'"

"The drunk?" Ion's tears hit the handle of his teacup, then splashed onto the red-checkered tablecloth. "She never used to drink. I never saw her. Never."

"It is the shame," Eva said. "You cannot imagine the shame. And drinking helps you forget."

Ion looked as if he were going to be sick. Anna wet a towel with cool water and began to pat his forehead with it.

"My sister kept me alive," he said. "When she had nothing else, she sold herself to keep me alive."

"We know, Ion. We know all about your Dora," Anna said.

"She was only twelve when she started. Twelve. Yes, Eva is right. It was shame. It was shame that drove Dora away and shame that…that killed her." Ion's voice was barely audible.

"It's not your fault. You were only a little boy when your parents were arrested. You cannot blame yourself."

"But if I were older…if only I had been the older one, then I could've taken care of her."

"But you were not. We cannot keep wishing for things to be what they are not." Anna hugged him again and she was crying.

Ion shook his head and tears dripped into his teacup. "She renounced her faith. Did I ever tell you that? But she didn't mean what she said. She was angry with God. It was the shame. I could see it in her eyes. She didn't mean it."

"Only God knows what transpired in Dora's mind and heart before she died," Teofil said, placing one hand on the young man's arm. "She loved Him once. It's possible she returned to her Savior at the end."

"Yes, it's possible," Ion said. "All things are possible with God. But it hurts. My heart hurts for my poor, sweet Dora." Then he dropped his face into his hands and sobbed.

Quietly, the others gathered around and cried with him.

❦

Alexander Wainwright, along with Donald Walters and Arni Houser, had been at the embassy for forty-eight hours straight. Most of the staff observed their normal routine, but leaving and returning was extremely difficult. The Securitate stopped all cars, and all embassy employees were delayed and harassed by lengthy questions. The ambassador registered a formal complaint with Ceausescu's government, but predictably, heard nothing.

In addition, Mrs. Tulasi's wound had become infected and she was running a fever. One-half of the embassy looked like a makeshift hotel, with rollaway cots and blankets everywhere. All the Marines had also remained at the compound and slept in shifts.

Alexander's office was rearranged, his desk pushed from the center of the room to one side, so a cot could fit in the other. There were plenty of bathroom and shower facilities, but no one had spare clothes, so those who had stayed were walking around in rumpled outfits.

Outside, forty Securitate sharpshooters maintained their vigil with their AK-47s. Each morning and evening forty fresh replacements took their places.

Alexander Wainwright held the phone to his ear. In front of him sat Arni Houser. "Yes, Rodger, I understand. I'll be on the plane first thing in the morning...Yes, I know you were disappointed that I had to cancel the meeting with the Japanese ambassador...I'll be able to give you a full briefing of my proposal tomorrow...right...good-bye."

"I take it you're going to the Seventh Floor tomorrow?"

Alexander nodded.

"In that suit, sir?"

Alexander looked down at his jacket and trousers and laughed. "A little too ripe?"

"Yes, sir."

Alexander picked up the phone and dialed the number of his residence.

A worried-sounding female voice answered. "Hello?"

"Loretta, I need you to pack my bag. I'm flying to Washington tomorrow, and I want the gray suit, not the double-breasted. And put my gray loafers in a separate bag before you pack them. Give it to...give it to the driver when you're finished and have him bring it to me as soon as possible."

"Darling, why can't you come home? What's happening?"

"Can't talk now," Alexander said and hung up.

"Maybe I should run to my place and pack a bag too," Houser said. "With fresh clothes, I can stay and man the fort while you're gone."

Donald Walters charged into the room. "Phones are down."

"I was just on mine," Alexander said.

"So was I, but everything's dead now. I stuck my head in some of the other offices on the way here. Same thing."

Alexander picked up his phone and began punching numbers. Nothing happened. Houser rose quietly and left the room. A few minutes later he returned.

"We're out. All the lines are down," Houser said. "I guess we won't be able to call the Diplomat's Club for take-out."

Walters rolled his eyes. "The Diplomat's Club doesn't do take-out."

Alexander laughed. He just realized he hadn't had a

stomachache in forty-eight hours. "Yeah, and I think they're doing us all a favor."

Loretta Wainwright carefully wrapped each of her husband's gray shoes in a towel, then placed them in the suitcase. She had packed everything she thought he would need: plenty of socks, underwear, shirts, pajamas, casual clothes, shaving equipment, cologne, hair dryer, toothbrush and paste, deodorant. Two suits were zipped in a garment bag, Alexander's favorite gray and a brown one. No telling how long he was going to be gone. She hoped she had everything. She rechecked her mental list and was sure it was all there. Quickly, she scribbled a note and placed it on top: *I love you. We must talk when you return. Loretta.*

Loretta looked out the bedroom window to see if Yuri had returned with the car. It was nearly dark, but she could make out the figure of a tall man leaning against the limo. She opened the window. "Meet me in the foyer."

Loretta struggled down the stairs, dragging the large suitcase with one hand and clutching the garment bag with the other. As soon as Yuri saw her, he came over and took everything. Loretta followed him out to the car.

"What's going on?" she asked him in a whisper. "Do you know?"

"Yes. It is serious."

"Is…is Alex all right?"

"I have no reason to think otherwise."

"When you see him, be careful."

"Why?"

Loretta looked away. "I'm ashamed to say it, but he thinks we're having an affair."

"I know."

"You know? How?"

"It is of no importance. Do not worry, Loretta. Trust God. He will see that things come out right in the end."

Anna hugged and kissed Mirela, then began passing out thick slices of freshly baked bread. Out of the corner of her eye she watched Ion move among the girls. She had tried to keep him from coming; it was dangerous having him here. He was still overwrought about Dora, and unpredictable, and he had insisted they come earlier than usual. It was barely dark and Anna glanced around nervously. She had hoped that between her and Eva, they could keep a close watch on Ion, but already Eva was surrounded by the other girls.

"No, this cannot be that sick, ugly rag woman!" Simona said to the others. "This isn't possible!"

"Yes, it is I, come back from the edge of death. Brought back by my beautiful Jesus."

"Oh, now we'll have two of them trying to indoctrinate us," Simona said.

"It's a miracle!" Mirela said. "Is it not, girls? A miracle!"

"You're too gullible, child. Too easily led," Simona said. "When are you going to grow up?"

Ion's loud voice suddenly thundered down the alley. "Come, gather round, ladies. I need to speak with you."

Anna saw the curious prostitutes begin to form a circle around him. She began praying fervently, quietly, under her breath. She watched as Ion's eyes grew large, then a peace came over him like a vapor. Anna prayed for God's direction, then she began praying for each of the prostitutes by name. She prayed their hearts would be opened and softened by the hand of God. She prayed that only God's words would proceed from Ion's lips, words of life that would be dropped into these hungry open hearts. She prayed these words would take root like a seed and grow into something new and beautiful, fresh and life giving. Then she held her breath.

"I need to tell you about my sister," Ion shouted into the crowd. "My sister was one of you, a lady of the streets. That's how she took care of us, both of us, for many years. That's how she put food on the table, kept a roof over our heads. Her name was Dora, and she was beautiful and sweet and very young. Today I learned that she has died. It was in a dark, cold alley like this one, and she died, all alone, with no one to comfort her. I was told it was pneumonia. But I know differently. I know that she died from shame."

Anna opened her eyes and saw Mirela move closer to Floare, like a little bird looking for protection. And she could see that Mirela had begun to cry. She watched as Eva moved silently toward the young girl and put her arm around her. In her spirit, Anna could sense a moving of God. But she could also sense something else and was instantly afraid. She began to pray harder.

"Why did my beautiful Dora die in an alley?" Ion's voice rang out clear and loud. Large tears dripped from his cheeks. "I will tell you why. She died all alone in an alley because she wouldn't come home to Jesus. She wouldn't let Him forgive her and heal her and…and *love* her. Ladies, do not stay any longer without your beautiful Savior. Come to Him. He knows every evil you've ever committed and still He loves you. Yes, He loves you! And He has paid the price for all your sins with His precious blood. His blood will wash you clean. Only accept and believe."

Mirela began to cry into her hands. "No, please don't lie to us."

Floare and the others also had tears in their eyes but made no move of any kind.

"Come! Come!" Ion was shouting at the top of his voice now and beckoning the women to come forward. "Don't let pride or doubt or…or fear steal you from your Jesus. Listen to Him as He calls your name today. He won't trick you. He won't deceive you. You are loved and you can come home again."

Suddenly three men rounded the corner of the alley. They had clubs in their hands and two of them had guns bulging beneath their jackets. Anna heard Simona say, "Securitate!"

They sprang upon Ion and dragged him to the alley wall. He offered no resistance but tried to shield himself from the blows from the clubs, then finally was unable and dropped to his knees. Anna saw him fall. There was a smile on his face and he spoke only one word over and over again, "Jesus," until finally he said nothing at all.

"No, no!" Anna shouted. "Please, no!" She tried to move toward the men, but the women pressed together and she could not pass. Suddenly a hand covered her mouth, and she found herself being pulled deep into the alley. Her abductors stopped next to Eva's old crate. Even with her mouth covered and her head in a rigid lock, Anna could see out of the corner of her eyes that it was Simona and Felicia who held her captive.

"Say nothing and stay absolutely quiet," Simona ordered in a whisper. "If they find you, they'll kill you! Will you stay here quietly?"

Anna nodded, and only then did Simona and Felicia let go of her. Simona pointed to the crate. "Hide behind it. And do not come out until I say!" And then both prostitutes were gone.

Quickly, Anna moved behind the crate, but even from where she now crouched against the alley wall, she could hear shouting. She strained to hear what was going on and heard crying.

"Why the tears, little one?" one of the Securitate said as he watched Mirela weep into her hands. He was dark and thin and stood wheezing against the wall. Blood splatters streaked his shirt and trousers, and there was blood on his hands, which he began to wipe on a handkerchief. "You're not one of them—one of these detestable sects—are you?"

"She's young. You must excuse her," Simona said, coming up to him as bold as lightning. Her arms were folded across her generous chest. "She's not used to such sights. But all this rough business, was it necessary?"

The stranger put his soiled handkerchief into his back pocket with only a glance at Simona. "This is none of your concern." Then he returned his full attention to Mirela. "But this tender little bird interests me. I think I'd enjoy plucking her feathers."

Simona stepped between him and the weeping girl and pushed roughly against his chest. "Just because you're Securitate, don't think you can get away without paying. It'll cost you, like anyone else. But first go and wash off this blood. Disgusting. This whole rough business is disgusting, and bad for business too. You're scaring away the customers."

The man laughed, then pulled out a flashlight and shone it into the dark end of the alley. "What's in there?"

"Just an old crate."

He began walking toward it.

"It belonged to an old prostitute with tuberculosis," Floare said.

The man stopped and backtracked. "Yes, I've heard about her." He studied the faces of the ladies around him, looking at each one carefully as though memorizing them for later. "I'll be back," he said suddenly. He turned to look at his two comrades and laughed. "Perhaps my friends would also like a little diversion. We'll all return later and compensate you for any loss to your business. Just make sure this tender little bird is here."

Then he walked to where his two companions stood, one on either side of the collapsed bloody body. With his foot he nudged Ion. When he heard a moan, he pulled out the gun from beneath his jacket and fired two bullets into Ion's head.

As Yuri Deyneko turned the corner of Str. Dionisie Lupu he saw two armed guards with flashlights waving their arms for him to stop. He pulled over to the side and lowered his window.

"I'm in a hurry," he snapped. "Why am I detained?"

One of the guards rested his arm on the open window and peered into the limo. "Orders," he said, shining his flashlight into the car.

The second guard inspected the other side of the car. He opened the back door and looked in, then closed the door and walked around to where the first guard stood. "State your business," he shouted through the window.

"This is the official limousine of the U.S. ambassador. I'm his driver."

"What's in the trunk?" the first guard asked.

"Luggage."

"Whose luggage?"

"Ambassador Wainwright's."

"We will see it."

Yuri pushed the button in the glove compartment to pop the trunk. Then he got out of the car and watched one of the guards scan the trunk with his light, then run a hand around the interior.

"Open it," guard number two ordered, pointing to the suitcase.

Yuri unzipped the bag and pulled the top back. The first thing he saw was Loretta's note. The guard saw it too and as he reached for it, Yuri clamped down on his arm.

"Leave it!"

"What does it say?"

"It's only a note from his wife."

The guard looked at his comrade, who was moving up behind Yuri.

"Stay where you are!" Yuri ordered, and at once the guard stopped. "I am Colonel Yuri Deyneko. I am on special assign-ment by order of General Tulasi. Call headquarters if you wish, but you will stop this search now and you will let me pass."

Both guards backed off at once.

"Colonel, our apologies!" the second guard said. "We were only following orders. We did not know…we meant no disre-spect." Then he snapped the trunk closed and saluted.

Yuri did not return the salute, but pushed past the guards and climbed back into the car. "I will speak to General Tulasi of this," he said and saw panic in the guards' faces. "I'll be sure to tell him how thorough and alert you were. You're to be commended."

After parking, Yuri pulled out a pen and wrote something on a piece of paper. Then he got out, zipped up the bags, pulled them from the trunk, and went to the back door. An armed Marine blocked the way.

"Halt!"

"I am Yuri Deyneko, the ambassador's chauffeur."

"I'm sorry, sir, you are unauthorized personnel."

"I have been instructed to bring the ambassador's luggage."

"One moment, sir." The Marine rang the bell, and seconds

later the door was opened by another Marine. The sentry outside spoke briefly to the one inside, then turned to Yuri. "He will bring the suitcases inside."

Yuri backed away with the bags. "Tell Ambassador Wainwright I will surrender these bags only to him."

"Sir?" The Marine looked puzzled.

"Get Ambassador Wainwright!"

The sentry inside disappeared. He gave the message to a nearby undersecretary, who went directly to the ambassador's office. The door was open, but he knocked politely on the wall. Inside, Ambassador Wainwright sat talking with Don Walters.

"Sir, your bags have arrived," the undersecretary said.

"Great, just bring them in here, will you?"

"Well, I don't have them, exactly."

"Then tell whoever has them to bring them here."

"I can't, sir. It's your driver, and you left strict orders not to let him in the building."

"What are you talking about?"

"Your driver, sir, has the bags."

"Then get them from him."

"He says he won't give them to anyone but you."

"What the…" Alexander rose from his chair. "We have armed Marines all over the place. For heaven's sake, have them take the bags by force!"

"I think he'll put up a fight, sir."

"Then shoot him!"

Walters stood up and began ushering the undersecretary out the door. "I'll handle this, Mr. Ambassador."

"No, Don, forget it," Alexander said, then cursed under his breath. "I'll take care of it myself." He began walking down the hall in a rage.

"Mr. Ambassador, please be careful. It could be a trick," Walters said, following him.

"Don't worry. You just tell the sentry to aim at Colonel Deyneko's head and if there's one false move, fire!"

"Mr. Ambassador, I don't think this is a good idea. I don't…"

Alexander pushed the back door open with such force that it would have swung back and hit him had Walters not stopped it with his foot. But Alexander couldn't see anything except the tall, burly man who stood several feet away, laden with luggage. For an instant Alexander considered provoking a situation that would cause the Marine to fire, but he just took a few steps and stopped.

"Well, you wanted to see me; here I am!"

Yuri moved very slowly, very carefully forward. He placed the suitcase near Alexander's right leg, then laid the garment bag on top of it. Then he handed Alexander a piece of paper and turned away.

Alexander watched Yuri open the limo door and get in. "I will be at the residence if you need me, sir," he heard him say. Then he watched as the car drove off. Only then did he open the note: *Do not worry about Loretta. All is not as it seems.*

Alexander stared down at the note and read it several times.

"Everything all right, sir?" Walters asked.

Alexander nodded and dismissed the first secretary with a wave of his hand. Walters shrugged and walked back inside.

Tears welled up in Alexander's eyes as he folded the note and put it in his jacket pocket. *All is not as it seems! All is not as it seems!* How he had longed to hear those words. How he had *prayed* to hear those words. Maybe they were true. And maybe there was a God after all.

8

ALEXANDER WAINWRIGHT'S LIMOUSINE PULLED INTO a semicircular driveway. In front of him stood an eight-story minicity of white stone. An aide to the secretary of state waited under the concrete canopy to welcome him, and after a hearty handshake and inquiries into the state of his health and the tedious nature of his trip, Ambassador Wainwright was led through a glass door and into a two-story-high reception room. A receptionist, who looked more like a fashion model, sat at a circular desk. The area behind her was barred by iron lattice that had only one opening, at which stood a guard. Past the guard were the elevators and passage to the Seventh Floor.

The aide flashed a badge, and the guard nodded rather pretentiously, then let them pass. Alexander was glad the aide had met him. As many times as he had been here, the two-city-block-long State Department was still a maze. Even with the internal corridors and color-coded walls he had trouble. He smiled appreciatively at his companion and hoped he didn't look too harried.

The elevator they boarded took them to the Seventh Floor, where it opened into a large reception suite. Settings of federal and colonial style furniture atop oriental carpets gave off a feeling of graciousness. The walls were covered with nineteenth-century American paintings, as well as with portraits of former secretaries of state. This reception suite formed the center of the reception hall, with partial glass dividers separating areas on both sides.

The aide led Alexander past the middle reception area and down a narrower wallpapered corridor. More portraits of secretaries of state hung on the walls, along with exhortations to "keep right" so as to avoid collisions. The hallway widened at various intervals and formed niches, here and there, where security men sat at desks.

As Ambassador Wainwright walked through the corridor, he saw a huge painting on the wall to his left. He stopped. It was an H. E. Bryant piece with snowy mountains as the backdrop and a cowboy as the central figure, pushing his horse uphill on an icy path. On the frame was a thin metal plate engraved with the title: *A Slippery Push on a Slippery Trail.* Alexander smiled. Inspiration or warning? Both was his guess. He wondered how hard he'd have to push before this Tulasi business was finished. And if something bad happened? Well, he hoped he wouldn't be under that horse, that's all.

The aide knocked, then opened the door and ushered Alexander into a large office that resembled the center reception area with its colonial furniture, oriental rugs, and huge oil paintings. Only this room smelled of tobacco.

Behind the desk sat the white-haired secretary of state, and to the right sat a balding Rodger McAllen, puffing vigorously on a half-smoked Camel.

"Mr. Secretary," Alexander said as the white-haired statesman rose and shook his hand. "Rodger." Alexander turned to the bureau director and offered him his hand, then took the chair directly in front of the desk, facing the secretary of state. He opened his briefcase and pulled out several sheets of paper. "You might want to see these first," he said, handing the papers to the secretary of state.

"What are they?"

"A copy of my official protest to Ceausescu."

The secretary nodded.

"I drafted it just before leaving for D.C. Don Walters will see it's delivered. It's our second protest regarding the troops outside the embassy, and the first regarding the downed telephone lines."

The secretary read them quickly, then passed them on to McAllen. "Alex, while you were en route, Doug Anderson was able to come up with something on the Tulasis. It seems that you are playing host to the parents of the number two man in the Securitate."

Alexander whistled. "Incredible. If it was anyone but Doug, I might be inclined to question it, but his information's always solid. Guess that explains why they're playing hardball. How is the number two man going to stay number two if his parents defect?"

"Exactly."

"It could get rougher."

"Well, give me your assessment, Alex," the secretary said.

"Worst-case scenario?"

"Go for the jugular."

"Well, sir, I don't think they'll let them out of the country alive. I think any attempt to bring them out will be met with armed resistance. And I don't think they'll worry about hitting one of ours."

"For heaven's sake, Alex, we can't have a gun battle in the streets of Bucharest!"

"I understand that, sir. But I'm trying to tell you I think this could get out of hand and I need to know my parameters. How far can I go?"

"You're to maintain a peaceful posture at all times. No military or paramilitary activities."

"And what about self-defense, sir? Am I to tell my staff and the Marine guards they can't defend themselves?"

"Your job, Alex, is to see that you don't have to defend yourself," McAllen said. "You're a *diplomat,* remember? Use some diplomacy!"

"That's fine to say when you're sitting behind a desk and the hottest thing you have to handle is a cigarette."

"Gentlemen, please," said the secretary, putting up his hand like a pontiff. "Let's not get sidetracked. The issue here, as I see it, Alex, from your previous dispatch and from what we've learned from Anderson, is that you have two aging Romanians who wish to defect. This defection will be a great embarrassment to the Securitate and therefore they're more than likely to use extreme measures to stop it. Have I stated the case clearly so far?"

"Yes, Mr. Secretary."

"You, on the other hand, are concerned about your embassy staff. You're also concerned about having this situation drag on and on. I mean, how long can you be expected to protect and care for these people at the embassy? In addition to the enemy outside, you need to guard the couple from possible assassination by secret police planted in your staff. It'd be embarrassing for the U.S. if they were to get killed inside the embassy. Correct so far, Alex?"

"Yes, sir."

"I'd like to meet with Anderson within the next forty-eight

hours to discuss possible strategy and see if we have any way of removing these people without gunplay and without loss of American lives."

"Yes, sir, but if there isn't any way, if there isn't a chance of getting them out without force, what are my parameters?"

McAllen cursed under his breath. "How much clearer do you want it? If the CIA can't get them out, then you do it, *without* force."

Alexander straightened in his chair. "You don't seem to understand. If the CIA can't do it, and we try it without firepower or at least a show of strength, they'll gun the Tulasis down." Alexander looked at McAllen, then at the secretary. Neither said a word. "The bottom line is that these people will get killed."

"Yeah," McAllen said, "they'll get killed. But they'll get killed *outside* the embassy."

"You mean to tell me you don't want the embassy to defend these people?" Alexander's neck began to blotch and redden. "You can't seriously mean that you want me to let them get killed?"

"What we're telling you," the secretary said, "is that we don't want to make a big thing out of this. We're beginning to make some headway with the Russians, with perestroika and glasnost, and in the wake of all this, we don't want to cause them too much embarrassment. There are things in the works, and the less waves we make right now, the better. You understand that, don't you, Alex?"

"Yes, sir."

"Good. Now follow this. On the other hand we don't want to appear soft on human rights. We're committed to fighting such violations, and of course that policy still stands. But we don't want to slap anyone in the face right now either. So that's the big picture. Do you see it, Alex?"

"Actually, sir, no. I'm a bit confused."

"Do you have the papers the doctor gave you?" McAllen asked.

Alexander nodded and pointed to his briefcase.

"Then we have everything we need. What other information can the doctor and his wife give us? If they live or die, it's the same."

"You can't possible be implying—"

"Alex, no one wants these people to die," the secretary said. "You're misinterpreting what Rodger's saying. Doug Anderson and the CIA will do their best. But if there's no way out and these people get killed...well, there's nothing we can do about it. Their blood will be on the hands of the Securitate, not on ours."

"Mr. Secretary, I respectfully disagree. If you refuse to let us use force and there's a showdown at the embassy, the Tulasis' blood will most assuredly be on our hands if they die."

The secretary frowned and looked thoughtfully at Alexander. "I'm sorry you see it that way. But you've asked for parameters and I've given them. You simply must understand that we are reluctant at this time to embarrass the Soviets."

"Sir, I don't see how this would embarrass the Soviets. It would be more of an embarrassment to the Ceausescu regime, and quite frankly, they need to be embarrassed. Besides, you may well be doing the Soviets a favor. Ceausescu has thumbed his nose at glasnost, and in doing so, at Gorbachev. There's no way Ceausescu wants to be more open or relinquish any power. I don't think Gorbachev will care if Ceausescu gets a little egg on his face."

The secretary smiled thinly. "Alex, I think we here at State are in a better position to determine what the big picture is or should be. The bottom line is that we're not prepared to start an international incident over two people looking to cleanse their conscience. Should we give them absolution by spilling innocent American blood? What if some of your staff were killed or some of those young Marine guards? How would you appease your own conscience? What would you tell their families?"

"I'd tell them they died doing their job."

The secretary of state sighed. "I have counseled you. Now you must do *your* job. You're a good man, with a promising future. This is a tough one, Alex, but you'll get through it. Just remember, long after this incident is over, you'll still have a career to think about."

The little brass bell announced the arrival of Pastor Gheorghe Vladimescu. His worn black suit appeared more crumpled than last time, and his hair was already in need of a trim. He was all smiles and politeness as he stepped into the shop. He nodded to Teofil, then walked directly to Anna's side of the room.

"Good day, Anna." Pastor Vladimescu peered over the counter and watched her finish basting the hem of a dress. "I wanted to see how you were feeling, and to once again offer my condolences."

Anna put down her work and forced a smile, then she rose and went to the counter. When she leaned her elbows on the countertop, she could see that the pastor's shoes were old and scuffed. She had not seen him wear that new, expensive pair since the first time he'd come into the shop. She noticed too that his shirt collar was more frayed today, and she leaned over and lightly touched it. "I'd be happy to mend this for you without cost."

"Well, yes…I mean, no, not necessary. We all have to make do, is that not so?"

Anna smiled sweetly. *What did he want?*

"Yes, well. I must say I am touched. Here I've come to be of service to you and it's you who try to assist me. I am touched, yes, very, but allow me to complete my ministry to you."

Anna prayed silently for God to fill her with love for this pretender, to help her forgive him for being part of the barbarians who had killed Ion.

"Yes, allow me to minister to you in your time of grief," Vladimescu continued.

"It's good of you to come," Anna said slowly, "but I'm quite fine. God is healing me of my pain."

"Oh? And how is He doing that?"

"The same way He's taking care of yours," Anna said, walking around the counter to stand next to the pastor. "For although you are new to us, I'm quite certain you share our grief over Ion's death."

"Yes, well. To be sure…to be sure." Vladimescu backed away and began edging toward Teofil's side. He accidentally kicked a pile of leather scraps and tried to remound it with his shoe. "Yes, well, if you are not in need of condolences, perhaps I can be of some comfort to Eva Stanciu. I understand she's still living with you."

"Yes."

"She took Ion's death badly, I hear."

"She barely knew him, but it's always a little sad when someone so young dies."

"Yes, well, then someone misinformed me. I cannot be sure

who but…well, never mind." Vladimescu began picking at his nails. They were clean and neatly trimmed, the hands of a careful man, a man too careful to be misinformed. "How's she doing otherwise?"

"She is well."

"Then perhaps I can visit, extend my concerns and gratitude that her health is improving."

"She's resting and cannot be disturbed."

"Yes, well. I've also heard that Eva has been the recipient of a miracle. They say—some say—God has healed her." He continued to pick at his nails. "Has God healed Eva Stanciu?"

"It would seem so."

"Oh?"

"She grows stronger every day."

"Yes, well. Then perhaps another day, when it's more convenient, I can speak with her and she can share this wonder?"

Anna nodded. "Yes, I'm certain she would like that."

Vladimescu sighed, and he was about to turn and leave when a sudden thought struck him. "I must commend you, Anna Rosu, for your tolerance, your capacity to forgive. It just struck me how much you've lost recently—first your pastor and the elders, and now a good friend. Perhaps there's some small matter of forgiveness you haven't addressed. I mean, a loss so large. I could help you with…perhaps I can pray with you about something?"

The seamstress looked over at Teofil, who had been sitting quietly at his bench listening. He rose when their eyes met.

"Yes, Pastor. I'm grateful for your condescension and care. And I do want to pray."

Vladimescu's eyes lit up. "Ah, so happy to be of service. So happy. What is it you want to pray for?"

"I'd like to pray for you," Anna said, and before Vladimescu could protest, Teofil and Anna both laid their hands on him and began to pray.

"No, Anna, I won't listen! I've made up my mind. Tonight I leave Ploiesti."

Anna sat on the cot, watching Eva Stanciu pace in front of her. "But he doesn't suspect you of anything. He only looks for information, hoping you'll slip and tell him something he can take back to headquarters and use."

"Exactly right, and that's why I must go." Eva stopped pacing and smiled at her friend. The dark circles under her eyes had almost disappeared, and there was a blush to her cheek. "You've become a dear friend, Anna. I'll love you always, wherever I go. I'll never forget you, what you did for me when I was so sick. How you cared for me. And I'll be eternally grateful to you for sharing your Jesus with me."

Tears welled up in Anna's eyes. "But what of your ministry to the other ladies? They're listening to you now. You're beginning to make an impact, especially on Mirela. And your study of Scripture, what of that? How can you give up so much?"

"I must leave all this in the hands of God. He'll make what He will of it. But I cannot stay. Of that I'm certain."

Anna wiped her cheeks with the back of her hand. "Are you sure this is necessary?"

"Yes. I've known many…I've known many Securitate. They're ruthless and will never let go. They know I've been an informer in the past, and they'll never let go, Anna. Never. This Gheorghe Vladimescu wants to question me in the hope I can give evidence against you and Teofil, against the others. And he'll twist and probe and pull until he gets something."

"But we're all prepared for this. We know the price we must pay to follow our Lord. I'm not afraid of what you'll tell them."

Eva took a seat next to Anna and picked up her hand and squeezed it. "I'll go to prison one day, I know this. Maybe it'll be a work camp, maybe prison, but I will go. God has shown me this. And I willingly suffer for my wonderful Lord. He's given me so much. How can I give less? But when they come for me...when they come, I must be far from here. There must be no connection to this place. Then no one will question me about you. No one will know there's any connection. I'm not afraid, Anna, not for myself."

Anna leaned her head against Eva's thin shoulder. "You're afraid you'll expose me as Anna Volkovoy?"

"Not that, Anna, but something else. Something I saw when we were in the field of sunflowers that wonderful day God touched me. It was Yuri, Yuri Deyneko. I didn't recognize him at first, but after a while I knew who he was. And then when I saw you and Yuri together...well, I *know*, Anna. I know about you and Yuri. The whole village always said you two would end up together. And they were right, were they not?"

Anna caught her breath as though a knife had been plunged into her heart. "Yes," she said in a near whisper.

"So then, you see how it is?" Eva said, squeezing Anna's hand and rising from the bed.

"Yes."

"We will probably never see each other again."

"No, I think not."

Eva laughed, then strutted across the room. "So gloomy we are! Listen to us! But of course we'll see one another. In the end we'll all be together."

Anna nodded and tried to smile, but she could not.

Eva began shoving her few possessions into a cloth bag. "Be assured, we will all be together again, you and me and Ion and Teofil, and your Yuri, all of us, and then there'll be no more crying. Our sweet Savior will wipe away all our tears." Eva tied the cloth bag with a string, then looked at her friend sitting on the cot. "Yes, we'll all be together one day. But for now I'll miss you, Anna Rosu Volkovoy; I'll miss you very, very much."

Alexander Wainwright walked around the walled grounds of the American embassy. He couldn't stay inside any longer. He missed his garden at the residence, even the weeds and crab-grass. He missed the bench where he could sit in silence and listen to the birds or pick a ripened plum from his fruit trees, where he could smell the flowers along the walkways. A garden, even one in disrepair, held promise. There was always another spring, always another growing season where weeds could be tamed, where fruit trees could be more productive, the fruit sweeter.

He hadn't been to the residence since the appearance of the doctor and his wife. Even when he returned from D.C., he had not returned home. He was still living out of a suitcase and his appearance was beginning to show it. Brown socks were worn with gray slacks. Dress shirts served two days in a row. Jackets and pants needed pressing. But he hardly noticed what he wore or how he looked.

His meeting with the secretary of state had shaken him badly. He thought of that painting at State. He was that lone cowboy shoving against a horse's posterior with nothing but ice under his feet. Maybe that was the purpose of the picture. A

visual illustration of the unwritten creed of so many bureau-
crats. *When the going gets tough, don't expect help from us!*

The disastrous possibilities consumed nearly all his
thoughts. Loretta consumed the rest. She lurked there, in the
shadows of an anteroom, where he had put her until he could
cope. He had only spoken to her once since his return, a one-
sided conversation when he told her he wouldn't be home for
several days. The phone lines were going up and down like a
berserk elevator, so he doubted he'd be hearing from Loretta
anytime soon. Which was fine with him.

He sighed as he listened to the chirping of a sparrow. He
watched the little male with its gray crown and black throat
courageously perch on the high fence. Below, two sentries with
loaded rifles kept watch. The sparrow continued his serenade
without regard to the rifles, and produced such a gay melody
that Alexander almost forgot them himself.

"Just what do you have to be so happy about, my brave little
fellow?" Alexander said, smiling in spite of himself.

He watched the bird fly off, then continued his rounds,
stopping here and there to smell a flower, to handle a tree
branch, to gaze at an especially lovely shrub. The flower beds
were in bloom. Blues, yellows, pinks, greens swirled together
to form a giant masterpiece of harmony, beauty, perfection.
Why couldn't his life be more like that, instead of the present
dark, ugly chaos?

Arni Houser had met with Doug Anderson at State and had
given Alexander a short cryptic message of doom over the
phone, when the lines were briefly in service. Even now, Don
Walters was picking Arni up at the airport; then Don was going
to drive them all somewhere to talk.

Alexander glanced back at the flower bed. Next spring it

would start all over again and next summer a new canvas would be created. He wondered if he'd still be here to see it.

Three men walked along the narrow footpath, passing dense forest and foliage on both sides. The footpath formed an *S* shape and emptied into a small clearing that contained a few wooden tables with benches and two large pits for cooking. The pits hadn't been used for some time and were free of ashes.

"Let's sit over there," Arni Houser said, pointing to a table in the right-hand corner of the clearing. It was the farthest from all the others, yet still not too close to the wooded area where someone could lurk unseen and overhear their conversation.

Alexander Wainwright and Donald Walters followed obediently, and after brushing some dirt and leaves off the seats, they sat down, Wainwright and Walters on one side, Houser on the other. The three huddled over the table and spoke quietly. During their ride to Herastrau Park, Houser had confirmed his earlier message. The embassy could expect little help from the CIA.

"Don't be too harsh, sir," Houser said after Alexander had cursed the agency. "Doug Anderson's a good man. Believe me, we brainstormed for hours trying to figure an angle. The fact is the CIA is expert at clandestine or covert operations, but our situation here has a bloody spotlight on it. Just too many eyes watching. We need a Special Operations team, but that's not going to happen. State doesn't want a bloodbath. Anderson said he'd keep working on it, and if they came up with a plan, we'd be notified."

"Don't call us, we'll call you," Alexander said.

"Something like that. But Anderson will try, that's one thing

I'm sure of. But right now it looks like we're on our own."

Alexander looked at the man next to him. "Our necks are way out on this one, and yes, Don, we could all lose something over it. Thing is, we need to come up with a game plan that everyone can live with."

Walters smiled weakly. "I'm with you on this all the way, sir."

Alexander laughed. "Well, then, try not to look so depressed."

"Do you have a plan, sir?" Houser asked.

"No. I was hoping you could come up with something."

"My advice is wait. Do nothing. Time is on our side. Two months, six months, what difference does it make? We need to wait until our Securitate friends begin to tire of the game, when they begin to get careless or sloppy, that's when we make our move. Sooner or later there'll be an opening, and then we can slip our little defectors through it."

"You're right, Arni. Time is about the only thing we have going for us right now." Alexander glanced at the first secretary. "Don? Anything to add?"

"I don't see an alternative to Arni's scenario. But you know State." He looked anxiously at Alexander.

"You know State, and I know State, but bless Arni for not," Alexander said. "At least someone can be objective."

At the end of the hall a Marine guard stood as straight and motionless as a flagpole, while Alexander Wainwright knocked on the closed door next to him. The door opened slightly and an elderly man timidly poked out his head. He smiled when he saw it was the ambassador himself.

"Ah, Mr. Ambassador! You have news for me!"

"How is Mrs. Tulasi?" Alexander asked in a whisper.

Dr. Tulasi inched his way through the door and closed it behind him. "I do not want Marian to hear. She is not well."

"Has the infection gotten worse?"

"No, no, the penicillin is doing its job. Again I thank you, Mr. Ambassador, for requesting that from your country."

"Forget it," Alexander said, waving his hand. "What seems to be the problem?"

The doctor looked around nervously and pointed to his head. "Up here, that is where Marian is not well. She cries every night. I cannot comfort her. She says we will never get out of here. She says we are here too long and that means trouble. But every night I tell her that the American ambassador has made a promise and he will keep it."

"You've only been here a week."

"I do not complain. I tell her each night not to complain. That resolution of such serious matters takes time. But no, she just cries and cries. Do you not hear her?"

"No." The last two nights he hadn't been able to sleep because of the crying.

"It is up here," the doctor said, pointing to his head again. "She has fixed her mind on this point and I cannot convince her otherwise. She has finally fallen asleep. But tonight I know it will be the same all over again. Would it be improper to ask you…to ask you to come later when she is awake and give her some small assurance? Perhaps if you tell her that all is well, that you have given your word, then maybe she will believe."

"Well, I—"

"You see, Marian does not know any better. All her life she has lived in a country where the government says one thing and does another. It is hard for her to understand that not all governments are alike; that if an American ambassador gives his word, then it is a matter of honor. Is that not true?"

"Well, yes, but—"

"See, this is what I cannot make her believe. But she will listen to you. You can explain. Reassure her. Then maybe she will stop her crying."

"I'll come see her."

The doctor's face beamed. "Thank you, thank you. I am so appreciative!" Then he grew somber again. "Marian says something else. I…I have tried to dispel this also, but I am at a loss. What would you say to her, Mr. Ambassador?"

"About what?"

"We are Communists, my wife and I. We do not believe in the existence of God. We have accepted this all our lives. Now Marian says she thinks there might be a God. More correctly, she *fears* there might be a God. She is afraid that this God is angry with us for living so long in comfort with our eyes closed to the horrors of what was happening in…in those dungeons." The doctor closed his eyes. "I have seen too much. But I cannot think of it anymore. I will not think of it anymore! So terrible, so terrible!" When Dr. Tulasi opened his eyes he seemed almost surprised to see the ambassador standing in front of him. He cleared his throat nervously. "Yes, my wife is afraid. No, I tell her, there is no God. We were good citizens. We did our duty, as we knew it. We were not the torturers. We were not the tormentors. Day after day, I came with my bag to mend the bodies that had been broken and torn. I did not break them. I did not tear them. I did what I was told, no more, no less. But she does not listen. She says this God will punish us by never allowing us to leave Romania. Do you believe this?"

Alexander looked at him in numb silence. Finally he

shrugged. "I'm not God, Doctor. I can't answer for Him."

"Well then, perhaps you can tell her there is no God. That you do not believe. That will reassure her."

"I will visit your wife; that's all I can promise."

"That is sufficient, Mr. Ambassador. That is more than sufficient. I thank you." Then, just as he was opening the door to his room, he stopped. "Oh, pardon, pardon. You came to tell me some news and I have made you forget."

"Well, I don't think—"

"Ah yes! Of course." The doctor looked around, his eyes scanning the ceiling and the corners. "I understand. You cannot speak freely. I understand." With that, he disappeared.

Alexander Wainwright stood frozen outside the closed door. He thought of the repulsive little man on the other side, a man who had played it safe, never made waves; who did what he was told, "no more, no less." Suddenly he shuddered. Was this the man he could become? Was this a self-portrait?

Alexander had always envisioned his portrait to be more like Dorian Gray's. Youthful, constant. He had always been content with himself as he was. There was no motivation for change, except, of course, in his career. To expect it to perpetually spiral upward was a given. Everything else could stay. Change was Loretta's department. She was always using words and phrases such as *maturity* and *coming to terms*. To him it was just silly prattle. Actually he thought it rather mature of him to be able to pacify and indulge her without really having to participate. So what was this cold breath that pierced his heart like an icicle? Perhaps he had been foolish to link himself in thought to someone like Dorian Gray. After all, Gray had, in one afternoon, changed completely. But that was fiction. This was real life. Self-portraits didn't change so suddenly.

He was having a bad day, that's all; feeling overcome and betrayed. And why shouldn't he? Hadn't State let him down? And what about his wife? The jury was still out on her. He was like that cowboy, all alone, struggling. So why didn't London and Paris ring his bells anymore? Once they'd been his dream. Surely a man couldn't give up his dream so easily? Could he? Maybe that's what bothered him most, the fact that *nothing* seemed so important anymore, except Loretta.

Slowly he walked back to his office, trying to forget the little man behind the door. Yes, that was it. A man needed a goal, something to conquer. He'd get his vision back. He'd be all right.

Glumly, he sat down at his desk, still unable to shake the portrait of that pathetic little man. In thirty years would he have to ask a stranger to lie to Loretta so she wouldn't cry at night? The thought was loathsome.

"Sorry to bother you, sir," came the intimidated voice of an undersecretary who stood in the doorway, "but your wife is here to see you."

A series of emotions washed over Alexander. He tried to compose himself and couldn't.

"Sir, your wife is here to see you," the nervous undersecretary repeated.

Alexander pretended to be busy reading something on his desk, then without looking up said, "Show her in."

"She won't come in, sir. Said you were to meet her outside."

Alexander rose from the chair and followed the undersecretary to the end of the hall. The secretary opened the back door, and Alexander looked into the face of his wife.

"Hello, darling," Loretta said with a smile. "The mountain has come to Mohammed." She gave him an affectionate hug and pulled him down the outside stairs. "A week is about all I can stand without you. And I bet you weren't even planning to come home tonight either?"

Alexander shook his head. His heart was melting, and he was beginning to feel as though he had played the biggest of fools until he saw Yuri Deyneko standing by the black limo. Immediately he pulled himself free.

"What's he doing here?"

Loretta took her husband's hand again and began leading him toward the car. "Did you want me to walk?"

Alexander followed reluctantly, balking every few steps. "What are you doing?"

Loretta kept pulling her unwilling husband until they stood next to the limo. "Get in," she said.

Alexander was about to pull away and tell Loretta it was impossible for him to leave the embassy, when he looked into her eyes and saw such tenderness and compassion. Her eyes spoke forgiveness, understanding, love. He was disarmed. With a slight wave of his arm and a shout to the undersecretary who still stood by the exit, Alexander disappeared into the back seat of the limo.

"No tails," Loretta said, as she slid next to her husband.

"What?"

"We don't want to be followed."

"What about the Securitate?"

"Yuri has fixed it. No more tails on you for a while."

"*Yuri* has fixed it? I don't like the sound of this, Loretta. What's going on?"

"Trust me."

"That's all I get, 'trust me'?"

"That's all."

Alexander looked into Loretta's eyes again and felt as if he were falling into a pool of gentian water. He had no defense against her. If he drowned, so be it. He stuck his head out the window and shouted to the undersecretary who still stood on the steps watching. "Keep the CIA boys here."

"But sir—"

"No tails!"

The limo pulled out of the gated embassy driveway and passed the Securitate's roadblock. Alexander looked out the back window. No one followed. *Yuri has fixed it.* Fixed what? He supposed he'd find out soon enough.

For the next fifteen minutes, no one spoke as the car whizzed through Bucharest and out past the suburbs. Alexander kept watching Loretta who sat quietly holding his hand and gazing out the window.

"Where are we going?" Alexander asked finally.

She gave him one of her sweet smiles and just looked at him for a moment.

"Where are we going?" he said, with agitation in his voice.

Loretta squeezed his hand. "To the countryside past Sitiu. Relax, darling, we have another half hour ride."

Alexander sulked quietly in his seat.

Soon they passed the quiet streets of Sitiu. Two-story buildings wedged against each other formed a charming and picturesque array of shops and dwellings. Smokestacks, sometimes as many as ten on a roof, pierced the shimmering tile like sooty square periscopes. If a hidden underground culture used them for spying out the land, they would have seen only a large sleepy town where little had changed in decades. In the center of town the same domed clock tower rose upward in a point and stood twice as tall as all the other buildings. The clock that had told a previous generation when to rise, eat, close shop, and rest, now instructed their great-grandchildren. The sun's rays hitting the lead tile roofs gave off a fiery light visible miles away and suggested the town was burning. But the town neither burned with fire nor activity. Aside from the occasional pedestrian, the narrow cobbled streets were deserted. It appeared that commerce in this area of Sitiu was conducted indoors out of the hot summer sun.

Alexander opened his eyes in time to see an old woman, draped in black, enter a church. As she disappeared into the vestibule he thought of Dr. Tulasi. How many times had the secret police emptied these churches and filled their prisons? How many times had Tulasi been a willing observer of their torture? This woman seemed not to care who saw. Perhaps her age made her fearless. She looked as if she had little time left and could afford to squander it on conscience.

As the car passed, Alexander looked into the dark entryway of the cathedral. It seemed to open like a huge mouth and swallow the woman. These people were eaten alive by their faith. What kind of God required such devotion? Or what kind of God inspired it?

"Why?" he asked absently, several minutes later.

"Why what, darling?" Loretta said.

"Nothing."

"Come on, why what?"

Alexander sighed. "Why are we here?"

"Are you being profound?"

"Why are we in this car? And why are we driving a zillion miles?"

Loretta laughed. "And just when I thought you wanted to explore the larger issues of life."

"We have enough of our own garden variety to explore. My plate, as they say, is full."

"Yes, darling, but not with wilted lettuce, I hope."

"Loretta, not now. I'm not in the best of moods."

His wife laughed again and squeezed his hand. "I can see that."

"Sometimes you're infuriating. You drag me away from my office when I'm in the middle of a crisis, and then you have the gall to patronize me. I hate when you do that, Loretta. I hate being treated like a child."

Loretta squeezed his hand again. "Humor me just a little longer." Her voice was sweet and kind, but she didn't look at him.

"You always did play a mean game of poker."

"I know. I'm sorry."

"That's because you never bluff."

"No, never." Loretta opened the glass partition between the driver and backseat. "Do you think that place will do, Yuri?" she asked, pointing to a dirt road to the right that led into a thicket.

Yuri nodded and turned off the main road. They were several miles outside Sitiu and the countryside here was lush with rolling hills and dense forests. They had not seen a living soul for the past several miles.

Alexander watched his wife with renewed agitation. He didn't like the familiar way she had said Yuri's name. When the car stopped, both Yuri and Loretta turned to face Alexander, and he watched as his wife gave Yuri a look that seemed to transmit some secret signal. All the fear and dread of his suspicions resurfaced.

"We needed to take you to a place where we could speak

freely, without fear of being bugged or overheard," Loretta said. "Obviously what we have to discuss is very important. Lives are at stake here, Alex. But first I need to confess my indiscretion."

Alexander Wainwright bit into the inside of his mouth. His heart thumped so hard he wondered if the entire population of Sitiu several miles back could hear it. Certainly Loretta and her lover could; the heart of the cuckold husband that beats pathetically as the erring wife confesses. For this they had to drive fifty miles? Did they want to see him squirm? What could he expect from a Romanian? They were all vampires, sucking the blood from their victims, draining the life out of them little by little.

"Yuri has been giving me information about Gustov Volkovoy, and I've been turning this information over to Charles Riley. And Yuri has taken me to a meeting of the Underground church. Oh, Alex, I'm sorry to have deceived you in this way, but the situation is so serious, so critical, I just couldn't stand idly by and do nothing. If you could only see these people, see how precious their faith is, see how—"

Alexander vaulted from the car and began to walk down the dirt road. He didn't want Loretta to see him cry. Large tears filled his eyes and ran down his cheeks. *She wasn't having an affair!* How long he walked, he did not know, but finally, when his heart began to beat normally, when his eyes no longer flooded over, he turned around and headed back toward the car.

Yuri and Loretta were still waiting in the limo. Alexander slipped into the backseat and glanced from one anxious face to the next. "I'm really angry with you, Loretta," he finally said, trying hard not to let his joy bubble over into his voice. "I've always been indulgent of your unorthodox behavior and given you plenty of slack. I've let you follow your conscience. Even when I didn't think it was in your best interest, I never interfered. But this time...*this time* you've crossed the line. You know that, don't you?"

Loretta nodded.

"This time you were reckless. So reckless, in fact, that it could mean my career." Alexander tapped his leg nervously with his fingers. "What do you plan to do?" he finally said.

"There's no turning back now, Alex."

"What does that mean?"

"It means I can't forget what I've seen and heard. It means I want to do something; I want *you* to do something."

"Me? What can I do? You know the embassy is like a fishbowl with the Tulasis there. I don't think you realize how serious the situation is."

"Now who's patronizing whom?"

"Sorry, but you just need to understand what's at stake."

"I know what's at stake. That's why you need Yuri."

Alexander looked over at the driver. "Oh, that's right, how could I forget? Colonel Deyneko is Gusto Volkovoy's brother-in-law," he said sarcastically.

"He is, Alex," Loretta said.

"You believe him?"

"I have every reason to believe him. I've met his wife, Anna Volkovoy."

"Anyone could claim to be Anna Volkovoy."

"Yes, but seeing her and...well, seeing them together and all, I just know. You've always trusted my judgment before. Please trust me in this."

"You're asking me to take a giant leap of faith on your say-so."

"Yes."

"Even knowing the consequences? Knowing what this could do to my future?"

"Yes."

Alexander looked into Loretta's eyes, and he could hardly bear the love and trust he saw in them. He never wanted those eyes to cry themselves to sleep. "What did you have in mind?" he finally said, turning to Yuri.

"You have an embarrassing problem and I have the solution."

"The Tulasis?"

"Yes, I will take them off your hands."

"And just how do you plan to do this?"

"The secret police will not stop me or search my car. I can bring them out, in the trunk, and then someone I know in the Underground church will see to the rest of it."

"Do you know who the Tulasis are?"

"Yes."

"You're a Christian?"

"You know that I am."

"You know what he's done? You know that he's supervised experiments on Christians? That he's kept prisoners alive so they could be tortured longer?"

"I know all this."

"And you're still willing to help?"

"Yes."

"Why?"

"Because in God's eyes we are all the same; we are all sinners. The Tulasis are no exception. And His love for them is no less real."

"But how...how can you forgive them?"

Yuri smiled. "I fear my forgiveness is somewhat tainted with selfishness."

"What do you mean?"

"I mean I will remove this embarrassment from your embassy, to the satisfaction of everyone and in a manner that will make you appear a hero to your superiors, and you will do something for me."

"What's your price?" There was satisfaction in Alexander's voice and just a hint of contempt.

Yuri sighed. "Yes, I bargain like a common thief with his fence. But when you have seen what I have seen, it is a small price to pay to save someone you love. I speak of Gustov Volkovoy. You do not know this man. He is nothing to you. But he is like a brother to me. We grew up together. I have never known a sweeter, kinder man or one who has endured so much suffering. His crime—to love the Lord. He preaches Jesus. For many years he has been in and out of prison for this horrible offense. Now he is in a psychiatric hospital because the State says he has a Christ complex and needs help. Do you know what his treatment is? What the prescribed cure is? I will tell you. He is beaten twice a day, drugged until he cannot even say his own name. Then on Sundays he is strapped to a cross and laid on the floor. Several hundred inmates are required to urinate and defecate on him. After that, the cross is put upright and Gustov, dripping and smeared in filth, is made to hang there all day. The guards jeer and say, 'Look at the beautiful Christ!' But Gustov never curses them. This goes on day after day, Sunday after Sunday. This is what my contact at the mental hospital tells me. And this is why I am not ashamed to come to you, to make of myself a worm in your eyes."

Alexander sat white faced and shaken. Beside him, Loretta

cried softly into a tissue. "What do you want from me?" he finally said in a hushed voice.

"I want you to get Gustov out of that hospital."

"How?"

"The hospital is like a fortress, but I know your CIA can do it. My inside contact will provide details—how many guards, positions of surveillance cameras, and the like. Once Gustov is free, I know those who can smuggle him out of the country."

Alexander reached over and took his wife's hand. "I'll have to clear this with Washington, but I'll see what I can do."

Loretta's eyes were red, but she had stopped crying. She squeezed her husband's hand and smiled.

"It may take time," Alexander said as he watched her.

"Do not take long," Yuri said. "Gustov has little time left. He will not be able to take such abuse much longer."

Alexander Wainwright still held his wife's hand, and from time to time gave it a gentle squeeze. Loretta responded with a smile, but said nothing. The partition between the front and backseat was open, but Yuri Deyneko drove silently, oblivious to their presence. Everyone was absorbed in thought.

Alexander had promised Loretta he would come home with her, but he wanted to make one quick stop at the embassy first.

"I won't be long," he promised, breaking the silence as the limo drove past the double iron gates and onto the large driveway of Str. Dionisie Lupu 9.

He stopped first at Donald Walters's office and poked his head in the doorway. "Any word on our supplies?"

"For the glass room?"

"Right. We need to get it built."

Walters nodded and smiled. "Yes, sir, arriving tomorrow."

"Good. Keep on top of it, Don. Things are heating up."

"Yes, sir. Highest priority, sir."

Next Alexander went to the room at the end of the hall. The sentry was still posted by the door with his rifle. Alexander knocked loudly and waited several minutes before the door opened.

"Dr. Tulasi, I've come to have a few words with your wife."

The doctor smiled broadly. "A man of his word, a man of his word," he murmured as he let Alexander in. An elderly woman with her arm in a sling sat in an office chair. She tried to rise when she saw the ambassador.

"No, please don't get up," Alexander said. "I've just come to see how you are, Mrs. Tulasi, and to tell you that things are looking up. I think I can say with confidence that this present situation will be changing in the near future. So take courage, we have everything under control."

Mrs. Tulasi looked at him through swollen lids and nodded her head. "How soon?"

Dr. Tulasi jumped between them and put his finger to his lips. "Now, we must not ask our host such questions. It is not polite. In due time he will advise us. It is enough that he assures us now. He is a man of his word. Did I not tell you that? Did I not say to you this morning, 'The ambassador will be here to see you later'? Did I not tell you that?"

Mrs. Tulasi shrugged. She seemed uninterested in humoring her husband.

The doctor's smile widened, and Alexander was amazed at how far this little man could spread his lips across his face.

"Ah, yes. I told you. I told you," the doctor said. "Everything is going to be satisfactory. Is that not correct, Mr. Ambassador?"

Alexander returned the smile. "Yes, everything's going to be satisfactory."

The smile was still frozen on Alexander's face when he closed the door. What were his chances of any of this working? He didn't know. He only knew they'd have to be very, very lucky for everything to come out all right. But he was in it now, and as Loretta said, "There was no turning back."

Alexander thought of Gustov Volkovoy and was glad it wasn't Sunday. Yuri had said that Gustov was "like a brother." Yes, for a brother you would do this…and for a wife.

9

LORETTA LAY CURLED NEXT TO ALEXANDER as he twisted the blond strands of her hair around his finger.

"Your hair is really getting long," he said, taking in the fragrance of fresh shampoo. "I like it. It looks good on you."

"Why, thank you, darling. Thank you for noticing." She had been growing her hair for months now, and it was finally long enough to pull straight back. That's how she was wearing it more and more, pulled back in a loose ponytail or knotted in a chignon. "But then you notice everything."

"If it concerns you, yes, everything."

"That drives the other wives mad, you know. Some of these husbands notice nothing at all. Makes you wonder if they really understand anything about diplomacy. It certainly makes me appreciate you."

"Pride," the ambassador said, continuing to play with his wife's hair.

"What?"

"It's understood that an attractive woman is an asset to a diplomat. That's why I notice everything. You're good for my career."

Loretta giggled. "And all this time I thought it was because you were crazy about me."

"That too," Alexander whispered.

She snuggled closer to him. "This time you've surprised even me."

"How's that?"

"With everything that's been going on, I didn't think you'd notice. You really are a dear."

"It makes you look sophisticated," he said, bending closer and kissing her face. It was so good to be with her, to touch as lovers, to speak as friends. His heart ached whenever he thought of the loneliness and uncertainty of the past several weeks. He felt sick when he recalled his mistrust of her, his ugly visions of her and Yuri. He didn't think he could ever live through that again.

Making love to her had been sweet; more tender than passionate because he was still so grateful she hadn't really broken his heart. Now, holding her in his arms, he was able for a while at least to forget that other world of uncertainty at the embassy.

Loretta sensed this and lay quietly at his side.

"How would you like to go to Hawaii on vacation?" he said suddenly, as though injected with a shot of adrenaline. He pulled his travel folder from the drawer of his nightstand.

"Sounds wonderful."

"I thought we'd stay at Maui," he said, spreading the brochures over the bed. "Honolulu's too crowded."

"Tell me more." Loretta stretched lazily against him.

"Well, the first few days at Maui we'll just sit on the beach and do nothing, *absolutely nothing*. We'll let the sun do all the work and tan us until we look like two coconuts. Then we'll go sightseeing and visit Needle Point and Lahaina. Did you know that Herman

Melville stayed at Lahaina before writing *Moby Dick*?"

"Really? Isn't that where they filmed the Elvis Presley movie, *Blue Hawaii*?"

"Noooo. Hanauma Bay in Oahu." Alex pretended to be annoyed. He'd given Loretta this same information a dozen times and each time she'd forget.

"Oh, right. Hanauma Bay. That was going to be my next guess."

"Liar."

"Bikini or one-piece?"

"What?"

"Should I get a new bikini or one-piece for our trip?"

"We'll both get bikinis."

"Great idea! Twins. His and hers, and we'll have them made special with writing on them, something like 'Danger, cranky diplomats. Do not disturb.'"

"You plan on getting all that on one bikini?"

"Oh, right. How about muumuus? We could get a lot of writing on those. Very therapeutic. We could really ventilate and get a lot off our chests."

"Like what?"

"Well, we could say stupid things because nobody'll know who we are and will never see us again. Things like, 'Two, four, six, eight, we *don't* appreciate the State.'"

Alexander hesitated, thinking about the bugs in their room. "Yeah, I like that," he finally said. "Or how about 'Roses are red, violets are blue, you can count on State to make a fool out of you.'" For the first time since coming to Bucharest, he felt giddy and carefree.

"Bravo, darling. Here's one. 'Star light, star bright, whose head is on the "rod" tonight'?"

"I have a better idea. Let's forget the bathing suits."

"And wear what?"

"Large tattoos."

"Very original. And what would they say?"

"Mine would say, 'Alex loves Loretta.'"

"And mine would say, 'Loretta loves Alex'?"

"Exactly."

Loretta opened the drawer of the nightstand, pulled out a pen, and handed it to her husband. "Care to do a rough draft?"

Alexander laughed, took the pen and tossed it on the floor, then pulled her to him and kissed her neck. "I do love you, Loretta. I love you terribly."

Alexander Wainwright and Charles Riley walked side by side through Palace Square. Alexander spoke in low tones and from time to time looked around to see how far away his tails were. Four men in suits followed at a distance. And a few paces behind, four more men in suits followed them. The first set was CIA, the second, Securitate.

"Charles, I need a favor. A big one."

"What is it, Ali?" Riley said, a look of concern on his face. He had never seen his friend so agitated.

"I want you to write about Volkovoy nonstop. I want articles on him every day. And for those papers that don't use your stuff, I want you to contact them and give their reporters information. In short, Charles, I want you to do everything in your power to see that Gustov Volkovoy becomes a household name in the U.S."

"What're you up to, dear boy?"

"It's best you don't know."

"That serious?"

"Yes, that serious. I know Loretta's been giving you information about Volkovoy."

Riley's eyebrows went up. "Oh, you know about that?"

"Thanks for helping her, and for trying to keep me out of it. Although I think I would've been better off had I known from the start. It would've saved me a lot of heartache."

"Trouble in Paradise?"

"Not anymore."

"She was only trying to protect you, you know."

"That's not it. But never mind; it's all cleared up."

"Have I missed something?"

"Yes, but don't worry about it."

"Right, dear boy. If you say so."

"But this Volkovoy thing…can you do it, Charles?"

"Of course I can do it. I've been doing it so far, haven't I? He's still hot news and I can make him hotter. But a word of advice, Ali. Be careful. You don't know what these people are capable of."

"Yes, I do."

"Well, however bad you think they are, just realize they're worse. Much worse. There's an ugly mood here, Ali. This country's in big trouble and it's going down. Glasnost has the entire Ceausescu clan worried. More openness and freedom for the people means less power for them. They're fighting it tooth and nail. So now they have pressure from all sides: the Soviets, the U.S., and internally from their own people. And you know what they say about a cornered rat."

"Yes, but what about a cornered bat?"

"A what?"

"Bat, as in vampire. Do bats react the same as rats, I mean?"

"Now don't go loony on me. What's this about bats?"

"They call Ceausescu, 'Draculescu.'"

"And for good reason. That's what I've been trying to tell you. Be careful! Remember that a Draculescu is not an ordinary man. It's not easy to kill."

"I know. That's why we need a silver bullet."

"Ali, you're scaring me. Stop talking drivel."

Alexander smiled. "You're the silver bullet, Charles. Rather, your articles are. You're what I need if I'm going to succeed."

"Well, dear boy, I don't know what you're up to, but you can count on me. I'll make Gustov Volkovoy as famous as Lindbergh."

"Thanks, Charles. Let's hope that'll be wings enough for Volkovoy."

Three men sat around a rectangular table in the center of the glass room. The floor was bare of carpet and the table and three chairs were the only furniture in the room. The U.S. Navy crew had built this glass room within a soundproof room within a regular room in just seventy-two hours. They had also completed a similar though smaller room at the residence.

Ambassador Wainwright had just finished briefing Arni Houser and Don Walters about Colonel Yuri Deyneko's proposal. For one week he had kept everything to himself, trying to give Charles Riley time to whip up sentiment in the States. Riley had been relentless. Every major paper in the U.S. carried daily accounts of the Romanian pastor. Alexander had, for good measure, leaked some of the information from the Tulasi documents. Politicians found their phones clogged with calls demanding action. Human rights advocates, along with dozens of Christian and Jewish groups, all held demonstrations of protest. Gustov Volkovoy was on his way to becoming a household name.

"So what do you think, gentlemen?" Alexander asked his two associates.

"Well, public opinion is certainly on our side," Walters said. "If ever we could expect State's full cooperation on anything, it's now. With the presidential election coming up, no one wants to be viewed as soft on human rights. And if we get both the Tulasis and Volkovoy out, we'll be heroes."

Houser nodded. "You're one lucky hombre, if you don't mind my saying so, Mr. Ambassador. This Volkovoy mania's the ticket out for both the Tulasis and the preacher. State can't refuse. I say we go for broke."

Alexander smiled. "Then I take it we're all in agreement?"

Both Walters and Houser nodded.

"Okay. Arni, you and I will fly to D.C. tomorrow. While I'm on the Seventh Floor, you talk with Doug Anderson. Let's nail things down fast and get on with operation Lindbergh."

"Lindbergh, sir?" Houser said.

"Doesn't every clandestine operation have a name? Or is that only in the movies?"

"No, we like to give them names. And I like this one, sir. It's a winner's name. Maybe I'm superstitious, but that makes me think our operation will be successful."

Alexander laughed. "You also like to win." It was the first time in a week he had been able to laugh.

"I think we all like that, sir," Walters said.

Alexander nodded. "The first principle of success—the desire to win. I just hope we're as committed to the second principle."

"And what's that, sir?" Walters asked.

"Willingness to pay the price."

Alexander Wainwright stopped in front of a large painting and smiled. The cowboy and his horse had not made any progress up that slippery slope since the last time he was here. Demoralizing, he thought, and a poor choice for this wall leading to the office of the secretary of state.

Alexander pretended not to notice the impatient coughing coming from the nervous undersecretary next to him. Finally, the undersecretary nudged Alexander's arm.

"*Please,* sir, the secretary of state is waiting."

So is Gustov Volkovoy. Two Sundays had already passed since Yuri Deyneko had described the ritual of the cross. Alexander had endured those Sundays only because of Loretta. They had spent many hours in their tiny glass room at the residence. She told him of the prayer meeting near the field of sunflowers and of Yuri's experience at Tirgu-Ocna prison. He told her of the Tulasi documents. They both cried. Sundays had become a day of tears.

"Your boy, Gustov, is counting on You, God," Alexander said to himself, as he looked at Bryant's painting. "If you want him out, You're going to have to give us a little push up that slope."

"*Mr. Ambassador.*"

Alexander turned to face the undersecretary. "Does this picture say anything to you?"

"I...I don't know. It's just a picture."

"Nothing?"

The undersecretary shook his head, his face reddening.

268

"Naturally."

"Sir, can we go now?"

Alexander nodded and followed the man down the hall and into the secretary of state's office.

It was déjà vu for Alexander. The white-haired secretary sat behind his desk. To the right sat Rodger McAllen. The same salutations were made, the same stiff handshakes. Then Alexander found himself sitting in the same chair in precisely the same position as last time.

"Thank you for seeing me on such short notice, Mr. Secretary."

The white head bobbed up and down. "That's what I'm here for, Alex."

"Well, thank you, sir. I appreciate it."

"So, what's the urgent matter you referred to?"

"A solution to our Tulasi problem has presented itself."

"I thought we made it clear that this was *your* Tulasi problem," McAllen said.

The secretary waved his hand in the air. "Rodger, let him talk."

"Thank you, Mr. Secretary," Alexander said. "This solution I spoke of…I think you'll like it. I believe it will show off State in a positive light, while at the same time accomplishing our objective of removing a potentially embarrassing situation from our embassy."

"Well, if this solution is all you say, I can't wait to hear it."

"My driver, Yuri Deyneko, is a colonel in the regular Romanian army. He's also the brother-in-law of Gustov Volkovoy."

"Volkovoy's a name I didn't expect to hear in conjunction with all this," the secretary said.

"It's a name I'm sick of hearing," McAllen said.

"But it's a name that's on the hearts of many Americans, and politically speaking, is a hot potato," Alexander said.

"Fine, but how does he figure in with your problem at the embassy?" the secretary asked.

"It's really quite simple. Yuri Deyneko will get the Tulasis out for us if we get Gustov Volkovoy out for him."

"Ridiculous!" McAllen said. "Even the most junior diplomat would be able to see that you're being set up. I can't believe you've fallen for this."

Alexander stared straight ahead, waiting for the secretary of state to comment.

"Alex, you must admit this does seem a bit preposterous. I mean, can you really trust this Colonel Deyneko? And how can you be so sure that he'll do what he says, that this isn't a trap?"

"Twenty years of experience."

The secretary sighed. "Yes, that is something. But if you're wrong…"

"I'm not wrong."

"But *if* you are, Alex, it's going to be your hide. You need to understand that."

"I understand."

"You're willing to risk it all?"

"That's right."

"Then you must be pretty certain."

"Positive."

The secretary leaned back in his chair, and a smile reappeared on his face. "I must confess to you, Alex, that I like the idea. Whoever ends up in the White House after the election is going to look very kindly on the agents of Volkovoy's liberation. Everyone who had a hand in it is going to look mighty good. And there'll be enough room for all those on stage to take a bow."

"I say it's too risky and we're going to get caught with our pants down," McAllen said.

"Never mind, Rodger. I appreciate your concern, but never mind. All right, Alex, let's get down to it. Let's get to the details."

An hour later, after Alexander Wainwright finished his meeting with the secretary of state, he passed his friend the cowboy. He knew it was his imagination, but for a split second, he thought the cowboy and horse had moved just a little further up that slope.

10

Yuri Deyneko stopped the limousine at a remote spot in the parking lot, the nose of his car pointed toward a short runway a few yards away. Baneasa Airport had many such runways. A small prop plane took off in front of him and he watched as it ascended.

"Were we followed?" Alexander Wainwright asked from the backseat.

"No. It seems Tulasi is still giving me great latitude under the assumption that I will be more effective. He is a desperate man."

"I understand the feeling."

"Sir?"

"If we're going to be in cahoots, you might as well stop calling me sir."

"What is cahoots?"

"It means we are partners. Call me Alex."

A curious look passed over Yuri Deyneko's face, a look of both surprise and pleasure. "Very well…Alex." The name stuck in his throat as he remembered his mother's scolding, and he turned away.

"My entire career is riding on this," Alexander said. "I just want you to know that. There can't be any mistakes."

"Is it not the lives of Gustov and the Tulasis that are 'riding on this'?"

"Look, I understand this means a lot to you, that you're personally involved. But you've got to realize that for me it's not personal. It's not even my job. It's…well, it stretches far above what I would normally do, or even think of doing. That's not to say I don't want to do it. Maybe my level of commitment seems a bit shallow to you, but believe me, it's there."

"Yes, I understand that. And under the circumstances, you are quite committed."

"What circumstances?"

"Your circumstances. It is not your fault you have had everything given to you—that your life has been one of ease."

"Ease! You think you Romanians have a monopoly on suffering?"

Yuri shook his head. "No. Forgive me. I have offended you. Romanians are serious people. We feel deeply. Sometimes I have difficulty in understanding that others do not have the same level of passion. But that is my problem, not yours. I have been told that sometimes my passion makes me negate the feelings of others. Please accept my apology."

"Forget it. Americans love to win, that's all."

"Then I am fortunate," Yuri said, "because I want to win this."

"Let's go on the assumption we will."

"But if we do not?"

"See, that's the difference. I don't allow myself any other assumption. I *expect* to win." There was more bravado in Alexander's voice than he actually felt, and he wondered if Yuri could detect this.

"I see now why God has put us together."

"Oh? I didn't realize it was God. I thought it was two people who rammed their car into our embassy gate one morning."

"I want to take the Tulasis out tonight," Yuri said suddenly.

"We're ready on our end."

"And the Tulasis? They are ready as well?"

"They will be."

"Their health? What is the state of their health?"

"The doctor seems fine, but the wife…I don't know."

"What is wrong?"

"Her wound is healing nicely; it's her mental condition I'm concerned about. She's…well, I can't say exactly. Neurotic? Unstable? I don't know, but she could give us trouble."

"Then sedate her. We cannot take the chance she will panic and become hysterical in the trunk."

"Fine, I'll see to it. What time?"

"Ten. There will be no moonlight tonight and darkness will provide a satisfactory covering. And make certain that only Americans are present."

"Naturally."

"Follow normal routine. Do not deviate."

"Don't worry, we're not exactly new at this. We won't do anything to tip our hand." Alexander sank back in the seat. He was finally beginning to feel a little relaxed. "I'm glad I'm not CIA. I'd hate doing this for a living."

Yuri smiled. "It is not my desire, either."

Alexander stared at the Romanian. He had rarely seen him smile. There was something friendly and pleasant in that smile. For the first time he did not see a foreigner or an enemy. He saw only a man. Perhaps under different circumstances they might have become friends.

"After they're out of the embassy, what then?" Alexander asked.

"I will take them to my contact at the *Industrialexport*. He is a secret Christian, and in charge of the exportation of railway rolling stock and heavy industrial equipment transported by ship. He will see that the Tulasis get to the port of Constanta. From there they go on a cargo carrier. Once in the Black Sea, they will be put on a small raft with a signaling device. You must have a submarine waiting. I will give you coordinates later."

"The Tulasis aren't young. This is a rigorous ordeal you propose."

"It is the only proposal I have."

"I suppose it's their best chance. Although if they knew what lay ahead perhaps they'd prefer to stay at the embassy. Of course, I can't offer that as an option."

"It is not an option."

"What do you mean?"

"Dr. Tulasi would never want to stay at the embassy, no matter how dangerous the escape."

"How can you be so sure?"

"Because he knows his son. He knows that sooner or later someone will assassinate him."

"I wondered about that. If push came to shove, would Tulasi really order a hit on his own parents?"

"Do not wonder. He has already done so."

"You sound pretty positive."

"I am. Tulasi has ordered me to do it, and he is not a patient man. He will tire of my failure rather quickly. Sooner or later, he will recruit another agent."

"I'm glad Loretta trusts you because all my instincts tell me not to. I'm going strictly on hers right now."

"I cannot fault you. If I were in your shoes, I would feel uneasy myself. But fortunately, your wife has good instincts. They will not fail you."

"That's what I'm counting on."

"Is this what you Americans call 'spreading your cards on the table'?"

"Ah...what do you mean?"

"You have revealed that you do not trust me. Have you considered that I may not trust you? I also have much to lose."

"No...actually..."

"It never entered your mind?"

"No. It seemed unimportant to the mission. I'm sorry, but that's the way it is."

"Yes, that is the way it is." Yuri looked at Alexander's hands tapping nervously on his knee. He smiled to himself as he remembered how fidgety Alexander was as a child, always moving about like one of those ants they would find in their mess kits. Even those times when they used to watch their mother for hours and Alexander seemed to be still, he was moving his eyes or fingers or mouth.

"But do you? Do you trust me, I mean?" Alexander asked.

"Does it matter?"

"I guess not. I was just curious."

Yuri watched as two men walked between the terminals. Friends? Brothers? His heart suddenly ached. "I share some of your doubts," he said slowly, "and some of your insecurity, but yes, I trust you."

"Strange how I never even thought about it."

Yuri pulled his eyes off the strangers and looked hard at Alexander. *Your love for me never matched mine for you. Even when you were small, Alexander, you thought only of yourself.*

277

"That may be one of the truest statements I have ever heard you make," Yuri said.

Alexander was surprised by the passion in Yuri's voice. He had just missed something. What was it?

"I guess we've spread our cards out enough," he said, feeling strangely unsettled. "How about telling me about this contact of yours?"

"He is a high-ranking official," Yuri said slowly, thinking of that last day they had together in the refugee camp. Remembering how he had saved half of his bread for Alexander, how he had scrambled on the floor looking for his mess kit. For years Yuri had stored his memories in a high tower protected from the siege-works of reality. Now reality had managed to batter an opening he could see through. *He had always loved Alexander more.* How else could he account for the fact that one brother remembered and the other sat like a stranger, oblivious? He wanted to weep. Instead he faced the front and watched a plane taxi down the runway. Lord, not now, he groaned as he began to understand the root of his resentment. Since that first meeting in the residency garden, Yuri had been storing resentment in his heart toward the ambassador. Now he understood why. *I forgive you, Alexander. I forgive you for not caring enough.*

"Yes, a high-ranking official. What else? Your contact, are you going to tell me about him?" There was undisguised impatience in Alexander's voice.

"He has the power to see that all necessary papers are signed and appropriate connections are made," Yuri said in a low uneven voice, desperately fighting for control. "He has done this before."

"I guess he's been successful."

Yuri nodded. "Yes, he has been very successful." God would get him through this. He must think only of Gustov now. What came later would be up to God.

"I guess that was a stupid question."

Yuri nodded again.

"Are all Romanians this candid?"

"Usually."

"All right, now that we have the Tulasis covered, what about Gustov?"

"Gustov is too weak. He will not survive this kind of ordeal."

"What's your plan then?"

Yuri pulled several folded papers from his shirt. "Here, this is the schedule at the hospital—times when guards make their rounds, how many are posted, the layout of the hospital, the location of Gustov's cell, the position of the security cameras. It is all here."

"You didn't answer my question. How do you propose to get Gustov out of the country?"

"I do not plan to get him out of the country. Not yet. When he is well, then we will try."

"We?"

"Cahoots, yes?"

Alexander laughed. "I'm not so sure, Yuri. I thought you were taking responsibility for that end."

"That is true, but my contact at the hospital has assured me this is impossible. Gustov hangs by a thread. After his rescue, he will be taken to a safe place to recuperate."

"What safe place?"

"Perhaps in a month or two, my contact at the Industrial-export can smuggle him out."

"What safe place?"

"He will need much care. If he gets it, and by God's grace, he will survive."

Alexander shifted uncomfortably in his seat. "Where is the CIA supposed to take him?"

"To the embassy."

Alexander suddenly envisioned a grinning Rod McAllen signing his transfer to some outpost on a sand dune. "No, not possible," he said shaking his head. "Forget it, Yuri. I'm just getting rid of two hot potatoes. I don't want another."

"We have no alternative."

"There you go with 'we' again."

"You said cahoots, partners. Did you not mean it?"

"Yes, but—"

"Either we are in this together or we are not. Which way is it?"

"Do you have any idea of the position you're putting me in? My orders are to get this matter expedited, not have it snowball." He remembered that cowboy and horse. *When the going gets tough don't expect help from us.* Was that what he wanted his creed to be? Did he want to be another Rod McAllen? "You have to understand that I've been ordered not to use force."

Yuri nodded thoughtfully. "Your government wishes to curry favor with the Soviets."

"Something like that."

"And it will go badly for you if something happens and Gustov dies."

"Yes, very badly."

"What will they do if things fall apart?"

"Crucify me."

Yuri flinched as though someone struck him. "Then wait until Monday and your problem will be solved."

"How's that?"

"Gustov will not live through another Sunday."

Alex looked away. "I'm sorry. That was a poor choice of words. I must sound like a real jerk to you."

"Jerk?"

"Fool, idiot, jerk, same thing."

Yuri nodded. "Yes, most times."

"Don't you know *any* diplomacy?"

Yuri shrugged. "I am a soldier, not a diplomat."

"Yes, you're the lance that cuts to the heart of a boil. I'm the ointment that covers and draws. Maybe that's what it's going to take, a soldier and a diplomat to do this job."

"I have been offensive again."

"I think I'm getting used to it."

"It is not intentional."

"I believe you."

"I think only of Gustov now."

"You two are very close."

"Yes. I do not want to lose him."

"He's fortunate to have a brother who cares so much."

Yuri gave Alexander a strange look. "Do you not have a brother?"

"No...well, yes, but actually no. It's too complicated to explain. Let's just say I did, but I don't anymore."

"It seems we both have had loss in our lives. I am sorry I was so hard on you, so offensive. It was not intentional."

"I know. But you're also right."

"About what?"

"Things have come pretty easy for me. I'm not good at losing."

"And if you should lose your post, your career, how will you manage?"

"Like everyone else who's faced with something tough. You just manage, that's all."

"It will not destroy you?"

Alexander chuckled. "Do I really seem that shallow? No, don't answer that!"

Yuri laughed. It was the first time Alexander had heard him laugh.

"So, the colonel has a sense of humor."

"A small one."

"Maybe when this is over, I can buy you a drink and then we can have a really good laugh."

Yuri smiled, and there was kindness in his eyes. "I would like that."

"Okay." Alexander took a deep breath. "We do the Tulasis tonight and Gustov Volkovoy tomorrow night, provided that Arni Houser gives me the green light. And...we bring Gustov back to the embassy."

Yuri's eyes teared. "It is a good thing you do. God will bless you."

Alexander looked away. That momentary feeling of euphoria in the Seventh Floor hall was crushed completely. And that horse looked more and more as if it were going to slide on top of him. "Have we covered it all?" he finally asked.

"Only one thing more."

"You don't have a sister somewhere that needs rescuing, do you?"

"What? I have no sister, no. Why?"

"Forget it, bad joke. What is it?"

"I need Loretta to come with me tomorrow night. She must dress as though she is out for the evening. Then, when everything is settled with the Tulasis, she must come to my dwelling for a short period."

Alexander shook his head. "Out of the question. I won't have Loretta involved in this."

"She is already involved."

"No!"

"She is already involved."

"How? How is she involved?"

"The Securitate thinks we are having an affair. I need her for cover. If someone should see me driving around, I will have a satisfactory explanation with Loretta present."

"How could you expect me to put my wife in such danger?"

"She will not be in danger."

"Can you *guarantee* that?"

"No, but I have great certainty that she will not be harmed."

"How can you make such a statement?"

"Because I have prayed much on this."

"And?"

"And I believe in my heart that God will protect her."

"Why?"

"Because I do."

"Not good enough!"

"Because...because a while past, God showed me that our lives would be interwoven, that He would use you for His purposes to help the church here in Romania. I did not understand then that Loretta would be the real instrument. That she would be the catalyst."

"You know, the Securitate wasn't the only one who thought you and Loretta were having an affair." Alexander watched the wind outside blow up a cloud of dust. "I thought so too."

"I know," Yuri said, with a new tenderness in his voice. "But you do not think so now?"

"No."

"That is good. I do not know if we are very alike or not. But this much I know: When it comes to women, we love only our wives."

At first Anna did not see Mirela's bony little frame standing by the counter. She had gone upstairs for something and not heard the jingling of the brass bell over the door. Teofil looked up when he heard Anna enter.

"She will speak only to you," the old shoemaker said, his eyes directing Anna to the wisp of a figure standing like a pale shadow against the counter.

Anna walked around the counter and gave the young girl a hug. "Is everything all right?"

Mirela nodded then looked shyly at Teofil. "I want to speak to you in private. Is there a place we can go?"

Anna smiled down on Mirela, then led her upstairs to her bedroom and closed the door. "Now, what is all this secrecy?"

Mirela reached inside her blouse and pulled out two envelopes and handed them to Anna.

"What's this?" Anna did not recognize the handwriting, and neither envelope had a postmark. Both were addressed to Simona—no last name, just Simona—and under the name was the address of a rundown hotel many prostitutes called home.

"They're letters," Mirela said in a hushed tone as though speaking about something sacred. "An old woman dropped them off. No one knows who she is. We've never seen her before. She hand delivered these letters without saying a word, then disappeared. They're letters from…from Eva."

Anna directed Mirela to sit down in the corner chair, while

she sat on the edge of her cot. Her hands trembled as she opened the one on top and began to read.

My dearest friend,

I am sending this letter to you through a mutual friend, and trust God that it will reach you.

I have been arrested for speaking about our wonderful Savior. Mostly it was to other prostitutes, but when I began to speak on the streets in daylight, some police took notice of me. I have been sent to a labor camp in Arges. You cannot imagine how many believers are here with me. They are all so beautiful and full of the love of Jesus. The camp guards work us very hard and there is never enough food, so we are hungry and tired at night, but as soon as some of us get together and sing psalms and quote Scriptures we begin to feel new strength and forget our hunger and the pain in our bodies.

Oh, dear friend, how happy I am! I never imagined that serving our Lord, that suffering for Him, could bring so much peace, so much joy! My heart grows sad when I see the hardness of the guards and know they are without hope. I know their hardness covers their own emptiness. God has given me a great love for these guards, a love I cannot explain. But why am I telling you, you who are so full of God's love? I pray for these guards day and night and also for some of the other inmates who do not know Jesus as we do. But I know I also need prayer. Please do not forget me! Please remember to pray for me. I will need great strength in the days ahead, for I do not want to fail my Lord. There is so much to be done here.

Yours in Christ,
Eva

Anna carefully folded the letter and slipped it into its envelope, then looked over at Mirela. The young girl was sitting perfectly straight in her chair, not moving a muscle.

"You have read this?"

Mirela nodded.

"And Simona and the others, they too have read this?"

Again Mirela nodded.

"What did they say?"

Mirela's eyes misted. "After you read the next one, then we'll talk."

With an unsteady hand, Anna pulled the second letter from its envelope.

Dear friend,

I have been sent to prison for not obeying my guards when they instructed me to stop speaking to them about my Jesus. But how could I obey such a cruel order? How could I not share the love of Jesus with them? If I failed to share what I know, how could I face my sweet Savior? To whom much is given, much is required. So I continued speaking about my Lord until finally they had enough of me and now here I am in Tirgu-Ocna.

Conditions are very hard here. There is much cruelty and always there is hunger. But there is joy and beauty too, for here, as in Arges, there are many Christians and we spend every free moment in fellowship and prayer. We continually pray for our guards and the other prisoners who do not know Christ. The other day a woman who had been convicted of killing her husband with a butcher knife came to the Lord. She cried like a baby and we wept with her, holding her and kissing her like a mother. But we are all mothers here. We have, all of us Christians here, conceived new believers for Christ, and have spiritual children we must nurture and protect. I praise God that I have had the privilege to be part of this. It is worth any price to see one of these hurting souls find hope and new life.

I do not know how much more time my Lord will give me to do this work. God's ways are higher than our ways. The time He has added to my life was for a purpose. And now I believe that purpose may be drawing to an end. My dear friend, I must tell you this, but I do not want you to worry. My cough has returned, and I have begun to spit up blood. I do not think I will be sending you any more letters. But do not be sad. Remember we will all be together again in heaven. But for now, please pray and ask God to help me be faithful to the end and not shame Him in any way. It is my only desire. I continue to pray for you daily and ask God to bless you.

Your Eva

For a long time, Anna held the letters in her lap and looked at Mirela, saying nothing.

"Simona wanted to wait and give them to you when you next brought your bread," Mirela said. "But I couldn't wait. I wanted you to read them. We all read them. All of the girls." Mirela looked down at her feet. "I hope you don't mind."

Anna shook her head, then stared at the letters. Perhaps Eva was dead even now. *To live is Christ, to die is gain.* Anna was surprised she did not cry, that she did not want to cry, that she actually felt joy though it was a bittersweet joy. When a kernel of wheat fell it produced new life.

"What did you think?" Anna finally asked.

Mirela continued to sit rigid in her chair, but her eyes were now fixed on Anna, and they were filled with tears. "I think I want to know this Jesus," she said quietly, not moving a muscle, hardly breathing, watching Anna's face, terrified that she would hear her say she couldn't know Him, that she was beyond hope or help, that she could never be forgiven, that no heavenly Father could ever, ever love her.

Anna rose slowly from the cot, walked over to Mirela, and gathered her into her arms. "Jesus has been waiting such a long time for you," she finally said, hugging and kissing her at the same time. "He has waited such a long time."

Alexander Wainwright watched Donald Walters drum his fingers nervously on the tabletop. Next to him sat Arni Houser, thoughtfully staring through the glass wall at a point only he knew.

"So there you have it," Alexander said, wrapping up his account of the morning with Yuri Deyneko. "Another houseguest."

Walters shook his head. "Very bad news, sir."

"How about telling me something I *don't* know."

"Well, our agents are in place," Houser said, smiling and finally directing his gaze to the others. "Got verification while you were out enjoying yourself, sir. They can go on a moment's notice."

"This is bad business, sir," Walters said. "I strongly advise against it."

"I understand. You can go on record and put it in writing. I won't blame you if you do. Arni, care to cover your posterior?"

"Sorry, sir, but my gut feeling tells me we should stay away.

I'll put that in my report, but I'll do my best for you, sir. You can count on that."

Alexander folded his arms across his chest. "All right, now that that's settled, can we proceed?"

Houser leaned over the table as though ready for action. "Yes, sir. Like I said, our boys are in place and waiting for my word."

Alexander handed him several sheets of folded paper. "Make sure they get these. Schedules, layouts, the whole bit. It's all there. With this information, it should be a piece of cake."

Houser spread the papers in front of him. "They probably have most of this already. They always do their homework, sir."

"I wouldn't want them on our team if I thought otherwise."

"No, sir. And Mr. Ambassador…"

"Yes, Arni?"

"No operation is ever considered cake, sir. There's always that unexpected element that can spring up suddenly and bite you."

"I'm just trying to be optimistic."

"Yes, sir, but maybe it'd be best to be realistic."

"For instance, how is Colonel Deyneko planning to get Volkovoy to the embassy?" Walters asked.

"The same way he gets the Tulasis out."

"That's what I like—simplicity," Houser said with a smile. "It's a good thing we have those additional oxygen units."

"Providence may be taking more of a hand in this than I had realized," Alexander said.

"Perhaps, sir," Walters said. "But if it's all the same, I'd like to leave as little to Providence as possible. Should I bring the Tulasis in now?"

Alexander nodded, and Walters left the room.

"He'll pull out of it, sir," Houser said, gesturing to the door that closed behind Walters. "He's a good man, and he'll come around."

"You know, Arni, I'm feeling awfully alone right now. I'm way out on a limb, and there's no one out here with me."

"I know, sir. Sorry about that. But I'll do my best for you anyway, and so will Don."

"I'm not worried about that."

"I know, sir. It's rough. But I have to compliment you."

"On what?"

"On being man enough to go out so far. Not many in your position would do it."

"But you think I'm foolish?"

Houser smiled as Don returned with the Tulasis. "I'd rather not comment on that, sir. One on a limb is enough."

Alexander grunted, then watched an undersecretary carry in a chair, then return with another. There was a shuffling of chairs as Walters positioned the new arrivals so that all five now sat around the table. Walters looked at Alexander and smiled, and Alexander responded with a smile of his own. "Welcome aboard, Don."

"Thank you, sir," Walters said, then rolled his eyes in a way that only Arni Houser could see it.

Josef Tulasi settled in his chair and looked around, taking in every detail. "Very interesting room. Very interesting. Is it *safe* to speak?" Alexander's nod sent the doctor into ecstasy. "Americans are so ingenious! Haven't I always said that, Marian? Haven't I?"

His wife, who sat next to him, seemed distant. Her arm was still cradled in a sling, and periodically she would stroke it with her free hand, as though it were an infant. Every time she did, her husband would lean closer and give her a little comforting pat.

"How is your shoulder, Mrs. Tulasi?" Alexander asked.

She gave a weak smile and began stroking her injured limb. "I do well," she said, in a voice and demeanor that said the opposite.

"We're taking you out tonight," Alexander said in a voice hard as a bullet. "I hope you're up to it."

"See, what did I tell you?" Josef said, nudging his wife. "The American ambassador will get us out. Did I not say this?" His wife nodded weakly and continued to stroke her arm. "Did I not tell you that Ambassador Wainwright is a man of his word? Yes, a man of his word." The doctor beamed proudly, as though all the credit for their pending liberation belonged to him.

"You have a tough trip ahead," Alexander said. "But if all goes well, you'll be in the U.S. next week."

"Next week! Do you hear that, Marian? Next week in America! Land of the free! Home of the brave!"

Alexander tried to reign in his disgust by compressing his lips. It only made him appear more disgusted.

"And, Marian, you do not need to worry," the doctor said. "I am sure even America can use an extra doctor. Is that not right, Ambassador?"

"I'm sure it is. And when this is all over, you'll have plenty of time to discuss your future plans."

"Marian is a worrier. I wish to reassure her." He turned to his wife and began patting her hand. "You will be well provided for. American doctors make excellent money. I have even heard it said that most are rich." He paused and looked at the faces around him. "Women can be rather delicate." He focused once again on his wife. "They say the streets in America are paved with gold. Of course, we know this is not true. It is only a way of saying that things are good in America. You will see. We will live well. It will be good for us there. You will see."

Alexander shifted uncomfortably in his chair and looked at his staff. Houser blew air between his lips and Walters just rolled his eyes.

"You both should rest as much as possible," Alexander finally said. "It's going to be a long night."

"How will you accomplish our escape?" the doctor asked.

"One step at a time."

"Oh, yes, yes, you are correct. Perhaps it is best that we do not know the details."

"Yes, it's best. The only thing you need to know is that later we'll be giving Mrs. Tulasi a little pain medication for her shoulder."

"Pain medication? Is that necessary?"

"The trip might be a bit uncomfortable for her."

"But that will make her…drowsy. She will not have her wits."

"Comfort is more important in this case than wits."

"Ah, yes, of course. It is best. Yes, medication would be in order. Women can be rather delicate."

Mrs. Tulasi sat quietly looking up at the ceiling.

"Don Walters will see that you get your wife's medication. I leave it to you to administer it," Alexander said, giving his first secretary a sign to remove the couple.

Walters rose from his chair and ushered them out.

"He's a tough old bird," Arni Houser said when they were alone. "And so is lady bird, no matter how delicate he might want to paint her. They're both survivors. My instincts tell me they'll come out of this all right."

"Yes, they're both tough birds," Alexander said. "Now, if Gustov Volkovoy were only as tough."

"I'm afraid, sir, that he's a different species altogether."

"And what do your instincts say about him?"

"You don't want to know, sir."

"Have you ever been wrong?"

"No, sir. Never. But there's always a first time. I've been following the Volkovoy story in the press, and I'd sure like to be wrong on this one."

Colonel Yuri Deyneko pulled the limo onto the grass and backed the car up to the steps as far as it could go. Within seconds the trunk was opened and two people, wearing small oxygen masks, were ushered out the back door of the embassy. They were then half lifted, half pushed into the well of the trunk, their oxygen tubes connected to a tank and the trunk lid closed. Then the limo pulled away.

No one stopped him as he neared the checkpoint at the end of Str. Dionisie Lupu, but Yuri slowed the car and gave the guards a casual salute allowing them to peek in the window. One of the guards was distracted by a slight sparkle in the back seat, and gave Yuri a sly smile when he saw the jewel-bedecked ambassadress.

Yuri went through the side streets of Bucharest, taking all the shortcuts he knew. Before long, he pulled down Str. Gabriel Peri 2, where the Industrialexport conducted business. The street was deserted. Not one other car could be seen anywhere. He popped the trunk when he heard three long toots on a bosun's whistle. Then he saw four men, dressed completely in black, appear out of nowhere. In a blink of an eye the four men and the Tulasis disappeared into the shadows. The entire operation had taken less than thirty minutes.

Another fifteen minutes of driving and Yuri was in front of his apartment complex. He parked the car and smiled as he opened the door for Loretta Wainwright.

"Thank you for looking so lovely tonight," he said, as he helped her out of the car.

"You're welcome," she said, offering him a trembling hand. Her blond hair was pulled straight back and tied into a bun, and large emerald and diamond earrings sparkled on her lobes. A black silk spaghetti-strap dress wrapped her trim figure, and a choker of emeralds and diamonds that matched her earrings glittered around her throat.

Yuri led her up the steps of the complex and down the hall toward his room.

"A thousand pardons, Yuri Deyneko," said a voice suddenly behind him. "It's late, and when I heard footsteps, I thought an intruder was among us. But I see it's only you. A thousand pardons. I'm not a man who pries."

"Good evening, comrade," Yuri said, forcing a smile.

"Oh, my manners. What has become of them? Good evening to you too. And to your friend. I see she's visiting again. But I must say, Yuri, for a man who prizes tranquillity so highly, you're keeping very long hours."

"Good night to you," Yuri returned abruptly, as he unlocked his door and pushed Loretta into the opening.

"Oh, where are my manners? I just said I wasn't a man who pried, yet I seek explanation to something that doesn't concern me. A thousand pardons. Do enjoy your evening with your friend. She's very lovely, Yuri Deyneko. And I think you're not such a dull fellow after all. Good night."

Loretta could see by the look on Yuri's face that he was upset. "Please don't tell me what he said. I don't want to know," she whispered.

"You do not need to whisper here. There are no bugs."

Loretta laughed. "I'm so conditioned not to talk anymore, except in the glass room. I'm beginning to believe that the whole of Romania is wired from end to end. It's really an awful feeling."

"You are not used to it."

"Are you?"

"When you have lived with such a thing for so long, you adjust. But I think that is somewhat different from saying I am used to it."

"That man in the hall is the same one I saw last time. A friendly neighbor?"

Yuri shook his head. "No. Secret police."

"I was afraid of that. What was he doing?"

"Just checking up. We have secret police that check on ordinary citizens and secret police that check on other secret police. It is Romania's own 'check and balance' system."

"Do you think he suspects something?"

"No." Yuri gestured for Loretta to take a chair. Then he went to the sink and filled the kettle. "I will make us some tea."

Loretta placed her hands on top of the oilclothed table and looked at her wedding ring. "He saw my ring. The man in the hall. Why don't you think he suspects something?"

Yuri smiled kindly. "Because of how shy and embarrassed you looked."

"That's because I was…or am. Well, you know what I mean."

"Yes. It is your true feeling. That is why you are believable.

And he sees this. And he thinks here is the guilty ambassador's wife, embarrassed to be seen going into her lover's apartment. It is perfect really."

Loretta sighed. "I hate it."

"I know," Yuri said, placing a cup in front of her. "But you were wonderful tonight. You are very brave, Loretta Wainwright."

"I was petrified."

"Being brave does not mean that you lack a sense of danger. No, you were perfect. And tomorrow night you will be so again."

Twenty-four hours later the official limousine for the U.S. ambassador to Romania pulled onto a dirt road exactly 3.25 miles past Sitiu. Another .75 miles and it left the road and pulled into a clearing. Yuri Deyneko flashed his lights, off and on three times, then waited. A black Dacia responded with three flashes of its own, then pulled slowly alongside the limo. All four doors of the Dacia flew open at once, a man jumping from each of them. Two of the men pulled out a body and carried it to the rear of the limo. The other two held guns and squinted into the darkness. Yuri stood by the open trunk with an oxygen mask in one hand and a light blanket in the other.

Quickly and quietly the CIA agents lowered the bony frame into the trunk well. Yuri placed the mask over Gustov Volkovoy's face, adjusted the oxygen flow from the tank, then tenderly covered him with the blanket. Yuri could see two large bruises covering both sides of Gustov's neck. A large gash dented one brow, and every hair on the frail man's head was completely white. Volkovoy was almost ten years younger than

Yuri, but he looked at least twenty years older.

"What have they done to you?" Yuri whispered as he bent over and kissed the thin, pale face.

Gustov's lids blinked open to reveal glazed, dull eyes.

"Rest easy, Gustov. God has delivered you," Yuri said, then closed the trunk.

"Is he alive?" Loretta Wainwright asked from the backseat when Yuri returned.

"Barely."

All the way to the embassy, Yuri drove faster than he should. But God was with him and he encountered no one on the road. And the ride that should have taken forty-five minutes took only thirty.

He slowed the car as he turned onto Str. Dionisie Lupu and stopped at the blockade. It was almost one in the morning.

"You are up late, Colonel," the guard said in Romanian.

Yuri nodded and rolled his eyes in a suggestive way, and felt sick as he did it. "I have been entertaining the ambassadress. She is a most bored and lonely woman. I am afraid all my training as a soldier is minor compared to the rigors she has put me through."

The guard peered through the window and saw Loretta Wainwright in a revealing green silk dress. Her hair hung in loose waves around her, and the only jewelry she wore was a single cameo brooch on a long gold chain. She looked more sensual and reckless than she had the night before.

"I should be so fortunate," the guard said to Yuri. "But why have you come here? Her *husband* is here."

"It is a curiosity, but I think the more unfaithful this woman is, the more devoted she becomes to her husband."

"Yes, I've heard this about other women. But won't the

husband suspect something is wrong, you coming at this hour?"

Yuri leaned out the window as if he were about to share some great confidence. "This situation at the embassy has worked to my advantage. The ambassador is preoccupied. She'll give him some excuse and he'll believe her." Yuri waved one hand in front of his eyes. "Blind. The man is blind."

The guard nodded knowingly. "Yes, and the wife is guilty. So go, let her appease her conscience. And with any luck, you'll be back here tomorrow night."

Yuri shook his head. "No, no. I don't have the strength. With any luck, tomorrow night I'll be resting in my bed, *alone*."

The guard laughed as he waved him through. "I should have such problems. At night, I have neither a woman nor rest."

Yuri Deyneko's hands shook as he backed the limo up to the embassy steps. The car had barely rolled to a stop when he popped the trunk and jumped out.

"Please, God, let Gustov still be alive."

The back door of the embassy was already open and Ambassador Wainwright stood at the top step. Several Marine guards had swarmed around the car and two of them picked up the bundle of rags and bones. Yuri stopped them as they were ready to carry Gustov Volkovoy inside.

"Is he still alive?" he asked, looking down on the gaunt face, which he touched lightly with his big hand.

A young Marine answered, "Yes, I saw the air bag move."

"We don't have a doctor, but we have a trained medic to look at him," Alexander said from the top of the stairs. He moved aside as the Marines carried Gustov and the oxygen equipment through the door.

But Yuri had not heard the ambassador. He had fallen to his knees and began to weep into his hands and pray.

Loretta quietly slipped from the backseat of the car and went to her husband. She took one of his hands and pressed it to her lips. There were tears in her eyes, tears of triumph, pride, and love.

"There's no turning back now," Alexander said softly as he put his arm around her.

"No, there's no turning back."

11

A BEAMING DONALD WALTERS STOOD in the ambassador's door-way. "The doctor was able to get a little broth down 'Tulasi,' sir. And he's actually starting to say a few words."

This new "Tulasi" created interest of a sort the old one never had. There wasn't an American in the embassy who hadn't been reading Charles Riley's account of the Volkovoy story. Major American newspapers came daily, by courier, along with mail from the home office. Riley was a most persuasive writer and had captivated millions of readers. Every day he recounted one man's heroic struggle for personal and religious freedom in the face of a tyrant viciously opposed to such freedoms. Gustov Volkovoy became the national symbol of Romania's persecuted. It was no wonder that every American at the embassy was pulling for him.

Alexander Wainwright had requested that an American physician be sent to the embassy to care for Gustov. The request was granted, but it came with a caustic note of disap-proval from Rodger McAllen and an order to come to D.C. as soon as possible. A second caustic note followed when Alexander did not come as quickly as expected, and the note contained a postscript: "Lindberghs arrive safely."

The safe arrival of Dr. Tulasi and his wife had not appeased any of State's wrath toward Alexander for his involvement with Gustov Volkovoy. Even so, Alexander remained in Bucharest. He, like the other embassy personnel, was pulling for Gustov, and he wanted to stay until the pastor's condition could be determined. For the past four days, he had not left the embassy. He had managed to share a few cryptic words with Loretta over the phone before the lines were once again disconnected.

The first thing the doctor did after checking the semiconscious Volkovoy was to hook him up to an IV of glucose and water. Then he pronounced Volkovoy's condition as "grave."

Now, seeing the smiling face of Donald Walters telling him that Gustov was able to consume some broth, Alexander felt profound relief. Perhaps the pastor's condition was not so grave after all.

"I'd like to see him," Alexander said.

"The doctor won't like it. He's worse than a mother hen. Shoos everyone away who tries to come in."

Alexander rose from his chair. "We'll see about that."

His long strides brought him to Gustov's door in seconds. He knocked twice and entered. On a cot against the far wall lay a man propped on pillows that appeared oversized compared to the head and shoulders that rested there. A small, birdlike breast moved up and down in irregular breathing. Gustov looked shriveled, like an old man or a cloth doll kept in the dryer too long. Alexander looked at the ruined body and saw little difference since the first night Gustov was brought to the embassy. Only now he was washed and bandaged, and clean pajamas had replaced the rags.

It wasn't until Alexander stood near Gustov that he noticed

a change. The agitated doctor signaled with his hands that he was not welcome, but Alexander ignored him as he gazed at the feeble Romanian. It was in the eyes where the difference lay. They were no longer glazed and unable to focus, but were now large, open, alert. If a man's eyes were truly the windows of his soul, then Gustov Volkovoy's soul was made of pure love. Warm light emanated from them and ignited the atmosphere with fire that seemed to both heat and purify. Alexander had never encountered anything like it.

Gustov smiled and nodded when Alexander put a finger to his lips. "Walls have ears," he said in heavily accented English. Then he placed the half-finished cup of broth on the floor and struggled to rise.

"Don't. Just stay as you are. I'm sorry I interrupted your meal."

"Ambassador, *please*. He's weak and has to rest," the doctor said.

"Ambassador? *Slava domnului*, bless the Lord!" The smile on Gustov's face deepened. "Let me think a little. I have had a difficult time piecing everything together. But I believe I understand. God has wrought a miracle."

"That's what a relative of yours thinks too, but we won't name him."

Gustov's hazel eyes twinkled, belying the white hair and wasted body. "He...he had a part in this?"

Alexander nodded.

"He is well?"

"He's certainly in better shape than you are."

Gustov laughed. It was an almost boyish sound, light and giggly, like bubbles out of a bottle. "You must not judge by appearances, Mr. Ambassador."

"You had us worried for a while," Alexander said with a smile.

"No need to worry. You think you look upon a broken man, a man who has nothing, who has had everything taken from him, but you are wrong. I am rich. Very rich. All of heaven waits to greet me, to open wide its arms."

"From what I understand, it doesn't have a more faithful son."

Gustov shook his head. "No, I am nothing. Dust. Jesus is all. It is because of His love for me that I know that where I have received blows, heaven will tenderly embrace me; where I have been spat upon, heaven will bestow kisses."

"Then you *are* a fortunate man. I don't know anyone with such assurance, such faith."

"Do you not?" Gustov gave Alexander a strange look, then with his chest heaving, he pulled himself to a sitting position. "Then I am sorry."

"What?"

Gustov raised a bony hand in dismissal of the query. "I must confess that when I first opened my eyes, I was disappointed. I thought for certain that I would never wake up in this earthly realm again. I was so sure that Jesus had called my name. But here I am. I have been praying and asking the Lord why. There is some purpose I do not yet understand. But soon I will know, because there is little time left."

"You'll pull out of this. You'll be all right in no time. You'll see. The doctor will help build up your strength."

Gustov looked kindly at Alexander. "You must not concern yourself. God has ordained my season. It will be as long or as short as He commands."

The doctor stepped closer to Alexander and pulled his arm.

"This man needs rest. I'm not God, but if you want me to help him, then you've got to cooperate and let me do my job."

"We'll talk another time," Alexander said, looking down on the frail body and wondering if there would be another time.

"Yes, I would like that," Gustov said, closing his eyes.

"Is there anything I can get you?"

"Actually, yes, there is something."

"What is it?"

"A Bible. I would like to have a Bible, in Romanian, if such a thing is possible."

"Is that all?"

Gustov opened his eyes. "It is such a great thing; I feel shame asking." He picked his head up for a moment then let it fall back onto the pillows. The pillows and sheets all seemed to swallow up his pale bony frame like a shroud and made him look like someone who had already died.

"That's enough for now," the doctor said, taking Alexander by the arm and leading him to the exit.

Alexander glanced back at the bed as he opened the door. "He doesn't look good. How is he really?"

The doctor frowned.

"Should I bother getting him that Bible?"

"You mean, will he have time to read it? I don't know."

"Well, what *do* you know, doctor?"

"Like I said, I'm not God. I can't work miracles. And I know that's what it's going to take, a miracle."

"Kindly tell me why it took three telegrams to get you here!" Rod McAllen said as he half sat, half hung out of his chair. One arm swung rhythmically over the side; his other arm rested on his heaving chest. The lip of a nearby ashtray cradled the butt of a cigarette. In the center of the ashtray the charred remains of a pack and a half of Camels formed a small pyramid. It had taken McAllen only five hours to build it. His face was flushed with anger.

Alexander Wainwright watched McAllen light another cigarette with the stub of his last one. No wonder he had such a raspy voice. He watched McAllen inhale, exhale, inhale, exhale. A cloud of smoke gathered over the bald head like a cloud over the crater of a volcano. Finally, McAllen returned his cigarette to the ashtray.

"He won't see you, you know."

"Why not?"

Air escaped from McAllen's lips in a sound of disgust. "You've got to be kidding. Do you have any idea how *ticked* he is? You promised him an underdog and didn't deliver."

"He has the Tulasis. Isn't that enough?"

"The newspapers haven't been writing about the Tulasis. It's Volkovoy the public wants. Nobody's ever heard of Tulasi, and quite frankly, if they knew who he really was, they'd wonder why you bothered. You can't promise filet mignon then dish out hamburger and expect anyone to be happy."

"Rodger, are we talking about meat here or people?"

"You're not impressing me, Alex, so save it. You know in this business perception is everything."

"You act as if the mission is a complete failure. I think you're losing sight of the fact that we had a successful escape."

"It is a failure. Getting close only counts in horseshoes. You've scored no points here."

"The secretary feels the same way?"

"No, Alex, he feels worse. Mad as a hornet, actually. You

made him look bad. The press thinks we have Volkovoy and that he's eating a Big Mac somewhere in the good ol' U.S. of A."

"You leaked the story?"

McAllen shrugged and looked defiantly at his subordinate.

"He's extremely sick, Rodger. He's been through a lot, and it's going to take time to put the pieces back together. You don't go through what he's been through without it taking a toll. That was very premature of the secretary. I mean, doesn't anyone *think* around here?"

"Alex, you're on thin ice. I'd be careful about what you say, if I were you. You can't afford to alienate anyone right now, any more than you already have. Okay? Eat a little humble pie and hope that's all you have to eat."

Alexander watched McAllen take another drag on his cigarette. He looked like a neurotic mess, lighting one Camel after the other. The charred pyramid was its own testimony. Then he thought of the Alka-Seltzer cocktails, of his mountain of empty foil packets. Maybe he and McAllen were more alike than he cared to admit. They both had spent the last twenty years polishing their own nameplate, always with an eye for a larger one, not minding the heads that fell along the way; not caring about the million Volkovoys who suffered and died.

So why was this suddenly so nauseating? A year ago, wouldn't he himself have considered his present mission a failure? Wouldn't his only reason for getting Volkovoy out have been to rack up points? When had all that changed? When had he taken one path and McAllen another? He thought of Loretta and Yuri Deyneko and their part in all this. He thought of the thin frail man with the blazing eyes. Maybe, like Dr. Tulasi, he needed absolution for all the posts he had had and never cared one lick about. Maybe that's why he would go the distance this time, why he *needed* to help the broken Gustov Volkovoy.

"Look, Alex," McAllen said. "I know what people say about me behind my back. I know I'm tough, but I don't want to do you harm, in spite of what you might think. Work with me. Let's see what we can salvage."

Alexander watched McAllen play with his cigarette, first flicking the ashes then rolling the burning tip around the ashtray. Always the politician. Always the lapdog. McAllen didn't give a hoot about helping him. McAllen was damage control, looking for a way to salvage something out of this mess. If McAllen could scrape the egg off the secretary of state's face, there was no telling what size of bone he'd get.

"Well? You want my help or not?" McAllen took a long drag on his cigarette and expelled the smoke directly into Alexander's face.

Alexander swallowed a cough and winced as his eyes burned. "If you can," he finally said.

"Fine. Then let's put our heads together and see what we can come up with. First of all, how soon can Volkovoy travel?"

"I don't know. Like I said, he's in bad shape."

"Well, what does the doctor say?"

"He said he's not God. He can't perform miracles."

"For crying out loud, what's that supposed to mean?"

"It means that after a man has been brutalized, starved, tortured, and drugged, he can't be pasted together like some torn paper doll. It means it'll be a miracle if Volkovoy lives."

McAllen cursed as he smashed his cigarette into the ashtray. "You didn't say anything about this in your reports. You just said he needed to recuperate. You didn't say one word about Volkovoy dying!"

"I didn't know it myself."

"You can't let him die in the embassy," McAllen finally said. "You must avoid that at all costs. The press will kill us."

"And how do you propose I stop him?"

"The Tulasi scenario, remember?"

"You can't be serious."

"No?"

"This is low, even for you, Rodger. The man's a national symbol, for heaven's sake!"

"No hearts and flowers, Alex. I'm talking to you man to man. I'm talking reality. If he's going to die, what difference does it make?"

"No difference at all if you don't have a conscience."

McAllen retrieved his smashed cigarette from the ashtray. He spent a moment straightening it out, then relit it and began to blow smoke rings into the air. "We need to make this work for us. If we play it right we can still come out looking like heroes and the secretary will have his underdog. Everyone wins. The press, because they'll get a good story; the Securitate, because they'll have saved face; the secretary of state, because he gets taken off the hot seat; and you because you don't get your hide pasted to an envelope and airmailed to Togo. Relations may even improve between Ceausescu and our government. He may suddenly become more accommodating on other issues. You get the picture. Everyone's happy. Everyone wins something. But if Volkovoy just fades away under *our* watch…well, where's the benefit? I mean, you said he was beyond help. That he didn't have a chance. A miracle, that's what you said he needed."

"I won't do it."

"No one's asking you to do anything. I'm *ordering* you to send Gustov Volkovoy back to the States for much-needed medical treatment. What happens en route, happens."

"I won't do it."

"You can't disobey an order."

"I'm not disobeying. I'm using my own discretion and the counsel of a licensed physician. I'm telling you Volkovoy can't be moved. I'll put that in my report and I'll see that every branch of the United States government, including the IRS, gets a copy. And for good measure, I'll send a copy to every major newspaper. Gustov Volkovoy will be moved only if and when he is certified able by a physician."

The bald volcano began to redden, going from a light pink to deep rose, all within seconds. "You're in trouble, *Mr. Ambassador,* and you don't even have enough sense to realize it. Heard the expression, 'dead meat'? Well, you're it! You'll be lucky to even get Togo after this. And God help you if this pastor dies in the embassy!"

"Well, there's two of us now that must depend upon God's help—Gustov Volkovoy and me. It looks like I'm finally in good company."

Yuri Deyneko walked alongside his wife. The sun streamed between the rows of fruit trees and settled like spotlights on them. Red highlights blazed in Anna's hair, and Yuri could not resist touching it. "You're so beautiful," he said. She smiled a warm, caressing smile, and that fire seemed to leap into Yuri's breast and consume him. "I have such love for you!"

She stopped and they embraced. "And I for you," she said.

They continued walking among the trees just as they used to do when they were children, exploring and stooping, here and there, to pick up something from the ground. They had the entire afternoon and evening to spend together. The couple at the farmhouse was serving as host. It had been so long since they had had this much time together that both were a little afraid of it, worried that such a gift might come at a great price. Had God made a way for them to have this time because He knew it would be their last? These were the thoughts that burdened them, that filtered from the brain to the eyes in anxious, worried looks that studied the other as though taking a picture.

"My heart is still praising God for Gustov's deliverance," Anna said, taking her husband's hand in hers. "Sometimes I wake up at night with such joy and I cannot go back to sleep."

"You haven't listened to my caution, Anna. You must understand how sick Gustov is."

Anna tilted her head upward toward the trees and laughed. Rich, full, throaty sounds came from her delicate throat and seemed almost not to fit. "You're such a worrier, my husband. You think I delude myself and don't understand that Gustov is near death. I know better than anyone! For hours my heart has cried to God for his life. But I have peace. I don't know what God's pleasure is in this, but I do know He'll use it for good. And…I'm grateful that if Gustov is soon to be with the Lord, his last days will be spent in peace and comfort. It's enough to know that no one will hurt him anymore."

"You're an astonishment, my Anna. I fear at times I underestimate you."

Anna laughed again and began running through the trees. She felt so gay, so carefree. Today she was not going to think about little Mirela, who was growing so beautifully in the Lord and who had become her apprentice seamstress. She was not going to think about Simona and Floare and the other ladies, who still went empty in soul and body. And she was not going to think about Gheorghe Vladimescu, who still floated ominously around her and Teofil and the rest of the believers with his poison tendrils. Teofil had said that jellyfish were at the mercy of the currents, and currents were at the mercy of God. Then let God think about them. Today…today was hers and Yuri's, and she would drink it in to the last drop.

She stopped by an old plum tree and sat against the trunk. Yuri followed and sat beside her. The scent of grass and dirt and plum trees swirled in the air and produced a potpourri of nostalgia.

"For a second I almost believed we were back on the farm."

Yuri smiled at her, pulled his car keys from his pocket, and began to use one of the keys to dig into the tree bark.

"What're you doing?"

"You'll see." He blocked his work with his body so she couldn't watch. Finally, when he finished, he moved aside. There, etched in the bark, was A V & Y D.

"Just like the first time you wrote them," Anna said, clasping her hands together in joy. "Oh, how angry your mother was with you for scarring her favorite tree! I can still see that look on her face. She was so stern. But, secretly I think it pleased her. I know that was the day I fell in love with you. I was only seven years old, but I knew right then and there that you, Yuri Deyneko, would be my husband; that I would have no other."

Yuri laughed. "And I loved you even before that. I have loved you always, Anna. I cannot remember a time when I didn't love you."

His wife stretched out and put her head on her husband's lap. Her fingers combed the tender shoots of grass. She watched a bird in the overhead branches fly here and there in search of food.

"We had a wonderful life together growing up, didn't we? You and Gustov and me. We were so happy. We didn't even understand that life was hard or that we were so poor. If it weren't for Mama always telling us so, I don't think I'd have any idea of it today."

"No, we had each other and that was enough for us."

"The first time I was truly unhappy was when you left for the army. Oh, how I cried!"

"I don't remember you crying."

"No. All you could see was yourself in that uniform."

"I remember you couldn't keep your eyes off me, little Anna."

"You did look handsome. But what a peacock."

Yuri squeezed her hand. "It's a wonderment that you could've loved me then. I often feel shame when I remember how proud I was."

"But I did love you and so did Gustov. Poor Gustov. He was so pathetic. He cried for days, and I called him a big baby. I was so cruel."

"It's hard to think of you as cruel."

"That's because you have a kind memory. But I was, and only to Gustov. He had such a tender heart, even then. How he missed you! You've always been a brother to him."

"I missed you both too."

"But you never cried."

"No, I was such a vain fellow. My ambition was like a flame. I was going to ignite the world with it."

"Well, I cried for both of us. I cried almost every day, but I never let Gustov see. I'd sneak off to the barn at night and cry in the loft after he was asleep. We lived for your letters."

"I didn't write many."

"No, you didn't, but we read and reread every one of them for months. We knew them by heart, but I pretended I didn't. Gustov knew better, though he never said anything whenever I taunted him about having memorized your words. I didn't know that the Lord had already begun to drizzle His sweetness over Gustov. I didn't know that Gustov was interested in the things of God or that he'd been memorizing a book that Mama's Communist friend had left at the house years before."

"A book that made fun of Christians and quoted Scriptures and then tried to show how ridiculous they were?"

"Yes, that's the one."

"I read it too, but it didn't speak to my heart."

"No, your heart was too hard then. But Gustov, oh, how he loved to read the Scriptures in that book. It wasn't long before the Lord had won his heart."

"I noticed a change in Gustov right away, the first time I came home on leave."

"Did you? It took me longer. I suppose because he was always there, always under my nose. But frankly, I'm surprised you noticed anything. Oh, that day you came home, what a sight! Such an angry and hard man you were, Yuri. It was the only time in my life, since I had decided to love you forever under that tree, that I wasn't so sure I wanted to be Mrs. Deyneko." Anna laughed as she thought of him. "For two weeks you were with us and for two weeks I was sure that some impostor had come home in your place. I even told Gustov that."

Yuri ran his fingers through his wife's hair and smiled down at her. He had heard this story a hundred times but never tired of it. "And what did Gustov say?"

"He said you needed Jesus."

"Gustov was always wiser than both of us, even though he was so much younger."

"I think that's why I always called him a baby and why I was so mean sometimes. I was supposed to be the older sister and he always made me feel as though he were older. But when you left the second time—when you had to report back to duty—how he cried again. I didn't call him a baby this time. When I spoke to him about it, he said he wept because you and I were breaking the heart of God. Oh, how he prayed! Night after night I would hear him in his room as he knelt beside his bed. And he'd be like that for hours. I don't think he even realized how long he prayed, but there he'd be, beside his bed, weeping before God. It wasn't long before I too came to the Lord."

"Yes, and it wasn't long after that I was assigned to Tirgu-Ocna."

"Oh, what a stubborn man you were, Yuri Deyneko! Even the sights at Tirgu-Ocna didn't bring you to your knees before God."

"No, but they softened my heart, like a plow through dry, crusty soil. It was your sweet face and your sweet lips that spoke about your love for Jesus that finished it," Yuri said, as he bent over his wife and kissed her. "If my Anna had such a love for Jesus, I told myself, then He must be a very wonderful fellow indeed."

Anna lazily ran her hand over the marks on the tree, then began tracing the letters with a finger. "I don't think I could go on living if there was no Yuri," she said in a low, melancholy tone. "The thought of losing Gustov is so difficult for me, but I couldn't bear it if I lost you. Tell me you won't leave me. Tell me this isn't our last time together."

"I'm not God, my love. Can I see into the future? But it may be the last time for a while anyway, that we meet."

Anna sat up and held Yuri's face between her hands. "You must not deceive me. You must tell me outright; has something gone wrong? Are you in danger?"

Yuri removed his wife's hands from his face and pressed them between his own hands. "No, nothing has gone wrong. But soon the Securitate will discover that the Tulasis have fled the country and that Gustov is being held at the embassy, if they don't know it already. They're not stupid, Anna. Sooner or later, I'll fall under suspicion and be put under surveillance. That's why we cannot see each other again for a while. I can't take the chance of leading them to you."

Anna snuggled against her husband's broad, strong shoulder. How many times had she rested her head on it? Even when she was little, if she skinned her knee or lost her only toy or was punished by her mother, it was Yuri's shoulder that had absorbed her tears.

"It's reasonable and sound, Yuri, even though I don't like it. By God's grace, our separation will be short and you can come to me once again. If God was able to use this foolish Ambassador Wainwright to help Gustov, then allowing a lonely wife to see her husband isn't such a difficult thing."

"Anna, I must…I must tell you something about this foolish Ambassador Wainwright."

Anna lifted her head from his shoulder. She did not say a word but stared into his face, not blinking for fear she would miss a sign or clue he might give away. She was not used to hearing anxiety in his voice. What had he been keeping from her?

"Ambassador Wainwright is my brother."

Relief spilled from Anna's mouth as a sigh, then she began to laugh. "It's not possible."

"Anna, I speak the truth."

She resisted the urge to laugh again when she saw the pained look on Yuri's face. "How is that possible?"

"You've always told me that God has a sense of humor."

"Yes, but this is too incredible. It's beyond belief."

"Incredible, yes. But also true."

"If this is so, why don't you seem happy?"

"At first I was upset. I judged him and scoffed at his weakness. How could a man who's had all the advantages of life be so puny and shallow, I asked myself? I played God, Anna, and God did not like it. I was ashamed to think this cowardly man could be my brother. There was pride in my heart, or I wouldn't have felt such loathing. But there was one afternoon, the afternoon he and I talked about freeing Gustov, that God let me see something very deep. He let me see Alexander through His eyes. He let me see what kind of man Alexander could become. I felt shame for my attitudes and I felt that I'd like very much to get to know this man. But this won't be possible. Now I feel sad. I feel like I've lost him all over again."

Anna put her arms around Yuri. A pair of birds had come to rest in the overhead branches and made a sweet melody that floated down around them. In the distance, past the fruit orchard, Anna could see a field of buttercups, heaving like a yellow sea in the breeze. How sweet life could be. How wonderful to be alive to share the beauty of God's world with someone you loved. At this moment, she couldn't feel sad, not for Gustov or for Yuri or for Alexander Wainwright or for herself.

"God is so big. Don't limit Him, Yuri. Who can tell what He'll do? You said so yourself. Can you foresee the future?

Don't be sad, my love. It's enough to be together, now, this moment. But you must tell me everything, how all this came about, how you discovered that Ambassador Wainwright was your brother."

Yuri smiled at his wife and kissed her face. Then he placed her head on his lap again and began to stroke her hair. "Yes, I'd like to tell you. It mystifies me still. It all began in Tulasi's office. You should've seen him, he was so angry with me, removing and replacing his glasses."

Anna laughed and brought her husband's hand to her lips and kissed it. "Yes, I can see it. What then?"

"Well, he began to talk about my assignment…"

Ambassador Wainwright asked about Gustov Volkovoy the second he stepped off the plane at Baneasa Airport and saw Donald Walters.

"Going downhill, sir," Walters said.

So instead of going directly to his residence, Alexander asked Walters to first stop at the embassy.

The doctor shook his head and gave a thumbs-down sign when Alexander entered the makeshift hospital room, but he didn't try to stop him from going over to Gustov's cot.

The IV still dripped into Gustov's arm, the last charade that hope still existed for recovery. On the small chest lay a Romanian Bible, embraced by bony arms that seemed too feeble even to hold it in place. The white hair on Gustov's head blended into the white of the pillow making it look as if only a small shrunken face lay there. His eyes were closed and Alexander was about to leave when suddenly Gustov opened them.

"Slava domnului! Bless the Lord! It is you, Mr. Ambassador. Please sit down."

Alexander shook his head, but when he saw Gustov try to rise, he found a nearby chair and pulled it next to the cot.

"You look well." Alexander could see that Gustov's eyes were no longer blazing but dark and receding. Only a small fire burned within.

Gustov smiled. "You are a true diplomat, sir. But not to worry. All is well. I can hardly contain the happiness that is within me." He patted the Bible on his chest. "I bless your name by the hour. I praise God for you and your great gift. I—" Gustov's voice broke and he paused to compose himself. "I never dreamed I would have my own Bible. This gift is too large, too wonderful!"

"I'm happy we were able to get it for you."

Gustov's eyes swam and he hugged the book closer to his chest. "You do not understand. This is enough food to feed a hundred, five hundred. In my village, one Bible would be cut into a hundred sections, maybe more, and distributed to all believers; the spiritual loaf cut into pieces so that many could feast. Each villager kept a portion for several months, then traded it with a neighbor for his copy. It would take years for a believer, trading his Scriptures back and forth in this manner, to read the Bible completely. I have met, in my lifetime, only a handful of people who have ever done so." Gustov closed his eyes again and smiled. "Yes, this is a very great gift. But I do not think I will have time enough to read it all. When I am gone, will you see that someone else gets it?"

"Yes, of course. But isn't there something else I could get you? Something else you want?"

"God has given me everything I could ever want, and I

praise His name. And I am so grateful to you, Mr. Ambassador, so very grateful!"

Alexander just stared down at the collection of skin and bones and groped for something to say. Finding nothing, he awkwardly reached out and began to stroke Gustov's head.

Alexander Wainwright fixed himself an Alka-Seltzer as his wife watched him anxiously. He took a few sips and made a face, then put the glass to his mouth again and drained it without coming up for air.

"Looks like your trip was a doozy," Loretta said, going up to him and giving him a hug.

"A nightmare. I kept seeing food and body parts. McAllen called me dead meat."

"He didn't!" Loretta tried to sound horrified, but there was a smile on her face.

"Your husband's life is going down the toilet and you don't seem to be too upset."

"Career, darling. Your career may be going down the drain but not your life. Big difference. Tell me what happened."

Alexander led Loretta down the hall and into the glass room. The first time they had used the glass room was when Loretta told him about Tirgu-Ocna prison, about the pastor and the stolen bread, about the field of sunflowers and the life-changing prayer meeting. The same two chairs were still in the middle of the room, and he pulled them closer together. After his wife sat down, he began to replay the scene in McAllen's office.

"You were brilliant, darling! I especially liked the part about you letting the IRS in on this. *The IRS!* Now that's a stroke of genius. You know how cranky they can get about losing potential revenue. If nothing else, that had to melt McAllen's heart with fear."

"You're making fun of me."

Loretta cupped her husband's chin in her hand and kissed him. "No, darling. I'm teasing, not making fun. The fact is, I'm very proud of you."

"Would you mind terribly being the wife of a stock clerk? I mean, if it should come to that?"

Loretta laughed so loudly Alexander was sure, soundproof or not, everyone in the house heard it. "Darling, a stock clerk? Well, if that's what you want to be when you grow up, it's fine with me. I want you to be happy. But just for the record, I didn't marry an ambassador or a stock clerk, I married Alexander Wainwright."

"Thanks for that." He leaned over and kissed her. "Then you won't mind terribly if you no longer find yourself the ambassadress?"

"You know in your heart of hearts that part of me would be profoundly relieved."

"I knew there was a reason I've loved you all these years." A small smile began to appear on his face, then quickly disappeared. "The worst part is that I wouldn't know what to do with myself. What would I *do*?"

"You're a West Point graduate. You'll figure something out."

"I suppose so."

"Of course you will, darling. And all of this may be premature. Perhaps the worst won't happen. Perhaps Gustov will live and be successfully smuggled out of the embassy."

"Sure, and 'they all lived happily ever after.' No, Loretta, I don't think so. Although I want him to desperately." Alexander saw the look on his wife's face and said, "Believe it or not, it's not because of my career. It's because of Gustov himself. There's something very special about him."

"I wish I'd gotten a chance to know him. How much longer?"

"What?"

"How much longer do you think Gustov has?"

"He could go anytime."

"That soon?"

"I think the doctor's surprised he's lasted this long."

"Does Yuri know?"

"I haven't talked to him about it, but I'm sure he suspects."

"Has he seen him yet?"

"No. If he comes into the embassy, he'll blow his cover." Alexander flushed with embarrassment and looked away. "We're still using 'he's having an affair with the ambassador's wife' ploy. We've certainly gotten a lot of mileage out of that one. I know you already know there was a time when I thought the two of you were actually…well, were actually having an affair. I'd like to apologize for that. Forgive me?"

Loretta smiled and squeezed his hand. "There's nothing to forgive. I'm flattered that you're still jealous."

"You want more honesty?"

"Dare we?" Loretta said, her eyes showering him with affection.

"I'm still a little jealous."

"But why?"

"Because there's something between the two of you. Oh, I know it's innocent. I'm not suggesting anything. But you share something together. I don't know what, I only know I'm not part of it. I guess I'm acting like a child because I feel left out. I've never felt like that before, not when it concerns you. We've always been so close. Shared everything. There's nothing I haven't told you. I always believed the same applied to you. But now, I think that's changed." He looked into her eyes, wide and imploring, hoping she would tell him he was behaving foolishly.

Loretta rose from the chair and began to pace around the glass enclosure. It was a small space, six feet by eight feet, a closet really, and left little room for walking.

"Loretta, please, you're making me dizzy," Alexander said. "If you've got something to say, just say it. You've got my stomach going nuts, and either you stop and talk now, or I'll have to go and get another Alka-Seltzer."

"I don't know how to tell you this, Alex, except to be direct. There's no way to soften it. I've racked my brain for weeks trying to think of a way."

"Loretta, I'm begging you! If you have any love for me left, or if you ever loved me, *please* stop pacing and talk to me."

She looked at her husband and shook her head, then slid quietly back into her chair and took a deep breath. "Yuri is your brother."

Loretta stared into her husband's face; he stared back and said nothing.

She grabbed his arm and shook it. "Did you hear what I said? Yuri Deyneko is your brother."

"You're not in love with him?"

"What? Alex!"

Alexander began to rub his head. Finally he said, "My brother? How do you know?"

"Wait here." She rose quickly and left the room. When she returned, she held an old, yellowed photograph. She placed it in her husband's shaking hands.

Alexander looked at it for some time. It had been years since he'd seen it. There was a time, long ago, when this picture meant something, when he kept it under his pillow at night, when he cried himself to sleep with grief. That time was only a blurred memory now because he had buried it like one would bury a corpse. He stared down at the picture. It evoked no emotion. Who were these people? A thin, worried-looking woman with two small boys? They meant nothing to him. If he had been that skinny little boy once, he was no longer.

"I showed this to you the first year we got married," he said, his mouth dry.

"Yuri has one, only you're not in it. But your mother and this little boy, a few inches taller maybe, but *this* boy was in it."

Alexander teared as he looked at his wife. "I don't remember them," he said slowly. "I don't remember either one of them."

Loretta leaned over and put her forehead against his. "I know."

"And I don't think I want to remember. I think I'm a little frightened of all this."

Loretta kissed her husband's face. "Nonsense, darling. A man who tells Rod McAllen he won't do something is not afraid of anything."

Yuri Deyneko walked up the six gray concrete steps leading to the office of the Securitate, taking two steps at a time. It was not that he was in a hurry to see Tulasi, but the sooner he saw the general, the quicker he would be able to leave. The large, gray stone building seemed to leer down at him as he walked through the mammoth double door. Yuri continued along a gray hall that contained no pictures, then through another wood door and to the left. Armed guards were everywhere, and even though he had been here several times before, he had his ID badge clipped to his suit pocket in full view. Down another gray hall and Yuri was now only a few yards from Valentine Tulasi's office.

There was one thing Yuri found consistent with all Communists; they were colorless. Everything their hands touched left a gray imprint, whether it was a building, clothing, the arts. It revealed a stinginess of spirit, so unlike God's generous creations of endless variety and color.

Tulasi's door was open, and even from where Yuri stood he could see that the Securitate officer was agitated.

"I've been waiting for you!" Tulasi said, the moment he saw Yuri in the doorway.

"I'm early." Yuri remained standing until Tulasi indicated he should take a seat. Tulasi continued to stand.

"I am extremely vexed! I can hardly contain myself! Today my sources informed me that there is good reason to believe Dr. Tulasi and his wife—" he coughed as though the names stuck in his throat—"that Dr. Tulasi and his wife have already fled the country and that *Gustov Volkovoy* has been smuggled into the American embassy. I have told them this is impossible. Impossible! I have told them that you would have informed me of this the instant it happened; indeed, that you would have prevented this from happening! What do you have to say?"

Yuri calmly folded his hands and looked at Tulasi. "Ambassador Wainwright is a very jealous man. I'm not allowed in the embassy, sir. I do not know what goes on inside."

Tulasi threw up both hands and began waving them wildly

in the air. "I grow weary of this affair between you and the ambassador's wife. What purpose does it serve? Where are the pictures? What humiliating blow have you delivered to the Americans? No, Yuri, I think this affair only serves your purposes. You have been pleasuring yourself while all around you has fallen into ruin."

"I have been following orders."

"Then how did my—how did the Tulasis escape? How has Gustov Volkovoy escaped?"

"The objective of my mission was to discredit or embarrass the American ambassador. His wife was the one weak spot I was able to discover. I followed through on that. Was I incorrect in my assessment of my orders?"

"Yes! No." Tulasi shook his head. "Do not play the fox with me, Yuri. *I* am the inquisitor here. And you can rest assured that I will discover exactly what you have been up to, because I do not believe you have been following orders at all, at least not *my* orders."

Yuri's lips parted in a slight smile. "Am I being charged with some crime?"

"You are either a clever man, Yuri Deyneko, or a complete fool."

Yuri stared straight ahead. "Am I being charged with a crime?"

Finally Tulasi sat in his desk chair. He removed his glasses and began wiping each lens in a circular motion. "No, you are not being charged with a crime, but I hold you responsible for what has happened. Do you understand that? I hold *you* responsible. And I will be watching you, Yuri Deyneko. One mistake. That is all I wait for. One mistake. I will be watching!"

꒰∽o∽꒱

It was nearly dark when Yuri returned to his apartment complex. Already the night air was becoming brisk from the first breath of fall. Shadows danced in corners and alleyways, and noisy children scampered home for dinner. Kitchen smells drifted through open windows. Cabbage soup mostly or cornmeal mush. Food ration cards did not go far when there were several mouths to feed. He remembered the days when smells other than cabbage soup floated from these windows, when the aroma of *sarmale* or *ciorba pescareasca* or *tocana* filled the air.

Suddenly, the aroma of grilled sausage floated past him. Someone was having a feast. No doubt for a special occasion, a birthday perhaps. Mothers would save their coupons for such an event.

But the smell of militei did not tempt him. He was not hungry. Maybe later in the apartment he would prepare a simple dinner of cornmeal mush and salt carp. Now, a walk was what he wanted. Perhaps this would be his last walk without a tail.

He walked a few blocks south and wished he lived closer to Herastrau Park. A stroll there would have made a pleasant end to the day, but that was way across town. A few blocks farther Yuri changed direction and began heading east. He was not particularly fond of Bucharest. Situated on the river Dimbovita and lying halfway between the foothills of the Carpathian highlands and the Danube, it had all the natural setting one would expect to see on a picture postcard. But repeated wars and fires had destroyed most of the old buildings, along with the old charm and character. Only a few relics remained: the open-air central market, an old inn or two, the dilapidated periphery. Most of the six hundred and fifty-four square miles of the city contained drab modern buildings and thoroughfares. And ugly high-rise apartments had replaced the picturesque single-family homes.

In spite of this, Bucharest remained essentially Romanian. Yuri was glad of that. He loved his homeland and the simple, good-natured people. But more and more, the people were losing hope. Too many years under Ceausescu had almost broken his countrymen. Melancholia filled the air. The economy was in a shambles. The pressure was on to produce more. Industries dotted the city like measles and operated double shifts. In addition, the city was becoming overcrowded with peasants as the government continued its demolition of villages, another attempt to redistribute population and to goose its citizens into the twenty-first century.

Yuri was still a country boy at heart, and he missed his farm outside Cluj. He even missed Cluj itself, with its quaint mix of Hungarian and Romanian culture and its Central European architecture. In its old-world charm and character, it provided a perfect contrast to Bucharest. He suddenly felt homesick and began to think about the farm. He had been happy there, where his mother and Aunt Sonia raised vegetables and sheep. He thought of the home-baked pies on the windowsill, the sound of rain on the barn roof, the smell of wet hay, the sound of bleating sheep. Oh, how he, Anna, and Gustov loved to listen to the songs of the shepherds during cheese making! Anna especially loved the sound of the long alpine horn as it marked the time for the mountain descent of the flocks. The first time he ever danced with Anna was at harvesttime when they did the *dragaica*. He had a treasure chest of memories such as these.

If only he had not been so restless! Why had he stayed in

the army after his mandatory service was finished? Why had soldiering appealed to him? Traveling, security, glory, all had lured him, but they seemed like such frivolous reasons now. He possessed a farmer's heart. He always had. How he yearned for the old life. But now there was no farm, there was no old life. And only God knew where Yuri would end up.

It had grown dark and the sidewalks were empty. There were no sounds of children or chatter, just the gray empty streets that seemed to moan and sigh, or was that just the wind? He had walked farther than he realized and began to retrace his steps.

He thought of Alexander Wainwright. So much had happened since the beginning of this assignment. Both their lives had been turned upside down. God had had His joke, but He had yet to share the punch line. What would become of them? Both their lives seemed to hang over a cliff.

Yuri took long strides over the gray walkways. How different things looked in the dark. The shapes of day became unfamiliar when wearing black cloaks. The future was like that. It too dressed in black. Only God could distinguish what lay ahead.

He was still thinking about this when he reached his apartment. He continued to think about it as he prepared his cornmeal mush and salt carp. Only when there was a knock at the door did he stop. He opened it and was surprised to see Nadia. Her eyes were swollen from crying.

"Nadia, what—"

She pushed Yuri into the apartment and closed the door behind her.

"No one must see! I should not be here."

"Nadia, what is it? What's wrong?"

The frail young woman began to cry, then wiped her tears on her sleeve. She looked more worn than the last time Yuri had seen her. He led her to a kitchen chair and tried to make her sit down, but she shook her head.

"No, no. My children are alone. I cannot stay. I should not even be here. But I had to come. I had to come and tell you. You've been so kind to me and my family, Yuri. I just had to tell you."

"What must you tell me?"

"They were here today. They came to me." Nadia shuddered as she recalled the visit. "They're horrible, Yuri, horrible!"

"Who, Nadia?"

"The secret police! They asked about you. I told them what I could, but it wasn't much. Then they said bad things—that you're a traitor, a deceiver. But I said, no. No, you must be mistaken. Yuri Deyneko is a kind and gentle man, a good man. But they just kept talking and talking. They wouldn't listen to me!" Nadia looked at the door nervously. "My children, I must go. They're alone."

Yuri led her back to the door. "Go home. It'll be all right."

Nadia started crying again and shook her head. "No, you don't understand. They were very angry with me for not saying anything against you. They said they would prepare a statement and that I *must* sign. I asked what was this statement, and they said it was a statement denouncing you. I told them, never! I couldn't do such a thing, that I didn't believe what they said about you was true."

Nadia wept into her hands, and Yuri placed his arms around her. "You're very brave, Nadia. Don't cry. Everything will be fine. You'll see."

She shook her head. "No, Yuri. I haven't told you the worst of it. They said I must come down to Securitate headquarters in three days and sign. They're giving me three days to make up my mind, and if I don't come, they'll return for my children. My *children,* Yuri! They said they would take away my children if I don't denounce you. They said anyone who didn't care about the welfare of their country, who wasn't willing to look out for their nation's interest, wasn't fit to raise children. I must do it. I must! Can you understand that? Please say you understand!"

Yuri continued holding her. "I understand, Nadia."

"I don't want to, Yuri. I don't want to."

Yuri released her and smiled into her tearful eyes. "I know that."

Nadia's face contorted with pain. "I will go to them in three days, like they asked. Forgive me. Please forgive me," she said, her voice sounding like a wail.

"I forgive you."

Nadia's hand moved to the doorknob. "I must go now. My children...they're alone."

Yuri stopped her from opening the door. "Wait." Quickly he went to the kitchenette and wrapped the salt carp that was on the counter. Then he went to the metal shelves over the sink and picked up five food ration cards.

"Take these," he said, placing them into her hand.

Nadia shook her head. "This is your dinner, and the cards...oh, it's too much!"

"I'm not very hungry tonight, and the coupons...well, a man living as a bachelor, he doesn't need much."

She reluctantly closed her fingers around the gift. "I don't know how to thank you."

Yuri smiled. "You do me an honor by coming here. That is thanks enough."

Nadia began to cry again. "I don't know if there is a God, but if there is, I pray He will bless and protect you, Yuri Deyneko." Then she opened the door and was gone.

12

Donald Walters entered Ambassador Alexander Wainwright's office in a trot. "He's still at it, sir. The doctor can't get him back to bed."

Alexander threw up his hands. "This is out of my league, Don. You know that. What am I supposed to do, tell him to *stop* praying?"

"I understand, sir, but the doctor would like you to come just the same."

Alexander sighed and rose from his chair. Immediately following Alexander's last visit, Gustov Volkovoy had begun a nonstop prayer vigil. That was twenty-four hours ago. Gustov had neither eaten nor slept in that time, and the doctor was extremely worried.

"I don't know how he's doing it, Mr. Ambassador," the doctor whispered when Alexander entered. "He should be dead on the spot. He's too sick and weak for this, but I don't know what to do about it." The doctor shook his head. "I give up."

Alexander looked across the room. There, kneeling by the cot, was Gustov Volkovoy, his face buried in his hands.

"What are you doing?" Alexander said, walking over to the cot. "Why aren't you in bed?"

At the sound of the ambassador's voice, Gustov looked up and smiled. "I am praying. God has put you on my heart, Mr. Ambassador, and I cannot get you out. I must continue."

"Don't you think God can hear you just as easily if you were lying down? I mean, you could do this in bed, couldn't you?"

Gustov shook his head and turned away, but not before Alexander got a close look at his face. Gustov's eyes were red and swollen.

"Are you in pain?" Alexander asked.

Gustov nodded. "Yes…here." He stabbed his chest with a bony finger. "I wear the broken heart of God, and He weeps for you."

Alexander placed his hand on Gustov's shoulder. "Then if all this is for me," he said in a shaken voice, "won't you please stop now, for a little while at least, and rest? I don't want you on my conscience."

A deep sigh escaped Gustov's lips, and for a second, Alexander thought he had taken his last breath. But then Gustov rose from the floor and climbed into bed. As Alexander adjusted the covers, a gray shadow fell across the bed, and he shuddered.

"Try to rest," he said.

Gustov smiled weakly, then closed his eyes. "You are right. God can hear me just as easily from here."

"I'll check back with you later," Alexander said, swallowing hard. "Keep me posted," he said to the doctor as he left the room. Then he walked slowly back to his office.

Why was this frail Romanian spilling out life's last precious moments for *him*? Why? Alexander had never felt so shaken; not when he thought Loretta was having an affair; not even when he found out that Yuri Deyneko was his brother.

"Your driver is waiting outside, sir," said an undersecretary who had slipped nervously beside him. "He'd like to see you. What should I tell him?"

The color drained from Alexander's face. "Nothing. I'll take care of it myself."

The walk to the back door seemed to take forever, and when Alexander finally got there, he felt he had reached it too soon. He braced himself, then opened the door. There, only inches away, stood his brother.

"I'd like to see him," Yuri said.

"It won't be healthy for you. Things won't line up anymore." Alexander's eyes were riveted on Yuri's face as he resisted the urge to scream, *How could you be my brother! I don't know you!*

"That is of no consequence now."

Alexander just stared and said nothing.

"Loretta has told you," Yuri finally said.

"Yes, and before you go in, I think we should talk."

Yuri nodded and waited while Alexander notified someone in the embassy that he was leaving. Alexander ordered the CIA not to follow them, then the two got into the limo. It took several minutes and numerous hairpin turns before Yuri lost his tail. They headed for the Baneasa Airport.

"I see Tulasi has revoked his latitude," Alexander said.

"Yes," Yuri said, pulling to a stop in an obscure corner of the parking lot. "But we have other things to discuss now, such as your unhappiness over our situation, little brother." Yuri turned to face Alexander. "You are distressed that your past has come and sits before you."

Alexander shook his head. "I don't know what I am, or what I feel right now. And why did you call me little brother? Aren't we supposed to be twins? Although for the life of me, I can't see one chromosome of mine in you."

Yuri laughed. "Fraternal twins do not necessarily look alike. And I am older. I was born first, or that's how Aunt Sonia always told it."

"I don't remember Aunt Sonia. I don't remember you. I'm…I'm sorry."

"I understand. I am sorry too, because now there is no time to get acquainted. I am afraid that after I see Gustov, I will be disappearing from Bucharest."

"What's happened?"

"Tulasi."

"He suspects you? That's why the tail?"

"Yes. I imagine that within forty-eight hours someone will come to arrest me, but I do not plan on being available."

"Tulasi hasn't found out you helped us?"

"No. If he had, I would be dead. But his parents' defection is more than he can bear. It will probably ruin his career. He hopes to save it by giving Ceausescu a scapegoat, and he is already in the process of fabricating evidence against me."

"What will you do? How will you survive?"

"I do not know. I put that in God's hands. My one pressing desire is not to get caught. If I do, I can harm many people. I know much, and they have ways. Believe me, they have ways of breaking a man. I would rather die than fall into their hands. This much I have decided; they will never capture me alive."

It had suddenly become stuffy and Alexander opened the window. "No," he found himself saying.

"What?" Yuri saw the distraught look on Alexander's face.

"No. I don't want you to do it, to go running off into the forest somewhere, living like one of your Romanian bears."

"Do you have a better idea?"

"Yes. We can smuggle you out of the country. You said yourself you have forty-eight hours before Tulasi makes his move. In forty-eight hours we can have you out of the country and safely in the U.S."

"I am grateful, little brother. Your offer is touching, but I cannot accept."

"Why not? And stop calling me little brother!"

Yuri smiled remembering a young boy in a refugee camp. "Thank you for caring enough to want to help me, but I can never leave Anna. It is unthinkable."

"Of course. I should've realized that. But we can get her out too. Arni Houser can arrange it. Between our CIA agents and your contacts at the Industrialexport, we could manage it."

"I do not know…"

"You said yourself you can't afford to be taken alive. What about the people you could betray? What about their wives, their children? Staying here is too much of a risk. You have no choice. Besides, it'll be a feather in my cap having a colonel defect."

"It is a poor attempt, Alexander, to make it seem that this is good for you. You know that once things settle down, your State Department will figure it all out, and then it will go badly, very badly indeed."

"But by then it'll be too late. By then you and Anna will be out of Romania and safely in America."

Yuri studied his brother. Alexander sat lean and dignified with his expensive brown suit and closely cropped hair. He looked every inch an ambassador.

"What will you do afterward?" Yuri asked.

"I don't know. Start over, I guess."

"It seems that we will both be starting over."

337

Alexander hesitated. "Maybe…maybe we can start over together."

"I would like that."

"Then it's settled? Your leaving the country, I mean?"

"Yes, I suppose it is, as long as you promise me that Anna will not be left behind."

"I give you my word," Alexander said, offering Yuri his hand.

Yuri laughed heartily. "Even when you were little, you were stiff like a tree." He reached over the backseat and drew Alexander forward, then kissed him on both cheeks.

Alexander did not pull away. "You were always kissing me, like I was a sissy or something."

Tears filled Yuri's eyes. "Yes, little brother. There was such little love in the camp. Most of the time we only had each other. I always felt older than you. I always wanted to protect you."

"I wish I could remember more, but I can't. It's all so new to me."

"It will come in time. Maybe that is one reason God has brought us together again, Alexander. In this hostile world, it will be good for you to have a brother."

Alexander looked out his window. Yes, it would be good to have a brother, he thought, as he watched a small jet take off in the distance. The metal wings caught the sun and glinted like mirrors. Where were these people going? Was there a fugitive among them looking down at his country for the last time? He could never imagine permanently leaving America. He loved it too much. How does one pull up roots and transplant? With anguish, certainly. He looked at his brother and felt compassion.

"Where do you want to go in America?"

"What?"

"Where do you want to settle?"

"I do not know. I have never thought of it."

"But if you could choose, what kind of place would you want to live in?"

Yuri leaned his head against the door and closed his eyes. "I think some place where I can grow vegetables and raise sheep, maybe have fruit trees. Anna would like that."

"A little farm. Yes, that shouldn't be difficult," Alexander said, smiling at his brother. "You don't ask for much."

"It is enough. It is everything I want."

"Sometimes dreams do come true, Yuri."

"I have had this dream so long I am almost afraid to believe it possible."

"Believe it."

"I will try. I will think of nothing else for the next several days. It will help me while you are getting Anna out. I will picture Anna and me standing on our own little farm, together and free. Then I can endure whatever it takes to make it happen."

"It's going to happen, Yuri."

"Yes, you are making me believe. But what of you, Alexander? What is your dream?"

Alexander stared out the window again, watching the dust swirl in the wind as another plane took off. He watched as the nose pulled up and the plane gracefully rose in the air. There was something thrilling about watching a plane take flight. It spoke of power, freedom, promise, and even uncertainty. If he had the power and freedom to change his life, to do anything he wanted, what would it be? He watched as the plane climbed until it was only a speck, then disappeared.

"I don't know," he finally said. "I have no idea what I want."

When they arrived back at the embassy, Donald Walters greeted them with the glum pronouncement that Volkovoy was dying. Yuri followed Alexander into the makeshift hospital room where Gustov lay gasping for air.

Gently, Yuri picked up Gustov's hand and felt it recoil. With his other hand, Yuri began to stroke the perspiring forehead. Gustov opened his eyes and for a moment struggled to identify the person who leaned over him so tenderly. He smiled when he recognized Yuri.

"My brother," he whispered, "God is calling me and I must not delay."

Tears rolled down Yuri's cheeks and he made no attempt to stop them. "Then you must obey, as always."

Gustov raised a frail, shaking hand into the air and touched Yuri's face. "Then why the tears? Why are you not happy?"

"I rejoice for you but weep for myself. I will miss you."

"No brother could have been more loving or kind. You have been a great blessing to me. We will see one another again." Gustov closed his eyes, then suddenly opened them again. "Yuri," he called out in a quavering voice, as though he could not see the man standing over him.

"I'm here."

Gustov blinked several times, then smiled weakly. "One last thing I ask. Pray for this man," he said, pointing to Alexander. "Pray for him."

Yuri squeezed the trembling hand. "God has played a little joke and He will tell you all about it when He sees you. But yes, I will pray for him."

Gustov closed his eyes once more, then his chest stopped

heaving and he was perfectly still.

Yuri let out a sob and knelt beside the bed. His head was very close to the still, white face and his lips moved as though he were speaking to his dead friend. Finally, he leaned closer and kissed him. "You will take care of everything?" Yuri asked, looking up at Alexander. "You will see to it that he has a proper Christian burial?"

"Yes, I'll handle it. Don't worry." Alexander picked up the Bible from the stand and handed it to his kneeling brother. "Take this. I'm sure Gustov would've wanted you to have it."

Yuri took the Bible from Alexander and rose to his feet. He ran a rough thumb over the black leather. "You made Gustov very happy before he died. Thank you."

Alexander placed a hand on Yuri's shoulder. "Now make me happy and come see Arni with me."

At Arni Houser's signal, three men ignited a small amount of blasting powder previously placed in special metal containers, then set off smoke bombs. In a matter of minutes, the embassy halls were filled with coughing employees scrambling to get out of the building. The secret police began to run along the perimeter of the embassy trying to stop those who were fleeing from passing through the gate.

When someone shouted, "It's a bomb," not even the threats of the secret police could contain the panic. People ran everywhere. In the dusk and confusion, no one noticed a tall burly man slip out the embassy side gate. No one noticed the man hug the shadows and disappear around the corner. And no one noticed when he stepped into a waiting Dacia that quickly sped away. And hours later, when all the buildings on Str. Gabriel Peri were deserted, no one saw the Dacia stop in front of the Industrialexport or the tall burly man slip out of the car and into the back of the building.

"Your stitching on the flap is excellent and your seam allowance perfect. I couldn't have done better."

"That's not what gives me the trouble." Mirela took the cotton fabric from Anna and slapped the muslin against it. "Why must we use two fabrics when one should do?"

"Because one will not do," Anna said, tousling Mirela's hair. "Lightweight fabrics must be interfaced with—" Anna looked up when she heard the doorbell jingle. Color drained from her face as two men entered. Each wore a long, black leather coat and wide-brimmed hat pulled low over his face, casting a shadow across his eyes. Behind them, almost crouching, stood Gheorghe Vladimescu.

"Identify her," one of the men said.

Gheorghe stepped forward and pointed a shaking finger at Anna.

"You're certain this is Anna Rosu?"

"Yes," Gheorghe said.

"Then you may go, your job is finished here."

Gheorghe took a few steps backward. "I don't understand this. I should've been informed. I am her pastor."

"We know who you are!"

"Yes, well, perhaps I can be of assistance to…to Anna. Perhaps I should stay."

"Suit yourself." One of the black-clad men leaned on the counter. "Anna Rosu, you are under arrest!"

Mirela clutched Anna's arm. "No, please! She has done nothing!"

"Stay quiet," Anna whispered.

Mirela began to sob. "Please don't take her."

"You must stay quiet. There is nothing you can do for me now." She forced Mirela into a nearby chair, then turned to face the intruder leaning over the counter.

"Don't be foolish, old man," the intruder said to Teofil, who had been moving quietly toward the group. "Or you'll force me to use these."

Anna watched in horror as the stranger slipped on a pair of brass knuckles.

"I won't cause trouble," Teofil said. "I only wish to end it, to clear up this misunderstanding."

"Not your business," the second man said as he intercepted Teofil and roughly pushed him away.

Anna stepped up to the counter. "What is the charge? Why am I being arrested?"

"We'll do the questioning!"

"Can't you just tell me what I've done?"

The man at the counter fingered his brass knuckles. "Don't make this unpleasant. Come quietly now and maybe, if this is a misunderstanding like the old man says, you'll be home for supper."

Anna swallowed hard and nodded, then went to where Mirela sat. "Everything is yours. I give it to you. Only promise me you'll stay and work hard and keep at your study of Scripture."

Mirela sobbed into her hands. "I promise."

Teofil had managed to slip past the second man and was now standing beside Anna. Tears streamed down his face. "God go with you." He hugged her tightly.

"Enough of this!"

The two black-clad men tore Teofil away and began leading Anna out the door. Gheorghe Vladimescu looked on, a mix of horror and confusion on his face, as the two men shoved Anna into the back of a black Dacia and drove away.

Anna looked back at the leather shop for what she believed would be the last time, then closed her eyes and prayed. Her heart jumped when she felt something touch her hand. She opened her eyes. The man who had, only moments before, threatened her with brass knuckles, now smiled broadly and shoved a piece of paper into her hand. Anna's heart jumped again when she opened the paper and saw the familiar hand-writing.

Dearest, you must trust the man who gives you this note. Do not be afraid to go with him. All is well.

"Don't worry so. I've sent my best men. They won't fail me. Soon your Anna will be walking through that door, you'll see."

Yuri's fingers tapped nervously against his leg. For twenty-four hours he had been hiding in this secret room at the Industrialexport. Yuri stilled his fingers, then rested them on his friend's shoulder. "I will never be able to repay you."

"We are brothers in the Lord. Repayment is not a word we should use."

"No, but it is something I'd still want to do."

"Then let your payment be in the form of prayers. Remember me when you are safe in America."

"I cannot imagine what it must be like for you, being hated by your own family, your friends."

"It is difficult."

"Are you ever tempted to tell them?"

The friend nodded.

"You've saved many lives. Many are indebted to you."

"Even so, it's difficult to wear the hated uniform of the Securitate. Sometimes when I see the loathing in my wife's eyes, when I touch her and she recoils, it's hard to stay silent."

Yuri rose from his chair and began to pace. "I don't know if I could endure that."

"God's grace is sufficient. In the end, it is always sufficient."

"This business won't cause you any harm?"

The friend laughed. "My rank protects me from a great deal. Few are brave enough to question me."

"And what of Anna's friends in Ploiesti?"

"They'll all be safe. I've taken precautions."

"And how will you handle things on your end?"

"There'll be no trail. By the time I'm done, Anna Rosu will have disappeared forever in the bowels of Tirgu-Ocna. No one will see or hear of her again. She'll be completely forgotten. And you and Anna Volkovoy will be free to begin a new life in America."

Alexander Wainwright sat behind his desk staring at the blank sheet of paper in front of him. He had been staring at it for hours, ever since Arni Houser called him with the good news that the "twins" were delivered safely. He laughed at the code word for Anna and Yuri Deyneko. Not even Houser knew the irony of those words. He tried to picture his face when he found out. Then he pictured Rodger McAllen's and threw down his pen.

He had to write that report to State, but what should he

say? What could he say? McAllen would be mad as a hornet when he found out the truth. He pictured smoke pouring from the bald head. And the secretary of state? He would turn this whole affair into a victory. After all, it gave him two trophies on the mantel: a Romanian colonel and Gustov Volkovoy's sister. That should be good for a few brownie points. Funny thing was, Alexander didn't care. He didn't care what Rod McAllen thought, he didn't care what the Secretary thought, and suddenly he laughed with joy.

He didn't care.

Alexander Wainwright strolled alongside Charles Riley, and from time to time he turned to look at the eight tails—four from the CIA, four from the Securitate—behind them.

"Rod McAllen called me dead meat, but frankly, Charles, I'm more like roadkill. For the life of me I don't understand why anyone would want to continue surveillance."

Riley looked over his shoulder and laughed. "The Securitate will follow anything—sorry, dear boy, I mean anyone. But our boys are keeping them at bay."

"I guess they haven't heard that I'm yesterday's news."

"Are we being cryptic?"

"I've been recalled, Charles."

Riley whistled. "Tough break, dear boy. Where are they sending you?"

"Nowhere. I'm resigning."

"You're not serious, Ali? After all your hard work these many years to get where you are?"

"Where am I, Charles?"

"Oh, we are in a mood, aren't we? But I won't play; you'll

have to tell me straight-out. Are you sorry that you stuck out your neck? Are you sorry about Volkovoy?"

"No. Not at all."

"But what'd you get out of all this? Where did it get you?"

"You'd be surprised."

"No riddles, Ali. Just give it to me plain and simple."

"Did you know I have a brother?"

"Since when?"

"Since I've been here in Romania."

"Not surprised. Strange country, Romania. Have I met him?"

Alexander looked at his longtime friend and laughed. "Always the cool cucumber. Doesn't anything faze you, Charles?"

"I'm a journalist, remember? We see it all, dear boy. And I mean all. But back to this brother of yours. Who is he?"

"My driver, Yuri Deyneko."

"*Colonel* Deyneko?" Riley whistled again. "Now here's a story! But where is he? I haven't seen him for some time."

"In the States with his wife, Anna."

"They both defected?"

"Not exactly."

"Then what exactly?"

"Anna is Gustov Volkovoy's sister."

"Then…that makes Colonel Deyneko Gustov's brother-in-law."

"Right."

"I'm beginning to see the picture, Ali. Very intriguing. It was Deyneko who helped the CIA with Volkovoy's escape."

"And the Tulasis."

"Very hot property. No wonder you got him out. I want an

exclusive, dear boy. You talk to me and no one else."

"Okay, it's yours."

"But really, Ali, do you need to do this? Your resignation, I mean. You've given State several big fish, and that should help smooth some of those ruffled feathers. Do you have to be so drastic and chuck everything? Can't you go on in the same way as before?"

"No."

"But why?"

"Because *I'm* not the same."

Riley groaned. "A reformed sinner can be very tedious."

"I'll try not to bore you."

"So, you're starting over."

"That's right."

"What do you plan to do with the rest of your life?"

"I've been giving it a lot of thought lately, and I think I'd like to do something with Yuri. I'm not sure what just yet, but I think the two of us can come up with something. America's still the land of opportunity."

"Well, there is something exciting about new beginnings. They are ever so hopeful, at least at the start. But Ali, sooner or later the new becomes old. Then what?"

"Some things never get old, Charles."

Riley sighed. "I don't understand you. You have everything and you're throwing it all away. What is it you want? Do you know?"

Alexander smiled. Yuri had asked him that question two weeks ago and he hadn't had an answer. Since then he had thought a lot about that pastor at Tirgu-Ocna. Loretta had shared every detail, and at the time he thought surely this story was an exaggeration. No one would do such a thing. It wasn't until he met Gustov Volkovoy that he was able to believe that such love was real. Twenty-four hours, that's how long Gustov had stayed on his knees for him. He didn't know how to go about getting that kind of love, or if he'd ever have it, but that was what he wanted.

"Well, dear boy, are you going to answer?" Riley said.

Alexander put his arm around his friend's shoulder and smiled. "Yes, Charles. I know what I want."

Author's Note

On December 15, 1989, a group of Christians in Timisoara demonstrated to protest both the pending shutdown of their church and the deportation of their pastor, Laslo Tokes. The Christians were fired upon by security forces and hundreds were slaughtered. This sparked a national revolution. On December 22, the Council of the National Salvation Front declared it had overthrown the government. The Ceausescus were arrested and tried by a military tribunal. On December 25, 1989, Nicolae Ceausescu and his wife, Elena, were executed by a three-man firing squad.

Printed in the United States
by Baker & Taylor Publisher Services